THE MABINOGION

The Mabinogion is the title given to eleven medieval Welsh prose tales preserved mainly in the White Book of Rhydderch (*c.*1350) and the Red Book of Hergest (*c.*1400). They were never conceived as a collection—the title was adopted in the nineteenth century when the tales were first translated into English by Lady Charlotte Guest. Yet they all draw on oral tradition and on the storytelling conventions of the medieval *cyfarwydd* ('storyteller'), providing a fascinating insight into the wealth of narrative material that was circulating in medieval Wales: not only do they reflect themes from Celtic mythology and Arthurian romance, they also present an intriguing interpretation of British history.

SIONED DAVIES is Chair of Welsh at Cardiff University. Her special interest is the interplay between orality and literacy, together with the performance aspects of medieval Welsh narrative. Her publications include *Crefft y Cyfarwydd* (Cardiff, 1995), which is a study of narrative techniques in the *Mabinogion, The Four Branches of the Mabinogi* (Llandysul, 1993), and a co-edited volume, *The Horse in Celtic Culture: Medieval Welsh Perspectives* (Cardiff, 1997).

OXFORD WORLD'S CLASSICS

*For over 100 years Oxford World's Classics have brought
readers closer to the world's great literature. Now with over 700
titles—from the 4,000-year-old myths of Mesopotamia to the
twentieth century's greatest novels—the series makes available
lesser-known as well as celebrated writing.*

*The pocket-sized hardbacks of the early years contained
introductions by Virginia Woolf, T. S. Eliot, Graham Greene,
and other literary figures which enriched the experience of reading.
Today the series is recognized for its fine scholarship and
reliability in texts that span world literature, drama and poetry,
religion, philosophy, and politics. Each edition includes perceptive
commentary and essential background information to meet the
changing needs of readers.*

OXFORD WORLD'S CLASSICS

The Mabinogion

Translated with an Introduction and Notes by
SIONED DAVIES

OXFORD
UNIVERSITY PRESS

OXFORD
UNIVERSITY PRESS

Great Clarendon Street, Oxford ox2 6DP

Oxford University Press is a department of the University of Oxford.
It furthers the University's objective of excellence in research, scholarship,
and education by publishing worldwide in

Oxford New York

Auckland Cape Town Dar es Salaam Hong Kong Karachi
Kuala Lumpur Madrid Melbourne Mexico City Nairobi
New Delhi Shanghai Taipei Toronto

With offices in

Argentina Austria Brazil Chile Czech Republic France Greece
Guatemala Hungary Italy Japan Poland Portugal Singapore
South Korea Switzerland Thailand Turkey Ukraine Vietnam

Oxford is a registered trade mark of Oxford University Press
in the UK and in certain other countries

Published in the United States
by Oxford University Press Inc., New York

British Library Cataloguing in Publication Data

Data available

Library of Congress Cataloging in Publication Data

Data available

Typeset by Cepha Imaging Private Ltd., Bangalore, India
Printed in Great Britain by
Clays Ltd., St Ives plc

ISBN 978–0–19–921878–3

8

CONTENTS

ACKNOWLEDGEMENTS

IN the tale of 'How Culhwch Won Olwen', we are presented with a roll-call of the Arthurian court, with characters ranging from Gilla Stag-Leg to Isberyr Cat-Claw. Judith Hawk-Eye would take her place well among these. I thank Judith Luna not only for her scrupulous editing, but also for her subtle reminders, her gentle prodding, and for her constant patience and encouragement.

My debt to Brynley F. Roberts is immense; he read the entire manuscript and offered advice and insightful criticism. Ceridwen Lloyd-Morgan, together with my colleague Dylan Foster Evans, also made valuable suggestions which I have taken on board. I must thank colleagues at Cardiff University, and in particular the staff of the School of Welsh who have had to live with this translation for more years than they care to remember; I am particularly grateful to Cath Pugh for easing my administrative burdens and for being so supportive at all times.

There are many others who have made this translation possible: my friends Manon Rhys and Christine James who have been a constant inspiration; my wonderful neighbours who would voice great concern at seeing the burning of the midnight oil; my parents—my father, whose gift as a storyteller first awakened my interest in these medieval tales, and my mother who commented on the entire translation; and finally, Smwt and Mao, who would curl up at my feet and purr whenever I settled down at my desk. Translating the *Mabinogion* has been a challenging, but one of the most rewarding experiences ever. Diolch o galon i bob un ohonoch.

In memory of Yolande, who loved performing

INTRODUCTION

BROTHERS transformed into animals of both sexes who bring forth children; dead men thrown into a cauldron who rise the next day; a woman created out of flowers, transformed into an owl for infidelity; a king turned into a wild boar for his sins—these are just some of the magical stories that together make up the *Mabinogion*.

The tales, eleven in all, deal with Celtic mythology, Arthurian romance, and a view of the past as seen through the eyes of medieval Wales. They tell of love and betrayal, shape-shifting and enchantment, conflict and retribution. Despite many common themes, they were never conceived as an organic group, and are certainly not the work of a single author. Their roots lie in oral tradition, and they evolved over centuries before reaching their final written form: as such, they reflect a collaboration between the oral and literary culture, and give us an intriguing insight into the world of the traditional storyteller.

What is the Mabinogion?

The *Mabinogion* is the collective name now given to eleven medieval Welsh tales found mainly in two manuscripts, the White Book of Rhydderch (Aberystwyth, National Library of Wales, MS Peniarth 4–5), dated *c.*1350, and the Red Book of Hergest (Oxford, Bodleian Library, MS Jesus College 111), dated between 1382 and *c.*1410. The term is a scribal error for *mabinogi*, derived from the Welsh word *mab* meaning 'son, boy'. As a result, some have suggested that *mabinogi* was a tale for boys, or perhaps a tale told by young or apprentice storytellers; however, the general consensus is that its original meaning was 'youth' or 'story of youth', confirmed by the appearance of the term as a translation of the Latin *infantia*, and that finally it meant no more than 'tale' or 'story'.

The term *Mabinogion* was popularized in the nineteenth century when Lady Charlotte Guest translated the tales into English, between 1838 and 1849. She regarded it as the plural form of *mabinogi*,[1] and

---

[1] The suffix -*(i)on* is a common plural ending in Welsh. Guest also included the tale

an ideal title for her collection. As her translation was published time and time again, the title became established, and by now has become an extremely convenient way to describe the corpus. However, it needs to be emphasized that the term *Mabinogion* is no more than a label, and a modern-day one at that: the stories vary as regards date, authorship, sources, content, structure, and style. Having said that, ever since Lady Guest's achievement the *Mabinogion* have taken on a life of their own, and earned their place on the European and world stage.

Of the eleven tales, it is clear that four of them form a distinct group, generally known as 'The Four Branches of the *Mabinogi*'. These are the *mabinogi* proper, as it were, so called because each one ends with the same formula in both the White and the Red Books: 'and so ends this branch of the Mabinogi.'[2] They are the only tales in the corpus that refer to themselves as *mabinogi*, divided into 'branches', a term used in medieval French narrative also to denote a textual division, suggesting the image of a tree with episodes leading off from the main narrative or 'trunk'. Even so, the link between them is fairly tenuous; the only hero to appear in all four is Pryderi—he is born in the First Branch and is killed in the Fourth. Resonances of Celtic mythology are apparent throughout these four tales, as mortals come into contact with characters who possess supernatural powers, from Gwydion the shape-shifter, who can create a woman out of flowers, to Bendigeidfran the giant, who lies across the river as a bridge for his men to cross; from Math the magician, whose feet must lie in the lap of a virgin, to the beautiful Rhiannon, whose magical white horse is impossible to catch. Yet, despite drawing on much older material, the author of the 'Four Branches' attempts to make the tales relevant to his own time, and indeed to any period, by using them to convey his views regarding appropriate moral behaviour, doing so by implication rather than by any direct commentary.

Manuscript evidence does not suggest any particular groupings for the remaining seven tales, although scholars and translators have indeed attempted to classify them, based on certain critical judge-

of *Taliesin* in her translation. However, since the earliest copy of this tale is not found until the sixteenth century, subsequent translators have omitted it from the corpus.

[2] The scribal error in the formula at the end of the First Branch—'And so ends this branch of the Mabinogion'—gave rise to Lady Guest's title.

ments. Traditionally, the tales of 'Peredur son of Efrog', 'Geraint son of Erbin', and 'The Lady of the Well' have been known as 'the three romances', partly because they correspond to the late twelfth-century metrical romances of Chrétien de Troyes—*Perceval*, *Erec et Enide*, and *Yvain*. They have as their focus the court at Caerllion on Usk, home to the emperor Arthur and his queen, Gwenhwyfar. In each tale the hero embarks on a journey in order to prove himself; once he has moved beyond the parameters of Arthur's realm, he comes across shining castles with grey-haired hosts and the most beautiful maidens who bestow lavish hospitality; threatening knights who must be overpowered and widowed countesses who must be defended. But in each tale the emphasis is different, so that although the three share common themes, which indeed set them apart from the other *Mabinogion* tales, they should not be regarded as an organic group, the work of a single author. Indeed, they have not been copied as a group in the extant manuscripts; neither do they share a common manuscript tradition. Moreover, although they exhibit some of the broad characteristics of romance, such as concerns regarding chivalric modes of behaviour and knightly virtues, they do not lie comfortably within that genre, so that the term 'the three romances' is both misleading and inappropriate; while they may well be very loose retellings of Chrétien's poems, they have been completely adapted to the native culture, and remain stylistically and structurally within the Welsh narrative tradition.

Of the remaining four tales, two are again Arthurian in content, while the other two deal with traditions about early British history. 'How Culhwch Won Olwen' portrays a world far removed from that of European romance, a world where Arthur holds court in Celli Wig in Cornwall, and heads a band of the strangest warriors ever—men such as Canhastyr Hundred-Hands, Sgilti Lightfoot, and Gwiawn Cat-Eye—who, together with Arthur, ensure that Culhwch overcomes his stepmother's curse and marries Olwen, daughter of Ysbaddaden Chief Giant. The interest throughout is in the action, with the hunting of the magical boar Twrch Trwyth reminiscent of a fast-moving film as he and his piglets are chased by Arthur and his men from Ireland, across South Wales, and eventually to Cornwall. All characters are stereotyped—the beautiful Olwen, the handsome Culhwch, the treacherous Ysbaddaden; talking to ants, owls, stags, and salmon poses no problem as one of Arthur's men, Gwrhyr

Interpreter of Languages, is there to translate. Indeed, the story, with its rhetorical set-pieces and burlesque scenes, is a world apart from the restraint and control of the 'Four Branches', and is, without doubt, a tale to be performed—vocality is of its essence.

Whereas all the other tales draw directly from oral tradition, 'Rhonabwy's Dream' probably only ever existed in a written form, as suggested by its colophon which claims that 'neither poet nor storyteller' knew the Dream 'without a book'. While the author is aware of traditional material, he uses this to create something completely new—a sophisticated piece of satirical writing which parodies not only the traditional storytelling techniques but also the Arthurian myth and its values. Indeed, as soon as Rhonabwy and his companions enter the house of a certain Heilyn Goch, and are up to their ankles in cows' urine and dung, and try to get to sleep in flea-infested beds, we realize that all is not as it should be! Moreover, having slept for three days and three nights on the yellow ox-skin, neither Rhonabwy nor the reader is offered an explanation, leaving the tale open to a variety of interpretations. This certainly is the most literary tale of them all, satirizing not only the elaborate descriptions of Arthurian knights, their horses, and their trappings, but also the structure of medieval romance itself.

The two short tales of 'Lludd and Llefelys' and 'The Dream of the Emperor Maxen' combine pseudo-historical traditions with folk-tale motifs, and offer an intriguing interpretation of British history. Lludd, who according to tradition was king of Britain shortly before Julius Caesar's invasion, overcomes three plagues that threaten the land, with the help of his brother Llefelys, king of France. All three plagues have parallels elsewhere in Welsh literature, and can be seen as variants on the theme of the historical invaders who threatened the sovereignty of the Island of Britain. However, despite great potential, the treatment throughout is rather dull and unimaginative. Maxen's story, on the other hand, is skilfully crafted, as he travels to Wales to marry the maiden he met in his love-dream. Maxen is the historical Magnus Maximus, proclaimed emperor by his troops in Britain in AD 383, and who became an important figure in Welsh historiography. The author of the tale clearly had antiquarian interests, for he then proceeds to give an onomastic account of the founding of Brittany by Cynan, Maxen's brother-in-law. Both tales are heavily indebted to historical sources and, like 'Rhonabwy's Dream', reflect a distancing from the oral tradition and a more conscious literary activity.

The *Mabinogion*, therefore, are a 'collection' of independent and extremely diverse tales. They provide a snapshot of the storyteller's repertoire, and give us an insight into the wealth of narrative material that was circulating in medieval Wales. Not only do they reflect themes and characters from myth and legend, they also show how Wales responded to conquest and colonization, and in so doing made a unique contribution to European literature.

Storytelling and the Oral Tradition

Although the *Mabinogion* have come down to us in written form, they clearly draw heavily on oral tradition and on the narrative techniques of the medieval storyteller. Of course, they are not merely written versions of oral narratives, but rather the work of authors using and shaping traditional material for their own purposes. Unlike the poetry of the period, none of the tales is attributed to an identified author, suggesting that there was no sense of 'ownership' as such, and that the texts were viewed as part of the collective memory. Indeed, on several occasions the final redactors (which may perhaps be a more correct term than 'authors' in many cases) draw attention to their sources, a common feature of medieval literature, but in so doing they distance themselves from those sources and set themselves up as merely the mouthpiece of tradition.

Although we have some evidence regarding the performance of poetry in medieval Wales, together with references to musicians such as harpists, crowthers, and pipers, and entertainers such as tumblers and magicians, very little is known of the performance of prose narrative. There is little evidence within the tales themselves—there are no requests for silence, no introductory remarks to the audience, and very few authorial asides. However, the Fourth Branch of the *Mabinogi* contains two passages that give a tantalizing glimpse of a storyteller in action. Upon entering the court of Pryderi, in the guise of a poet, the shape-shifter Gwydion receives a warm welcome and is offered the place of honour at table. When Pryderi asks some of Gwydion's young companions for a story, Gwydion offers his own services:

'Our custom, lord . . . is that on the first night we come to a great man, the chief poet performs. I would be happy to tell a story.'

Gwydion was the best storyteller in the world. And that night he entertained the court with amusing anecdotes and stories, until he was admired by everyone in the court, and Pryderi enjoyed conversing with him. (p. 48)

Later in the tale, Gwydion gains entrance to Aranrhod's court, again in the guise of a poet, and after dinner he and his host talk of tales and storytelling—'And Gwydion was a good storyteller' (p. 57).[3]

In both examples, there is a clear indication of an integral relationship between the poet and storytelling. According to the medieval Welsh laws, there were three types of poet—the *pencerdd* ('chief poet'), the *bardd teulu* ('household bard'), and *cerddor* (*joculator*), a generic term for poets and musicians rather than the more specific 'jester' or 'buffoon'. However, the laws make no reference at all to storytelling, implying perhaps that this was a secondary bardic function, given much less priority than elegy and eulogy, the predominant domains of the poet. Certainly, poets were acquainted with traditional stories, as reflected in the many allusions scattered throughout their work; yet it would seem from the surviving evidence that verse itself was not used for extended narrative in medieval Wales—the preferred medium, unlike most Indo-European countries, was prose. The situation, therefore, was not only a complex, but surely a dynamic one: despite the hierarchical legal structure, one could expect a certain degree of interaction between the various professional 'performers' as they entertained at feasts and gatherings. Moreover, there are examples within the *Mabinogion* themselves of personal narratives arising out of informal conversation at table, as in the Second Branch when Matholwch, king of Ireland, tells his table-companion Bendigeidfran the history of the Cauldron of Rebirth (pp. 26–7). It would appear, therefore, that storytelling was the domain of both the professional and the amateur, while the numerous words for 'story', as reflected in the tales themselves, point to a wide range of forms within the narrative genre.

In order to fully appreciate the *Mabinogion*, we have to understand the effect that this oral milieu had on the written tales. Oral and

---

[3] The Welsh word for 'storyteller' is *cyfarwydd*, which originally meant 'the well-informed person, expert', while the term *cyfarwyddyd* developed from its original sense of 'lore, the stuff of stories' to mean simply 'tale'.

performance features are an integral part of their fabric, partly because the authors inherited pre-literary modes of narrating, but also because the written tales were composed for oral delivery, so that their reception and dissemination continued to have an influence on both style and structure. Indeed, one of the overriding concerns of this new translation has been the attempt to communicate to readers the exhilarating power of performance.

Many features related to the tales' structure are inexorably linked to memorability: after all, if an oral tale is impossible to remember it will not survive. The structure of each tale is divided into manageable episodes, as reflected in manuscript layout and decoration, where large initials divide the manuscript texts in many instances. A more common technique is for tales to be divided by scene-setting phrases such as 'one day', 'one afternoon', which function as a boundary between one event and the next, or for episodes to be framed by verbal repetition, which acts as a 'chorus' of sorts and functions as a signal to a listening audience.[4] Indeed, one could argue that the episode was the all-important narrative unit, and that the authors were the first to combine such units into long composite texts, although the audience might well have been aware of an immanent whole. The chronological structure of each episode is again linked to memory, while the overwhelming presence of the conjunction 'and' may well be a reflection of the fragmented nature of spoken language. This, together with features such as the use of the present tense as the action intensifies, is a constant reminder of the crucial role played by oral performance in shaping the grammar and linguistic structure of vernacular narratives from the Middle Ages.

The onomastic tags that conclude several episodes point again to narrative that is memory-friendly: the three major episodes of the First Branch of the *Mabinogi*, for example, can be remembered by recourse to three onomastic explanations: (i) Why was Pwyll called Head of Annwfn? (ii) When was 'Badger in the Bag' first played? (iii) How did Pryderi get his name? Onomastic tales linked with place-names are a common feature of much of the corpus, too—they are a constant reminder of the significance of the place and the legends connected with it.

---

[4] For example, the beginning of the second major episode in the First Branch of the *Mabinogi* echoes the opening of the tale: 'Once upon a time Pwyll was at Arberth, one of his chief courts' (p. 8).

Repetition of events, with a high dependency on verbal repetition, is a common feature of any oral tale. This makes sense in practice, due to the ephemeral nature of oral prose or poetry. Tripartite repetition is particularly prevalent in the *Mabinogion*, employed to create suspense, and to focus. As well as verbal repetition within individual tales, one finds that certain phrases are common to more than one tale in the corpus, suggesting that the authors are drawing on a common pool of formulae or traditional patterns. Much has been written on the significance of the formula in oral poetry, ever since the work of Milman Parry and Albert Lord on Homeric diction and South Slavic heroic songs. Although metre is an integral part of the Parry–Lord formula, many scholars have shown that formulae, or stereotyped forms of expression, are also a distinctive feature of orally transmitted *prose*. In the *Mabinogion* they are employed to describe physical appearance, combat, horses, approach to a building, feasting, transition from one day to the next, and openings and endings of tales, so that although composition was in writing, formulae facilitated the retention, and therefore the reception, of the written text when read or heard.

Many passages in the *Mabinogion* demand a voiced performance. This is particularly true in the case of dialogue, which in some tales constitutes almost half the narrative. Often the action calls for a wide range of voices, from the giant Ysbaddaden to the drunken Peredur, from the ferocious boar Twrch Trwyth to the distressed Lady of the Well. Indeed, characters come alive through their words rather than through any descriptions which, if they exist at all, are in the main highly stereotyped. There are many other examples in the tales where a silent reading does not do them justice. This is particularly so in the case of 'How Culhwch Won Olwen', of which it has often been said it is a tale to be heard. The long rhetorical passage describing in detail Culhwch's steed, hounds, and equipment in a rhythmical fashion is highly reminiscent of the elaborate style of the court poets of medieval Wales, a style linked inexorably with public declamation, and found elsewhere throughout the corpus, not in extended paragraphs but as isolated descriptive phrases, especially with reference to horses, knights, squires, and in descriptions of combats, physical or verbal. The two lists in the tale also need to be read out loud for full effect. The first, a roll-call of those present at Arthur's court (pp. 184–9), is highly alliterative and descends into farce at times, with the rhetorical effect taking on more importance than the personalities themselves. Inserted in the list, too, are tantalizing fragments of narrative—the triad of the three men who escaped from the battle of Camlan, for example, or Teithi the Old whose lands were submerged by the sea—challenging the listeners' knowledge of traditional narrative. The second list is placed within a formulaic dialogue between Ysbaddaden and Culhwch (pp. 195–200), where the giant challenges Culhwch to perform forty seemingly impossible tasks in return for the hand of Olwen, his daughter. Upon hearing each task, Culhwch replies, 'It is easy for me to get that, though *you* may think it's not easy', to which the giant retorts, 'Though you may get that, there is something you will not get', and proceeds to describe the next challenge. The formulae therefore act as a chorus of sorts between the naming of each task, easing the listing, and also the listening, process.

The Tales and the Medieval Context

This is the milieu, therefore, in which the *Mabinogion* developed before they were committed to writing. Although the tales appear in the fourteenth-century Red and White Book manuscripts, fragments of individual tales occur in manuscripts earlier by a hundred years or so. It is unclear whether the texts represent the earliest attempts at recording narrative prose in the Welsh language, or whether they are merely the earliest surviving examples. The dating and chronology of the tales are also problematic, which complicates issues concerning the relationship between individual texts. However, we can probably assume that they were written down sometime between the end of the eleventh and the beginning of the fourteenth centuries, against a background of vast change in the history of Wales.[5] During this period the Welsh struggled to retain their independence in the face of the Anglo-Norman conquest which ultimately transformed the society, economy, and church of Wales. Wales was divided into four major kingdoms—Gwynedd in the north-west; Powys, which stretched from the borders of Mercia into central Wales; Deheubarth in the south-west; and Morgannwg or Glamorgan in the

---

[5] For an authoritative analysis of the history of the period, see R. R. Davies, *Conquest, Coexistence, and Change: Wales 1063–1415* (Oxford, 1987).

south-east. These were further divided into smaller units ruled by independent princes who vied with each other for supremacy. There was, therefore, no central unity, largely due to the difficulties imposed by physical geography, so that Wales did not develop into a single kingdom or kingship. With the erosion of Welsh authority in the south of the country, together with the establishment of the rule of the Anglo-Norman barons along the Welsh–English border, known as the March, there was an attempt to create a single Welsh principality under the leadership of the native princes of Gwynedd, figures such as Llywelyn ap Iorwerth (otherwise known as Llywelyn the Great, who was married to Joan, illegitimate daughter of King John), and Llywelyn ap Gruffudd, whose death at the hands of the English in 1282 brought any hopes of Welsh independence to an end. But even without the emergence of a common polity, Wales had an identity of its own, as exemplified by its language, culture, customs, and laws. Moreover, the Welsh had a shared sense of the past, and pride in a common descent from the Britons, the rightful owners of the Island of Britain.

This clear view of their own past is attested in sources such as *Trioedd Ynys Prydain* (The Triads of the Island of Britain), a catalogue of stories and characters listed in groups of three similar episodes or themes which would have facilitated the recall of the material for storytellers and poets. Some of the references are corroborated by surviving narratives. According to the triads, one of the 'Three Fortunate Concealments of the Island of Britain' is the head of Bendigeidfran, concealed in the White Hill in London with its face towards France to ward off Saxon oppression; indeed, the account in full is given in the third part of the Second Branch of the *Mabinogi*. As for other references, however, they will forever remain cryptic. Some of the triads deal with mythological themes and figures from the Welsh heroic age, but many, including the reference to Bendigeidfran, are concerned with the traditional history of Britain, focused on the notion of Britain as a single entity. The basic concept of medieval Welsh historiography was that the Welsh, descendants of the Britons, were the rightful heirs to the sovereignty of Britain, symbolized by the crown of London; despite invasions by the Romans and the Picts, and despite losing the crown to the Saxons, the Welsh would eventually overcome and a golden age of British rule would be restored. The theme of the loss of Britain can be traced back to the sixth century, to the work of the British monk Gildas; it is seen again some 300 years later in the anonymous *History of the Britons* (often ascribed to Nennius), and reaches its zenith in the twelfth century, in Geoffrey of Monmouth's highly influential, and largely fictional, *History of the Kings of Britain*—all these were works that helped forge the *Mabinogion*.

The tale of 'Lludd and Llefelys' and 'The Dream of the Emperor Maxen' closely mirror these themes. Indeed, the former is unique among the tales of the *Mabinogion* in that it first appears as an addition incorporated into a mid-thirteenth-century Welsh transla-tion of Geoffrey of Monmouth's work. There is no doubt that it was taken originally from the oral storytelling tradition, as testified by the translator himself. However, even in its slightly embellished form in the White and the Red Books, the tale owes more to a translation style than to the oral storytelling style of the other tales: there is almost no dialogue, the treatment of the tripartite repetition is unimaginative, while there is overall very little attention to detail and no desire to dwell on the magical qualities of the three plagues that threaten the Island of Britain. In the tale, after all, these are not represented as historical invaders; rather, they have been trans-formed into the realm of folk-tale and presented as supernatural oppressors: the Coraniaid, a race of people who are able to hear every word that is spoken; fighting dragons whose screams every May eve cause women to become barren and men to lose their senses; and a powerful magician who can lull the court to sleep. The tale can be read as an alternative rendering of a triad, in which the invaders are the Romans, the Picts, and the Saxons. Indeed, the episode of the dragons, who are eventually captured and laid to sleep at Dinas Emrys in Snowdonia, is related to the ninth-century *History of the Britons*, and linked with the development of the red dragon as a symbol of Welsh identity.

It may be no coincidence that 'The Dream of the Emperor Maxen' precedes 'Lludd and Llefelys' in both the White and the Red Books: the island is left at the mercy of foreign invaders as a result of Maxen's action for it was he who deprived Britain of her military resources when he led them away to fight on the Continent. Unlike the Latin chroniclers, however, the native Welsh tradition shows Maxen in a favourable light, a symbol of the relationship between Rome and Wales, and someone from whom medieval Welsh dynasties claim to derive their descent. As with 'Lludd and Llefelys', the author again combines historical facts with folk-tale motifs, the hero's quest for his true love, together with love-sickness, being common themes in Indo-European literature. This author, however, is much more skilful in his handling of the narrative, and especially in his imaginative treatment of the triple journey. When Maxen travels in his dream, the description of the journey itself is realistic, but actual geographical locations are imprecise. When his messengers go in search of the maiden, however, place-names are introduced and the journey is localized, although the maiden's name is not revealed. The third journey is over in a few lines, as Maxen himself travels to the Island of Britain, invades and defeats the inhabitants, and makes for the castle at Caernarfon in Gwynedd. It is only then that we learn the identity of the maiden and her family: she is Elen of the Hosts, daughter of Eudaf and sister of Cynan. The remainder of the tale is far less integrated, consisting of a collection of onomastic tales and an account of the founding of Brittany— Maxen travels to the Continent to defend his throne, and grants land in Brittany to Elen's brother, Cynan, in return for military support. The identity of the author is unknown, although interest in Caernarfon, together with dialect features, suggest that he might have come from North Wales. Indeed, the author may have been motivated by the historical circumstances of the reign of Llywelyn ap Iorwerth at the beginning of the thirteenth century, and the legend used 'as a contemporary declaration of the long-standing Gwynedd policy of Welsh hegemony', such a political motivation being in line with other attempts to fabricate or manipulate the past to justify the claims of Gwynedd.[6] Indeed, it may be significant that 'The Dream of the Emperor Maxen' is preceded by 'Peredur' in both the White and the Red Books—they could both be vestiges of the powerful court of Gwynedd.

Although very different in their approach, both 'How Culhwch Won Olwen' and 'Rhonabwy's Dream' look back to a time when Britain was under the rule of one leader—Arthur. In the former he is described as 'chief of the kings of this island'; in the latter, he is 'emperor'. 'Rhonabwy's Dream' is unique in that it survives only in the Red Book of Hergest. Moreover, in that manuscript some fifty-six

---

[6] Brynley F. Roberts (ed.), *Breudwyt Maxen Wledic* (Dublin, 2005), p. lxxxv.

columns separate it from the nearest *Mabinogion* tale—it is grouped
with a prophetic text and a version of the tale of the Seven Sages.
The opening suggests a pseudo-historical tale, where Madog ap
Maredudd, ruler of Powys, sends men to seek out his troublesome
brother Iorwerth; however, one of the envoys, Rhonabwy, falls asleep
on a yellow ox-skin and is granted a vision, reflecting the ritual of the
Irish poet-seers who were said to lie on the hides of bulls to acquire
hidden knowledge. But any comparison ends there, for Rhonabwy's
action occurs completely by chance—it is not premeditated—and he
is granted a vision of the distant Arthurian past rather than of future
events. Perhaps the most remarkable feature of this tale is that nothing really happens—there are digressions and detailed descriptions,
where the author combines every known formula possible, but very
few actions that lead to any clear outcomes. In fact, time runs backwards: Rhonabwy is guided through his dream by Iddog, who
has just completed seven years penance for causing the battle of
Camlan, Arthur's final battle; yet Arthur himself is then introduced,
and we are informed that the battle of Badon has not yet taken place!
Indeed, the account of that battle is replaced by a long and perfectly
balanced set-piece where Arthur plays *gwyddbwyll*, not against his
enemy, which may well have been an acceptable motif, but against
one of his own men, Owain son of Urien. As the board-game progresses Arthur and Owain's men attack and kill each other offstage,
and it is only when Arthur crushes all the pieces on the playing board
that a truce is finally called. When Rhonabwy wakes up to discover
that he has slept for three days and three nights, the tale comes to an
abrupt end—no commentary whatsoever is offered, and nothing
more is said of Rhonabwy, Madog, or Iorwerth.

The meaning of the dream and its purpose have been interpreted
in a variety of ways, much depending on views regarding the date of
the tale and the nature of the satire contained within it. The frame-
work is set in Powys during the reign of the historical Madog ap
Maredudd. The comparative stability of his reign (1130–60) was
followed by a period of unrest as Powys was divided between Madog's
sons, brother, and nephew. The tale may well have been composed in
the thirteenth century, when the author, surely someone from Powys,
was looking back to a golden age under Madog's rule; or it may be a
product of Madog's lifetime (he died in 1160), and the satire
aimed at contemporaries, even perhaps at Llywelyn ap Iorwerth of

Gwynedd, whose political ambition was to become, like Arthur, a national leader. On the other hand, Arthur himself and all his trappings seem to be mocked, so that the satire may be directed not so much at the past as at stories about the past, and against those who take the Arthurian myth and its values seriously.[7]

Whereas the author of 'Rhonabwy's Dream' may well have a cynical view of national leaders, the author of 'How Culhwch Won Olwen' sees Arthur as the model of an over-king, physically strong, decisive, focused, and leader of a band of ferocious warriors. The tale was probably first written down in south-east Wales, perhaps at Carmarthen, in the first half of the twelfth century; whatever its date, it certainly bears no resemblance to the Arthurian history of Geoffrey of Monmouth. Rather, the atmosphere is akin to that seen in early Welsh poems such as 'What Man is the Gatekeeper?', where Arthur and his band of warriors roam the country fighting witches, chasing monsters, and overpowering supernatural opponents. The action in the tale is centred on two classical international themes: the Jealous Stepmother and the Giant's Daughter. When the young Culhwch refuses to marry his stepmother's daughter, she puts a curse on him that he will marry no one save Olwen, the daughter of Ysbaddaden Chief Giant. At the mere mention of Olwen's name Culhwch falls in love with her, and sets off for Arthur's court to seek help. There he comes face to face with a host of men and women whose names are presented in a florid list—some 260 names in all—drawn from a variety of sources, reflecting both historical and legendary characters. Six warriors are enlisted as Culhwch's helpers, and they accompany him to Ysbaddaden's court, where we are presented with a list of forty tasks or marvels which Culhwch must achieve before he can win Olwen's hand. Some of these involve the provision of food, drink, and entertainment for the wedding feast, while many focus on the hunting of Twrch Trwyth, a magical boar (*twrch*) who has between his ears a comb and scissors required by Ysbaddaden to trim his hair for the special occasion. The account of how the tasks are accomplished forms a series of independent episodes in which Arthur, together with warriors such as Cai and Bedwyr, help Culhwch win his bride.

---

[7] See Edgar M. Slotkin, 'The Fabula, Story, and Text of *Breuddwyd Rhonabwy*', *Cambridge Medieval Celtic Studies*, 18 (1989), 89–111.

The underlying structure of the tale is, therefore, quite simple, and is a focus for a myriad of international motifs—grateful animals, magical helpers, horns and hampers of plenty. However, we are presented with an inconsistent, undisciplined, and lengthy composition. The main flaw in the structure is that the listing of the tasks and their ultimate completion do not form a balanced unity—of the forty tasks that are set by the giant Ysbaddaden, only twenty-one are accomplished. But was there ever a version of the tale in which all forty tasks were successfully executed? As was suggested earlier, the long prose form may never have existed at all in the oral medium, and may have only come into being with the development of literary writing. Indeed, perhaps the male and female protagonists—the stereotyped Culhwch and Olwen—were a deliberate creation on the part of the author as a vehicle to bring together numerous episodes that were already in circulation concerning Arthur and the Arthurian world. The hunting of Twrch Trwyth certainly has a long history—a reference is made to Arthur's hunting of the supernatural creature in the ninth-century *History of the Britons*, while allusions in medieval poetry show that traditions concerning the animal were well known all over Wales. Indeed, it might be no coincidence that Culhwch himself takes his name from the pig-run in which he was born. Or was this onomastic merely another creation on the part of an author who delighted so much in words and word-play? For, more than anything else, this is what makes the tale unique, together with its unbounding energy, its humour, and sheer panache.

The Arthurian world presented in 'How Culhwch Won Olwen' is very different to that found in 'Peredur son of Efrog', 'Geraint son of Erbin', and 'The Lady of the Well'.[8] In the former Culhwch and Arthur's men encounter giants, witches, and magical creatures; Arthur is a proactive figure, leading by example; his court, home to archaic social and legal customs, is at Celli Wig in Cornwall; the atmosphere is one of aggression and heroic machismo. In the later tales, however, his court is relocated at Caerllion on Usk, under the influence of Geoffrey of Monmouth, and Arthur's role is similar to

---

[8] For an overall survey of Arthurian references in medieval Welsh literature, see O. J. Padel, *Arthur in Medieval Welsh Literature* (Cardiff, 2000). For a more detailed analysis of individual Arthurian texts, see *The Arthur of the Welsh: The Arthurian Legend in Medieval Welsh Literature*, ed. Rachel Bromwich, A. O. H. Jarman, and Brynley F. Roberts (Cardiff, 1991).

that found in the Continental romances—as a shadowy, fairly passive figure, who leaves adventure and danger to his knights. There are no clear geographical or political boundaries to his kingdom, and the action takes place in a somewhat unreal, daydream-like world. On the surface the three tales convey a common theme, in that the young hero embarks on a journey and goes in search of adventure; a string of events follow, usually in no particular order—their *raison d'être* is to put the hero to the test. Owain wins his bride, but he neglects her, preferring to remain at Arthur's court with his companions; however, he is reminded of the error of his ways and the couple are eventually reunited. Geraint wins his bride, but becomes preoccupied with her and deserts his knightly responsibilities; he misinterprets her anxiety as love for another man, and takes her on a gruelling journey, but eventually, after a series of trials, they are reconciled. In *Peredur*, on the other hand, the hero's initial journey transforms him from a country bumpkin into a skilful knight; he then wins a reluctant love, Angharad, before gaining the admiration of the empress of Constantinople, with whom he stays for fourteen years; finally he embarks on a perilous journey that takes him to the Castle of Wonders, where the witches of Caerloyw (Gloucester) are slain and vengeance is his. The treatment tends to be uncourtly, with no interest in the characters' feelings or motives, no authorial asides or comments; rather, the emphasis throughout is on the action, with no attempt whatsoever at psychological digressions. What seems to have occurred, therefore, is that Wales accepted certain themes prevalent in the romance tradition, such as the education of the knight, and moderation between love and military prowess; however, other features were rejected as being too foreign, culminating in three hybrid texts, typical of a post-colonial world.

Structurally, the three tales are different: 'The Lady of the Well' is concise and well proportioned, based on three journeys to the magic well; 'Geraint' is longer and slightly more complex, especially in the opening section, where the narrative alternates between different protagonists; but the overall structure is clear and linear. 'Peredur', however, is a different matter, due perhaps to its textual instability which raises questions regarding the nature of the tale itself. A 'full' version is preserved in the White and the Red Books, an incomplete fragment in the manuscript Peniarth 14 (*c.* 1300–50), which breaks off in mid-sentence during Peredur's visit to his second uncle, while an earlier version has survived in Peniarth 7 (*c.*1300), which lacks the opening paragraphs and ends the story, deliberately so it would seem, when the hero settles down to reign with the empress of Constantinople. This short version is the earliest, and probably the closest to the oral milieu; indeed, it may have been circulating for a while before some individual added further episodes in an attempt to explain the unresolved events of the first part of the tale. Both long and short versions can be regarded as authentic and complete in themselves, raising significant issues regarding the notion of 'authorship' and 'version' in the medieval context.

With 'The Four Branches of the *Mabinogi*' we return to a familiar geographical landscape and a society apparently pre-dating any Norman influence. Indeed, the action is located in a pre-Christian Wales, where the main protagonists are mythological figures such as Lleu, cognate with the Celtic god Lugus, and Rhiannon, whose horse-imagery has led her to be equated with Epona, the Celtic horse-goddess. Even though it is doubtful whether their significance was understood by a medieval audience, the mythological themes make for fascinating stories: journeys to an otherworld paradise where time stands still and mortals do not age; the Cauldron of Rebirth, which revives dead warriors but takes away their speech; shape-shifting, where an unfaithful wife is transformed into an owl or a pregnant wife into a mouse. Such events are interwoven with well-known themes and motifs from the world of storytelling. Both Rhiannon's and Branwen's penances are variations on the theme of the Calumniated Wife: when her son disappears on the night of his birth, Rhiannon is forced to act like a horse and carry people on her back to court, while Branwen is made to suffer for her half-brother Efnysien's insult to the king of Ireland. A monster hand, a cloak of invisibility, a magic mist—these are all elements that contribute to making the Four Branches examples of some of the best storytelling ever.

But these are more than mere tales of magic and suspense. Despite the absence of a clear, overarching structure, there is within them a thematic unity that gives a consistency to the tales and suggests a single author working with traditional material to put forward a consistent view regarding appropriate moral behaviour. In the first three branches the nature of insult, compensation, and friendship are explored, and acts of revenge are shown to be totally

destructive—legal settlement and hard bargaining are to be preferred. In the Fourth Branch, however, further considerations are
raised. Math, lord of Gwynedd, is not only insulted but also dis-
honoured, as his virgin foot-holder is raped and his dignity as a
person is attacked. The offenders, his own nephews, are transformed
into animals—male and female—and are shamed by having offspring from one another. However, once their punishment is complete Math forgives them in the spirit of reconciliation. As noted by
Brynley F. Roberts, 'legal justice is necessary for the smooth working
of society, but without the graces of forgetting and forgiving, human
pride will render the best systems unworkable'.[9] Throughout the
Four Branches, therefore, the author conveys a scale of values which
he commends to contemporary society, doing so by implication
rather than by any direct commentary. The listeners are left to draw
their own conclusions, and to realize that the image of a man alone,
at the end of the Fourth Branch, with no wife and no heir, does not
make for a promising future.

It is this genuine interest in human nature that makes the Four
Branches stand out, suggesting that we are here dealing with an
author in the true sense of the word. Although he is deeply indebted
to oral narrative techniques, he has begun to move away from the
one-dimensional world of the storyteller, creating strongly delineated
characters that he uses to convey his views—the wise and cautious
Manawydan; the warped Efnysien; the complex Gwydion; and the
impetuous Pwyll, who gradually discovers the true meaning of his
name—'wisdom' or 'caution'. Even so, it is probably the women
who are the most memorable; between them Rhiannon, Branwen,
Blodeuedd, and Aranrhod place the men in situations where they
must make decisions, and their choice determines the fate of all
concerned. The characters come alive not through any authorial
comments, but through lively dialogue which becomes more than
simply pleasantries, and is harnessed to create intense drama. The
identity of this medieval author is, of course, unknown. He may have
been a cleric, or perhaps a court lawyer, as suggested by the legal
terms and concepts reflected in the tales. However, any conjecture
rests on dating, and although the general consensus is that the tales

---

[9] Brynley F. Roberts, *Studies on Middle Welsh Literature* (Lewiston, Queenston, and
Lampeter, 1992), 101.

were first committed to writing between *c.*1060 and 1120, nothing is certain. But the author, whoever it was, had an extraordinary ear for dialogue, created unforgettable characters, and conjured up the most dramatic scenes; all in all, he gave us stories unparalleled in the literature of the Middle Ages.

Re-creating the Mabinogion

After the medieval period the *Mabinogion* were mainly the preserve of copyists and antiquarians until the nineteenth century, when they were 're-created' in the wake of the Romantic Revival and the rediscovery of medieval literature. By then King Arthur had returned from Avalon, with his legend reinvented through Victorian eyes. Writers—and artists too—projected their own ideals and values onto the legendary characters and events, so that the chivalric past became a vehicle for educating the present, as reflected in the works of Walter Scott and Tennyson. The time was ripe, therefore, to introduce the *Mabinogion* to an English-speaking audience.

Lady Charlotte Guest (1812–95) was not only responsible for publishing the first translation of the *Mabinogion* into English, but she must be given credit, too, for popularizing the tales and, of course, their title. Daughter of the ninth earl of Lindsay, she grew up in Lincolnshire, but in 1833 married the industrialist Josiah John Guest, owner of the Dowlais Iron Company in South Wales. Her detailed journal, from 1822 to 1881, relates how, among other things, she gave birth to ten children, founded schools for the education of the working classes in the Dowlais area (for both male and female pupils), and translated all eleven tales of the *Mabinogion* (together with the tale of Taliesin) into English.[10] Her huge, multi-volume work (1838–46) presents the text in English and in Welsh, with detailed scholarly notes, variant versions in other languages of the three Arthurian romances, illustrations, and facsimiles from the Red Book of Hergest and from manuscripts of other

[10] For a detailed study of her life, see Revel Guest and Angela John, *Lady Charlotte: A Biography of the Nineteenth Century* (London, 1989). After her husband's death Lady Guest married Charles Schreiber, her eldest son's tutor, and travelled extensively on the Continent with him, collecting eighteenth-century ceramics; the Schreiber Collection can be seen today in the Victoria and Albert Museum.

versions.[11] Apart from translating in the spirit of the Romantic Revival, she had another reason for wanting to turn these medieval Welsh tales into English: she wanted to reveal to the English-speaking world the supremacy of the 'ancient' Celtic literature, of the 'venerable relics of ancient lore'. In her opinion, Welsh literature had an intrinsic worth, and the tales of the *Mabinogion* deserved a place on the European stage; indeed, Guest went so far as to argue that 'the Cymric nation . . . has strong claims to be considered the cradle of European Romance'. Similar views are expressed by nineteenth-century translators, translating from Irish into English, as outlined by Michael Cronin, where he argues that 'translation relationships between minority and majority languages are rarely divorced from issues of power and identity'.[12] Indeed, in Wales, as in Ireland, associations emerged to promote scholarship in the language—ancient texts were resurrected from manuscripts and translated to show the 'colonizers' that the 'colonized' were civilized and in possession of a noble literary heritage.

Despite its lack of rigour, there is no doubt that Guest's translation had far-reaching consequences. The texts were translated quickly into both French (1842 and 1889) and German (1841); John Campbell compared the Welsh tales with those he had collected in the West Highlands, while Alfred Nutt pointed out resemblances between the story of Branwen and the Nibelung and Gudrun sagas. The translation also stimulated further scholarship on Celtic literature, such as Ernest Renan's *Essai sur la poésie des races celtiques* (1854)—the first attempt at any kind of comparative study of the Celtic literatures—and Matthew Arnold's *Lectures upon the Study of Celtic Literature* (1867). The work also had a direct impact on the literature of the target language—Tennyson founded his poem 'Geraint and Enid' in his *Idylls of the King* on her translation of 'Geraint son of Erbin'. Indeed, through the endeavours of Charlotte Guest the tales of the *Mabinogion* were given their rightful place on the European stage and assumed a prestige far beyond that which they might have achieved had they remained in the Welsh language alone, lending

[11] However, revised editions of her translation were condensed, and the Welsh text omitted; in other words, the text became appropriated by the culture of the English target language.

[12] Michael Cronin, *Translating Ireland: Translation, Languages, Cultures* (Cork, 1996), 4.

support to Lefevere's argument that 'rewritten texts can be as important for the reception and canonization of a work of literature as its actual writing'.[13]

Since then three other English translations have appeared, most notably the rigorously accurate, if overtly literal, translation of Gwyn Jones and Thomas Jones (1948), which replaced Guest's version in the renowned Everyman's Library.[14] In spite of the performance potential of the *Mabinogion*, dramatic genres have been slow to exploit the material. *The Cauldron of Annwn*, an operatic trilogy loosely based on the Four Branches, was composed and performed in the first quarter of the twentieth century—Lord Howard de Walden (T. E. Scott-Ellis) wrote the librettos, with music by Josef Holbrooke. Its three operas are concerned with the effects of a cauldron whose fumes magnify emotion to the point of obsession: *The Children of Don*,[15] *Bronwen*, and *Dylan: Son of Wave* (staged in London at Drury Lane in 1914, with the sets and costumes designed by the English artist Sidney Herbert Sime and the orchestra conducted by Thomas Beecham).[16] Welsh dramatists Saunders Lewis and Gareth Miles have also turned to the Four Branches, while the tales in general continue to inspire Welsh poets and novelists, as well as English-language writers such as Evangeline Walton, Anthony Conran, Gillian Clarke, and Alan Garner. In each case the modern authors have interpreted the tales according to their own personal vision, tangible proof of their lasting significance and resonance. More recent ventures in re-creating the *Mabinogion* have included a foray into film: 2002 saw the release of a ninety-minute animated version of the Four Branches under the title *Y Mabinogi* (*Otherworld* in the English-language version), produced by Cartŵn Cymru for the Welsh television channel S4C. The scriptwriters decided that the animated version should not only entertain but also educate and

---

[13] André Lefevere, *Translation, Rewriting, and the Manipulation of Literary Fame* (London, 1992), back cover.

[14] See T. P. Ellis and John Lloyd, *The Mabinogion: A New Translation* (Oxford, 1929), and Jeffrey Gantz, *The Mabinogion* (Harmondsworth, 1976). In his *The Mabinogi and Other Medieval Welsh Tales* (Berkeley, Los Angeles, and London, 1977), Patrick K. Ford included a translation of the Four Branches of the *Mabinogi*, 'Lludd and Llefelys', 'Culhwch and Olwen', 'The Tale of Gwion Bach', and 'The Tale of Taliesin'.

[15] First staged in the London Opera House in 1912, this was also translated into German and performed in Vienna in 1923.

[16] The trilogy is in clear emulation of Wagner's *Der Ring der Nibelungen*.

inspire; there is a genuine attempt, therefore, to reflect the ideological perspectives of the literary narrator.[17] Transmitting the Four Branches to the screen offers a return to the oral and the aural, but at the same time it offers wider dissemination and an international audience. This 'new' orality has a striking resemblance to the old in its fostering of a communal sense, its invitation to a shared experience, its focus on the actual moment; but, of course, it is a more deliberate and self-conscious orality, where communication is strictly one-way, with no *inter*action between listener and performer.

We have travelled a long way from the storytellers of medieval Wales, yet the *Mabinogion* retain their fascination, captivating us not only with their fantastic glimpses of the surreal world of magic and enchantment, but also through their sheer inventive fecundity—the pleasure the narratives take in fabrics and colour, in weapons and horses, in people and places. Individually, each tale is unique; together, they form a collection that is unsurpassed. With stories such as these to draw upon, it is no wonder that Gwydion, in the Fourth Branch of the *Mabinogi*, is described as 'the best storyteller in the world'.

[17] For further details see www.S4c.co.uk/otherworld/.

TRANSLATOR'S NOTE

THE present translation is based largely on current editions of the eleven tales (see the Select Bibliography), although paragraphing and sentence division have been modified in line with my own interpretation of narrative structure and punctuation—the two manuscripts which form the basis for most of the edited versions (the White Book of Rhydderch and the Red Book of Hergest) present the tales in blocks of continuous prose, with large capitals, rubrications, and opening/ending formulae segmenting the narrative. My debt to all the editors will be apparent, as will the benefit received from the most recent linguistic scholarship in the field.

The overriding aim of this translation has been to convey the performability of the surviving manuscript versions. As emphasized in the Introduction, the *Mabinogion* were tales to be read aloud to a listening audience—the parchment was 'interactive' and vocality was of its essence. Indeed, many passages can only be truly captured by the speaking voice. The acoustic dimension was, therefore, a major consideration in this new translation: every effort has been made to transfer the rhythm, tempo, and alliteration of the original to the target language. The repetitive element in all eleven tales has been preserved, with due regard for the formulaic content, while the present tense, employed to describe dramatic events in the source-language text, has been retained where possible to convey the excitement of the narration. In 'How Culhwch Won Olwen' the rhetorical passages have been divided into short lines in an attempt to transmit the rhythm of the oral performance visually to the printed page. Yet, inevitably, the demands of modern English usage have overridden choices in certain areas: for example, the connective 'and', an integral part of the tales' micro-structure, has sometimes been omitted where it was felt to be too intrusive; and where speakers are not identified, their names have sometimes been added to the lines of direct speech, for clarification. Many of the proper names, especially in 'How Culhwch Won Olwen', embody meanings that give an insight into the characters, and are often associated with onomastic explanations, although to what extent this was always apparent to a medieval audience is unclear.

In an attempt to weigh up the loss to the English-speaking reader
if personal names are in Welsh only, against the loss of authenticity
if they are translated, I have chosen to retain the original Welsh
name (in modern orthography), but to provide a translation, and
often a further explanation, in the Explanatory Notes at the first
occurrence of the name. At subsequent occurrences the reader is
able to turn to the Index of Personal Names, which repeats the
English translation and refers to the relevant notes. The long Court
List of 'How Culhwch Won Olwen', with its 260 proper names,
proved a challenge worthy of the giant Ysbaddaden's impossible
tasks. I decided to give the reader a choice—the original Welsh
names are retained in the main text, so that the reader can appreciate
the rhythm and alliterative quality, while an alternative list is
provided in the notes, where all names, as far as possible, have been
translated into English.

In the translation by Gwyn Jones and Thomas Jones (1948), the
tales are presented in the following order: *The Four Branches of the
Mabinogi* ('Pwyll prince of Dyfed', 'Branwen daughter of Llŷr',
'Manawydan son of Llŷr', 'Math son of Mathonwy'); *The Four
Independent Native Tales* ('The Dream of Macsen Wledig', 'Lludd
and Llefelys', 'Culhwch and Olwen', 'The Dream of Rhonabwy');
The Three Romances ('The Lady of the Fountain', 'Peredur son of
Efrawg', 'Gereint son of Erbin'). Because of the immense popularity
of their translation, these artificial groupings have, to a large extent,
influenced our reading of the tales. In the White and Red Book
manuscripts the following groupings are common to both: (i) The
Four Branches of the *Mabinogi*; (ii) 'Peredur son of Efrog', 'The
Dream of the Emperor Maxen', 'Lludd and Llefelys'; (iii) 'Geraint
son of Erbin', 'How Culhwch Won Olwen'. There may well be no
particular rationale behind this—perhaps certain groupings already
existed in the scribe's exemplars. However, it seemed appropriate,
for the purpose of the current translation, to reflect the groupings of
the extant manuscripts. I also decided to follow the order of the
earliest manuscript, placing 'Rhonabwy's Dream', which is not
included in the White Book, at the end of the 'collection' due to
its apparent literary context. The aim, therefore, is to challenge
any preconceived notions and to provide a platform from which to
re-examine the relationship between the individual tales.

In an attempt to understand the resonances of these medieval

Welsh texts, Explanatory Notes and Indexes of Personal and Place-Names are provided; their aim is to enhance the reading experience by placing the tales in a wider cultural and literary context, and by highlighting the intertextuality of medieval Welsh prose narrative. We can never expect to recover the tradition of reception that existed in medieval Wales. But we can try to recognize the signals, understand the cues, in order to transmit to a modern-day reader these unique theatrical experiences.

GUIDE TO PRONUNCIATION

Since the emphasis in this translation is on performance, it is important that readers think about how the texts would have sounded to a listening audience, especially the alliterative personal names. Welsh spelling is largely phonetic, with the stress falling almost always on the penultimate syllable, e.g. Mabinógion, Perédur, Máxen, Llefélys, Géraint, Rhonábwy. The following is meant to be a very rough guide rather than an accurate phonetic description.

Welsh consonants

As in English, except for the following:

c	*carol*; never as in *cider*
ch	*loch*; never as in *chair*
dd	*this*; never as in *thorn*
f	as in *of*
ff	as in *off*
g	*girl*; never *gem*
ng	*sing*; never *angel* or *finger*
h	*hat*; never silent in Welsh
ll	articulated by putting the tongue in the *l* position and producing a voiceless breathy sound
r	trilled/rolled as in Italian
rh	articulated by putting the tongue in the *r* position and producing a voiceless breathy sound
s	*sit*; never *rose*
	si + vowel is pronounced as *sh*, as in *shop*
th	*thin*; never *the*

i and *w* can also be used as consonants:

i	*yes*
w	*water*

Welsh vowels can be short or long

a	*cat*	*father*
e	*pet*	*bear*
i	*sit*	*machine*

o	*pot*	*more*
u	*sit*	*machine*
w	*cook*	*pool*
y	*sit*	*machine*
		cut (in all positions except monosyllables and final syllables)

Diphthongs

ae, ai, au	*aye*
aw	*ah + oo*
ei, eu, ey	*eye*
ew	*eh + oo* (*well* backwards)
iw, uw	*dew*
oe, oi	*oil*
ow	*Owen*, not *down*
yw	*bough*
wy	*gooy* (with the two vowels compressed into one syllable)

Mutations

The beginnings of Welsh words change (or mutate) under certain circumstances; for example, *Cymru* (Wales) can appear as *Gymru*, *Chymru*, and *Nghymru*. A mutation also takes place in the second of two words joined together as a compound, thus affecting many of the proper names found in the *Mabinogion* (e.g. Glewlwyd < glew + llwyd; Ewingath < ewin + cath).

Pronunciation of Common Names (an accent denotes stress)

Aranrhod	Arr-ánn-hrod
Bendigeidfran	Ben-dee-géyed-vran
Blodeuedd	Blod-éye-ethe
Branwen	Brán-wen
Cai	Kaye
Cigfa	Kíg-vah
Culhwch	Kíll-hooch
Enid	Énn-id
Gilfaethwy	Gill-váye-thooee
Gronw	Gróh-noo
Gwenhwyfar	Gwen-hóoy-varr
Gwydion	Góoyd-eeon

Llefelys	Llev-él-iss
Lleu	Ll-eye
Lludd	Lleethe
Luned	Lýn-ed
Manawydan	Man-ah-wúd-an [*wud* as in *bud*]
Matholwch	Math-óll-ooch
Olwen	Ól-wen
Owain	Ów-aye-n
Peredur	Per-éd-eer
Pryderi	Prud-érry [*Prud* as in *bud*]
Pwyll	Pooy-ll
Rhiannon	Hree-án-on
Rhonabwy	Hron-áb-ooee
Ysbaddaden	Us-bath-ád-en [*th* as in *then*]

SELECT BIBLIOGRAPHY

Editions (including a substantial introduction and notes)
* denotes a Welsh-language edition

Rachel Bromwich and D. Simon Evans, *Culhwch and Olwen: An Edition and Study of the Oldest Arthurian Tale* (Cardiff, 1988).

Patrick K. Ford, *Math uab Mathonwy* (Belmont, Mass., 1999).

—— *Manawydan uab Llyr* (Belmont, Mass., 2000).

Glenys Witchard Goetinck, *Historia Peredur vab Efrawc* (Cardiff, 1976).*

Ian Hughes, *Math uab Mathonwy* (Aberystwyth, 2000).*

Melville Richards, *Breudwyt Ronabwy* (Cardiff, 1948).*

Brynley F. Roberts, *Cyfranc Lludd a Llefelys* (Dublin, 1975).

—— *Breudwyt Maxen Wledic* (Dublin, 2005).

Derick S. Thomson, *Branwen Uerch Lyr* (Dublin, 1976).

R. L. Thomson, *Pwyll Pendeuic Dyuet* (Dublin, 1957).

—— *Owein or Chwedyl Iarlles y Ffynnawn* (Dublin, 1968).

—— *Ystorya Gereint Uab Erbin* (Dublin, 1997).

Ifor Williams, *Pedeir Keinc y Mabinogi* (Cardiff, 1930).*

Translations

T. P. Ellis and John Lloyd, *The Mabinogion: A New Translation* (Oxford, 1929).

Patrick K. Ford, *The Mabinogi and Other Medieval Welsh Tales* (Berkeley, Los Angeles, and London, 1977).

Jeffrey Gantz, *The Mabinogion* (Harmondsworth, 1976).

Lady Charlotte Guest, *The Mabinogion from the Llyfr Coch o Hergest, and other Ancient Welsh manuscripts* (London, 1836–49).

Gwyn Jones and Thomas Jones, *The Mabinogion* (London, 1948).

Critical Studies

Rachel Bromwich, A. O. H. Jarman, and Brynley F. Roberts (eds.), *The Arthur of the Welsh: The Arthurian Legend in Medieval Welsh Literature* (Cardiff, 1991).

Sioned Davies, *The Four Branches of the Mabinogi* (Llandysul, 1993).

—— *Crefft y Cyfarwydd: Astudiaeth o dechnegau naratif yn Y Mabinogion* (Cardiff, 1995).

—— and Peter Wynn Thomas (eds.), *Canhwyll Marchogyon: Cyd-destunoli Peredur* (Cardiff, 2000).

Glenys Goetinck, *Peredur: A Study of Welsh Tradition in the Grail Legends* (Cardiff, 1975).

W. J. Gruffydd, *Rhiannon: An Inquiry into the First and Third Branches of the Mabinogi* (Cardiff, 1953).

Ceridwen Lloyd-Morgan (ed.), *Arthurian Literature XXI: Celtic Arthurian Material* (Cambridge, 2004).

Proinsias Mac Cana, *The Mabinogi* (Cardiff, 1977; revised edn. 1992).

O. J. Padel, *Arthur in Medieval Welsh Literature* (Cardiff, 2000).

Brynley F. Roberts, *Studies on Middle Welsh Literature* (Lewiston, Queenston, and Lampeter, 1992).

C. W. Sullivan III (ed.), *The Mabinogi: A Book of Essays* (New York and London, 1996).

Cultural and Social Background

Rachel Bromwich (ed. and trans.), *Trioedd Ynys Prydein: The Triads of the Island of Britain* (Cardiff, 1961; revised edn. 2006).

R. R. Davies, *Conquest, Coexistence and Change: Wales 1063–1415* (Oxford, 1987).

Sioned Davies and Nerys Ann Jones (eds.), *The Horse in Celtic Culture: Medieval Welsh Perspectives* (Cardiff, 1997).

Miranda Green, *The Gods of the Celts* (Gloucester, 1986).

Daniel Huws, *Medieval Welsh Manuscripts* (Cardiff, 2000).

Dafydd Jenkins (ed. and trans.), *The Law of Hywel Dda* (Llandysul, 1986).

—— and Morfydd E. Owen (eds.), *The Welsh Law of Women* (Cardiff, 1980).

Proinsias Mac Cana, *Celtic Mythology* (London, 1968; revised edn. 1983).

Huw Pryce (ed.), *Literacy in Medieval Celtic Societies* (Cambridge, 1998).

Anne Ross, *Pagan Celtic Britain* (London, 1967).

Lewis Thorpe (trans.), *Geoffrey of Monmouth: The History of the Kings of Britain* (Harmondsworth, 1966).

Further Reading in Oxford World's Classics

Eirik the Red, ed. Gwyn Jones.

Wolfram von Eschenbach, *Parzival*, trans. Cyril Edwards, introduction by Richard Barber.

Elias Lönnrot, *The Kalevala*, trans. Keith Bosley.

Thomas Malory, *Le Morte Darthur*, trans. Helen Cooper.

The Poetic Edda, ed. Caroline Larrington.

Sir Gawain and the Green Knight, ed. Keith Harrison and Helen Cooper.

Tales of the Elders of Ireland, ed. Ann Dooley and Harry Roe.

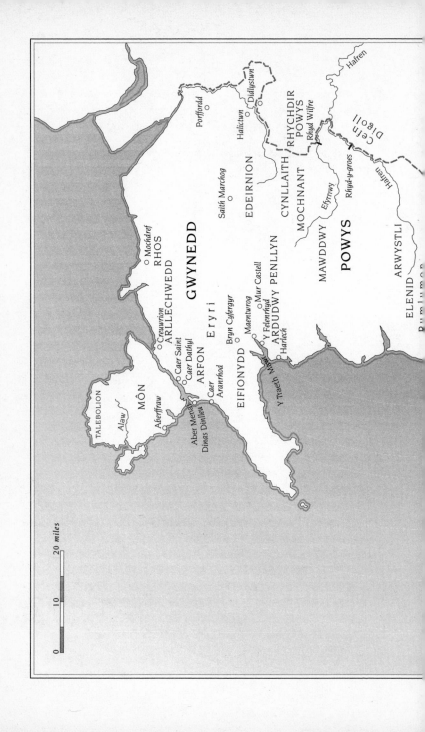

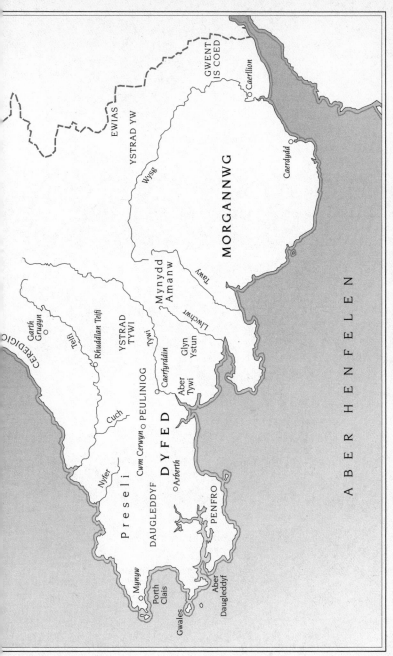

The Wales of the *Mabinogion*

THE
MABINOGION

The First Branch of the Mabinogi

PWYLL, prince of Dyfed, was lord over the seven cantrefs of Dyfed.* Once upon a time he was at Arberth, one of his chief courts, and it came into his head and his heart to go hunting. The part of his realm he wanted to hunt was Glyn Cuch.* He set out that night from Arberth, and came as far as Pen Llwyn Diarwya, and stayed there that night. And early the next day he got up, and came to Glyn Cuch to unleash his dogs in the forest. And he blew his horn, and began to muster the hunt, and went off after the dogs, and became separated from his companions. And as he was listening for the cry of his pack, he heard the cry of another pack, but these had a different cry, and they were coming towards his own pack. And he could see a clearing in the forest, a level field; and as his own pack was reaching the edge of the clearing, he saw a stag in front of the other pack. And towards the middle of the clearing, the pack that was chasing caught up with the stag and brought it to the ground.

Then Pwyll looked at the colour of the pack, without bothering to look at the stag. And of all the hounds he had seen in the world, he had never seen dogs of this colour—they were a gleaming shining white, and their ears were red.* And as the whiteness of the dogs shone so did the redness of their ears. Then he came to the dogs, and drove away the pack that had killed the stag, and fed his own pack on it.

As he was feeding the dogs, he could see a rider coming after the pack on a large dapple-grey horse, with a hunting horn round his neck, and wearing hunting clothes of a light grey material. Then the rider came up to him, and spoke to him like this: 'Sir,' he said, 'I know who you are, but I will not greet you.'*

'Well,' said Pwyll, 'perhaps your rank is such that you are not obliged to.'

'God knows,' he said, 'it's not the level of my rank that prevents me.'

'What else, sir?' said Pwyll.

'Between me and God,' he said, 'your own lack of manners and discourtesy.'

'What discourtesy, sir, have you seen in me?'

'I have seen no greater discourtesy in a man,' he said, 'than to drive away the pack that had killed the stag, and feed your own pack on it; that', he said, 'was discourtesy: and although I will not take revenge upon you, between me and God,' he said, 'I will bring shame upon you to the value of a hundred stags.'

'Sir,' said Pwyll, 'if I have done wrong, I will redeem your friendship.'*

'How will you redeem it?' he replied.

'According to your rank, but I do not know who you are.'

'I am a crowned king in the land that I come from.'

'Lord,' said Pwyll, 'good day to you. And which land do you come from?'

'From Annwfn,' he replied. 'I am Arawn, king of Annwfn.'*

'Lord,' said Pwyll, 'how shall I win your friendship?'

'This is how,' he replied. 'A man whose territory is next to mine is forever fighting me. He is Hafgan, a king from Annwfn. By ridding me of that oppression—and you can do that easily—you will win my friendship.'

'I will do that gladly,' said Pwyll. 'Tell me how I can do it.'

'I will,' he replied. 'This is how: I will make a firm alliance with you. What I shall do is to put you in my place in Annwfn, and give you the most beautiful woman you have ever seen to sleep with you every night, and give you my face and form so that no chamberlain nor officer nor any other person who has ever served me shall know that you are not me. All this', he said, 'from tomorrow until the end of the year, and then we shall meet again in this place.'

'Well and good,' Pwyll replied, 'but even if I am there until the end of the year, how will I find the man of whom you speak?'

'A year from tonight,' Arawn said, 'there is a meeting between him and me at the ford. Be there in my shape,' he said, 'and you must give him only one blow—he will not survive it.* And although he may ask you to give him another, you must not, however much he begs you. Because no matter how many more blows I gave him, the next day he was fighting against me as well as before.'

'Well and good,' said Pwyll, 'but what shall I do with my realm?'

'I shall arrange that no man or woman in your realm realizes that I am not you, and I will take your place,'* said Arawn.

'Gladly,' said Pwyll, 'and I will go on my way.'

'Your path will be smooth, and nothing will hinder you until you get to my land, and I will escort you.'

Arawn escorted Pwyll until he saw the court and dwelling-places.

'There is the court and the realm under your authority,' he said. 'Make for the court; there is no one there who will not recognize you. And as you observe the service there, you will come to know the custom of the court.'

He made his way to the court. He saw sleeping quarters there and halls and rooms and the most beautifully adorned buildings that anyone had seen. And he went to the hall to take off his boots. Chamberlains and young lads came to remove his boots, and everyone greeted him as they arrived. Two knights came to remove his hunting clothes, and to dress him in a golden garment of brocaded silk. The hall was got ready. With that he could see a war-band and retinues coming in, and the fairest and best-equipped men that anyone had ever seen, and the queen with them, the most beautiful woman that anyone had seen, wearing a golden garment of shining brocaded silk. Then they went to wash, and went to the tables, and sat like this,* the queen on his one side and the earl,* he supposed, on the other. And he and the queen began to converse. As he conversed with her, he found her to be the most noble woman and the most gracious of disposition and discourse he had ever seen. They spent the time eating and drinking, singing and carousing. Of all the courts he had seen on earth, that was the court with the most food and drink and golden vessels and royal jewels. Time came for them to go to sleep, and they went to sleep,* he and the queen. As soon as they got into bed, he turned his face to the edge of the bed,* and his back to her. From then to the next day, he did not say a word to her. The next day there was tenderness and friendly conversation between them. Whatever affection existed between them during the day, not a single night until the end of the year was different from the first night.

He spent the year hunting and singing and carousing, and in friendship and conversation with companions until the night of the meeting. On that night the meeting was as well remembered by the inhabitant in the remotest part of the realm as it was by

him. So he came to the meeting, accompanied by the noblemen of
his realm. As soon as he came to the ford, a knight got up and
spoke like this:

'Noblemen,' he said, 'listen carefully. This confrontation is between the two kings, and between their two persons alone. Each one
is making a claim against the other regarding land and territory; all
of you should stand aside and leave the fighting between the two
of them.'

With that the two kings approached each other towards the
middle of the ford for the fight. And at the first attack, the man
who was in Arawn's place strikes Hafgan in the centre of the boss of
his shield, so that it splits in half, and all his armour shatters, and
Hafgan is thrown the length of his arm and spear-shaft over his
horse's crupper to the ground, suffering a fatal blow.*

'Lord,' said Hafgan, 'what right did you have to my death? I was
claiming nothing from you. Nor do I know of any reason for you to
kill me; but for God's sake,' he said, 'since you have begun, then
finish!'

'Lord,' said the other, 'I may regret doing what I did to you. Find
someone else who will kill you; I will not kill you.'

'My faithful noblemen,' said Hafgan, 'take me away from here; my
death is now certain. There is no way I can support you any longer.'

'And my noblemen,' said the man who was in Arawn's place, 'take
advice and find out who should become vassals of mine.'

'Lord,' said the noblemen, 'everyone should, for there is no king
over the whole of Annwfn except you.'

'Indeed,' he said, 'those who come submissively, it is right to
receive them. Those who do not come willingly, we will force them
by the power of the sword.'

Then he received the men's allegiance, and began to take over the
land. And by noon the following day both kingdoms were under his
authority.

Then Pwyll set off for his meeting-place, and came to Glyn Cuch.
And when he got there Arawn, king of Annwfn, was there to meet
him. Each one was glad to see the other.

'Indeed,' said Arawn, 'may God repay you for your friendship; I
have heard about it.'

'Well,' said the other, 'when you yourself return to your country
you will see what I have done for you.'

'What you have done for me,' he said, 'may God repay you for it.'

Then Arawn gave to Pwyll, prince of Dyfed, his proper form and features, and he himself took back his own. And Arawn set off to his court in Annwfn, and he was happy to see his men and his retinue for he had not seen them for a year. They, however, had not missed him, and his arrival was no more of a novelty than before. He spent that day pleasurably and happily, sitting and conversing with his wife and his noblemen. When it was more appropriate to sleep than carouse, they went to sleep. He went to his bed, and his wife went to him. The first thing he did was to converse with his wife, and indulge in affectionate play and make love to her. And she had not been accustomed to that for a year, and reflected on that.

'Dear God,' she said, 'why is his mood different tonight from what it has been for the past year?'

And she deliberated for a long time. And after that he woke up, and spoke to her, and a second time and a third; but she did not answer him.

'Why won't you answer me?' he said.

'I tell you', she said, 'that I have not spoken as much as this for a year in this bed.'

'How can that be?' he said. 'We have always talked.'

'Shame on me,' she said, 'if there has been between us for the past year, from the time we were wrapped up in the bedclothes, either pleasure or conversation, or have you turned your face to me, let alone anything more than that!'

And then he thought, 'Dear Lord God,' he said, 'I had a friend whose loyalty was steadfast and secure.' And then he said to his wife, 'Lady,' he said, 'do not blame me. Between me and God,' he said, 'I have neither slept nor lain down with you for the past year.'

And then he told her the whole story.

'I confess to God,' she said, 'you struck a firm bargain for your friend to have fought off the temptations of the flesh and kept his word to you.'

'Lady,' he said, 'those were my very thoughts while I was silent just now.'

'No wonder!' she said.

Then Pwyll, prince of Dyfed, came to his realm and his land. And he began to question the noblemen of the land as to how he had ruled over them during the past year compared with how he had ruled before that.

'Lord,' they said, 'never have you been so perceptive; never have you been such a kind young man; never have you been so ready to distribute your wealth; never have you ruled better than during this year.'

'Between me and God,' he said, 'it is right for you to thank the man who was with you. This is the story, how it happened.'

Pwyll told them everything.

'Well, lord,' they said, 'thank God you had that friendship. And the rule we have had this year, surely you will not take it from us?'

'I will not, between me and God,' said Pwyll.

From that time on Pwyll and Arawn began to build up their friendship, and sent each other horses and hunting-dogs and hawks, and whatever treasure they thought would please the other. And because he had stayed that year in Annwfn, and had ruled there so successfully, and united the two realms through his courage and prowess, the name Pwyll, prince of Dyfed, fell into disuse, and he was called Pwyll Pen Annwfn* from then on.

Once upon a time Pwyll was at Arberth, one of his chief courts,* where a feast had been prepared for him, and there was a large retinue of men with him. After the first sitting Pwyll got up to take a walk, and he made for the top of a mound that was above the court, called Gorsedd Arberth.*

'Lord,' said one of the court, 'the strange thing about the mound is that whatever nobleman sits on it will not leave there without one of two things happening: either he will be wounded or injured, or else he will see something wonderful.'

'I am not afraid to be wounded or injured among such a large company as this. As for something wonderful, I would be glad to see that. I will go and sit on the mound,' he said.

He sat on the mound. And as they were sitting, they could see a woman wearing a shining golden garment of brocaded silk on a big, tall, pale-white horse coming along the highway that ran past the mound. Anyone who saw it would think that the horse had a slow, steady pace, and it was drawing level with the mound.

'Men,' said Pwyll, 'do any of you recognize the rider?'

'No, lord,' they said.

'Let someone go and meet her to find out who she is,' he said.

One of them got up, but when he came to the road to meet her, she had gone past. He followed her as fast as he could on foot. But the greater his speed, the further she drew away from him. When he saw that it was useless to pursue her, he returned to Pwyll and said to him,

'Lord,' he said, 'it is useless for anyone in the world to pursue her on foot.'

'Very well,' said Pwyll, 'go to the court, and take the fastest horse that you know of, and go after her.'

He took the horse, and off he went. He came to the open, level plain, and set spurs to the horse. And the more he spurred the horse, the further she drew away from him. She was going at the same pace as when she had started. His horse became tired; and when he realized that his horse's pace was failing, he returned to where Pwyll was.

'Lord,' he said, 'it is useless for anyone to pursue that rider over there. I know of no faster horse in the realm than this one, yet it was useless for me to pursue her.'

'Yes,' replied Pwyll, 'there is some magical explanation here. Let us return to the court.'

They came to the court, and passed that day.

The next day they got up, and passed that too until it was time to go and eat. And after the first sitting, 'Well,' said Pwyll, 'let those of us who went yesterday go to the top of the mound. And you,' he said to one of his young lads, 'bring along the fastest horse you know of in the field.' And the young lad did that. They made for the mound, together with the horse.

As they were about to sit down they saw the lady on the same horse, and wearing the same garment, coming along the same road.

'Here is yesterday's rider,' said Pwyll. 'Be ready, lad,' he said, 'to find out who she is.'

'Lord,' he said, 'I shall do that gladly.'

With that the rider drew level with them. Then the young lad mounted the horse, but before he had settled himself in his saddle she had gone past, putting a fair distance between them. Her pace was no different to the day before. He set his horse to amble, and he thought that although his horse was going slowly, he would catch up with her. But that was futile. He gave his horse its head; he was no closer to her than if he were on foot; and the more he spurred his horse, the further she drew away from him. Her pace was no faster than before. Since he saw that it was futile for him to pursue her, he returned, and came to where Pwyll was.

'Lord,' he said, 'the horse cannot do any better than you have seen.'

'I have seen that it is useless for anyone to pursue her,' Pwyll replied. 'And between me and God,' he said, 'she has a message for someone on this plain, had her obstinacy not stopped her from delivering it. Let us return to the court.'

They came to the court, and spent that night singing and carousing, until they were contented. The next day they amused themselves until it was time to go and eat. When they had finished eating, Pwyll said, 'Where are those who were with me yesterday and the day before on top of the mound?'

'Here we are, lord,' they said.

'Let us go to the mound to sit,' he said. 'And you,' he said to his groom, 'saddle my horse well, and bring it to the road, and bring along my spurs.' The groom did that.

They came to the mound and sat down. They were there hardly any time at all when they saw the rider coming along the same road, in the same manner, and at the same pace.

'Groom,' said Pwyll, 'I see the rider. Give me my horse.' Pwyll mounted his horse, and no sooner had he mounted his horse than she rode past him. He turned after her, and let his spirited, prancing horse go at its own pace. And he thought that at the second leap or the third he would catch up with her. But he was no closer to her than before. He urged his horse to go as fast as possible. But he saw that it was useless for him to pursue her.

Then Pwyll said, 'Maiden,' he said, 'for the sake of the man you love most, wait for me.'

'I will wait gladly,' she said, 'and it would have been better for the horse if you had asked that a while ago!'

The maiden stopped and waited, and drew back the part of her headdress which should cover her face, and fixed her gaze on him, and began to talk to him.

'Lady,' he said, 'where do you come from, and where are you going?'

'Going about my business,' she said, 'and I am glad to see you.'

'My welcome to you,' he said. And then he thought that the face of every maiden and every woman he had ever seen was unattractive compared with her face.

'Lady,' he said, 'will you tell me anything about your business?'

'I will, between me and God,' she said. 'My main purpose was to try and see you.'

'That, to me, is the best business you could have,' said Pwyll. 'Will you tell me who you are?'

'I will, lord,' she said. 'I am Rhiannon, daughter of Hyfaidd Hen,* and I am to be given to a husband against my will. But I have never wanted any man, because of my love for you. And I still do not want him, unless you reject me. And it is to find out your answer on the matter that I have come.'

'Between me and God,' replied Pwyll, 'this is my answer to you: if I could choose from all the women and maidens in the world, it is you that I would choose.'*

'Good,' she said, 'if that is what you want, before I am given to another man, arrange a meeting with me.'

'The sooner the better, as far as I'm concerned,' said Pwyll. 'Arrange the meeting wherever you want.'

'I will, lord,' she said, 'a year from tonight, in the court of Hyfaidd, I will have a feast prepared, ready for when you come.'

'Gladly,' he replied, 'and I will be at that meeting.'

'Lord,' she said, 'farewell, and remember to keep your promise, and I shall go on my way.'

They parted, and he went to his retinue and his men. Whatever questions they asked concerning the maiden, he would turn to other matters. Then they spent the year until the appointed time; and Pwyll got ready with ninety-nine horsemen. He set off for the court of Hyfaidd Hen, and he came to the court and they welcomed him, and there was a gathering and rejoicing and great preparations waiting for him, and all the wealth of the court was placed at his disposal. The hall was prepared, and they went to the tables. This is how they sat: Hyfaidd Hen on one side of Pwyll, and Rhiannon on the other; after that each according to his rank. They ate and caroused and conversed.

As they began to carouse after eating, they saw a tall, regal, auburn-haired lad enter, wearing a garment of brocaded silk. When he came to the upper end of the hall, he greeted Pwyll and his companions.

'God's welcome to you, friend, and come and sit down,' said Pwyll.

'No,' he said, 'I am a suppliant, and I will make my request.'

'Do so with pleasure,' said Pwyll.

'Lord,' he said, 'my business is with you, and I have come to ask you a favour.'

'Whatever you ask of me, as long as I can get it, it shall be yours.'

'Oh!' said Rhiannon, 'why did you give such an answer?'

'He has given it, lady, in the presence of noblemen,' said the lad.

'Friend,' said Pwyll, 'what is your request?'

'The woman I love most you are to sleep with tonight. And it is to ask for her, and for the preparations and provisions that are here that I have come.'

Pwyll was silent, for there was no answer that he could give.

'Be silent for as long as you like,' said Rhiannon. 'Never has a man been more stupid than you have been.'

'Lady,' he said, 'I did not know who he was.'

'That is the man to whom they wanted to give me against my will,' she said, 'Gwawl son of Clud, a powerful man with many followers. And since you have given your word, give me to him for fear of bringing disgrace upon yourself.'

'Lady,' he said, 'I do not know what sort of answer that is. I can never bring myself to do what you say.'

'Give me to him,' she said, 'and I'll see to it that he will never have me.'

'How will that be?' said Pwyll.

'I will give you a little bag,' she said, 'and keep it safely with you. And he is asking for the feast and the preparations and the provisions; those are not in your power to give. But I will give the feast to the retinue and the men,' she said, 'and that will be your answer on the matter. As for me,' she said, 'I will arrange a meeting, a year from tonight, for him to sleep with me; and at the end of the year,' she said, 'you be in the orchard up there, with ninety-nine horsemen, and have this bag with you. And when he is in the middle of his entertainment and carousing, come in on your own wearing ragged clothes, and carrying the bag,' she said, 'and ask for nothing but to fill the bag with food. I'll see to it', she said, 'that if all the food and drink in these seven cantrefs were put into it, it would be no fuller than before. And when they have thrown a great deal into it, he will ask you, "Will your bag ever be full?" You say, "No, unless an extremely powerful noble-man gets up and treads down the food in the bag with both feet, and says, 'Enough has been put in here'. " And I will see to it that he goes to tread down the food in the bag. And when he comes, turn the bag so that he goes head over heels in it; then tie a knot in the strings of the bag; have a good hunting-horn around your neck, and when he is tied up in the bag, give a blast on your horn, and let that be a signal between you and your horsemen; when they hear the blast of your horn, let them descend upon the court.'

'Lord,' said Gwawl, 'it is high time that I had an answer to my request.'

'As much of your request as it is in my power to give, you shall have,' said Pwyll.

'Friend,' said Rhiannon, 'as for the feast and the preparations that are here, I have given these to the men of Dyfed and to the retinue and men that are here. I will not let those to be given to anyone else. But a year from tonight, a feast will be prepared in this court when you, friend, shall sleep with me.'

Gwawl set off for his realm; Pwyll returned to Dyfed. Each of them spent that year until it was time for the feast in the court of Hyfaidd Hen. Gwawl son of Clud came to the feast that had been prepared for him, and he made for the court, and they welcomed him. But Pwyll Pen Annwfn went to the orchard, with ninety-nine horsemen, as Rhiannon had ordered, and the bag with him. Pwyll put on wretched rags, and big rag boots on his feet. And when he realized they were about to begin carousing after the meal he made for the hall; and when he had come to the upper end of the hall he greeted Gwawl son of Clud and his company of men and women.

'May God prosper you,' said Gwawl, 'and God's welcome to you.'

'Lord,' he said, 'may God repay you. I have business with you.'

'Your business is welcome,' he said. 'And if your request is reasonable, then gladly you shall have it.'

'Reasonable, lord,' he said. 'I ask only to ward off hunger. This is my request, to fill this little bag that you see with food.'

'That's a modest request,' he said, 'and you shall have it gladly. Bring him food,' he said. A great number of servants got up and began to fill the bag. But no matter what was thrown into it, it was no fuller than before.

'Friend,' said Gwawl, 'will your bag ever be full?'

'Never, between me and God,' he said, 'no matter what is put in it, unless a nobleman endowed with land and territory and power gets up and treads down the food in the bag with both feet and says, "Enough has been put in here".'

'My hero!' said Rhiannon to Gwawl son of Clud. 'Get up quickly.'

'I will, gladly,' he said.

He gets up and puts both feet in the bag, and Pwyll turns the bag so that Gwawl is head over heels in it, and quickly he closes the bag and ties a knot in the strings and sounds his horn. And immediately the retinue descends on the court, and then they seize the entire company that had come with Gwawl and tie each man up separately. And Pwyll throws off the rags and the rag boots and the untidy clothes.

As each one of Pwyll's men entered, he struck the bag a blow and asked, 'What's in here?'

'A badger,' the others said.

This is how they played: each one would strike the bag a blow either with his foot or with a stick; and that is how they played with the bag. Each one as he entered would ask, 'So what game are you playing?' 'Badger in the Bag', the others would say. And that was the first time that Badger in the Bag* was played.

'Lord,' said the man from the bag, 'if you would only listen to me, killing me in a bag is no fitting death for me.'

'Lord,' said Hyfaidd Hen, 'what he says is true. You should listen to him; that is not the death for him.'

'I agree,' said Pwyll; 'I shall follow your advice on the matter.'

'This is what I advise,' said Rhiannon. 'You are in a position where it is expected of you to satisfy suppliants and musicians. Let Gwawl give to everyone on your behalf,' she said, 'and let him promise that no claim or vengeance shall be sought; that is punishment enough for him.'

'He accepts that gladly,' said the man from the bag.

'And I, too, accept it gladly,' said Pwyll, 'on the advice of Hyfaidd and Rhiannon.'

'That is our advice,' they said.

'Then I accept it,' said Pwyll. 'Find guarantors for yourself.'

'We will answer for him,' said Hyfaidd, 'until his men are free to stand bail for him.'

Then Gwawl was released from the bag, and his chief followers set free.

'Now ask Gwawl for guarantors,' said Hyfaidd. 'We know who should be taken from him.'

Hyfaidd listed the guarantors.

'Draw up your own conditions,' said Gwawl.

'I am satisfied with what Rhiannon has drawn up,' said Pwyll.

The guarantors stood bail on those conditions.

'Lord,' said Gwawl, 'I am injured and have received many wounds, and I need to bathe, and with your permission I will depart. And I will leave noblemen here on my behalf to answer all those who may make requests of you.'

'Gladly,' said Pwyll; 'do as you propose.' Gwawl set off for his realm.

Then the hall was prepared for Pwyll and his company, and for the men of the court as well. They went to sit down at the tables, and just as they had sat the year before, each one sat that night. They ate and caroused, and time came to go to sleep. Pwyll and Rhiannon went to the chamber, and spent that night in pleasure and contentment.

Early the next day, 'Lord,' said Rhiannon, 'get up and begin satisfying the musicians, and do not refuse anyone who requests a gift today.'

'I will do that gladly,' said Pwyll, 'today and every day while this feast lasts.'

Pwyll got up, and called for silence, asking all the suppliants and musicians to present themselves, and telling them that each one would be satisfied according to his wish and whim; and that was done. They consumed the feast, and no one was refused while it lasted. When the feast came to an end,

'Lord,' said Pwyll to Hyfaidd, 'with your permission, I will set out for Dyfed tomorrow.'

'Well and good,' said Hyfaidd, 'may God ease your path; arrange a time and date for Rhiannon to follow you.'

'Between me and God,' said Pwyll, 'we will leave here together.'

'Is that your wish, lord?' said Hyfaidd.

'It is, between me and God,' said Pwyll.

The next day they travelled to Dyfed, and made for the court at Arberth where a feast had been prepared for them. The best men and women in the land and the realm assembled before them. Neither a man nor woman among them left Rhiannon without being given a notable gift, either a brooch or a ring or a precious stone. They ruled the land successfully that year, and the next. But in the third year the noblemen of the land began to worry at seeing a man whom they loved as much as their lord and foster-brother* without an heir, and they summoned him to them. The place where they met was Preseli in Dyfed.

'Lord,' they said, 'we know that you are not as old as some of the men of this land, but we are afraid that you will not get an heir from the wife that you have. And because of that, take another wife from whom you may have an heir. You will not live for ever,' they said, 'and although you may want to stay as you are, we will not allow it.'

'Well,' said Pwyll, 'we have not been together for long yet, and much may happen. Delay the matter until the end of the year. A year from now we will arrange to meet, and I will abide by your decision.'

The meeting was arranged. Before the whole period had elapsed a son was born to him, and he was born in Arberth. On the night of his birth women were brought to keep watch over the boy and his mother, but the women fell asleep and so, too, did the boy's mother, Rhiannon. Six women had been brought to the chamber. They kept watch for part of the night; however, before midnight each one fell asleep, and woke up towards cock-crow. When they woke up, they looked to where they had put the boy, but there was no sign of him there.

'Oh,' said one of the women, 'the boy has disappeared.'

'Truly,' said another, 'burning us alive or putting us to death would be too small a punishment for this.'

'Is there anything in the world we can do?' said one of the women.

'Yes, there is,' said another; 'I have a good plan,' she said.

'What is that?' they said.

'There is a stag-hound bitch here,' she said, 'and she has pups. Let us kill some of the pups, and smear Rhiannon's face and hands with the blood, and throw the bones beside her, and swear that she herself destroyed her son.* And the word of the six of us will prove stronger than hers.' They agreed on that.

Towards daybreak Rhiannon woke up and said, 'My women,' she said, 'where is the boy?'

'Lady,' they said, 'do not ask *us* for the boy. We are nothing but bruises and blows from struggling with you; and we are certain that we have never seen a woman fight like you did, and it was useless for us to struggle with you. You yourself have destroyed your son, and do not ask us for him.'

'You poor creatures,' said Rhiannon, 'for the sake of the Lord God who knows everything, do not tell lies about me. God, who knows everything, knows that to be a lie. And if you are afraid, by my confession to God, I will protect you.'

'God knows,' they said, 'we will not let ourselves come to any harm for anyone in the world.'

'You poor creatures,' she replied, 'you shall come to no harm if you tell the truth.' Whatever she said, out of fairness or pity, she received only the same answer from the women.

Then Pwyll Pen Annwfn got up, and his company and retinue, and the incident could not be concealed. The news spread throughout the land, and all the noblemen heard it. And they gathered together to make representations to Pwyll, to ask him to divorce his wife for having committed such a terrible outrage. But Pwyll gave this answer: 'They have no reason to ask me to divorce my wife, unless she has no children. I know that she has a child, and I will not divorce her. If she has done wrong, let her be punished for it.'

Rhiannon summoned wise and learned men. And when she thought it better to accept her punishment than argue with the women, she accepted her punishment. This is what it was: to stay at that court in Arberth for seven years. And there was a mounting-block* outside the gate—to sit by that every day, and tell the whole story to anyone whom she thought might not know it, and offer to carry guests and strangers on her back to the court if they permitted it. But rarely would anyone allow himself to be carried. And so she spent part of the year.

At that time Teyrnon Twrf Liant was lord over Gwent Is Coed,* and he was the best man in the world. In his house he had a mare, and throughout his kingdom no stallion or mare was more handsome. And every May eve* she would give birth, but no one knew at all what became of her foal. One evening Teyrnon spoke with his wife.

'My wife,' he said, 'we are careless, losing our mare's offspring every year without keeping one of them.'

'What can we do about it?' she said.

'God's vengeance upon me', he said, 'if I do not find out what fate befalls the foals—tonight is May eve.'

He had the mare brought indoors, and he armed himself, and began the night's vigil. As it begins to get dark the mare gives birth to a big, perfect foal which stands up on its feet immediately. Teyrnon gets up to examine the sturdiness of the foal. As he is doing this he hears a loud noise, and after the noise an enormous claw* comes through the window, and grabs the foal by its mane. Teyrnon draws his sword and cuts off the arm at the elbow so that that part of the arm, and the foal with it, are inside. Then he hears a noise and a scream at the same time. He opens the door and rushes off after the noise. He cannot see the cause of the noise because the night is so dark; but he rushes after it, and follows it. Then he remembers that he has left the door open, and he returns. And by the door there is a small boy in swaddling-clothes with a mantle of brocaded silk wrapped around him. He picks up the boy and sees that he is strong for his age.

Teyrnon fastened the door and made for the room where his wife was.

'My lady,' he said, 'are you asleep?'

'No, my lord,' she said. 'I was asleep, but when you came in I woke up.'

'Here is a son for you, if you want,' he said; 'something you have never had.'

'Lord,' she said, 'what happened?'

'I will tell you everything,' said Teyrnon, and he told her the whole story.

'Well, lord,' she said, 'how is the boy dressed?'

'In a mantle of brocaded silk,' he said.

'Then he is the son of noble people,' she said. 'Lord,' she said, 'it would be a pleasure and delight to me—should you agree—to take women into my confidence and say that I have been pregnant.'*

'I will agree with you gladly on the matter,' he said. This was done. They had the boy baptized in the way it was done at that time. This was the name that they gave him, Gwri Wallt Euryn:* all the hair on his head was as yellow as gold.

The boy was brought up at the court until he was a year old. And before he was a year old he was walking strongly, and was sturdier than a well-developed and well-grown three-year-old boy. The boy was reared a second year, and he was as sturdy as a six-year-old.* And before the end of the fourth year he was bargaining with the stableboys to be allowed to water the horses.

'Lord,' said his wife to Teyrnon, 'where is the foal you saved the night you found the boy?'

'I ordered it to be given to the stableboys,' he said, 'and told them to look after it.'

'Would it not be good, lord, for you to have it broken in, and given to the boy?' she said. 'For on the night you found the boy, the foal was born and you saved it.'

'I will not disagree with that,' said Teyrnon. 'I will let you give it to him.'

'Lord,' she said, 'may God repay you; I will give it to him.'

Then the horse was given to the boy, and she went to the grooms and stableboys to tell them to look after the horse, and to break it in for when the boy would go riding, and to report on its progress.

Meanwhile they heard news of Rhiannon and her punishment. Because of what he had found, Teyrnon Twrf Liant listened out for news and enquired constantly about the matter, until he heard increased complaints about the wretchedness of Rhiannon's misfortune and punishment from the very many people who visited the court. Teyrnon reflected on this, and looked closely at the boy. He realized that he had never seen a son and father so alike as the boy and Pwyll Pen Annwfn. Pwyll's appearance was known to Teyrnon, for he had previously been a vassal of his. Then grief seized him because of how wrong it was for him to keep the boy, when he knew that he was another man's son. As soon as he had the first chance to talk privately with his wife, he told her that it was not right for them to keep the boy, nor to let a noblewoman as good as Rhiannon be punished so terribly for it, when the boy was the son of Pwyll Pen Annwfn.

Teyrnon's wife agreed to send the boy to Pwyll.

'And we shall get three things, lord, as a result of that,' she said: 'thanks and gratitude for releasing Rhiannon from her punishment; and thanks from Pwyll for rearing the boy and restoring him; and thirdly, if the boy proves to be a considerate man, he will be our foster-son, and he will always do his best for us.'

They agreed on that.

No later than the next day Teyrnon prepared himself with two other riders, and the boy a fourth on the horse that Teyrnon had given him. They travelled towards Arberth, and it was not long before they arrived. As they approached the court, they saw Rhiannon sitting by the mounting-block. When they drew level with her, 'My lord,' she said, 'go no further. I shall carry each of you to the court. And that is my punishment for killing my own son and destroying him.'

'My lady,' said Teyrnon, 'I do not imagine that any one of these will ride on your back.'

'If anyone wants to, then let him do so,' said the boy; 'I certainly will not.'

'God knows, my friend,' said Teyrnon, 'neither will we.'

They made for the court, and there was great joy at their arrival. A feast was about to begin at court—Pwyll himself had just returned from a circuit of Dyfed. They went into the hall and to wash themselves. Pwyll welcomed Teyrnon, and they went to sit. This is how they sat—Teyrnon between Pwyll and Rhiannon, with Teyrnon's two companions above Pwyll, and the boy between them.

When they had finished eating, at the beginning of the carousal, they conversed. Teyrnon told the whole story about the mare and the boy, and how he and his wife had taken the boy into their charge, and how they had brought him up.

'And this is your son, my lady,' said Teyrnon. 'And whoever told lies against you did you wrong. And when I heard of your affliction, I was saddened, and distressed. And I imagine there is no one in this entire company who does not recognize that the boy is Pwyll's son,' said Teyrnon.

'No one doubts it,' said everyone.

'Between me and God,' said Rhiannon, 'what a relief from my anxiety if that were true.'*

'My lady,' said Pendaran Dyfed, 'you have named your son well—Pryderi; Pryderi son of Pwyll Pen Annwfn suits him best.'

'Make sure that his own name does not suit him better,' said Rhiannon.

'What is his name?' said Pendaran Dyfed.

'We called him Gwri Wallt Euryn.'

'Pryderi shall be his name,' said Pendaran Dyfed.

'That is most appropriate,' said Pwyll, 'to take the boy's name from the word his mother uttered when she received joyous news about him.' And they agreed on that.

'Teyrnon,' said Pwyll, 'God repay you for raising this boy until now. It is proper for him, if he proves to be a considerate man, to compensate you for it.'

'Lord,' said Teyrnon, 'as for the woman who raised him, there is no one in the world who is grieving after him more than her. It is right for him to remember what we did for him, for my sake and hers.'

'Between me and God,' said Pwyll, 'as long as I live I will maintain both you and your realm, as long as I am able to maintain my own. If he lives to maturity, it is more appropriate for him to maintain you than for me. And with your agreement, and that of these noblemen, since you have raised him until now, we will give him to Pendaran Dyfed to foster from now on. But you shall all be his companions and his foster-fathers.'

'That is sound advice,' said everyone.

Then the boy was given to Pendaran Dyfed, and the noblemen of the land allied themselves to him. Teyrnon Twrf Liant and his companions set off for his land and his realm, full of love and joy. And he did not depart without having being offered the fairest jewels and the best horses and the most highly prized dogs. But he wanted nothing.

They stayed in their own realm after that, and Pryderi son of Pwyll Pen Annwfn was brought up carefully, as was proper, until he was the most handsome lad, and the fairest and the most accomplished at every worthy feat in the kingdom. And so years and years passed, until Pwyll Pen Annwfn's life came to an end, and he died. And Pryderi ruled the seven cantrefs of Dyfed successfully, beloved by his realm and all those around him. After that he conquered the three cantrefs of Ystrad Tywi and the four cantrefs of Ceredigion, and these are called the seven cantrefs of Seisyllwch. Pryderi son of Pwyll Pen Annwfn was occupied with that conquest until he decided to take a wife. The wife he wanted was Cigfa daughter of Gwyn Gohoyw, son of Gloyw Walltlydan, son of Casnar Wledig, noblemen of this island.

And so ends this branch of the Mabinogion.*

The Second Branch of the Mabinogi

BENDIGEIDFRAN son of Llŷr was crowned king over this island* and invested with the crown of London. One afternoon he was in Harlech in Ardudwy,* at one of his courts; he was sitting on the rock of Harlech, above the sea, with his brother Manawydan son of Llŷr,* and his two brothers on his mother's side, Nysien and Efnysien, and noblemen too, as was appropriate around a king. His two brothers on his mother's side were the sons of Euroswydd by his own mother Penarddun, daughter of Beli son of Mynogan.* One of these was a good lad—he could make peace between two armies when they were most enraged; that was Nysien. The other would cause two of the most loving brothers to fight.

As they were sitting there, they could see thirteen ships coming from the south of Ireland, heading towards them easily and swiftly, the wind behind them, and they were approaching with speed.

'I can see ships over there, coming boldly towards the shore,' said the king. 'Tell the men of the court to put on their armour, and go and find out what their intentions are.'

The men armed themselves and went down to meet them. Having seen the ships at close quarters, the men were certain that they had never seen ships in a more perfect condition than these with their fair, beautiful, exquisite banners of brocaded silk.

Suddenly one of the ships overtook the others, and they saw a shield being raised above the ship's deck, with the point of the shield upwards as a sign of peace. The king's men approached them so that they were within speaking distance. The others put out boats, and approached the shore, and greeted the king. The king could hear them from where he was seated on the high rock above their heads.

'May God prosper you,' he said, 'and welcome. Whose are these ships, and who is their chief?'

'Lord,' they said, 'Matholwch, king of Ireland, is here, and these are his ships.'

'What does he want?' said the king. 'Does he want to come ashore?'

'No, lord,' they said, 'unless you grant him his request—he has business with you.'

'What sort of request does he have?' said the king.

'He wishes to unite your two families, lord,' they said. 'He has come to ask for Branwen daughter of Llŷr,* and if you agree, he wishes to join together the Island of the Mighty* and Ireland so that they might be stronger.'

'Very well,' he said, 'let him come ashore, and we will take advice on the matter.' That answer was taken to Matholwch.

'I will go gladly,' he said. He came ashore, and was made welcome. And there was a great crowd in the court that night, what with Matholwch's retinue and that of the court.

First thing the next day they took counsel. They decided to give Branwen to Matholwch. She was one of the Three Chief Maidens of this Island:* she was the most beautiful girl in the world. They set a date for Matholwch to sleep with her at Aberffraw,* and they left Harlech. They all set off for Aberffraw, Matholwch and his retinue in the ships, Bendigeidfran and his own retinue overland until they came to Aberffraw. There the feast began, and they sat down. This is how they sat: the king of the Island of the Mighty with Manawydan son of Llŷr on one side and Matholwch on the other, with Branwen daughter of Llŷr next to him. They were not in a house, but in tents. Bendigeidfran had never been able to fit inside any house.

They began the celebration, and continued to carouse and converse. When they thought it was better to sleep than continue carousing, they went to sleep. And that night Matholwch slept with Branwen. The next day, everyone in the court got up; and the officers began to discuss the billeting of the horses and grooms; and they billeted them in every region as far as the sea. Then, one day, Efnysien, the quarrelsome man of whom we spoke above, happened to come across the lodgings of Matholwch's horses, and he asked whose horses they were.

'These are the horses of Matholwch, king of Ireland,' they said.

'What are they doing here?' he said.

'The king of Ireland is here, and he has slept with Branwen, your sister, and these are his horses.'

'Is that what they have done with such a fine maiden, and my sister at that, given her away without my permission? They could not have insulted me more,' he said.

Then he went for the horses, and cut their lips to the teeth, and their ears down to their heads, and their tails to their backs; and where he could get a grip on the eyelids, he cut them to the bone. And in that way he maimed the horses, so that they were no good for anything.

The news reached Matholwch: he was told how his horses had been maimed and spoiled so that they were no good for anything.

'Well, lord,' said one, 'you have been insulted, and it was done deliberately.'

'God knows, but I find it strange, if they wanted to insult me, that they should have first given me such a fine maiden, of such high rank, so beloved by her family.'

'Lord,' said another, 'it's perfectly clear; there is nothing for you to do but return to your ships.' So Matholwch made for his ships.

The news reached Bendigeidfran that Matholwch was leaving the court, without asking, without permission. Messengers went to ask him why he was going. The messengers who went were Iddig son of Anarog and Hyfaidd Hir. Those men caught up with him, and asked him what was his intention, and why he was leaving.

'God knows,' he said, 'if I had known, I would not have come here. I have been completely insulted; no one has ever been on a worse expedition than this one. And a strange thing has happened to me.'

'What is that?' they said.

'I was given Bronwen daughter of Llŷr, one of the Three Chief Maidens of this Island, and daughter to a king of the Island of the Mighty, and I slept with her, but after that I was insulted. And I find it strange that the insult was not done before such an excellent maiden as that was given to me.'

'God knows, lord, that insult was not done to you with the approval of the one who rules the court,' they said, 'nor any one of his council. And although you consider it a disgrace, this insult and deception is worse for Bendigeidfran than it is for you.'

'Yes,' he said, 'perhaps so. But yet Bendigeidfran cannot undo the insult just because of that.'

The men returned with that answer to Bendigeidfran, and told him what Matholwch had said.

'Well,' said Bendigeidfran, 'it is no good if he goes away angry, and we cannot allow it.'

'We agree, lord,' they said. 'Send messengers after him again.'

'I will,' he said. 'Arise Manawydan son of Llŷr, and Hyfaidd Hir and Unig Glew Ysgwydd, and go after him,' he said, 'and tell him that he shall have a sound horse for each one that was maimed; and also he shall have as his honour-price a rod of silver as thick as his little finger and as tall as himself, and a plate of gold as broad as his face;* and tell him what sort of man did this, and how it was done against my will; and that a brother on my mother's side did it, and it is not easy for me either to kill him or destroy him. Let Matholwch come and see me,' he said, 'and I will make peace on whatever terms he wishes.'

The messengers went after Matholwch, and repeated those words in a friendly manner, and he listened to them.

'Men,' he said, 'we will take counsel.'

He took counsel. They decided that were they to refuse the offer, they would be more likely to get further shame than further compensation. So Matholwch made up his mind to accept. They came to the court in peace. The tents and pavilions were arranged as if they were laying out a hall, and they went to eat. And as they had sat at the beginning of the feast, so they sat now.

Bendigeidfran and Matholwch began to converse. But it seemed to Bendigeidfran that Matholwch's conversation was lifeless and sad, whereas he had always been cheerful before that. And he thought that the chieftain was downhearted because of how little compensation he had received for the wrong done to him.

'Sir,' said Bendigeidfran, 'your conversation is not as good as it was the other night. And if it's because you feel your compensation is too little, I shall add to it as you wish, and tomorrow your horses shall be given to you.'

'Lord,' he said, 'may God repay you.'

'I will increase your compensation, too,' said Bendigeidfran. 'I will give you a cauldron,* and the property of the cauldron is that if you throw into it one of your men who is killed today, then by tomorrow he will be as good as ever except that he will not be able to speak.'

Matholwch thanked him for that, and was extremely happy on account of the cauldron. The next day his horses were handed over to him, so long as there were tame horses to give. From there

Matholwch was taken to another commot and foals were handed over to him until his payment was complete. And for that reason, the commot was called Talebolion* from then on.

The second night, they sat together.

'Lord,' said Matholwch, 'where did you get the cauldron that you gave me?'

'I got it from a man who had been in your country,' said Bendigeidfran. 'And for all I know, that is where he found it.'

'Who was he?' he said.

'Llasar Llaes Gyfnewid,'* he said. 'And he came here from Ireland, with Cymidei Cymeinfoll, his wife, and they escaped from the iron house in Ireland when it was made white-hot around them, and they fled from Ireland. I am surprised that you know nothing about it.'

'I do, lord,' he said, 'and I will tell you as much as I know. I was hunting in Ireland one day, on top of a mound overlooking a lake called the Lake of the Cauldron. And I saw a large man with yellow-red hair coming out of the lake with a cauldron on his back. He was a huge, monstrous man, too, with an evil, ugly look about him; and a woman followed him; and if he was large, the woman was twice his size. And they came up to me and greeted me. "Well," I said, "how are things going with you?" "It's like this, lord," said the man, "in a month and a fortnight this woman will conceive, and the boy who is then born of that pregnancy in a month and a fortnight will be a fully armed warrior."

'I took them in to maintain them: they were with me for a year. During that year no one objected to them; but from then on people resented them. And before the end of the fourth month of the second year they were causing people to hate and loathe them throughout the land, insulting, harassing, and tormenting noble men and women. From then on my people rose against me to ask me to get rid of them, and gave me a choice, either my kingdom or these people.

'I left it to the council of my country to decide what should be done about them. They would not go of their own free will; they did not have to go against their will because of their ability to fight. And then, in this dilemma, it was decided to build a chamber completely of iron;* and when the chamber was ready, all the smiths in Ireland and all those who owned tongs and hammers were summoned there, and charcoal was piled up to the top of the chamber, and the woman and her husband and her children were served with plenty of food and drink. And when it was clear that they were drunk, the smiths began to set fire to the charcoal around the chamber, and blew the bellows that had been placed around the house, each man with two bellows, and they began to blow the bellows until the house was white-hot around them. And then the family took counsel in the middle of the chamber; and the husband waited until the iron wall was white. And because of the great heat, he charged at the wall with his shoulder and broke out through it, with his wife following. And only he and his wife escaped. After that, lord,' said Matholwch to Bendigeidfran, 'I suppose he came over to you.'

'He did indeed,' said Bendigeidfran, 'and he gave the cauldron to me.'

'What sort of welcome did you give them, lord?'

'I dispersed them throughout the land, and they are numerous, and prosper everywhere,* and strengthen whatever place they happen to be in with the best men and weapons anyone has seen.'

That night they continued to talk and sing and carouse as long as it pleased them. When they realized it was better to sleep than to sit up longer, they went to sleep. And so they enjoyed the feast. When it finished Matholwch, together with Branwen, set out for Ireland. They set out from Abermenai in their thirteen ships, and came to Ireland.

In Ireland they received a great welcome. Not one man of rank or noblewoman in Ireland came to visit Branwen to whom she did not give either a brooch or a ring or a treasured royal jewel, and it was remarkable to see such things leaving the court. Furthermore, she gained renown that year, and flourished with honour and companions. Meanwhile she became pregnant. After the appropriate time had passed she gave birth to a boy. They named him Gwern son of Matholwch. The boy was put out to be fostered to the very best place for men in Ireland.

Then in the second year, there was a murmuring of dissatisfaction in Ireland because of the insult that Matholwch had received in Wales, and the disgrace he had suffered regarding his horses. His foster-brothers and the men closest to him taunted him with it quite openly. And there was such an uproar in Ireland that there was no peace for Matholwch until he avenged the insult.* They took revenge by sending Branwen from her husband's chamber, and forcing her to cook for the court; and they had the butcher come to her every day, after he had chopped up meat, and give her a box on the ear.* And that is how her punishment was carried out.

'Now, lord,' said his men to Matholwch, 'set an embargo on the ships, and the rowing-boats and the coracles, so that no one may go to Wales; and whoever comes here from Wales, imprison them and do not let them return in case they find out what is happening.' They agreed on that.

This continued for not less than three years. In the meantime Branwen reared a starling at the end of her kneading-trough, and taught it to speak, and told the bird what kind of man her brother was. And she brought a letter telling of her punishment and dishonour. The letter was tied to the base of the bird's wings, and it was sent to Wales, and the bird came to this island. It found Bendigeidfran in Caer Saint in Arfon, where he was at a council of his one day. The bird alighted on his shoulder, and ruffled its feathers until the letter was discovered and they realized that the bird has been reared among people. Then the letter was taken and examined. When it was read, Bendigeidfran grieved to hear how Branwen was being punished, and there and then he sent messengers to muster the entire island. Then he had the full levy of one hundred and fifty-four districts come to him, and he complained personally to them of his sister's punishment. Then he took counsel. They agreed to set out for Ireland, and leave seven men behind as leaders, together with their seven horsemen, and Caradog son of Brân in command. Those men were left in Edeirnion, and because of that the name Saith Marchog* was given to the township. The seven men were Caradog son of Brân and Hyfaidd Hir, and Unig Glew Ysgwydd, and Iddig son of Anarog Walltgrwn, and Ffodor son of Erfyll, and Wlch Minasgwrn, and Llashar son of Llasar Llaesgyngwyd; and Pendaran Dyfed, then a young lad,* was with them. Those seven stayed behind as seven stewards to look after this island, and Caradog son of Brân was their chief steward.*

Bendigeidfran and the army we mentioned sailed towards Ireland, and the sea was not wide then; Bendigeidfran waded across. There were only two rivers, called the Lli and the Archan. Later the sea spread out when it flooded the kingdoms.* But Bendigeidfran walked carrying all the stringed instruments on his own back, and made for Ireland's shore.

Matholwch's swineherds were on the sea shore one day, busy with their pigs. And because of what they saw on the sea, they went to Matholwch.

'Lord,' they said, 'greetings.'

'May God prosper you,' he said, 'and do you have any news?'

'Lord,' they said, 'we have extraordinary news;* we have seen a forest on the sea, where we never before saw a single tree.'

'That's strange,' he said. 'Could you see anything else?'

'Yes, lord,' they said, 'we could see a huge mountain beside the forest, and it was moving; and there was a very high ridge on the mountain, and a lake on each side of the ridge; and the forest, and the mountain, and all of it was moving.'

'Well,' said Matholwch, 'there is no one here who would know anything about that unless Branwen knows something. Go and ask her.' Messengers went to Branwen.

'Lady,' they said, 'what do you think it is?'

'Though I am no "lady",' she said, 'I know what it is: the men of the Island of the Mighty coming over, having heard of my punishment and dishonour.'

'What is the forest they saw on the sea?' they said.

'Masts of ships and yardarms,' she said.

'Oh!' they said. 'What was the mountain they saw alongside the ships?'

'That was Bendigeidfran my brother, wading across,' she said. 'There was no ship big enough for him.'

'What was the very high ridge and the lake on each side of the ridge?'

'That was him, looking at this island,' she said. 'He is angry. The two lakes on either side of the ridge are his two eyes on each side of his nose.'

Then they quickly mustered all the fighting-men of Ireland and of the coastal regions, and took counsel.

'Lord,' said his men to Matholwch, 'the only advice is to retreat across the Liffey (a river in Ireland), and put the Liffey between you and him, and then destroy the bridge that crosses the river. There are loadstones on the riverbed—neither ships nor vessels can sail across.'* They retreated over the river, and destroyed the bridge.

Bendigeidfran landed with his fleet and approached the riverbank.

'Lord,' said his noblemen, 'you know the strange thing about the river, no one can sail across it, nor is there a bridge. What shall we do for a bridge?' they said.

'Nothing, except that he who is a leader, let him be a bridge,'* said Bendigeidfran. 'I will be a bridge,' he said. This was the first time that saying was uttered, and it is still used as a proverb.

Then after Bendigeidfran had lain down across the river, hurdles were placed on him,* and his men walked on top of him to the other side. Then, as soon as he got up, Matholwch's messengers approached him, and greeted him, and addressed him on behalf of Matholwch his kinsman who, they said, wished nothing but good to come Bendigeidfran's way.

'And Matholwch is giving the kingship of Ireland to Gwern son of Matholwch, your nephew, your sister's son, and will invest him in your presence, to make up for the injustice and injury that was done to Branwen. And make provision for Matholwch wherever you like, either here or in the Island of the Mighty.'

'Well,' said Bendigeidfran, 'if I myself cannot have the kingship, perhaps I should take advice regarding your message. But until a better response comes, you will get no answer from me.'

'Very well,' they said, 'we will bring you the best response we can get; wait for our message.'

'I will if you return quickly,' he said.

The messengers set off and went to Matholwch.

'Lord,' they said, 'prepare a better response for Bendigeidfran. He would not listen at all to the one we took him.'

'My men,' said Matholwch, 'what is your advice?'

'Lord,' they said, 'there is only one thing to do. He has never been able to fit inside a house,' they said. 'Build a house in his honour, so that there is room for him and the men of the Island of the Mighty in one half of the house, and for you and your troops in the other. And place your kingship at his disposal, and pay homage to him. And because of the honour in building the house (for he has never had one into which he could fit) he will make peace with you.'

The messengers took the offer to Bendigeidfran; and he took advice. He decided to accept; and that was all done on Branwen's advice because she feared that the country would be laid waste.

The terms of peace were arranged, and the house was built, large and spacious. But the Irish had a cunning plan. They placed a peg on either side of each column of the one hundred columns in the house, and hung a hide bag on each peg with an armed man in each one of them.* Efnysien entered the house ahead of the troops of the Island of the Mighty, and cast fierce, ruthless glances around the house. He caught sight of the hide bags along the pillars.

'What is in this bag?' he said to one of the Irishmen.

'Flour, friend,' he answered.

Efnysien prodded the bag until he found the man's head, and he squeezed the head until he could feel his fingers sinking into the brain through the bone. He left that one, and put his hand on another bag and asked, 'What have we here?'

'Flour, friend,' said the Irishman. Efnysien played the same game with each of them, so that not a man was left alive of the entire two hundred, apart from one. And he came to that one, and asked, 'What have we here?'

'Flour, friend,' said the Irishman. Efnysien prodded the bag until he found the man's head, and just as he had squeezed the heads of the others so he squeezed this one. He could feel armour on the head of this one. He did not let him go until he had killed him. And then he sang an *englyn*:

> 'There is in this bag a different kind of flour,
> Champions, warriors, attackers in battle,
> Against fighters, prepared for combat.'*

Then the troops entered the house. The men of the Island of Ireland entered the house on the one side, and the men of the Island of the Mighty on the other. As soon as they sat down they were reconciled, and the boy was invested with the kingship.

Then, when peace had been made, Bendigeidfran called the boy to him. The boy went from Bendigeidfran to Manawydan, and everyone who saw him loved him. From Manawydan, Nysien son of Euroswydd called the boy to him. The boy went to him graciously.

'Why does my nephew, my sister's son, not come to me?' said Efnysien. 'Even if he were not king of Ireland, I would still like to make friends with the boy.'

'Let him go, gladly,' said Bendigeidfran. The boy went to him cheerfully.

'I confess to God,' said Efnysien to himself, 'the outrage I shall now commit is one the household will never expect.' And he gets up, and takes the boy by the feet, and immediately, before anyone in the house can lay a hand on him, he hurls the boy head-first into the fire. When Branwen sees her son burning in the fire she tries to jump into the fire from where she is sitting between her two brothers. But Bendigeidfran seizes her with one hand, and seizes his shield with the other. Then everyone in the house leaps up. And that was the greatest uproar ever by a crowd in one house, as each one took up arms. Then Morddwyd Tyllion said, 'Hounds of Gwern, beware of Morddwyd Tyllion.'* As each went for his weapons, Bendigeidfran held Branwen between his shield and his shoulder.

The Irish began to kindle a fire under the Cauldron of Rebirth. Then they threw the corpses into the cauldron until it was full, and they would get up the next morning fighting as well as before except that they could not talk. When Efnysien saw the corpses, and no room anywhere for the men of the Island of the Mighty, he said to himself, 'Oh God,' he said, 'woe is me that I am the cause of this mountain of the men of the Island of Mighty; and shame on me,' he said, 'unless I try to save them from this.'

He creeps in among the corpses of the Irish, and two bare-backed Irishmen come up to him and throw him into the cauldron, as if he were an Irishman. He stretches himself out in the cauldron so that the cauldron breaks into four pieces, and his own heart breaks too. And because of that, such victory as there was went to the men of the Island of the Mighty. There was no real victory except that seven men escaped, and Bendigeidfran was wounded in the foot with a poisoned spear. The seven men who escaped were Pryderi,* Manawydan, Glifiau son of Taran, Taliesin, Ynog, Gruddieu son of Muriel, and Heilyn son of Gwyn Hen.

Then Bendigeidfran ordered his head to be cut off.* 'And take my head,' he said, 'and carry it to the Gwynfryn in London, and bury it with its face towards France. And it will take you a long time; you will feast in Harlech for seven years, with the birds of Rhiannon* singing to you. And you will find the head to be as good company as it ever was when it was on me. And you will stay for eighty years in Gwales in Penfro.* And so long as you do not open the door towards Aber Henfelen,* facing Cornwall, you can remain there and the head will not decay. But as soon as you open that door you can stay no longer. Make for London to bury the head. And now set off across the sea.'

Then his head was cut off, and they set out across the sea with the head, those seven men* and Branwen as the eighth. They came ashore at Aber Alaw in Talebolion. And then they sat down and rested. She looked at Ireland and at the Island of the Mighty, what she could see of them.

'Oh son of God,' she said, 'woe that I was ever born. Two good islands have been laid waste because of me!' She gives a mighty sigh, and with that her heart breaks. And they make a four-sided grave for her* and bury her there on the banks of the Alaw.

Then the seven men journeyed towards Harlech carrying the head. As they were travelling they met a company of men and women.

'Do you have any news?' said Manawydan.

'No,' they said, 'except that Caswallon son of Beli* has overrun the Island of the Mighty and is crowned king in London!'

'What happened to Caradog son of Brân and the seven men who were left with him on this Island?' they said.

'Caswallon attacked them and six men were killed, and Caradog's heart broke from bewilderment at seeing the sword kill his men and not knowing who killed them. Caswallon had put on a magic cloak so that no one could see him killing the men—they could only see the sword. Caswallon did not want to kill Caradog—he was his nephew, his cousin's son. (And he was one of the Three People who Broke their Hearts from Sorrow.)* Pendaran Dyfed, who was a young lad with the seven men, escaped to the woods,' they said.

Then they went to Harlech, and sat down and were regaled with food and drink. As soon as they began to eat and drink, three birds came and began to sing them a song, and all the songs they had heard before were harsh compared to that one. They had to gaze far out over the sea to catch sight of the birds, yet their song was as clear as if the birds were there with them. And they feasted for seven years.

At the end of the seventh year they set out for Gwales in Penfro. There was a pleasant royal dwelling for them there, above the sea, and there was a large hall, and they went to the hall. They could see two doors open; the third door was closed, the one facing Cornwall.

'See over there,' said Manawydan, 'the door we must not open.'

That night they stayed there contented and lacking nothing. And of all the sorrow they had themselves seen and suffered, they remembered none of it nor of any grief in the world. And there they spent eighty years so that they were not aware of ever having spent a more pleasurable or more delightful time. It was no more unpleasant than when they first arrived, nor could anyone tell by looking at the other that he had aged in that time. Having the head there was no more unpleasant than when Bendigeidfran had been alive with them.* Because of those eighty years, this was called The Assembly of the Noble Head. (The one which went to Ireland was The Assembly of Branwen and Matholwch.)

One day Heilyn son of Gwyn said, 'Shame on my beard* unless I open the door to find out if what they say about it is true.' He opened the door, and looked at Cornwall, and at Aber Henfelen. And when he looked, every loss they had ever suffered, and every kinsman and companion they had lost, and every ill that had befallen them was as clear as if they had encountered it in that very place; and most of all concerning their lord. And from that moment they could not rest but made for London with the head. Although the road was long, they came at last to London and buried the head on the Gwynfryn. And that was one of the Three Fortunate Concealments when it was concealed, and one of the Three Unfortunate Disclosures* when it was disclosed; for no oppression would ever come across the sea to this island while the head was in that hiding-place. And that is how the story goes: their tale is called 'The Men who Set Out from Ireland'.

In Ireland no one was left alive except for five pregnant women in a cave in the wilds of Ireland. Those five women, at exactly the same time, gave birth to five sons. And they reared those five sons until they were big lads, and their thoughts turned to women, and they lusted after them. Then each lad slept promiscuously with each other's mother, and lived in the land and ruled it, and divided it between the five of them. And the five provinces of Ireland still reflect that division.* And they searched the country where battles had taken place, and found gold and silver until they grew wealthy.

And that is how this branch of the Mabinogi ends, concerning the Blow to Branwen which was one of the Three Unfortunate Blows* in this Island; and the Assembly of Brân, when the army of one hundred and fifty-four districts went to Ireland to avenge the Blow to Branwen; and the Feasting in Harlech for seven years; and the Singing of the Birds of Rhiannon, and the Assembly of the Head for eighty years.

The Third Branch of the Mabinogi

AFTER the seven men we spoke of above* had buried Bendigeidfran's head on the Gwynfryn in London, with its face towards France, Manawydan looked at the town of London and at his companions, and heaved a great sigh, and immense sorrow and longing came over him.

'Alas Almighty God, woe is me!' he said. 'I am the only one who has no place to go tonight.'

'Lord,' said Pryderi, 'do not be so sad. Your cousin Caswallon* is king over the Island of the Mighty; and although he has done you wrong,' he said, 'you have never claimed land or territory—you are one of the Three Undemanding Chieftains.'*

'Well,' he said, 'although that man may be my cousin, I am extremely sad to see anyone take the place of Bendigeidfran my brother, and I could not be happy under the same roof as him.'

'Will you take any other advice?' said Pryderi.

'I need it,' he said, 'and what advice is that?'

'The seven cantrefs of Dyfed* were left to me,' said Pryderi, 'and Rhiannon, my mother, lives there. I shall give her to you, together with the authority over those seven cantrefs. Although it may be the only realm you have, there are no better seven cantrefs. My wife is Cigfa, daughter of Gwyn Gloyw,' he said. 'And although the realm will be mine in name, let the benefits be yours and Rhiannon's. And if you ever wanted a realm of your own, perhaps you could take that one.'

'I have never wanted one, lord,' he said, 'but may God repay you your friendship.'

'The best friendship I can give shall be yours, if you want it.'

'I do, friend,' he said. 'May God repay you. And I shall go with you to visit Rhiannon and the realm.'

'You are doing the right thing,' he said. 'I am sure that you have never heard a woman converse better than Rhiannon. When she was in her prime, there was no woman more beautiful, and even now you will not be disappointed with her looks.'

They set off. Although the road was long, they came at last to Dyfed. A feast had been prepared for them, ready for their arrival at Arberth, arranged by Rhiannon and Cigfa.

Then Manawydan and Rhiannon sat together and began to converse; and as a result of that conversation his head and heart grew tender towards her, and he was delighted that he had never seen a woman who was fairer or more beautiful than her.

'Pryderi,' he said, 'I will agree to your proposal.'

'What was that?' said Rhiannon.

'My lady,' said Pryderi, 'I have given you as a wife to Manawydan son of Llŷr.'

'I will agree to that gladly,' said Rhiannon.

'I am glad, too,' said Manawydan, 'and may God repay the man who gives me such firm friendship.' Before that feast finished, he slept with her.

'Continue with what is left of the feast,' said Pryderi, 'and I will go to England to pay homage to Caswallon son of Beli.'

'Lord,' said Rhiannon, 'Caswallon is in Kent, so you can continue with the feast and wait until he is closer.'

'Then we will wait for him,' said Pryderi. They finished the feast, and began to make a circuit of Dyfed where they hunted and enjoyed themselves.

As they wandered through the land they had never seen a place more pleasant to live in, nor better hunting ground, nor land more abundant in honey and fish. And during that time a friendship developed between the four of them, so that not one wished to be without the other, either day or night. In the meantime Pryderi went to pay homage to Caswallon in Oxford, where he was given a great welcome, and was thanked for paying homage. When he returned, Pryderi and Manawydan feasted and relaxed.

They began a feast at Arberth, for it was one of the chief courts, and every celebration originated from there. That night after the first sitting, while the servants were eating, they got up and went out, and the four of them proceeded to Gorsedd Arberth* and many people with them. As they were sitting there they heard a tumultuous noise, and with the intensity of the noise there fell a blanket of mist so that they could not see each other. And after the mist, everywhere became bright. When they looked to where they had once seen the flocks and herds and dwelling-places, they could now see nothing at all, neither building nor beast, neither smoke nor fire, neither man nor dwelling-place, only the court buildings empty, desolate, uninhabited, without people, without animals in them; their own companions had disappeared, with nothing known of their whereabouts—only the four of them remained.*

'Dear Lord God,' said Manawydan, 'where is the court retinue and our company, apart from us? Let us go and look.'

They came to the hall; there was no one. They went to the chamber and sleeping-quarters; they could see no one. In the mead-hall and kitchen, there was nothing but desolation.

The four of them continued with the feast; and they hunted, and enjoyed themselves. Each one of them began to wander through the land and realm to see whether they could find either a building or dwelling-place; but nothing at all did they see, only wild animals. When they had finished their feast and provisions, they began to live on meat they hunted, and on fish and swarms of wild bees. And so they spent a year happily, and the second. But at last they grew tired.

'God knows,' said Manawydan, 'we cannot live like this. Let us go to England, and seek a craft by which we may make our living.'

They set off for England, and came to Hereford, and took up saddlemaking. Manawydan began to shape pommels, and colour them with blue enamel in the way he had seen it done by Llasar Llaesgyngwyd, and he prepared blue enamel as the other man had done. And because of that it is still called 'Llasar's enamel', because Llasar Llaesgyngwyd* made it. As long as that work could be had from Manawydan, neither pommels nor saddles were purchased from any other saddler throughout all Hereford. All the saddlers realized that they were losing their profits, and that nothing was being bought from them unless it could not be supplied by Manawydan. So they got together and agreed to kill him and his companion. But in the meantime the two of them received a warning, and discussed whether they should leave the town.

'Between me and God,' said Pryderi, 'my advice is not to leave the town but rather to kill these churls.'

'No,' said Manawydan, 'if we were to fight them, we would get a bad reputation and would be imprisoned. It would be better for us to go to another town and earn our living there.' Then the four of them went to another city.

'What craft shall we take on?' said Pryderi.

'We will make shields,' said Manawydan.

'Do we know anything about that?' said Pryderi.

'We will attempt it,' he said.

They began making shields, shaping them after the design of good shields that they had seen, and colouring them as they had coloured the saddles. Their work flourished, so that no shield was being bought throughout the town unless it could not be supplied by them. They worked quickly and made vast quantities. And so they continued until their fellow townsmen became angry with them and agreed to try and kill them. But they received a warning and heard that the men were intent on putting them to death.

'Pryderi,' said Manawydan, 'these men want to kill us.'

'We will not take that from these churls. Let us go for them and kill them.'

'No,' he replied, 'Caswallon would get to hear of it, and his men, and we would be ruined. We will go to another town.' They came to another town.

'What craft shall we take up?' said Manawydan.

'Whatever craft you want of those we know,' said Pryderi.

'Not so,' he said, 'we will take up shoemaking. Shoemakers will not have the heart to fight us or forbid us.'

'I know nothing about that craft,' said Pryderi.

'But I do,' said Manawydan, 'and I will teach you how to stitch. And we will not bother to tan the leather but buy it already prepared, and work with that.'

Then he began to buy the finest Cordovan leather* he could get in town, and bought no other leather except leather for the soles. He began to make friends with the best goldsmiths in town and had buckles made for the shoes, and had them gilded, and watched the process himself until he knew how to do it. And because of that he was called one of the Three Golden Shoemakers.*

As long as a shoe or boot could be supplied by him, nothing was bought from any shoemaker throughout town. The shoemakers realized that they were losing their profits, for as Manawydan cut out the leather, Pryderi stitched it. The shoemakers came and took counsel; they agreed to kill them.

'Pryderi,' said Manawydan, 'the men want to kill us.'

'Why should we take that from the thieving churls, rather than kill them all?' said Pryderi.

'No,' said Manawydan, 'we will not fight them nor will we stay in England any longer. We will set off and go and visit Dyfed.'

Although the road was long, they came at last to Dyfed, and made for Arberth where they kindled a fire, and began to support themselves by hunting, and they spent a month like this; they gathered their hounds about them and hunted, and spent a year there in this way.

One morning Pryderi and Manawydan get up to hunt; they get their dogs ready and leave the court. Some of the dogs run ahead of them and approach a small thicket that is nearby. But as soon as they enter the thicket they come out again quickly, their hair standing on end with fear, and return to the men.

'Let us get closer to the thicket to see what is inside,' said Pryderi.

They approached the thicket. As they approached, a gleaming-white wild boar* rose from it. Encouraged by the men, the dogs charged at him. The boar then left the thicket and retreated a little way from the men. And until the men closed in on him, he would keep the dogs at bay without retreating; but when the men closed in he would retreat again and break away. They followed the boar until they saw a huge, towering fort, newly built, in a place where they had never before seen either stone or building. The boar was heading quickly for the fort, with the dogs after him. When the boar and the dogs had gone into the fort, the men marvelled at seeing the fort in a place where they had never before seen any building at all. From the top of the mound they looked and listened for the dogs. Although they waited for a long time, they did not hear the sound of a single dog nor anything at all about them.

'Lord,' said Pryderi, 'I will go into the fort to seek news of the dogs.'

'God knows,' replied Manawydan, 'it's not a good idea for you to go into the fort. We have never seen it before; if you take my advice, you will not enter. For whoever cast a spell on the land has caused the fort to appear.'

'God knows,' said Pryderi, 'I will not abandon my dogs.'

In spite of the advice he received from Manawydan, Pryderi approached the fort. When he entered, neither man nor beast, neither boar nor dogs, neither house nor dwelling-place could he see in the fort. But he could see in the middle of the floor, as it were, a well with marble-work around it. At the edge of the well there was a golden bowl fastened to four chains, over a marble slab, and the chains reached up to the sky, and he could see no end to them. He was enraptured by the beauty of the gold and the fine workmanship of the bowl. And he went to the bowl and grabbed it. But as soon as he grabs the bowl, his hands stick to it and his feet stick to the slab on which he was standing, and the power of speech is taken from him so that he could not utter a single word. And there he stood.

Manawydan waited for him almost until evening. Late in the afternoon, when he was certain that he would get no news about Pryderi or the dogs, he returned to the court. When he entered, Rhiannon looked at him.

'Where is your companion and your dogs?' she said.

'This is what happened,' he said, and told her the whole story.

'God knows,' said Rhiannon, 'you have been a poor companion, and you have lost a good friend.' And with those words out she went, going in the direction he had told her Pryderi and the fort could be found.

She found the gate of the fort open—it was ajar—and in she came. As soon as she entered she discovered Pryderi gripping the bowl, and she went up to him.

'My lord,' she said, 'what are you doing here?' Then she too grabbed the bowl. As soon as she grabs it, her hands too stick to the bowl and her feet to the slab, so that she too could not utter a single word. Then, as soon as it was night, there was a tumultous noise above them, and a blanket of mist, and then the fort disappeared and so did they.

When Cigfa, daughter of Gwynn Gloyw, wife of Pryderi, saw that she and Manawydan were alone in the court, she lamented that she did not care whether she lived or died. Manawydan saw this.

'God knows,' he said, 'you are mistaken if you are lamenting because you are afraid of me. I give you God as my guarantor,* that you will never find a truer friend than me, for as long as God wishes it so. I swear to God, even if I were in the prime of youth, I would be true to Pryderi. And for your sake, too, I will be true, and so have no fear at all,' he said. 'I swear to God,' he said, 'you shall have the friendship that you want from me, as far as I am able, for as long as God wants us to be in this misery and sorrow.'

'May God repay you; I thought as much,' said Cigfa. Then the maiden cheered up and took courage because of that.

'Well, my friend,' said Manawydan, 'there is no point our staying here. We have lost our dogs and we cannot support ourselves. Let us go to England—it will be easier for us to support ourselves there.'

'Gladly, lord,' she said, 'let us do that.' Together they journeyed to England.

'Lord,' she said, 'what craft will you choose? Choose one that is clean.'

'I will choose nothing but shoemaking, as I did before,' he said.

'Lord,' she said, 'that craft, as regards its cleanliness, is not suitable for a man of your skill and status.'

'Well that's the one I will follow,' he said.

He set about his craft and shaped his work from the fairest Cordovan leather he could get in town. As they had done in the other place, he began to fit the shoes with golden buckles, until the work of all the shoemakers in town was worthless and inferior compared to his. And as long as a shoe or boot could be supplied by him, nothing was bought from anyone else. And so he spent a year there until the shoemakers became envious and jealous of him, and until warnings reached him saying that the shoemakers had decided to kill him.

'Lord,' said Cigfa, 'why should we put up with this from the churls?'

'We will not,' he said, 'but we will return to Dyfed.'

They set out for Dyfed. When Manawydan set off, he took with him a load of wheat and made for Arberth and settled there. Nothing gave him more pleasure than seeing Arberth and the land where he had been hunting, he and Pryderi, and Rhiannon with them. He began to get used to catching fish and wild animals in their lairs. After that he began to till the soil, and then he sowed a small field, and a second, and a third. And indeed, the wheat sprang up the best in the world, his three fields flourishing alike so that no one had seen wheat finer than that. The seasons of the year passed by. Harvest time arrived, and he went to look at one of his fields; it was ripe.

'I will reap this tomorrow,' he said. He returned that night to Arberth.

In the grey dawn the next day, he comes intending to reap the field. When he arrives, there are only the bare stalks, each one having been broken off where the ear comes out of the stalk, and the ears have all been carried away, and the stalks left there, bare. He is greatly surprised at that and goes to look at another field; it is ripe.

'God only knows,' he said, 'I will reap this one tomorrow.'

The next day he comes with the intention of reaping the field. When he arrives, there is nothing but bare stalks.

'Oh Lord God,' he said, 'who is trying to destroy me completely? I know this much: whoever began this destruction is now bringing it to an end, and has destroyed the land along with me.'

He comes to look at the third field. When he arrives, no one has seen finer wheat, and all of it ripe.

'Shame on me,' he said, 'if I do not keep watch tonight. Whoever carried off the other wheat will come to take this, and I will find out who it is.'

He took his weapons, and began to keep watch over the field. He told Cigfa everything.

'Well,' she said, 'what have you in mind?'

'I will keep watch over the field tonight,' he said.

He went to keep watch over the field. While he was doing so, towards midnight, he heard the loudest noise in the world. He looked. There was a huge army of mice*—they could not be counted or measured. The next thing he knew, the mice were making for the field, and each one was climbing up along a stalk and bending it down, and breaking the ear and making off with the ears, and leaving the stalks behind. And as far as he knew there was not a single stalk there without a mouse to it. And they ran away carrying the ears with them. Then, enraged and angered, he charged in among the mice. He could no more keep his eye on one of them than on the gnats or the birds in the air. But he could see that one was very fat, and unlikely to be able to move quickly. He went after that one and caught it, and put it in his glove, and tied the mouth of the glove with string, and kept hold of it and made for the court.

Manawydan came to the chamber where Cigfa was, and he lit the fire, and hung the glove by its string on the peg.

'What do you have there, lord?' said Cigfa.

'A thief that I caught stealing from me,' he replied.

'What sort of thief, lord, could you put in your glove?' she said.

'I'll tell you everything,' he said, and he told her how his fields had been destroyed and laid waste, and how the mice had come to the last field before his very eyes.

'And one of them was very fat, and I caught it, and it's inside the glove, and I intend to hang it tomorrow. And by my confession to God, had I caught them all, I would hang them.'

'Lord,' she said, 'I'm not surprised. But yet it's not proper for a man of your status and rank to hang that sort of creature. If you were to do the right thing, you would not bother with the creature, but let it go.'

'Shame on me,' he said, 'if I would not have hanged them all had I caught them. But what I have caught I will hang.'

'Well, lord,' she said, 'there is no reason why I should help this creature, except to prevent you from being disgraced. So do as you will, lord.'

'If I knew of any reason in the world why you should help the creature, I would take your advice; but since I do not, my lady, I intend to destroy it.'

'Then do so gladly,' she said.

Then he made for Gorsedd Arberth, taking the mouse with him, and he pushed two forks into the highest point of the mound. As he was doing this, he could see a cleric* coming towards him, dressed in poor, threadbare, old clothes. And it was seven years since he had seen either man or beast, except for the four people who had been together until two of them disappeared.

'Lord,' said the cleric, 'good day to you.'

'May God prosper you, and welcome,' said Manawydan. 'Where do you come from, cleric?' he said.

'I come, lord, from England where I have been singing. And why do you ask, lord?' he said.

'Because for the last seven years I have not seen a single person here, apart from four exiled people, and now yourself.'

'Well, lord,' he said, 'I myself am just passing through on the way to my own country. But what sort of work are you engaged in, lord?'

'Hanging a thief I caught stealing from me,' he said.

'What sort of thief, lord?' he said. 'I can see a creature in your hand that looks like a mouse. It's not fitting for a man of your status to handle such a creature. Let it go!'

'I will not, between me and God,' he said. 'I caught it stealing, and I am punishing it in accordance with the law,* which is to hang it.'

'Lord,' he said, 'rather than see a man of your status involved in such work, I will give you the pound I received as charity to let that creature go.'

'Between me and God, I will neither sell it nor let it go.'

'As you wish, lord,' he said. 'If it were not improper to see a man of your status touching such a creature, it would not worry me.' And off went the cleric.

As Manawydan was placing the crossbeam on the forks, he saw a priest approaching on a well-equipped horse.

'Lord, good day to you,' he said.

'May God prosper you,' said Manawydan, 'and I ask for your blessing.'

'God's blessing upon you. And what sort of work, lord, are you engaged in?'

'I am hanging a thief I caught stealing from me,' he said.

'What sort of thief, lord?' he said.

'A creature in the shape of a mouse,' he said, 'and it stole from me, and I am putting it to death in the way one should a thief.'

'Lord, rather than see you handle that creature, I will buy it from you. Let it go.'

'By my confession to God, I will neither sell it nor let it go.'

'The truth is, lord, it is worth nothing. But rather than see you defile yourself with that creature, I will give you three pounds to let it go.'

'Between me and God,' he said, 'I want no payment except what is deserves—hanging!'

'Very well, lord, do as you please.' Off went the priest. Manawydan tied the string around the mouse's neck.

As he was hoisting it up, he could see a bishop's entourage and his baggage and his retinue, and the bishop himself approaching. So Manawydan postponed his work.

'Lord bishop,' he said, 'your blessing.'

'May God give you his blessing,' he said. 'What sort of work are you engaged in?'

'I'm hanging a thief I caught stealing from me,' he said.

'Isn't that a mouse I see in your hand?' he said.

'It is,' he said, 'and it stole from me.'

'Well,' said the bishop, 'since I have arrived just when you were about to destroy that creature, I will buy it from you. I will give you seven pounds for it, and rather than see a man of your status destroying such a worthless creature, let it go, and you shall have the money.'

'I will not let it go, between me and God,' he said.

'Since you will not let it go for that, I will give you twenty-four pounds in ready money to let it go.'

'By my confession to God,' he said, 'I will not let it go for as much again.'

'Since you will not release the creature for that,' he said, 'I will give you every horse you can see on this plain, and the seven loads of baggage that are on the seven horses.'

'No, between me and God,' he said.

'Since you do not want that, name your price.'

'I will,' he said: 'the release of Rhiannon and Pryderi.'

'You shall have that.'

'That's not enough, between me and God.'

'What else do you want?'

'Remove the magic and enchantment from the seven cantrefs of Dyfed.'

'You shall have that too, now let the mouse go.'

'I will not, between me and God,' he said. 'I want to know who the mouse is.'

'She is my wife, and if she were not, I would not free her.'

'How did she come to me?'

'Stealing,' he said. 'I am Llwyd son of Cil Coed, and it is I who placed the enchantment on the seven cantrefs of Dyfed, and I did so to avenge Gwawl son of Clud, out of friendship for him; and I took revenge on Pryderi because Pwyll Pen Annwfn played Badger in the Bag* with Gwawl son of Clud, and he did that unwisely at the court of Hyfaidd Hen. And having heard that you were living in the land, my retinue came to me and asked me to turn them into mice so that they could destroy your corn. The first night they came alone. And they came the second night too, and destroyed the two fields. But the third night my wife and the ladies of the court came to me and asked me to transform them too, and I did that. My wife was pregnant. And had she not been pregnant you would not have caught her. But since she was, and you did, I will give you Pryderi and Rhiannon, and I will remove the magic and enchantment from Dyfed. I have told you who she is, now let her go.'

'I will not let her go, between me and God,' he said.

'What else do you want?' he said.

'This is what I want,' he said: 'that there will never be any spell on the seven cantrefs of Dyfed, and that none will ever be cast.'

'You shall have that,' he said. 'Now let her go.'

'I will not let her go, between me and God,' he said.

'What else do you want?' he said.

'This is what I want,' he said: 'that no vengeance will ever be taken on Pryderi and Rhiannon, nor on me, because of this.'

'You shall have all of that. And God only knows, you have struck a good bargain,' he said. 'Had you not done so,' he said, 'all the trouble would have fallen on your own head.'

'Yes,' said Manawydan, 'that is why I made it a condition.'

'And now set my wife free.'

'I will not set her free, between me and God, until I see Pryderi and Rhiannon free with me.'

'Look, here they come,' he said. Then Pryderi and Rhiannon appeared. He got up to meet them, and welcomed them, and they sat down together.

'Sir, set my wife free now, for you have everything you asked for.'

'I will do so gladly,' he said. Then she was released, and he struck her with a magic wand, and changed her back into the fairest young woman that anyone had seen.

'Look around you at the land,' he said, 'and you will see all the houses and dwelling-places as they were at their best.'

Then Manawydan got up and looked around. And when he looked, he could see all the land inhabited and complete with all its herds and its houses.

'In what sort of captivity were Pryderi and Rhiannon?' said Manawydan.

'Pryderi had the gate-hammers* of my court around his neck, while around hers Rhiannon had the collars of the asses after they had been hauling hay. And that was their imprisonment.'

Because of that imprisonment, this story was called the Mabinogi of the Collar and the Hammer.* And so ends this branch of the Mabinogi.

The Fourth Branch of the Mabinogi

MATH son of Mathonwy was lord over Gwynedd,* and Pryderi son of Pwyll was lord over twenty-one cantrefs in the south, namely the seven cantrefs of Dyfed, and the seven of Morgannwg, and the four of Ceredigion, and the three of Ystrad Tywi.* At that time Math son of Mathonwy could not live unless his feet were in the lap of a virgin, except when the turmoil of war prevented him. The maiden who was with him was Goewin daughter of Pebin from Dol Pebin in Arfon. And she was the fairest maiden of her generation known at the time. Math found peace at Caer Dathyl in Arfon.* He was unable to circuit the land,* but Gilfaethwy son of Dôn and Gwydion son of Dôn,* his nephews, sons of his sister, together with the retinue would circuit the land on his behalf.

The maiden was always with Math. But Gilfaethwy son of Dôn set his heart on the maiden, and loved her to the extent that he did not know what to do about it. And behold, his colour and face and form were wasting away because of his love for her, so that it was not easy to recognize him. One day Gwydion, his brother, looked at him closely.

'Lad,' he said, 'what has happened to you?'

'Why,' said the other, 'what is wrong with me?'

'I can see that you are losing your looks and colour, and what has happened to you?' said Gwydion.

'Lord brother,' said Gilfaethwy, 'there is no point my telling anyone what has happened.'

'Why is that, my friend?' he said.

'You know of Math son of Mathonwy's special attribute',* said Gilfaethwy. 'Whatever whispering goes on between people—no matter how quiet—once the wind catches hold of it then Math will know about it.'

'That's true,' said Gwydion; 'say no more. I know your thoughts; you love Goewin.'

When Gilfaethwy realized that his brother knew what was on his mind, he heaved the heaviest sigh in the world.

'Friend, stop your sighing,' said Gwydion; 'you will not get anywhere like that. The only thing to do is for me to arrange that Gwynedd and Powys and Deheubarth gather for war, so that you can get the maiden; and cheer up, because I will arrange it for you.'

Then they went to Math son of Mathonwy.

'Lord,' said Gwydion, 'I hear that some kind of creatures that have never been in this island before have arrived in the South.'

'What are they called?' said Math.

'*Hobeu*, lord.'

'What sort of animals are they?'

'Small animals whose flesh is better than beef. They are small, and their name varies. They are called *moch* now.'

'Who owns them?'

'Pryderi son of Pwyll—they were sent to him from Annwfn by Arawn, king of Annwfn.'* (And to this day that name survives in the term for a side of pork: half a *hob*.)

'Well,' said Math, 'how can we get them from him?'

'I will go with eleven men disguised as poets, lord, to ask for the swine.'

'He could refuse you,' said Math.

'My plan is not a bad one, lord,' he said. 'I will not return without the swine.'

'Very well,' said Math, 'then go on your way.'

Gwydion and Gilfaethwy, together with ten men, travelled to Ceredigion, to the place now called Rhuddlan Teifi; Pryderi had a court there. They entered, disguised as poets.* They were made welcome. Gwydion was seated next to Pryderi that night.

'Well,' said Pryderi, 'we would like to have a story from some of the young men over there.'

'Our custom, lord,' said Gwydion, 'is that on the first night we come to a great man, the chief poet performs. I would be happy to tell a story.'

Gwydion was the best storyteller in the world. And that night he entertained the court with amusing anecdotes and stories, until he was admired by everyone in the court, and Pryderi enjoyed conversing with him.

When that was over, 'Lord,' said Gwydion, 'can anyone deliver my request to you better than I myself?'

'No indeed,' said Pryderi. 'Yours is a very good tongue.'

'Then this is my request, lord: to ask you for the animals that were sent to you from Annwfn.'

'Well,' he replied, 'that would be the easiest thing in the world, were there not an agreement between me and my people concerning them; namely, that I should not part with them until they had bred twice their number in the land.'

'Lord,' said Gwydion, 'I can free you from those words. This is how: do not give me the pigs tonight, but do not refuse me either. Tomorrow I will show you something you can exchange for them.'

That night Gwydion and his companions went to their lodging to confer.

'My men,' said Gwydion, 'we will not get the swine just by asking for them.'

'Well,' they said, 'what plan is there to get them?'

'I will make sure we get them,' said Gwydion. Then he drew on his skills, and began to demonstrate his magic, and he conjured up twelve stallions, and twelve hounds, each one black with a white breast, and twelve collars with twelve leashes on them, and anyone who saw them would think they were of gold; and twelve saddles on the horses, and where there should have been iron there was gold, and the bridles were of the same workmanship.

Gwydion came to Pryderi with the steeds and the dogs.

'Good day to you, lord,' he said.

'May God prosper you,' said Pryderi, 'and welcome.'

'Lord,' he said, 'here is a way out for you from what you said last night concerning the swine, that you would not give them away or sell them. You can exchange them for something better. I will give you these twelve horses, fully equipped as they are with their saddles and bridles, and the twelve hounds that you see with their collars and leashes, and the twelve golden shields you can see over there.' (He had conjured those up out of toadstools.)

'Well,' he said, 'we will take advice.' They decided to give Gwydion the swine and take from him in return the horses and hounds and shields.

Then they took their leave and set off with the swine.

'My brave men,' said Gwydion, 'we must move quickly. The magic will only last until tomorrow.'

That night they travelled as far as the uplands of Ceredigion, the place which for that reason is still called Mochdref. The next day they pushed on and crossed Elenid. They spent that night between Ceri and Arwystli, in the town which is also called Mochdref because of that. From there they continued, and that night they went as far as a commot in Powys which is also for that reason called Mochnant, and they stayed there that night. From there they travelled as far as the cantref of Rhos, and they stayed there that night in the town which is still called Mochdref.*

'Men,' said Gwydion, 'we will make for the strongest part of Gwynedd with these animals. They are mustering armies behind us.' So they made for the highest town in Arllechwedd, and there they made a pen for the pigs, and because of that the name Creuwrion* was given to the town. Then, having made a pen for the pigs, they made their way to Math son of Mathonwy, in Caer Dathyl.

When they arrived there, the country was being mustered.

'What is happening here?' said Gwydion.

'Pryderi is assembling twenty-one cantrefs to come after you,' they said. 'It is strange how slowly you have travelled.'

'Where are the animals you went after?' said Math.

'A pen has been made for them in the other cantref below,' said Gwydion.

Then behold, they could hear the trumpets and the mustering of people. They armed themselves at once and travelled until they came to Pennardd in Arfon.

But that night Gwydion son of Dôn and Gilfaethwy his brother returned to Caer Dathyl. And in the bed of Math son of Mathonwy, Gilfaethwy and Goewin daughter of Pebin were put to sleep together, and her maidens were forced out violently, and she was taken against her will that night.

At dawn the next day they travelled to where Math son of Mathonwy and his host were. As they arrived, the men were about to take counsel regarding where they would wait for Pryderi and the men of the South. So they too joined in the deliberation. They decided to wait in the strongest part of Gwynedd in Arfon. And they waited right in the middle of the two districts, Maenor Bennardd and Maenor Coed Alun.

Pryderi attacked them there; and that is where the battle took place, and there was a great massacre on each side, and the men of the South were forced to retreat. They retreated as far as the place which is still called Nant Call, and they were pursued as far as there. And then there was immeasurable slaughter. Then they fled as far as the place called Dol Benmaen. Then they rallied and attempted to make peace, and Pryderi gave hostages to secure peace: he gave Gwrgi Gwastra and twenty-three sons of noblemen.

After that, they travelled in peace as far as Y Traeth Mawr;* but as soon as they reached Y Felenrhyd, because the foot-soldiers could not be restrained from shooting at each other, Pryderi sent messengers requesting that both armies be called off, and that the matter be left to him and Gwydion son of Dôn, since Gwydion had caused all this. The messengers came to Math son of Mathonwy.

'I agree,' said Math, 'between me and God; if it pleases Gwydion son of Dôn, I will allow it gladly. I will not force any one to go and fight if we can prevent it.'

'God knows,' said the messengers, 'Pryderi says it is only fair for the man who did him this wrong to set his body against his, and let the two hosts stand aside.'

'By my confession to God,' said Gwydion, 'I will not ask the men of Gwynedd to fight on my behalf, when I myself can fight against Pryderi. I will set my body against his gladly.' That message was dispatched to Pryderi.

'I agree,' said Pryderi, 'I, too, will not ask anyone to seek compensation on my behalf.'

They set those men apart, and began to equip them with armour. And they fought. And because of strength and valour, and magic and enchantment, Gwydion triumphed and Pryderi was killed; and he was buried in Maentwrog, above Y Felenrhyd, and his grave is there.*

The men of the South set off for their land lamenting bitterly, and no wonder; they had lost their lord, and many of their best men, and their horses, and most of their weapons. The men of Gwynedd returned home elated and rejoicing.

'Lord,' said Gwydion to Math, 'should we not release to the men of the South their nobleman, the one they gave as hostage for peace? We should not imprison him.'

'Let him be released,' said Math. And that young man, and the hostages who were with him, were released to follow after the men of the South.

Then Math made for Caer Dathyl. Gilfaethwy son of Dôn and the retinue who had been with him gathered together to circuit Gwynedd as had been their custom, and they did not go to the court. Math went to his chamber, and had a place prepared for him to recline so that he could put his feet in the maiden's lap.

'Lord,' said Goewin, 'look for another virgin to hold your feet now—I am a woman.'

'How can that be?'

'I was assaulted, lord, quite openly, nor did I keep quiet—everyone in the court knew about it. It was your nephews who came, lord, your sister's sons, Gwydion son of Dôn and Gilfaethwy son of Dôn. And they forced me, and shamed *you*, and I was taken in your chamber and in your very bed.'*

'Well,' he said, 'what I can, I shall do. I will arrange recompense for you first, and then I will seek recompense for myself. And I will take you as my wife,' he said, 'and give you authority over my kingdom.'

Meanwhile Gwydion and Gilfaethwy did not come near the court, but continued to circuit the land until a ban went out denying them food and drink. At first, they would not go near Math. Then they came.

'Lord,' they said, 'good day to you.'*

'Well,' he said, 'have you come here to make amends?'

'Lord, we are at your will.'

'Had it been my will, I would not have lost all those men and weapons. You cannot compensate me for my shame, not to mention Pryderi's death. But since you have come to do my will, I will begin to punish you.'

Then he took his magic wand, and struck Gilfaethwy so that he changed into a good-sized hind, and he caught Gwydion quickly—he could not escape although he wanted to—and struck him with the same magic wand so that he changed into a stag.

'Since you are in league with each other, I will make you live together and mate with each other, and take on the nature of the wild animals whose shape you are in; and when they have offspring, so shall you. And a year from today return here to me.'

At the end of the year to the very day, behold, he heard a commotion under the chamber wall, and the dogs of the court barking at the commotion.

'Have a look what is outside,' he said,

'Lord,' said one, 'I have looked. There is a stag and a hind, and a fawn with them.'

Then Math, too, got up and went outside. And when he came he could see the three animals, namely a stag, a hind, and a sturdy fawn. He raised his magic wand.

'The one that has been a hind for the past year shall be a wild boar this year. And the one that has been a stag for the past year shall be a wild sow this year.' Then he strikes them with the magic wand.

'The boy, however, I will take, and have him fostered and baptized.' He was called Hyddwn.

'Now go, and let the one be a wild boar and the other a wild sow. And let the nature that is in wild swine be yours too. And a year from today be here under the wall with your offspring.'

At the end of the year, behold, they heard dogs barking under the chamber wall and the court gathering around them. Then Math, too, got up and went outside. When he came outside, he could see three animals, namely a wild boar, a wild sow, and a good-sized young one with them. And it was big for its age.

'Yes,' he said, 'I will take this one, and have him baptized.' He struck him with the magic wand so that he changed into a large, handsome, auburn-haired lad. That one was called Hychddwn.

'As for you, the one that has been a wild boar for the past year shall be a she-wolf this year, and the one that has been a wild sow for the past year shall be a wolf this year.' Then he strikes them with the magic wand so that they become a wolf and she-wolf.

'And take on the nature of the animals whose shape you are in. And be here a year from this very day, under this wall.'

That same day, at the end of the year, behold, he could hear a disturbance and barking under the chamber wall. He got up to go outside, and when he came he could see a wolf and a she-wolf and a strong wolf cub with them.

'I will take this one,' he said, 'and have him baptized, and his name is ready, Bleiddwn. The three boys are yours and those three are:

> The three sons of wicked Gilfaethwy,
> Three true champions,
> Bleiddwn, Hyddwn, Hychddwn Hir.'*

Then he strikes them both with the magic wand so that they are in their own form.

'Men,' he said, 'if you did me wrong, you have been punished enough, and you have been greatly shamed that each of you has offspring by the other. Prepare a bath for the men and wash their heads and have them properly dressed.' That was done for them.

After they had got themselves ready, they came to Math.

'Men,' he said, 'you have had peace and you shall have friendship.* Now give me advice as to which virgin I should seek.'

'Lord,' said Gwydion son of Dôn, 'it is easy to advise you— Aranrhod daughter of Dôn,* your niece, your sister's daughter.' She was brought to Math. The maiden entered.

'Maiden,' he said, 'are you a virgin?'

'That is my belief.'* Then he took his magic wand and bent it.

'Step over this,' he said, 'and if you are a virgin I shall know.'*

Then she stepped over the magic wand, and as she stepped she dropped a large, sturdy, yellow-haired boy. The boy gave a loud cry. After the boy's cry she made for the door, but as she went she dropped a small something. Before anyone could get a second glimpse of it, Gwydion took it and wrapped a sheet of brocaded silk around it and hid it. He hid it in a small chest at the foot of his bed.

'Well,' said Math son of Mathonwy, of the sturdy, yellow-haired boy, 'I will have this one baptized. I will call him Dylan.'

The boy was baptized. As soon as he was baptized he made for the sea. And there and then, as soon as he came to the sea, he took on the sea's nature and swam as well as the best fish in the sea. Because of that he was called Dylan Eil Ton—no wave ever broke beneath him. The blow which killed him was struck by Gofannon, his uncle. And that was one of the Three Unfortunate Blows.*

One day, as Gwydion was in his bed, and waking up, he heard a cry from the chest at his feet. Although it was not loud, it was loud enough for him to hear it. He got up quickly and opened the chest.

As he opened it, he could see a small boy waving his arms free of the folds of the sheet and throwing it aside. He took the boy in his arms and carried him to the town, where he knew of a woman who was nursing. And he struck a bargain with the woman to suckle the boy. The boy was reared that year. At the end of the year they would have been surprised at his sturdiness had he been two years old. And by the second year he was a large boy, and was able to go to court on his own. Gwydion himself took notice of him when he came to court. And the boy grew used to Gwydion and loved him more than anyone. Then the boy was reared at the court until he was four years old; and it would have been surprising for an eight-year-old boy to be as sturdy as that.

One day the boy followed Gwydion as he went out walking. He made for Caer Aranrhod and the boy with him. When he came to the court, Aranrhod got up to meet him, to welcome and to greet him.

'May God prosper you,' he said.

'Who is the boy behind you?' she said.

'This boy is a son of yours,' he said.

'Alas man, what has come over you, putting me to shame, and pursuing my shame by keeping him as long as this?'

'If you have no greater shame than that I should foster a boy as fine as this, then your shame is but a small matter.'

'What is your boy's name?' she said.

'God knows,' he said, 'he has no name yet.'

'Well,' she said, 'I will swear a destiny that he shall not get a name until he gets one from me.'

'By my confession to God,' he said, 'you are a wicked woman; but the boy shall have a name, though it displeases you. And you,' he said, 'it is because of him you are angry, since you are no longer called a virgin. Never again will you be called a virgin.'

Then he walked away angrily, and made for Caer Dathyl and stayed there that night. And the next day he got up and took the boy with him, and went walking along the seashore between there and Aber Menai. And where he saw dulse and wrack* he conjured up a ship. And out of the seaweed and dulse he conjured up Cordovan leather, a good deal of it, and he coloured it so that no one had seen more beautiful leather than that. Then he rigged a sail on the ship, and he and the boy sailed to the harbour entrance of Caer Aranrhod. Then they began to cut out shoes and stitch them. And then they were seen from the fort. When Gwydion realized they had been seen from the fort, he took away their own appearance and gave them another so that they would not be recognized.

'Who are the people in the ship?' said Aranrhod.

'Shoemakers,' they said.

'Go and see what kind of leather they have, and what sort of work they are doing.' They went. When they arrived, Gwydion was colouring Cordovan leather with gold. Then the messengers returned and told her.

'Good,' she said, 'measure my foot and ask the shoemaker to make shoes for me.' He made the shoes, not according to her size, but bigger. They bring her the shoes. Behold, the shoes are too big.

'These are too big,' she said. 'He shall be paid for these, but let him also make some that are smaller.' So he made others much smaller than her foot, and sent them to her.

'Tell him that not one of these shoes fits me,' she said. He was told that.

'Fine,' he said, 'I will not make shoes for her until I see her foot.' And she was told that.

'Fine,' she said, 'I will go to him.' Then Aranrhod went to the ship, and when she arrived he was cutting out and the boy was stitching.

'Lady,' he said, 'good day to you.'

'May God prosper you,' she said. 'I find it strange that you could not make shoes to fit.'

'I could not,' he said. 'But I can, now.' And suddenly a wren lands on the deck of the ship. The boy aims at it and hits it in the leg, between the tendon and the bone. She laughs.

'God knows,' she said, 'it is with a skilful hand that the fair-haired one has hit it.'

'Indeed,' he said. 'And God's curse upon you. He has now got a name, and it's good enough. From now on he is Lleu Llaw Gyffes.'*

Then everything vanished into dulse and seaweed. And Gwydion pursued the craft no more. But because of that occasion was called one of the Three Golden Shoemakers.*

'God knows,' she said, 'you will be none the better for treating me badly.'

'I have not treated you badly yet,' he said.

Then he changed the boy back into his own shape, and he himself took on his own form.

'Well,' she said, 'I will swear a destiny on this boy that he shall never get weapons until I arm him myself.'

'Between me and God,' said Gwydion, 'this stems from your wickedness. But he shall get weapons.'

Then they came to Dinas Dinlleu.* Lleu Llaw Gyffes was brought up until he could ride every horse, and until he had matured as regards appearance, and growth, and size. Then Gwydion noticed that he was pining for horses and weapons, and summoned him.

'Lad,' he said, 'you and I shall go on an errand tomorrow. So be more cheerful than you are.'

'That I will,' said the boy.

Early the next day they got up, and followed the coast up towards Bryn Arien. At the very top of Cefn Cludno they got ready on horseback and came towards Caer Aranrhod. Then they changed their appearance and approached the gate disguised as two young men, except that Gwydion looked more serious than the lad.

'Porter,' said Gwydion, 'go inside and say there are poets here from Morgannwg.' The porter went.

'God's welcome to them. Let them come in,' said Aranrhod. There was great rejoicing at their arrival. The hall was prepared and they went to eat. When they had finished eating, she and Gwydion talked of tales and storytelling. And Gwydion was a good storyteller.

When it was time to end the carousing, a chamber was prepared for them, and they went to sleep. Long before daybreak Gwydion got up. Then he called on his magic and his power. By the time day was dawning, there was rushing to and fro and the sound of trumpets and wailing throughout the land. When day broke, they heard knocking on the chamber door, and then Aranrhod asking them to open up. The young lad got up and opened the door. In she came, and a maiden with her.

'Men,' she said, 'we are in a bad situation.'

'Yes,' he replied, 'we can hear trumpets and wailing, and what do you make of it?'

'God knows,' she said, 'we cannot see the colour of the sea for all the ships tightly packed together, and they are making for land as fast as they can. And what shall we do?' she said.

'Lady,' said Gwydion, 'there is nothing we can do except to shut ourselves in the fort and to defend it as best we can.'

'I agree,' she said. 'May God repay you. You defend us. And you will find plenty of weapons here.'

Then she went to fetch the weapons. She returned, and two maidens with her carrying arms for two men.

'Lady,' he said, 'you arm this young man. And I will arm myself with the help of the maidens. I hear the clamour of men approaching.'

'I will do that gladly.' And she armed him gladly, and completely.

'Have you finished arming that man?' said Gwydion.

'I have,' she said.

'I have finished, too,' he said. 'Let us now remove our weapons; we have no need of them.'

'Oh,' she said, 'why not? Look, the fleet surrounds the place.'

'Woman, there is no fleet there.'

'Oh,' she said, 'then what kind of uprising was it?'

'An uprising to break your fate on your son,' he said, 'and to get weapons for him. And now he has weapons, no thanks to you.'

'Between me and God,' she said, 'you are an evil man. And many a lad could have lost his life in the uprising you brought about in this cantref today. And I will swear a destiny on him,' she said, 'that he will never have a wife from the race that is on this earth at present.'

'Yes,' he said, 'you always were a wicked woman, and no one should ever come to your aid. But he shall have a wife nevertheless.'

They came to Math son of Mathonwy, and made the most vehement complaint in the world against Aranrhod, and related how Gwydion had obtained all the weapons for Lleu.

'Fine,' said Math, 'let you and I try through our magic and enchantment to charm a wife for him out of flowers.' By then Lleu was a man in stature, and the most handsome lad that any one had ever seen.

Then they took the flowers of the oak, and the flowers of the broom, and the flowers of the meadowsweet, and from those they conjured up the fairest and most beautiful maiden that anyone had ever seen. And they baptized her in the way they did at that time, and named her Blodeuedd.*

After Lleu and Blodeuedd had slept together at the feast, 'It is not easy for a man without a realm to support himself,' said Gwydion.

'I know,' said Math. 'I shall give him the best cantref that a young man can have.'

'Lord,' he said, 'what cantref is that?'

'The cantref of Dinoding,' he said. That is now called Eifionydd and Ardudwy. Lleu set up a court in the cantref at a place called Mur Castell,* in the uplands of Ardudwy; he settled there, and ruled. And everyone was pleased with him and his governance.

Then one day Lleu went to Caer Dathyl to visit Math son of Mathonwy. On the day he left for Caer Dathyl, Blodeuedd was wandering around the court. And she heard the sound of a hunting-horn, and after the sound of the horn a weary stag passed by with hounds and huntsmen chasing it, and after the hounds and the huntsmen came a band of men on foot.

'Send a lad to find out who they are,' she said. The lad went, and asked who they were.

'This is Gronw Pebr, the man who is lord of Penllyn,'* they said. The lad told her that. Meanwhile Gronw went after the stag. And at the river Cynfael he caught up with the stag and killed it. And there he was, skinning the stag and baiting his hounds until night closed in on him. And as day was failing and night drawing near, he came past the gate of the court.

'God knows,' she said, 'the chieftain will pour scorn on us for letting him go at this hour to another land if we do not invite him in.'

'God knows, lady,' they said, 'it is only proper to invite him in.' Then messengers went to meet him and invite him in. He accepted the invitation gladly and came to the court, and she came to meet him, to welcome him and greet him.

'Lady, may God repay you your welcome', he said. He took off his riding clothes, and they went to sit down. Blodeuedd looked at him, and from the moment she looked there was no part of her that was not filled with love for him. And he gazed at her, and the same thought came to him as had come to her. He could not hide the fact that he loved her, and he told her so. She was overjoyed. And their talk that night was of the attraction and love they felt for one another. And they did not put off making love to each other any longer than that night—that night they slept together.

The next day he asked permission to depart.*

'God knows,' she said, 'you will not leave me tonight.' That night, too, they were together. And that night they discussed how they might stay together.

'There is only one thing to do,' he said; 'find out from him how his death may come about, and do that by pretending to be concerned about him.'

The next day he asked permission to leave.

'God knows, I do not advise you to leave me today.'

'God knows, since you do not advise it, I will not go,' he said. 'However, I would say there is danger that the chieftain who owns this court will return.'

'Yes,' she said, 'tomorrow I will let you leave.'

The next day he asked permission to leave, and she did not prevent him.

'Now,' he said, 'remember what I told you, and keep on talking to him as if you really loved him. And find out from him how his death might come about.'

Lleu returned that night. They spent the day in conversation, song, and carousal. That night they went to sleep together. He spoke to her, and a second time. But he got no reply.

'What's the matter,' he said, 'are you well?'

'I am thinking about something you would not expect of me,' she said. 'Namely, I am worried about your death, if you were to go before me.'

'Well,' he said, 'may God repay you your concern. But unless God kills me, it is not easy to kill me,' he said.

'Then for God's sake and mine, will you tell me how you can be killed? Because my memory is better than yours when it comes to avoiding danger.'

'I will, gladly,' he said. 'It is not easy to kill me with a blow. You would have to spend a year making the spear that would strike me, working on it only when people were at Mass on Sunday.'

'Are you sure of that?' she said.

'Sure, God knows,' he said. 'I cannot be killed indoors,' he said, 'nor out of doors; I cannot be killed on horseback, nor on foot.'

'Well,' she said, 'how can you be killed?'

'I will tell you,' he said. 'By making a bath for me on a riverbank, and constructing an arched roof above the tub, and then thatching that well and watertight. And bringing a billy-goat,' he said, 'and standing it beside the tub; and I place one foot on the back of the billy-goat and the other on the edge of the tub. Whoever should strike me in that position would bring about my death.'*

'Well,' she said, 'I thank God for that. That can be avoided easily.'

No sooner did she get the information than she sent it to Gronw Pebr. Gronw laboured over making the spear, and a year from that very day it was ready. That day he let Blodeuedd know.

'Lord,' she said, 'I am wondering how what you told me before could happen. Will you show me how you would stand on the edge of the tub and the billy-goat, if I get the bath ready?'

'I will,' he said.

She sent word to Gronw, and told him to be in the shadow of the hill which is now called Bryn Cyfergyr, on the bank of the river Cynfael. She had all the goats she could find in the cantref rounded up and brought to the far side of the river, facing Bryn Cyfergyr.*

The next day she said to Lleu, 'Lord, I have had the roof prepared, and the bath, and they are ready.'

'Fine,' he said, 'let us go and look at them, with pleasure.' The next day they came to look at the bath.

'You will get into the bath, lord?' she said.

'I will, with pleasure,' he said. He got into the bath, and washed himself.

'Lord,' she said, 'these are the animals you said were called billy-goats.'

'Yes,' he said, 'have them catch one and bring it here.'

A goat was brought. Then he got up from the bath and put on his trousers, and placed one foot on the edge of the tub and the other on the billy-goat's back. Then Gronw got up from the hill called Bryn Cyfergyr, and on one knee he aimed at Lleu with the poisoned spear, and struck him in his side so that the shaft stuck out of him but the head remained inside. And then Lleu flew up in the form of an eagle and gave a horrible scream, and he was not seen again.

As soon as Lleu disappeared they made for the court, and that night they slept together. The next day Gronw got up and took possession of Ardudwy. Having taken possession of the land, he ruled it so that Ardudwy and Penllyn were in his control. Then the news reached Math son of Mathonwy. Math felt sad and sorrowful, and Gwydion even more so.

'Lord,' said Gwydion, 'I will never rest until I get news of my nephew.'

'Yes,' said Math, 'may God be your strength.'

Then he set off and went on his way, and wandered through Gwynedd and the length and breadth of Powys. Having travelled everywhere he came to Arfon, and in Maenor Bennardd he came to the house of a peasant. Gwydion dismounted at the house and stayed there that night. The man of the house and his family came in, and last of all came the swineherd. The man of the house said to the swineherd, 'Lad,' he said, 'has your sow come in tonight?'

'Yes,' he said, 'she has just come to the pigs.'

'Where does this sow go?' said Gwydion.

'Every day when the pen is opened she goes out. No one can grab her, and no one knows where she goes, any more than if she sank into the earth.'

'For my sake, will you not open the pen until I am at the side of the pen with you?' said Gwydion.

'Yes, gladly,' he said. They went to sleep that night.

When the swineherd saw daylight he woke Gwydion, and Gwydion got up and dressed and went with him and stood beside the pen. The swineherd opened the pen. As soon as he opens it she leaps out and sets off at a brisk pace, with Gwydion following her. And she goes upstream and heads for a valley which is now called Nantlleu,* and there she slows down and feeds. Then Gwydion goes under the tree and looks to see what the sow is feeding on; and he can see the sow feeding on rotten flesh and maggots. He looks up to the top of the tree. And when he looks, he can see an eagle at the top of the tree. And when the eagle shakes himself, the worms and the rotten flesh fall from him and the sow eats them. He thinks that the eagle is Lleu, and sings an *englyn*:*

> 'An oak grows between two lakes,
> Very dark is the sky and the valley.
> Unless I am mistaken
> This is because of Lleu's Flowers.'

The eagle lowers himself until he is in the middle of the tree. Gwydion sings another *englyn*:

> 'An oak grows on a high plain,
> Rain does not wet it, heat no longer melts it;
> It sustained one who possesses nine-score attributes.
> In its top is Lleu Llaw Gyffes.'

And then he lowers himself down until he is on the lowest branch of the tree. Then Gwydion sings him an *englyn*:

'An oak grows on a slope
The refuge of a handsome prince.
Unless I am mistaken
Lleu will come to my lap.'

And he dropped down onto Gwydion's knee; then Gwydion struck him with his magic wand so that he changed back into his own shape. But no one had ever seen a man look more wretched—he was nothing but skin and bone.

Then he made for Caer Dathyl, and there all the good physicians that could be found in Gwynedd were brought to him. Before the end of the year he was completely recovered.

'Lord,' said Lleu to Math son of Mathonwy, 'it is high time for me to have recompense from the man who caused me this distress.'

'God knows,' said Math, 'he cannot continue like this, owing you recompense.'

'I agree,' he said. 'The sooner I get recompense the better.'

Then they mustered Gwynedd and set off for Ardudwy. Gwydion went ahead and made for Mur Castell. When Blodeuedd heard they were coming, she took her maidens with her and made for the mountain; and having crossed the river Cynfael they made for a court that was on the mountain. And they were so afraid that they could only travel with their faces looking backwards. And they knew nothing until they fell into the lake and were drowned,* all except Blodeuedd.

Then Gwydion caught up with her and said to her, 'I will not kill you. I will do worse. Namely, I will release you in the form of a bird,' he said. 'And because of the shame you have brought upon Lleu Llaw Gyffes, you will never dare show your face in daylight for fear of all the birds. And all the birds will be hostile towards you. And it shall be in their nature to strike you and molest you wherever they find you. You shall not lose your name, however, but shall always be called Blodeuwedd.'* *Blodeuwedd* is 'owl' in today's language. And for that reason the birds hate the owl: and the owl is still called *Blodeuwedd*.

As for Gronw Pebr, he made for Penllyn, and from there he sent messengers: he asked Lleu Llaw Gyffes whether he would take land or territory or gold or silver for the insult.*

'No, by my confession to God,' he said. 'And this is the least I will accept from him; he must come to where I was when he threw the spear at me, while I stand where he was. And he must let me throw a spear at him. And that is the very least I will accept from him.' That was relayed to Gronw Pebr.

'Yes,' he said, 'I must do that. My loyal noblemen and my retinue and my foster-brothers, is there any one of you who will take the blow on my behalf?'

'Certainly not,' they said. And because they refused to stand and take one blow for their lord, they are known from that day to this as one of the Three Disloyal Retinues.*

'Then I will take it,' he said.

Then they both came to the bank of the river Cynfael. Gronw Pebr stood where Lleu Llaw Gyffes was when Gronw aimed at him, and Lleu stood where Gronw was. Then Gronw Pebr said to Lleu, 'Lord,' he said, 'since it was through the deceit of a woman that I did to you what I did, I beg of you, in God's name: a stone I see on the riverbank, let me put that between me and the blow.'

'God knows,' said Lleu, 'I will not refuse you that.'

'Yes,' he said, 'may God repay you.'

Gronw took the stone and put it between him and the blow. Then Lleu threw the spear at him, and it pierced through the stone and through him too, so that his back was broken and Gronw was killed. And the stone is still there on the bank of the river Cynfael in Ardudwy, with the hole through it. And because of that it is still called Llech Gronw.*

Then Lleu Llaw Gyffes took possession of his land for a second time, and ruled over it prosperously. And according to the tale, he was lord over Gwynedd after that. And so ends this branch of the Mabinogi.*

Peredur son of Efrog

EARL EFROG held an earldom in the North,* and he had seven sons. Efrog made his living not so much from his land but from tournaments and battles and wars. And as often happens to those who follow battle he was killed, himself and his six sons. And his seventh son was called Peredur.* He was the youngest of his seven sons. He was not old enough to go to war or battle—had he been, he would have been killed as his father and brothers were killed. His mother was a wise and clever woman. She thought hard about her son and his territory, and decided to flee with the boy to wasteland and wilderness, leaving behind the inhabited regions. She took no one with her save women and children, and meek, mild men who could not and would not fight or wage war. In the boy's hearing no one dared mention horses or weapons in case he set his heart on them. And every day the boy would go to the long forest to play and throw holly darts.

One day Peredur saw a herd of goats that belonged to his mother, and two hinds near the goats. The boy stood and marvelled to see those two without horns, while all the others had horns, and he assumed the two had been missing for a long time and because of that they had lost their horns. With strength and speed he drove the hinds along with the goats into a building for the goats at the far end of the forest. He returned home.

'Mother,' he said, 'I saw a strange thing over there: two of your goats gone wild and they have lost their horns because they have been running wild for so long under the trees. And no one had more trouble than I had, driving them inside.' Then everyone got up and went to look. And when they saw the hinds they were greatly amazed that anyone had the strength or speed to catch them.

One day they saw three knights coming along a bridle-path by the side of the forest. Who were they but Gwalchmai son of Gwyar and Gwair son of Gwystyl and Owain son of Urien, and Owain bringing up the rear, pursuing the knight who had shared out the apples in Arthur's court.*

'Mother,' he said, 'what are those over there?'

'Angels, my son,' she said.

'I will go and be an angel with them,' said Peredur. And he went to the path to meet the knights.

'Tell me, friend,' said Owain, 'did you see a knight passing here either today or yesterday?'

'I don't know what a knight is,' he replied.

'The same as myself,' said Owain.

'If you tell me what I ask you, then I'll tell you what you want to know.'

'I will, gladly,' said Owain.

'What is that?' he said, pointing to the saddle.

'A saddle,' said Owain. Peredur asked what everything was, and what it was intended for, and how it was used. Owain told him in detail what everything was and how it was used.

'Continue on your way,' said Peredur. 'I have seen what you are asking about. And I will follow you as a knight immediately.' Then Peredur returned to his mother and the household.

'Mother,' he said, 'those over there are not angels, but knights.' Then she fell into a dead faint. But Peredur went over to where the horses were that carried firewood for them and brought food and drink from inhabited regions to the wilderness. And he took a bony, dapple-grey nag, the strongest in his opinion. And he pressed a pannier on it as a saddle, and went back to his mother. With that the countess recovered from her faint.

'So,' she said, 'are you wanting to set off?'

'I am,' he said.

'Wait for words of advice from me before you set off.'

'Then speak quickly,' he said. 'I will wait.'

'Go to Arthur's court,' she said, 'where you will find the best men and most generous and most brave. Wherever you see a church, chant the Our Father to it. If you see food and drink, if you are in need of it and no one has the courtesy or goodness to offer it to you, help yourself. If you hear a scream, go towards it, and a woman's scream above any other scream in the world. If you see a fair jewel, take it and give it to someone else, and because of that you will be praised. If you see a beautiful lady, make love to her even though she does not want you—it will make you a better and braver man than before.'

Peredur imitated with twisted branches all the horse-trappings he had seen. He set off with a fistful of sharp-pointed darts in his hand. And for two nights and two days he travelled wasteland and wilderness, without food and without drink. Then he came to a great, desolate forest, and far into the forest he could see a clearing of open ground, and in the clearing he could see a pavilion, and under the impression that it was a church, he chanted the Our Father to the pavilion. And he approached the pavilion. The entrance to the pavilion was open and there was a golden chair near the door, and a beautiful, auburn-haired maiden sitting in the chair with a frontlet of gold on her forehead, and sparkling stones in the frontlet, and a thick gold ring on her hand. Peredur dismounted and went inside. The maiden made him welcome and greeted him. At the far end of the pavilion he could see a table and two flagons full of wine, and two loaves of white bread, and chops of the flesh of sucking-pigs.

'My mother', said Peredur, 'told me that wherever I saw food and drink, to take it.'

'Then go, lord, to the table,' she said, 'and God's welcome to you.' Peredur went to the table, and he took half the food and drink for himself, and left the other half for the maiden. And when he had finished eating, he got up and went to the maiden.

'My mother', he said, 'told me to take a fair jewel wherever I saw one.'

'Then take it, friend,' she said. 'I certainly won't begrudge it to you.' Peredur took the ring. And he went down on his knee and kissed the maiden. And he took his horse and set off.

After that, the knight who owned the pavilion arrived—he was the Proud One of the Clearing. And he saw the horse's tracks.

'Tell me,' he said to the maiden, 'who has been here since I left?'

'An odd-looking man, lord,' she said. And she described Peredur's appearance and manner.

'Tell me,' he said, 'has he been with you?'

'No he has not, by my faith,' she said.

'By my faith, I don't believe you. And until I find him to avenge my anger and shame, you shall not stay two nights in one and the same place.' And the knight got up to go and look for Peredur.

Meanwhile Peredur continued his journey to Arthur's court. And before he arrived at Arthur's court another knight came to the court and gave a thick gold ring to a man at the gate to hold his horse. And he himself proceeded into the hall where Arthur and his retinue were, and Gwenhwyfar and her maidens, and a chamberlain* serving Gwenhwyfar from a goblet. And the knight grabbed the goblet from Gwenhwyfar's hand and poured the drink that was in it over her face and breast, and gave Gwenhwyfar a great clout on the ear.*

'If there is anyone', he said, 'who wants to fight with me for this goblet, and avenge this insult to Gwenhwyfar, let him follow me to the meadow and I'll wait for him there.' And the knight took his horse and made for the meadow. Then everyone hung his head for fear of being asked to avenge the insult to Gwenhwyfar. And they assumed that no one would commit such a crime as that unless he possessed strength and power or magic and enchantment so that no one could wreak vengeance on him.

With that Peredur comes into the hall on a bony, dapple-grey nag with its untidy, slovenly trappings.* And Cai* is standing in the middle of the hall floor.

'Tell me, you tall man over there,' said Peredur, 'where is Arthur?'

'What do you want with Arthur?' said Cai.

'My mother told me to come to Arthur to be ordained a knight.'

'By my faith,' said Cai, 'your horse and weapons are too untidy.' Then the retinue notices him, and they begin to make fun of him and throw sticks at him, and they are glad that someone like him has arrived so that the other incident can be forgotten.

Then the dwarf comes in, who had come a year earlier to Arthur's court, he and his she-dwarf, to seek Arthur's hospitality, which they received. But apart from that they had not spoken a word to anyone for the whole year. When the dwarf sees Peredur, 'Ah,' he said, 'God's welcome to you, fair Peredur son of Efrog, chief of warriors and flower of knights.'*

'God knows, lad,' said Cai, 'that's bad behaviour, to stay dumb for a year in Arthur's court, with your choice of men with whom to talk and drink, and to call such a man as this, in the presence of the emperor and his retinue, chief of warriors and the flower of knights.' And he gives him a clout on the ear until he falls headlong to the floor in a dead faint.

Then the she-dwarf comes. 'Ah,' she said, 'God's welcome to you, fair Peredur son of Efrog, flower of warriors and candle of knights.'

'Well, girl,' said Cai, 'that's bad behaviour, to stay dumb for a year in Arthur's court, without saying a word to anyone, and today to call such a man as this, in the presence of Arthur and his warriors, flower of warriors and candle of knights.' And he kicks her until she is in a dead faint.

'Tall man,' said Peredur then, 'tell me, where is Arthur?'

'Be quiet,' said Cai. 'Go after the knight who left here for the meadow, and take the goblet from him, and overthrow him, and take his horse and weapons. And after that you will be ordained a knight.'

'Tall man,' he said, 'I will do just that.' And he turns his horse's head and goes out to the meadow. And when he arrives the knight is riding his horse in the meadow, great his pride in his power and prowess.

'Tell me,' said the knight, 'did you see anyone from the court coming after me?'

'The tall man who was there', he said, 'told me to overthrow you, and take the goblet and the horse and the weapons for myself.'

'Quiet,' said the knight. 'Go back to the court, and in my name ask Arthur to come to fight with me, either he or someone else. And unless he comes quickly I will not wait for him.'

'By my faith,' said Peredur, 'you choose. Whether it is with or without your consent, I will take the horse and the weapons and the goblet.'

And then the knight attacks him angrily, and strikes him a powerful and painful blow with the butt of his spear between shoulder and neck.

'Young man,' said Peredur, 'that is not how my mother's servants would play with me. I will play with you like this.' And he aims a sharp-pointed dart at him, and hits him in the eye so that the dart comes out through the nape of his neck, and he falls stone-dead to the ground.

'God knows,' said Owain son of Urien to Cai, 'you behaved badly towards that foolish man you sent after the knight. And one of two things has happened, either he has been overthrown or killed. If he has been overthrown, the knight will consider him a nobleman, and Arthur and his warriors will be eternally disgraced. If he has been killed, they will still be disgraced, but more than that, it will have been your fault. And I will lose all face unless I go and find out what has happened to him.'

Then Owain made his way to the meadow. And when he arrived Peredur was dragging the man behind him along the meadow.

'Lord,' said Owain, 'wait. I will remove the armour.'

'This iron tunic will never come off,' said Peredur. 'It is part of him.' Then Owain removed the armour and the clothing.

'Here you are, friend,' he said, 'now you have a horse and armour that are better than those you had. Take them gladly and come with me to Arthur, and you will be ordained a knight.'

'May I lose all face if I go,' said Peredur. 'But take the goblet from me to Gwenhwyfar, and tell Arthur that wherever I go I will be his man. And if I can be of use to him, and serve him, I will do so. And tell him that I will never set foot in his court until I confront the tall man who is there, and avenge the insult to the dwarf and she-dwarf.'

Then Owain made his way to the court and told the story to Arthur and Gwenhwyfar and each one of the retinue, and of the threat to Cai.

Peredur went on his way. And as he was travelling, he met a knight.

'Where do you come from?' said the knight.

'I come from Arthur's court,' he said.

'Are you Arthur's man?'

'I am, by my faith,' he said.

'A fine place to acknowledge Arthur.'

'Why?' said Peredur.

'I will tell you why,' he said. 'I have always pillaged and plundered from Arthur, and I have killed every one of his men whom I have met.'

Without further delay they attacked each other. It was not long before Peredur struck him so that he was over his horse's crupper to the ground. The knight asked for mercy.

'You shall have mercy,' said Peredur, 'if you swear that you will go to Arthur's court and tell Arthur that it was I who overthrew you, in service and honour to him. And tell him that I will never set foot in his court until I confront the tall man who is there, and avenge the insult to the dwarf and she-dwarf.' The knight, having promised that, set off for Arthur's court. He told his story in full, and of the threat to Cai.

Peredur went on his way. And that same week he met sixteen knights, and he overthrew each one, and they made their way to

Arthur's court with the same tale as the first knight he overthrew, and the same threat to Cai. And Cai was reprimanded by Arthur and the retinue. And he was worried on account of that.

Peredur set off. And finally he came to a great, desolate forest, and at the edge of the forest was a lake, and on the other side of the lake was a large court and a fine fortress around it. And on the shore of the lake there was a grey-haired man sitting on a cushion of bro-caded silk and wearing a garment of brocaded silk, and young lads fishing in a small boat on the lake.* As the grey-haired man saw Peredur approaching, he got up and made for the court, and the man was lame. Peredur, too, made for the court, and the gate was open and he came into the hall. And when he entered, the grey-haired man was sitting on a cushion of brocaded silk, and there was a big, blazing fire starting to burn. And a number of the retinue got up to meet Peredur, and helped him to dismount and took off his armour. And the man patted the end of the cushion with his hand and asked the squire* to come and sit on the cushion. And they sat together and talked. And when it was time, they set up tables and went to eat. And he was put to sit and eat next to the man. When they had finished eating, the man asked Peredur if he knew how to strike well with a sword.

'I suppose', said Peredur, 'that if I were taught, then I would know.'

'If you know how to play with a stick and a shield,' he replied, 'you would know how to strike with a sword.'

The grey-haired man had two sons, a yellow-haired lad and an auburn-haired lad.

'Get up, lads,' he said, 'to play with the sticks and the shields.' The lads went to play.

'Tell me, friend,' said the man, 'which of the lads plays better?'

'I suspect', said Peredur, 'that the yellow-haired lad could have drawn blood long ago from the auburn-haired lad if he had wanted to.'

'Friend, take the stick and shield from the auburn-haired lad and draw blood from the yellow-haired lad if you can.'

Peredur got up and took the stick and the shield, and struck the yellow-haired lad until his eyebrow was down over his eye and the blood was streaming.

'Well, friend,' said the man, 'come and sit down now—you will be the best swordsman in this Island. And I am your uncle, your mother's brother. And you will stay with me for a while, learning manners and etiquette. Forget now your mother's words—I will be your teacher and make you a knight. From now on this is what you must do: if you see something that you think is strange, do not ask about it unless someone is courteous enough to explain it to you. It will not be your fault, but mine, since I am your teacher.' And they received every kind of honour and service, and when it was time they went to sleep.

As soon as it was daybreak Peredur got up and took his horse, and with his uncle's permission he departed. He came to a great forest, and at the far end of the forest he came to a level meadow, and beyond the meadow he could see a great fortress and a beautiful court. Peredur made for the court; and he found the door open and made for the hall. And when he entered, there was a handsome grey-haired man sitting to one side of the hall with many young men around him. And everyone got up to meet the squire, and the courtesy and service he received were excellent. He was placed to sit next to the nobleman who owned the court, and they talked. And when it was time to go and eat, he was placed to sit and eat next to the nobleman. When they had finished eating and drinking, for as long as it pleased them, the nobleman asked him if he knew how to strike with a sword.

'If I were taught,' said Peredur, 'then I'm sure I would know.'

There was a huge iron column in the hall floor, a warrior's embrace in circumference.

'Take that sword,' said the man to Peredur, 'and strike that iron column.' Peredur got up and struck the column so that it was in two pieces and the sword in two pieces.

'Put the pieces together and join them.' Peredur put the pieces together, and they became one, as before. And he struck the second time so that the column broke into two pieces and the sword into two pieces. And as before, they became one. And he struck the third time so that the column broke into two pieces and the sword into two pieces.

'Put them together again, and join them.' Peredur placed them together the third time, but neither the column nor the sword could be joined.

'Well, lad,' he said, 'go and sit down, and God's blessing on you. You are the best swordsman in the kingdom. You have gained two-thirds of your strength, and the third is still to come. And when you have gained it all, you will surrender to no one. And I am your uncle, your mother's brother, brother of the man whose court you were in last night.' Peredur sat down next to his uncle, and they talked.

Suddenly he could see two lads entering the hall, and from the hall they proceeded to a chamber, carrying a spear of huge proportions, with three streams of blood running from its socket to the floor. When everyone saw the lads coming in this way, they all began weeping and wailing so that it was not easy for anyone to endure it. Yet the man did not interrupt his conversation with Peredur. The man did not explain to Peredur what that was, nor did Peredur ask him about it. After a short silence, suddenly two maidens entered with a large salver between them, and a man's head on the salver, and much blood around the head.* And then they all shrieked and wailed so that it was not easy for anyone to stay in the same building. At last they stopped, and remained sitting as long as it pleased them, and drank. After that a chamber was prepared for Peredur, and they went to sleep.

Early the next day Peredur got up, and with his uncle's permission he set off. From there he came to a forest, and deep inside the forest he could hear crying. He went to where the crying was coming from. When he arrived he saw a beautiful auburn-haired woman and a saddled horse standing beside her, a man's corpse between the woman's hands. And as she tried to place the corpse in the saddle, the corpse would fall to the ground, and then she would give a cry.

'Tell me, sister,' he said, 'why are you crying?'

'Alas, accursed Peredur,' she said, 'little relief have you ever brought me from my misery.'

'Why should I be accursed?' he said.

'Because you are the cause of your mother's death, for when you set off against her will, a shooting pain leapt up within her, and she died from it. And you are accursed because you are the cause of her death. And the dwarf and she-dwarf you saw in Arthur's court, that was the dwarf of your father and mother. And I am a foster-sister of yours, and this is my husband, killed by the knight who is in the forest. And do not go near him in case you are killed too.'

'You are wrong, sister,' he said, 'to blame me. And because I have stayed with you as long as I have, I will scarcely defeat the knight;

and were I to stay longer I would never overcome him. And as for
you, stop your crying now, for help is closer than before. And I will
bury the man, and go with you to where the knight is, and if I can get
revenge I will do so.'

After burying the man, they came to where the knight was riding
his horse in the clearing. At once the knight asked Peredur where he
came from.

'I come from Arthur's court.'

'Are you Arthur's man?'

'I am, by my faith.'

'A fine place for you to acknowledge Arthur.' Without further
delay they attacked each other, and there and then Peredur overthrew
the knight. The knight asked for mercy.

'You shall have mercy on condition that you take this woman as
a wife, and treat her as well as you have treated other women, since
you killed her husband for no reason; and proceed to Arthur's
court and tell him that it was I who overthrew you in service and
honour to Arthur. And tell him that I will not set foot in his court
until I confront the tall man who is there, to avenge the insult to
the dwarf and the maiden.' And Peredur accepted his assurance on
that. The knight sat the woman properly on a horse beside him,
and came to Arthur's court and told Arthur of his adventure and of
the threat to Cai. And Cai was reprimanded by Arthur and the
household for having driven away from Arthur's court a lad as
good as Peredur.

'That squire will never come to the court,' said Owain. 'Nor will
Cai venture out.'

'By my faith,' said Arthur, 'I will search the waste lands of the
Island of Britain until I find him, and then let them do their worst to
each other.'

Meanwhile Peredur went on his way and came to a great, desolate
forest. He could see neither the tracks of men nor herds in the forest,
only thickets and vegetation. And when he comes to the far end of
the forest, he can see a great, ivy-covered fortress with many strong
towers. And near the gate the vegetation is taller than elsewhere.

Suddenly, a lean lad with reddish-yellow hair appears on the
battlement above him.

'Take your choice, lord,' he said; 'either I shall open the gate for
you, or I shall tell the man in charge that you are in the gateway.'

'Say that I am here, and if he wants me to enter I will.' The lad returned quickly and opened the gate for Peredur, and he proceeded into the hall. And when he came into the hall he could see eighteen lean, red-headed lads, of the same height and the same appearance and the same age and the same dress as the lad who had opened the gate for him. And their manners and their service were excellent. They helped him to dismount, and took off his armour. And they sat and talked.

Suddenly, five maidens came into the hall from a chamber. As for the principal maiden amongst them, he was sure that he had never seen such a beautiful sight. She wore an old dress of tattered brocaded silk that had once been good; where her flesh could be seen through it, it was whiter than the flowers of the whitest crystal; her hair and her eyebrows were blacker than jet; two tiny red spots in her cheeks, redder than the reddest thing. The maiden greeted Peredur and embraced him, and sat down next to him. Not long after that he saw two nuns entering, one carrying a flagon full of wine and the other six loaves of white bread.

'Lady,' they said, 'God knows, tonight the convent over there has only this amount again of food and drink.' Then they went to eat. Peredur saw that the maiden wanted to give him more of the food and drink than anyone else.

'Sister,' he said, '*I* will share out the food and drink.'

'No, friend,' she said.

'Shame on my beard', he said, 'if I don't.' Peredur took the bread and shared it equally among everyone, and likewise with the drink, to the cupful. When the meal was finished, 'I would be glad,' said Peredur, 'if I could have a comfortable place to sleep.' A room was prepared for him and Peredur went to sleep.

'Sister,' said the lads to the maiden, 'this is what we advise.'

'What is that?' she said.

'Go to the squire in the chamber nearby, and offer yourself to him however he wants, either as his wife or as his mistress.'

'That,' she said, 'is something which is not proper—I, who have never been with a man, offering myself to him before he courts me. I cannot do that on any account.'

'By our confession to God,' they said, 'unless you do that, we will leave you here to your enemies.'

With that the maiden got up in tears, and went straight to the chamber. And with the noise of the door opening, Peredur woke up. And the maiden had tears running down her cheeks.

'Tell me, sister,' said Peredur, 'why are you crying?'

'I will tell you, lord,' she said. 'My father owned this court, along with the best earldom in the world. Now the son of another earl was asking my father for me. I would not go to him of my own free will; my father would not give me against my will to him or to anyone else. And my father had no other children but me. And after my father died the realm fell into my hands. I was then even less eager to have the man than before. So what he did was to wage war against me and overcome my realm apart from this one house. And because the men you saw are so brave—they are my foster-brothers—and the house is so strong, we could never be overpowered as long as food and drink lasted. And now they have run out, were it not for the nuns you saw feeding us, as they are free to travel through the land and the realm. But now they too have neither food nor drink. And no later than tomorrow the earl and all his might will descend on this place. If he takes me, my fate will be no better than if I were given to his stable lads. So I come to offer myself to you, lord, in whatever way you please, in exchange for helping us to escape or else defending us here.'

'Go to sleep, sister,' he said. 'And I will not leave you without doing one or the other.' The maiden left and went to sleep.

Early the next day the maiden got up and went to Peredur, and greeted him.

'God be good to you, friend,' he said. 'Do you have any news?'

'None but good news, lord, as long as you're well—but that the earl and all his might have descended on the house. No one has ever seen a place with more pavilions or knights calling on each other to fight.'

'Very well,' said Peredur, 'prepare my horse, and I will get up.' They prepared his horse for him, and he got up and made for the meadow. And when he arrived a knight was riding his horse, having raised the signal for combat. Peredur threw him over his horse's crupper to the ground. And he threw many that day.

And in the afternoon, towards the end of the day, an exceptional knight came to fight him, and Peredur overthrew him too. He asked for mercy.

'Who are you then?' said Peredur.

'In truth,' he said, 'the head of the earl's retinue.'*

'How much of the countess's realm do you own?'

'In truth,' he said, 'a third.'

'Very well,' he said, 'tonight in her court return a third of her realm to her in full, together with all the profit you have made from it, and food and drink for a hundred men, and horses and weapons for them; and you will be her prisoner, but you shall not lose your life.'

That was done immediately. The maiden was joyously happy that night, a third of her realm hers, and plenty of horses and weapons and food and drink in her court. They rested for as long as it pleased them, and then went to sleep.

Early the next day Peredur made for the meadow, and overthrew large numbers that day. And at the end of the day an exceptional, arrogant knight came along, and Peredur overthrew him too. And he asked for mercy.

'Who are you then?' said Peredur.

'The court steward,'* he said.

'How much of the maiden's realm do you own?'

'A third,' he said.

'Then give a third of her realm back to the maiden, and all the profit you have made from it, and food and drink for two hundred men, and horses and weapons for them, and you will be her prisoner.' That was done immediately.

And the third day Peredur came to the meadow, and he overthrew more that day than on any other day. And finally the earl came to fight him, and Peredur threw him to the ground. And the earl asked for mercy.

'Who are you then?' said Peredur.

'I will not conceal myself,' he said. 'I am the earl.'

'Very well,' he said, 'then give the whole of her earldom back to the maiden and also your earldom, too, and food and drink and horses and weapons for three hundred men, and you yourself will be under her authority.'

And so for three weeks Peredur arranged tribute and submission to the maiden. And when he had settled and secured her in her realm, 'With your permission,' said Peredur, 'I shall be on my way.'

'Brother, is that what you want?'

'Yes, by my faith. And if I did not love you, I would have left long ago.'

'Friend,' she said, 'who are you then?'

'Peredur son of Efrog from the North. And if you are ever in distress or danger, let me know, and I will defend you if I can.'

Then Peredur set off, and far from there he was met by a lady rider on a lean, sweaty horse. She greeted the knight.

'Where do you come from, sister?' said Peredur. She explained her situation and the reason for the journey. She was the wife of the Proud One of the Clearing.

'Well,' said Peredur, 'I am the knight on whose account you have suffered this distress, and whoever brought this upon you will be sorry.' And with that a knight approaches, asking Peredur if he had seen such a knight as he was after.

'Be silent,' said Peredur. 'I am the one you are after, and by my faith, the maiden is innocent on my account.' But they fought each other, and Peredur overthrew the knight. He asked for mercy.

'You shall have mercy, by going back the way you came to let it be known that the girl has been found innocent, and that as recompense for the insult I overthrew you.' The knight promised to do that.

And Peredur went on his way. On a mountain not far from him he could see a castle. And he made for the castle and hammered on the door with his spear. Then behold, a handsome auburn-haired lad opening the door, in stature and strength a warrior, but in age a boy. When Peredur came into the hall there was a large, handsome woman sitting in a chair and numerous handmaidens about her. And the good lady made him welcome. And when it was time to go to eat, they went. And after eating, 'You would do well, lord,' said the lady, 'to go elsewhere to sleep.'

'Can't I sleep here?'

'There are nine witches here, friend,' she said, 'together with their father and mother. They are the witches of Caerloyw.* And by day-break we shall be no nearer to making our escape than to being killed. And they have taken over and laid waste the land, except for this one house.'

'Well,' said Peredur, 'here is where I want to be tonight, and if there is trouble and I can be of use, I will. I shall certainly do no harm.' They went to sleep.

And at dawn Peredur heard a scream. He got up quickly in his shirt and trousers, with his sword about his neck, and out he went. And when he arrived a witch was grabbing hold of the watchman, and he was screaming. Peredur attacked the witch and struck her on the head with a sword until her helmet and mail cap spread out like a dish on her head.

'Your mercy, fair Peredur son of Efrog, and the mercy of God.'

'How did you know, witch, that I am Peredur?'

'It was fated and foretold that I would suffer grief at your hands, and that you would receive a horse and weapons from me. And you will stay with me for a while as I teach you how to ride your horse and handle your weapons.'

'This is how I shall show you mercy,' he replied. 'Give your word that you will never do harm again to this countess's land.' Peredur took assurance to that effect, and with the countess's permission he set off with the witch to the witches' court. And there he stayed for three successive weeks. Then Peredur chose his horse and his weapons, and went on his way. At the close of day he came to a valley, and at the far end of the valley he came to a hermit's cell. And the hermit welcomed him and he stayed there that night.

Early the next morning he got up, and when he came outside a fall of snow had come down the night before. And a wild hawk had killed a duck near the cell. And what with the noise of the horse, the hawk rose and a raven descended on the bird's flesh. Peredur stood and compared the blackness of the raven and the whiteness of the snow and the redness of the blood to the hair of the woman he loved best, which was as black as jet, and her skin to the whiteness of the snow, and the redness of the blood in the white snow to the two red spots in the cheeks of the woman he loved best.*

Meanwhile, Arthur and his retinue were searching for Peredur. 'Do you know,' said Arthur, 'who is the knight with the long spear, standing in the valley above?'

'Lord,' said one, 'I shall go and find out who he is.' Then the squire approached Peredur, and asked him what he was doing there and who he was. But Peredur was thinking so hard about the woman he loved best that he gave no answer. The squire attacked Peredur with a spear, but Peredur turned on him and threw him over his horse's crupper to the ground. Twenty-four knights came in succession, and he would not answer one more than another, but treated each one the same—he threw each one with a single thrust over his horse's crupper to the ground. Then Cai came up to him, and spoke harshly and rudely to Peredur. And Peredur struck him with a spear under his jaw and threw him a long distance away, so that his arm and collar-bone were broken. And while he was in a dead faint—such was the pain he had received—his horse returned, galloping wildly. And when all the retinue saw the horse coming without its rider, they rushed to where the encounter had taken place. And when they got there, they thought Cai had been killed. They realized, however, that if he had a physician who could set his bone and bandage his joints well, he would be none the worse. Peredur was not distracted from his thoughts any more than before, despite seeing the crowd around Cai. And Cai was brought to Arthur's pavilion, and Arthur had skilful physicians brought to him. Arthur was sorry for the pain that Cai had received, for he loved him greatly. And then Gwalchmai said, 'No one should distract an ordained knight from his thoughts in a discourteous way, for perhaps he has either suffered a loss or he is thinking about the woman he loves best. Such discourtesy, perhaps, was shown by the man who saw him last. If you wish, lord, I shall go and see whether the knight has stirred from those thoughts, and if he has, I shall ask him kindly to come and see you.'

And then Cai sulked, and spoke angry, jealous words. 'Gwalchmai,' he said, 'I am certain you will lead him back by his reins. However, little praise and honour will you get from overcoming the tired knight, exhausted from fighting. Yet that is how you have overcome many of them, and while you have your tongue and fine words, a mantle of thin, fine linen will be armour enough for you. And you will not need to break a spear or a sword fighting the knight you find in that state.'

And then Gwalchmai said to Cai, 'You could have said something more pleasant had you wished. And it is not proper for you to vent your rage and anger on me. I expect, however, that I shall bring the knight back with me, without breaking either my arm or my shoulder.'

Then Arthur said to Gwalchmai, 'You speak like a wise and reasonable man. Go hence and put on plenty of armour, and choose your horse.'

Gwalchmai armed himself, and went forward leisurely at his horse's pace to where Peredur was. And he was resting on his spear-shaft, thinking the same thoughts. Gwalchmai approached him with no sign of hostility about him, and said to him, 'If I knew it would please you, as it pleases me, I would talk to you. Still, I am a messenger from Arthur, begging you to come and see him. And two men have come before me on that same errand.'

'That is true,' said Peredur, 'and they were discourteous. They fought with me, and that did not please me because I disliked being distracted from my thoughts. I was thinking about the woman I loved best. This is why I was reminded of her: I was looking at the snow and at the raven, and at the drops of blood from the duck which the hawk had killed in the snow. And I was thinking that the whiteness of her skin was like the snow, and the blackness of her hair and eyebrows was like the raven, and that the two red spots in her cheeks were like the two drops of blood.'

Gwalchmai said, 'Those thoughts were not dishonourable, and it is not surprising that you disliked being distracted from them.'

Peredur said, 'Tell me, is Cai in Arthur's court?'

'He is,' he replied. 'He was the last knight to fight you. And no good came to him from the confrontation: he broke his right arm and his collar-bone in the fall he took from the thrust of your spear.'

'Good,' said Peredur, 'I am happy that I have begun to avenge the insult to the dwarf and she-dwarf in that way.' Gwalchmai was surprised to hear him mention the dwarf and the she-dwarf. And he approached him and embraced him, and asked what was his name.

'I am called Peredur son of Efrog,' he said. 'And who are you?'

'I am called Gwalchmai,' he replied.

'I am pleased to see you,' said Peredur. 'I have heard of your reputation for military prowess and integrity in every land I have been, and I beg for your friendship.'

'You shall have it, by my faith, and give me yours.'

'You shall have it gladly,' said Peredur.

They set off together, in joyful agreement, to where Arthur was. And when Cai heard they were coming, he said, 'I knew that Gwalchmai would not need to fight the knight. Nor is it surprising that he has received praise. He does more with his fair words than we by force of arms.'

And Peredur and Gwalchmai went to Gwalchmai's pavilion to take off their armour. And Peredur put on the same kind of garment that Gwalchmai wore. And they went hand in hand to where Arthur was, and greeted him.

'Lord,' said Gwalchmai, 'here is the man you have been seeking for a long time.'

'Welcome to you, chieftain,' said Arthur; 'you shall stay with me. And had I known that your progress would be as it has been, you would not have left me when you did. Yet that was foretold by the dwarf and the she-dwarf, whom Cai harmed, and whom you have now avenged.'

Then the queen and her handmaidens approached, and Peredur greeted them. And they were happy to see him and made him welcome. Arthur showed Peredur great respect and honour. And they returned to Caerllion.

The first night Peredur came to Caerllion to Arthur's court, he happened to be strolling in the castle after dinner. Behold, Angharad Law Eurog met him.*

'By my faith, sister,' said Peredur, 'you are a dear, lovely girl. And I could love you best of all women if you wished.'

'I give my word,' she said, 'I do not love you and I will never want you, ever.'

'And I give my word', said Peredur, 'that I will never utter a word to any Christian until you confess that you love me best of men.'

The next day Peredur set off, and he followed the highroad along the ridge of a great mountain. At the far end of the mountain he could see a round valley, and the edges of the valley were wooded and stony, and on the floor of the valley were meadows, and ploughed land between the meadows and the forest. In the heart of the forest he could see large, black houses, roughly built. He dismounted and led his horse towards the forest. And at some distance in the forest he could see a steep rock, and the road leading to the side of the rock, and a lion tied to a chain, sleeping by the rock. He could see a deep pit, of huge proportions, below the lion, filled with the bones of men and animals. Peredur drew his sword and struck the lion, so that it fell, hanging by its chain above the pit. And with the second blow he struck the chain so that it broke and the lion fell into the pit.

Peredur led his horse along the side of the rock until he got to the valley. He could see in the middle of the valley a fair castle, and he went towards the castle. In a meadow near the castle was seated a large, grey-haired man—he was larger than any man he had ever seen—and two young lads were shooting at the whalebone handles of their knives, one an auburn-haired lad and the other a yellow-haired lad. Peredur went up to the grey-haired man and greeted him. The grey-haired man said, 'Shame on my gatekeeper's beard.'* Then Peredur realized that the lion was the gatekeeper. And then the grey-haired man, together with the lads, went into the castle, and Peredur went with them. A fair, noble place could he see there. They made for the hall, and the tables had been set out, with plenty of food and drink on them. Then he saw coming from the chamber an old woman and a young woman, and they were the largest women he had ever seen. They washed and went to eat. The grey-haired man went to the most important place at the top of the table, and the old woman next to him; Peredur and the maiden were placed next to each other; and the two young lads waited on them. The maiden looked at Peredur and became sad. Peredur asked the maiden why she was sad.

'Friend, since I first saw you, it is you I have loved best of men. And I am heartbroken to see the fate that will befall such a noble young man as you tomorrow. Did you see the many black houses in the heart of the forest? All those are vassals of my father, the grey-haired man over there, and they are all giants. And tomorrow they will set upon you and kill you. And this valley is called the Round Valley.'

'Fair maiden, will you arrange that my horse and armour are in the same lodging as me tonight?'

'I will, between me and God, if I can, gladly.'

When the time came to sleep rather than carouse, they went to sleep. And the maiden arranged that Peredur's horse and armour were in the same lodging as him.

The next day Peredur could hear the clamour of men and horses around the castle. Peredur got up and armed himself and his horse, and came to the meadow. The old woman and the maiden went to the grey-haired man.

'Lord,' they said, 'accept the squire's word that he will not say anything about what he has seen here, and we will ensure that he keeps it.'

'I will not, by my faith,' said the grey-haired man. Peredur fought against the host, and by midday he had killed a third of them without anyone harming him. Then the old woman said, 'The squire has killed many of your men. Show him mercy.'

'I will not, by my faith,' he replied. The old woman and the beautiful maiden were watching from the battlement of the castle.

Then Peredur attacked the yellow-haired lad and killed him.

'Lord,' said the maiden, 'show mercy to the squire.'

'I will not, between me and God.' Then Peredur attacked the auburn-haired lad and killed him.

'It would have been better for you had you shown mercy to the squire before your two sons were killed. And it will not be easy for you to escape, if indeed you do.'

'Go, maiden, and beg the squire to show us mercy, though we have not shown it to him.' The maiden went to Peredur and asked for mercy for her father and all his men who had escaped alive.

'Yes, on condition that your father and all those under him go to pay homage to the emperor Arthur, and tell him that it was Peredur, a vassal of his, who did this service.'

'We will gladly, between me and God.'

'And you will be baptized. I shall send word to Arthur and ask him to give this valley to you and your heirs after you forever.'

Then they came inside, and the grey-haired man and the large woman greeted Peredur. Then the grey-haired man said, 'Since I have owned this valley, I have never seen a Christian leave here alive, apart from you. And we shall go and pay homage to Arthur, and receive faith and baptism.'

And then Peredur said, 'Thanks be to God that I did not break my promise to the woman I love best, namely that I would not utter a word to a Christian.' They stayed there that night.

Early the next morning the grey-haired man went with his followers to Arthur's court, and they paid homage to Arthur, and Arthur had them baptized. The grey-haired man told Arthur that it was Peredur who had overcome him, and Arthur gave the valley to the grey-haired man and his followers to rule on his behalf, as Peredur had requested. And with Arthur's permission, the grey-haired man set off for the Round Valley.

Peredur, on the other hand, travelled the next morning through a long stretch of wilderness without coming across any dwelling. At last he came to a very poor, small house. And there he heard of a serpent that lay on a golden ring, leaving no dwelling standing for seven miles around. Peredur went to where he heard the serpent was, and he fought the serpent, furious and valiant, bold and proud, and eventually he killed it and took the ring for himself. For a long time he wandered in this way, without uttering a word to any Christian, until he began to lose his colour and appearance because of a deep longing for Arthur's court and the woman he loved best, and his companions.

From there he travelled to Arthur's court. On the way Arthur's retinue met him, with Cai riding ahead going on an errand for them. Peredur recognized them all, but no one in the retinue recognized him.

'Where do you come from, lord?' said Cai, and a second time, and a third. But Peredur would not answer. Cai struck him with a spear through his thigh, and lest he be forced to speak and break his word, Peredur rode past without taking vengeance on him. And then Gwalchmai said, 'Between me and God, Cai, that was bad behaviour, to set upon a squire like that just because he could not speak.' And Gwalchmai returned to Arthur's court.

'Lady,' he said to Gwenhwyfar, 'can you see how badly Cai has wounded this squire just because he could not speak? Let him have medical treatment by the time I return, and I shall repay you.'

Before the men returned from their errand, a knight came to the meadow near Arthur's court, demanding an opponent to do battle with. And an opponent was found. And the knight overthrew him, and for a week he overthrew a knight every day.

One day Arthur and his retinue were going to the church; they saw the knight with the signal raised for battle.

'Men,' said Arthur, 'by the bravery of men, I shall not leave here until I get my horse and weapons to overthrow that knave over there.'

Then the servants went to fetch Arthur his horse and weapons. Peredur met the servants as they were passing, and he took the horse and weapons, and made for the meadow. When everyone saw him get up and go and fight the knight, they went to the rooftops and hills and high places to watch the fighting. Peredur signalled to the knight with his hand, urging him to begin. And the knight charged at him; however, Peredur remained rooted to the spot. But then he spurred on his horse and set upon the knight, furious and valiant, violent and angry, eager and proud, and struck him a blow that was brutal and bitter, painful and bold in a warrior-like way under the chin, lifting him out of his saddle and throwing him a great distance away.* And

Peredur returned, leaving the horse and armour with the servants as before. And he made for the court on foot. And after that Peredur was called the Mute Knight. With that Angharad Law Eurog met him.

'Between me and God, lord, it is a shame that you cannot speak. And if you could, I would love you best of men. And by my faith, even though you cannot speak, I will still love you best.'

'May God repay you, sister. By my faith, I love you too.' And then they realized that he was Peredur. He renewed his friendship then with Gwalchmai and with Owain son of Urien and all the retinue. And he remained at Arthur's court.

Arthur was in Caerllion ar Wysg, and he went to hunt, and Peredur with him. And Peredur let his dog loose on a stag, and the dog killed the stag in a deserted place. Some distance away he could see signs of a dwelling, and he approached the dwelling. He could see a hall, and at the door of the hall he could see three swarthy, bald young men playing *gwyddbwyll*.* And when he entered he could see three maidens sitting on a couch, dressed in garments of gold as befits noblewomen. And he went to sit with them on the couch. One of the maidens looked at Peredur intently, and wept. Peredur asked her why she was weeping.

'Because it pains me so much to see such a handsome young man as you killed.'

'Who would kill me?'

'If it were not dangerous for you to stay here, I would tell you.'

'However great the danger if I stay, I will hear you out.'

'The man who owns this court is our father. And he kills everyone who comes to this court without permission.'

'What sort of man is your father, that he can kill everyone like that?'

'A man who is violent and malicious towards his neighbours, and he does not give recompense to anyone for it.'

Then Peredur saw the young men getting up and clearing the pieces from the board. And he heard a great noise, and after the noise he saw a huge, black-haired, one-eyed man coming in.* The maidens got up to meet him, and removed his armour, and he went to sit down. When he had collected his thoughts and rested, he looked at Peredur and asked who the knight was.

'Lord,' said the maiden, 'the fairest and noblest young man you have ever seen. And for God's sake, and your own pride, be patient with him.'

'For your sake I will be patient, and I will spare his life tonight.'

Then Peredur joined them by the fire. He took food and drink, and talked with the maidens. Then, when he had become drunk, Peredur said, 'I am surprised that you claim to be as strong as you do. Who pulled out your eye?'

'One of my rules is that whoever asks me that question will not escape with his life, neither as a gift nor for a price.'

'Lord,' said the maiden, 'although he is talking to you foolishly, because of being drunk and intoxicated, keep to your word and the promise you gave me just now.'

'I will do so gladly, for your sake. I will gladly spare his life for tonight.' And they left it at that for the night.

The next day the black-haired man got up and put on his armour, and told Peredur, 'Get up, man, to meet your death,' said the black-haired man.

Peredur said to the black-haired man, 'Black-haired man, do one of two things if you wish to fight me: either remove your own armour or else give me additional armour to fight you.'

'Man!' he said. 'Could you fight if you had weapons? Take whatever weapons you want.' Then the maiden brought Peredur the weapons he wanted. And he and the black-haired man fought until the black-haired man had to ask Peredur for mercy.

'Black-haired man, you shall have mercy on condition that you tell me who you are, and who pulled out your eye.'

'Lord, I shall tell you—fighting the Black Serpent of the Cairn. There is a mound called the Mound of Mourning, and in the mound there is a cairn, and in the cairn there is a serpent, and in the serpent's tail there is a stone. And these are the attributes of the stone: whoever holds it in one hand will have as much gold as he wishes in the other hand. And I lost my eye fighting that serpent. And my name is the Black Oppressor. The reason I was called the Black Oppressor is because I would not leave a man around me whom I did not terrorize, and I would never give recompense to anyone.'

'Well,' said Peredur, 'how far from here is the mound you mentioned?'

'I shall list the stages of your journey there, and tell you how far it is. The day you set off from here, you will come to the court of the Sons of the King of Suffering.'

'Why are they called that?'

'A lake monster kills them once each day. When you leave there, you will come to the court of the Countess of the Feats.'

'What feats does she perform?'

'She has a retinue of three hundred men. Every stranger who arrives at court is told of the feats of her retinue. That is why the retinue of three hundred men sit next to the lady, not out of disrespect to the guests, but in order to narrate the feats of her retinue. The night you set off from there you will get as far as the Mound of Mourning, and there, surrounding the mound you will find the owners of three hundred pavilions, guarding the serpent.'

'Since you have been an oppressor for so long, I shall make sure that you will never be so again.' And Peredur killed him. Then the maiden who had started to talk to him said, 'If you were poor arriving here, you shall now be rich with the treasure of the black-haired man you have killed. And can you see the many lovely maidens in this court—you may take whichever one you wish.'

'I did not come from my country, lady, to take a wife. But I see fine young men there—let each one of you pair up with another, as you wish. And I do not want any of your wealth—I do not need it.'

From there Peredur set off, and came to the court of the Sons of the King of Suffering. When he came to the court, he could see only women. The women got up and welcomed him. As they started to talk he could see a horse approaching with a saddle on it, and a corpse in the saddle. One of the women got up and took the corpse from the saddle, and bathed it in a tub of warm water* that was by the door, and applied precious ointment to it. The man got up, alive, and went up to Peredur, and greeted him, and made him welcome. Two other corpses entered on their saddles, and the maiden gave those two the same treatment as the previous one. Then Peredur asked the lord why they were like that. They replied that there was a monster in a cave who killed them every day. And that night they left it at that.

The next day the young men got up. Peredur asked to be allowed to go with them, for the sake of their lovers. They refused him. 'If you were killed there, no one could bring you back to life again.' Then they set off. Peredur followed them; but when they had disappeared so that he could not see them, behold, he came across the fairest woman he had ever seen, sitting on a mound.

'I know where you are going. You are going to fight the monster, but it will kill you. And not because it is brave but because it is cunning. It lives in a cave, and there is a stone pillar at the mouth of the cave, and it can see everyone who enters but no one can see it. And with a poisonous stone spear from the shadow of the pillar it kills everyone. And if you promise to love me more than all women, I will give you a stone so that you will see the monster when you enter, but it will not see you.'

'I promise, by my faith,' said Peredur. 'Since I first saw you, I loved you. And where would I search for you?'

'When you search for me, look towards India.'* Then the maiden disappeared, after placing the stone in Peredur's hand.

He continued to a river valley, and the edges of the valley were wooded and on each side of the river were flat meadows. On one side of the river he could see a flock of white sheep, and on the other side he could see a flock of black sheep: when one of the white sheep bleated, one of the black sheep would come across and turn white, and when one of the black sheep bleated, one of the white sheep would come across and turn black. He could see a tall tree on the riverbank, and one half of it was burning from its roots to its tip, but the other half had fresh leaves on it. Beyond that he could see a squire sitting on top of a mound with two spotted, white-breasted greyhounds on a leash, lying beside him; and he was certain that he had never seen such a royal-looking squire. In the forest facing him he could hear hunting-dogs raising deer. He greeted the squire, and the squire greeted Peredur. And Peredur could see three paths leading away from the mound, two were wide and the third was narrower. And Peredur asked where the three paths went.

'One of these paths goes to my court. And I advise you to do one of two things: either proceed to the court to my wife who is there, or stay here where you will see the hunting-dogs driving the tired deer from the forest to the open ground; and you will see the best grey-hounds you have ever seen, and the bravest to face deer, killing them by the water near us. And when it is time for us to go and eat, my servant will bring my horse to meet me, and you will be welcome there tonight.'

'May God repay you. I will not stay but I will be on my way.'

'The second path leads to the town that is close by. You can buy food and drink there. And the path that is narrower than the others goes to the monster's cave.'

'With your permission, squire, I shall go there.'

Peredur came to the cave, and took the stone in his left hand and the spear in his right hand. And as he entered he saw the monster and thrust a spear through him and cut off his head. And when he came out of the cave he saw, in the mouth of the cave, the three companions. And they greeted Peredur and said that it had been foretold he would kill that oppressor. Peredur gave the head to the young men, and they offered him his choice of their three sisters as a wife, together with half their kingdom.

'I did not come here to take a wife, but if I wanted a wife perhaps it's your sister I would choose first.'

Peredur went on his way. He heard a noise behind him, and he looked behind him, and could see a man on a red horse, dressed in red armour. The man drew level with him and greeted Peredur in the name of God and man. Peredur greeted the young man kindly.

'Lord, I have come to ask you something.'

'What do you want?' said Peredur.

'Take me as your man.'

'Whom would I be taking as my man, if I were to take you?'

'I will not conceal my identity from you. I am called Edlym Gleddyf Goch,* an earl from the eastern region.'

'I am surprised that you are offering yourself as a man to someone who has no more land than yourself. I too have only an earldom. But since you want to become my man, I will take you gladly.'

They came to the countess's court. They were made welcome in the court and were told that it was not out of disrespect to them that they were seated below the retinue, but that it was the custom of the court. For whoever overthrew her retinue of three hundred men would be allowed to eat next to her, and she would love him more than any man. When Peredur had overthrown her retinue of three hundred men and sat down beside her, she said, 'I thank God for having a young man so fair and brave as you, since I have not had the man I loved best.'

'Who was the man you loved best?'

'By my faith, Edlym Gleddyf Goch was the man I loved best, but I have never seen him.'

'God knows,' he said, 'Edlym is my companion, and here he is. And it was for his sake that I came to challenge your retinue. But he could have done it better than I, had he wanted. And I will give you to him.'

'God thank you, fair young man, and I will take the man I love best.' That night Edlym and the countess slept together.

The next day Peredur set off for the Mound of Mourning.

'By your hand, lord, I will go with you,' said Edlym.

They came to where they could see the Mound and the pavilions.

'Go to those men over there,' said Peredur to Edlym, 'and tell them to come and pay homage to me.' Edlym came to them and said, 'Come to pay homage to my lord.'

'Who is your lord?' they said.

'My lord is Peredur Baladr Hir,'* said Edlym.

'If it were lawful to kill a messenger, you would not return to your lord alive for making such an arrogant request of kings and earls and barons to come and pay homage to your lord.'

Edlym returned to Peredur. Peredur told him to go back to them and give them a choice, either to pay homage or fight him. They chose to fight him. And Peredur overthrew the owners of a hundred pavilions that day. The next day he overthrew the owners of another hundred. But the third hundred decided to pay homage to Peredur. He asked them what they were doing there. They said that they were guarding the serpent until it died.

'And then we will fight each other for the stone, and whichever one of us is victorious will get the stone.'

'Wait for me here, I will go and confront the serpent.'

'No, lord,' they said, 'we will go together to fight the serpent.'

'No,' said Peredur, 'I do not want that. If the serpent were killed, I would get no more praise than any one of you.' And he went to where the serpent was, and killed it, and returned to them.

'Add up what you have spent since you came here, and I will repay it to you in gold,' said Peredur. He paid them as much as each one said he was owed, and asked nothing of them save to acknowledge that they were his men.

And he said to Edlym, 'You shall go to the woman you love best, and I will go on my way and repay you for becoming my man.' And then he gave the stone to Edlym.

'May God repay you, and may God speed your journey.'

Peredur went on his way. He came to a river valley, the fairest he had ever seen, and he could see many pavilions there of different colours. But he was more surprised to see the number of watermills and windmills. A large, auburn-haired man came up to him with the look of a craftsman about him. Peredur asked him who he was.

'I am the head miller over all the mills over there.'

'May I have lodging with you?' said Peredur.

'Yes,' he replied, 'gladly.' He came to the miller's house, and saw that the miller had a fair and pleasant place. Peredur asked the miller if he could borrow money to buy food and drink for himself and the household, and he would repay him before leaving. He asked the miller why there was such a crowd of people. The miller said to Peredur, 'It is either one or the other: either you are a man from afar or else you are mad. The empress of great Constantinople is there, and she wants only the bravest man since she has no need of wealth. And it was impossible to carry food to the several thousands that are here, and that is why there are all these mills.' That night they rested.

The next day Peredur got up and armed himself and his horse to go to the tournament. He could see a pavilion among the other pavilions, the fairest he had ever seen. And he could see a beautiful maiden craning her head through a window in the pavilion. He had never seen a more beautiful maiden, dressed in a garment of gold brocaded silk. He stared at the maiden and was filled with great love for her. And he gazed at the maiden in this way from morning until midday, and from midday until it was afternoon. By then the tournament had ended. He came to his lodging and he took off his armour and asked the miller if he could borrow money. The miller's wife was angry with Peredur. But even so the miller lent him money. The next day he did the same as he had done the day before. That night he came to his lodging and borrowed money from the miller. The third day, when he was in the same place gazing at the maiden, he felt a large blow with the handle of an axe between his shoulder and neck. When he looked round at the miller, the miller said to him, 'Do one of two things,' said the miller, 'either turn your head away or go to the tournament.'

Peredur smiled at the miller and went to the tournament. He overthrew all those he encountered that day. Of those he overthrew, he sent the men as a gift to the empress, and the horses and armour as a gift to the miller's wife, as a guarantee of the money he had borrowed. Peredur took part in the tournament until he had over-thrown everyone. Those he overthrew, he sent the men to the empress's prison, and the horses and armour to the miller's wife as a guarantee of the money he had borrowed.

The empress sent word to the Knight of the Mill asking him to come and see her. But he rejected the first messenger. And the second went to him. And the third time she sent one hundred knights to ask him to come and see her, and unless he came voluntar-ily they were to take him against his will. They went to him and related their message from the empress. He fought well against them—he had them tied up as one ties a roebuck, and thrown into the mill ditch. And the empress asked the advice of a wise man who was in her council.

He said to her, 'I will go to him with your message.' He came to Peredur and greeted him, and asked him for the sake of his lover to come and see the empress. And Peredur and the miller went. He sat down in the first part of the pavilion to which he came, and she sat down next to him. They talked together for a while. Peredur took his leave and went to his lodging. The next day he went to visit her. When he came to the pavilion there was no part of it less well appointed than the rest, for they did not know where he would sit. Peredur sat next to the empress and talked lovingly. As they were sitting like that, they saw a black-haired man entering, with a golden goblet full of wine in his hand. He went down on his knee before the empress and told her to give it only to the man who would fight him for it. She looked at Peredur.

'Lady,' he said, 'give the goblet to me.' He drank the wine, and gave the goblet to the miller's wife. Meanwhile, behold, a black-haired man who was bigger than the other, with a wild animal's claw in his hand shaped like a goblet and full of wine. He presented it to the empress and told her to give it only to the man who would fight him.

'Lady,' said Peredur, 'give it to me.' And she gave it to Peredur. He drank the wine and gave the goblet to the miller's wife. Meanwhile, behold, a man with red curly hair who was bigger than either of the other men, and a crystal goblet in his hand, full of wine. He went down on his knee and placed it in the empress's hand and told her to give it only to the man who would fight him for it. And she gave it to

Peredur, and he sent it to the miller's wife. That night he went to his lodging.

The next day he armed himself and his horse, and came to the meadow. Peredur killed the three men and then went to the pavilion. The empress said to him, 'Fair Peredur, remember the promise you made me when I gave you the stone, when you killed the monster.'

'Lady,' he replied, 'what you say is true, and I remember it too.' And Peredur ruled with the empress for fourteen years, according to the story.*

Arthur was in Caerllion ar Wysg, one of his chief courts, and in the middle of the hall floor sat four men on a mantle of brocaded silk— Owain son of Urien, and Gwalchmai son of Gwyar, and Hywel son of Emyr Llydaw,* and Peredur Baladr Hir. Suddenly they saw a black, curly-haired maiden come in on a yellow mule, with rough reins in her hand urging the mule forward, and a rough, unfriendly look about her. Blacker were her face and her hands than the blackest iron daubed with pitch; and the colour was not the ugliest thing about her, but her shape—high cheeks and a sagging, baggy face, and a snub nose with flaring nostrils, and one eye mottled-green and piercing, and the other black, like jet, sunk deep in her head. Long yellow teeth, yellower than the flowers of the broom, and her belly rising from her breastbone higher than her chin. Her backbone was shaped like a crutch; her hips were broad and bony, but everything from there down was scrawny, except her feet and knees, which were stout.* She greeted Arthur and all his retinue except Peredur; for him she had angry, insolent words.

'Peredur, I will not greet you, for you are not worthy of it. Fate was blind when it gave you talent and fame. When you came to the court of the lame king and when you saw there the young man carrying the sharpened spear, and from the tip of the spear a drop of blood streaming down to the young man's fist, and you saw other wonders there, too—you did not question their meaning or their cause.* And had you done so, the king would have recovered his health and held his kingdom in peace. But now there is conflict and combat, knights lost and wives left widowed and young girls unprovided for, and all that because of you.'

And then she said to Arthur, 'With your permission, lord, my home is far away from here, in the Castle of Pride—I do not know if you have heard of it. There are sixty-six knights and five hundred ordained knights there,* each with the woman he loves best. And whoever wants to gain fame in arms and combat and conflict will do so there if he deserves it. But whoever wants the ultimate fame and admiration I know where he can get that. There is a castle on a prominent mountain, and in it there's a maiden, and the castle is under siege. Whoever could set her free would receive the highest praise in the world.'

And with that she set off. Gwalchmai said, 'By my faith, I will not sleep in peace until I know whether I can set the maiden free.' And many of Arthur's retinue agreed with him. Peredur, however, said otherwise, 'By my faith, I will not sleep in peace until I know the story and significance of the spear about which the black-haired maiden spoke.'

As everyone was getting ready, behold, a knight came to the gate, of the size and strength of a warrior, and equipped with horse and armour, and he came forward and greeted Arthur and all his retinue except for Gwalchmai. On the knight's shoulder there was a gold-chased shield with a cross-piece of blue azure, and all his armour was the same colour as that. He said to Gwalchmai, 'You killed my lord through your deceit and treachery, and I will prove it to you.'

Gwalchmai got up. 'Here is my pledge against you,' he said, 'either here or in a place of your choice, that I am neither a deceiver nor a traitor.'

'I want the combat between us to take place in front of my king.'

'Gladly,' said Gwalchmai. 'Go on ahead, I will follow you.'

The knight set off, and Gwalchmai got ready. He was offered many weapons, but he only wanted his own. Gwalchmai and Peredur armed themselves, and rode after him because of their friendship and the extent of their love for each other. But they did not continue together—each went his own way.

At daybreak Gwalchmai came to a valley,* and in the valley he could see a fort, and a large court inside the fort with very high, splendid turrets around it. And he could see a knight coming out through the gate to hunt on a shiny black, wide-nostrilled, swift-moving palfrey with a pace steady and stately, sure-footed and lively.* He was the man who owned the court. Gwalchmai greeted him.

'May God be good to you, lord, and where do you come from?'

'I come from Arthur's court,' he said.

'Are you Arthur's man?'

'I am, by my faith,' said Gwalchmai.

'I have good advice for you,' said the knight. 'I see that you are tired and weary. Go to the court and stay there tonight if you want.'

'I will, lord, and may God repay you.'

'Take a ring as a sign to the gatekeeper, and make for that tower; a sister of mine is there.'

Gwalchmai came to the gate, and showed the ring, and made for the tower. When he arrived there was a big fire blazing with a bright, tall, smokeless flame, and a fair noble maiden sitting in a chair by the fire. The maiden was glad to see him and welcomed him, and got up to meet him. And he went to sit next to the maiden. They had their dinner.

After their dinner they engaged in pleasant conversation. As they were doing so, a handsome grey-haired man entered.

'You wretched whore,' he said, 'if you knew how wrong it is for you to sit and amuse yourself with that man, you would not do so.' He withdrew his head, and left.

'Lord,' said the maiden, 'if you take my advice you will secure the door, in case the man has set a trap for you,' she said.

Gwalchmai got up, but when he got to the door the man was with thirty others, fully armed, climbing up the tower. Gwalchmai used a *gwyddbwyll* board so that no one could come up until the man returned from hunting. Then the earl arrived.

'What is this?' he said.

'It's not right', said the grey-haired man, 'for the wretched girl over there to sit and drink until evening with the man who killed your father—he is Gwalchmai son of Gwyar.'

'No more of this,' said the earl. 'I will go inside.'

The earl made Gwalchmai welcome.

'Lord,' he said, 'it was wrong of you to come to our court, if you knew you had killed our father. Since we cannot avenge that, may God avenge it.'

'Friend,' said Gwalchmai, 'this is the situation. I came here neither to admit to killing your father nor to deny it. I am on a quest for Arthur and myself. However, I ask for a year's respite until I return from my quest, and then, on my word, I will come to this court to do one of two things, either to admit it or deny it.' They granted him the respite gladly. He stayed there that night.

The next day he set off, but the story says no more than that about Gwalchmai on the matter.

But Peredur went on his way. He wandered the island searching for news about the black-haired maiden, but found none. And he came to land that he did not recognize in a river valley. As he was travelling through the valley, he could see a rider coming towards him with the mark of a priest on him. Peredur asked for his blessing.

'Miserable wretch,' he said, 'you do not deserve to receive a blessing, and it won't be of any use to you seeing that you are wearing armour on a day as exalted as this.'

'And what day is today?' said Peredur.

'Today is Good Friday.'

'Do not chide me, I did not know. A year from today I set off from my country.'

Then he dismounted and led his horse by the bridle. He walked part of the highway until he came to a by-road, and he took the by-road through the forest. On the other side of the forest he could see a fort with no towers, and he could see signs of habitation in the fort. He made for the fort. And at the gate of the fort he met the priest whom he had come across earlier. Peredur asked for his blessing.

'God's blessing on you,' he said, 'and it is better to travel thus. And you shall stay with me tonight.' And Peredur stayed that night.

The next day Peredur asked permission to leave.

'Today is no day for anyone to travel. You shall stay with me today and tomorrow and the day after. And I will give you the best information that I can as to what you are looking for.'

The fourth day, Peredur asked permission to leave, and begged the priest to give him information about the Fortress of Wonders.

'As much as I know, I shall tell you. Cross the mountain over there, and on the far side of the mountain there is a river, and in the river valley there is the court of a king, and the king was there over Easter. And if you are to get news anywhere about the Fortress of Wonders, you will get it there.'

Then he went on his way, and came to the river valley. And he met a number of men going to hunt. He could see among the crowd a man of high rank. Peredur greeted him. He said, 'It is your choice, lord, either go to the court or come hunting with me. And I will send one of the retinue to entrust you to the care of one of my daughters who is there, so that you can take food and drink until I return from hunting. And if your business is one that I can help you with, then I will do so gladly.'

The king sent a short, yellow-haired lad with him. And when they came to the court, the lady had got up and was going to wash. Peredur approached, and she welcomed him warmly and made room for him next to her. And they ate their dinner. Whatever Peredur said to her, she would laugh out loud so that everyone in the court could hear. Then the short, yellow-haired lad said to the lady, 'By my faith,' he said, 'if you have ever had a lover then it was this squire, and if you have not had a lover, then your heart and head are set on him.'

The short, yellow-haired lad went to the king, and told him that it was most likely that the squire he had met was his daughter's lover.

'And if he is not her lover, I am sure he will be her lover very soon unless you safeguard against it.'

'What is your advice, lad?'

'I advise you to set brave men on him and hold him, until you know it for sure.'

The king set men on Peredur to seize him and put him in prison. The maiden came to her father and asked him why he had had the squire from Arthur's court imprisoned.

'God knows,' he replied, 'he will not be set free tonight or tomorrow or the day after, and he will not be leaving where he is.'

She did not confront the king about what he had said, but went to the squire.

'Is it unpleasant for you being here?'

'I would prefer it if I weren't.'

'Your bed and your conditions will be no worse than the king's, and the best songs in the court you shall have at your command. And if you would prefer to have my bed here so that I could talk to you, you shall have that gladly.'

'I will not object to that.' He was in prison that night, and the maiden kept her promise to him.

The next day Peredur could hear a commotion in the town.

'Fair maiden, what is this commotion?'

'The king's host and his army are coming to this town today.'

'What do they want?'

'There is an earl nearby, and he has two earldoms, and he is as strong as a king. And there will be battle between them today.'

'I want you to arrange a horse and armour for me to go and look at the battle,' said Peredur, 'and on my word I will return to my prison.'

'Gladly,' she replied. 'I'll arrange a horse and armour for you.'

She gave him a horse and armour, and a pure red cloak over his armour, and a yellow shield on his shoulder. And he went to the battle. Those of the earl's men who encountered him that day, he overthrew them all, and he returned to his prison. She asked Peredur for news, but he did not utter a single word to her. She went to ask her father for news—she asked who of his retinue had performed best. He replied that he did not recognize him: 'He was a man with a pure red cloak over his armour, and a yellow shield on his shoulder.'

She smiled, and went to Peredur. And he was held in high regard that night. For three consecutive days Peredur killed the earl's men, and before anyone could find out who he was he would return to his prison. On the fourth day Peredur killed the earl himself. And the maiden went to meet her father, and asked him for news.

'Good news,' said the king. 'The earl has been killed,' he said, 'and I now own both earldoms.'

'Do you know, lord, who killed him?'

'I do,' said the king. 'The knight with the pure red cloak and yellow shield killed him.'

'Lord,' she said, 'I know who he is.'

'In God's name,' he replied, 'who is he?'

'Lord, he is the knight whom you imprisoned.'

The king went to Peredur, and greeted him, and told him that he would pay him whatever he wanted for the service he had rendered. When they went to eat, Peredur was placed next to the king, and the maiden on the other side of Peredur.

After eating, the king said to Peredur, 'I will give you my daughter in marriage, and half my kingdom with her, and the two earldoms I will give you as a wedding gift.'

'May the Lord God repay you. I did not come here to look for a wife.'

'So what are you seeking, lord?'

'I am seeking news of the Fortress of Wonders.'

'The lord's mind is on higher things than we expected,' said the maiden. 'You shall have news of the fortress, and someone to guide you through my father's land, and plenty of food and drink. And you, lord, are the man I love best.'

Then the king said to Peredur, 'Cross that mountain over there, and you will see a lake, and a fortress within the lake. And it is called the Fortress of Wonders. And we know nothing of its wonders, but that is what it's called.'

And Peredur came to the fortress, and the gate of the fortress was open. And when he came to the hall, the door was open. As he entered, he could see *gwyddbwyll* in the hall, and each of the two sides playing against the other. And the side he supported lost the game, and the other side shouted just as if they were men.* He got angry, and took the pieces in his lap and threw the board into the lake. As he was doing so, behold, the black-haired maiden entered.

'May you not receive God's welcome. You do evil more often than good.'

'Of what are you accusing me, black-haired maiden?'

'You have made the empress lose her board, and she would not wish that for her empire.'

'Is there a way to get the board back?'

'There is, if you were to go to the Fortress of Ysbidinongyl. There is a black-haired man there, destroying much of the empress's land; kill him and you would get the board. But if you go there, you will not come back alive.'

'Will you guide me there?'

'I will show you a way there.'

He came to the Fortress of Ysbidinongyl and fought the black-haired man. The black-haired man asked Peredur for mercy.

'I will be merciful—see that the board is where it was when I entered the hall.' Then the black-haired maiden arrived.

'God's curse on you for your effort, for leaving alive the oppressor who is destroying the empress's land.'

'I let him have his life,' said Peredur, 'in order to get the board.'

'The board is not where you first found it. Go back and kill him.' Peredur went and killed the man.

When he came to the court, the black-haired maiden was there.

'Maiden,' said Peredur, 'where is the empress?'

'Between me and God, you will not see her again unless you kill an oppressor that is in the forest over there.'

'What sort of oppressor is it?'

'A stag, as swift as the swiftest bird, and there is one horn in his forehead, as long as a spear-shaft, and as sharp as the sharpest thing.

And he eats the tops of the trees and what grass there is in the forest. And he kills every animal he finds in the forest, and those he does not kill die of starvation. And worse than that, he comes every day and drinks the fishpond dry, and leaves the fish exposed, and most of them die before it fills again with water.'

'Maiden,' said Peredur, 'will you come and show me this creature?'

'No, I will not. No man has dared enter the forest for a year. There is the lady's lapdog—it will raise the stag and bring him to you. And the stag will attack you.'

The lapdog went as Peredur's guide, and raised the stag, and brought it to Peredur. And the stag rushed at Peredur, but he let it charge past him and cut off its head with a sword. As he was looking at the stag's head, he could see a lady on horseback coming towards him and picking up the lapdog in the sleeve of her cape and placing the stag's head between herself and the saddle-bow, together with the collar of red gold that was round its neck.

'Lord,' she said, 'you did a discourteous thing, killing the most beautiful jewel in my land.'

'I was told to do that. And is there any way I can win your friendship?'

'Yes, there is. Go to the hillside and there you will see a bush. And at the base of the bush there is a slab. And ask for a man to fight you, three times—you would then have my friendship.'

Peredur went on his way and came to the edge of the bush and asked for a man to fight. A black-haired man arose from beneath the slab, on a scraggy horse, and big, rusty armour on him and his horse. And they fought. As Peredur threw the black-haired man to the ground, he would jump up again into his saddle. Peredur dismounted and drew his sword. With that the black man disappeared, and Peredur's horse and his own horse with him, so that he did not get a second glimpse of them.

Peredur walked along the mountain, and on the other side of the mountain he could see a fortress in a river valley, and he approached the fortress. And as he entered the fortress he could see a hall, and the hall door open, and he entered. And he could see a lame, grey-haired man sitting at the end of the hall, with Gwalchmai sitting on one side of him. And he could see Peredur's horse in the same stall as Gwalchmai's horse. They made Peredur welcome, and he went to sit on the other side of the grey-haired man. With that a

yellow-haired lad went down on his knee before Peredur and asked
him for his friendship.

'Lord,' said the lad, 'I came in the guise of the black-haired
maiden to Arthur's court, and when you threw away the *gwyddbwyll*,
and when you killed the black-haired man from Ysbidinongyl, and
when you killed the stag, and when you fought against the black-
haired man from the slab. And I brought the head on the salver, all
covered in blood, and the spear with the blood streaming along it
from its tip to its hilt. And the head was your cousin's, and it was
the witches of Caerloyw who killed him, and they made your uncle
lame. And I am your cousin, too, and it is foretold that you will
avenge that.'

Peredur and Gwalchmai decided to send for Arthur and his retinue, to ask him to set upon the witches. And they began to fight the
witches, and one of the witches killed one of Arthur's men in front
of Peredur, and Peredur told her to stop. A second time the witch
killed a man in front of Peredur, and a second time Peredur told her
to stop. A third time the witch killed a man in front of Peredur, and
Peredur drew his sword and struck the witch on top of her helmet, so
that the helmet and all the armour and the head were split in two.
She gave a scream and told the other witches to flee, and said that it
was Peredur, the man who had been learning horsemanship with
them and who was fated to kill them. Then Arthur and his retinue
attacked the witches, and all the witches of Caerloyw were killed.
And that is what is told of the Fortress of Wonders.*

The Dream of the Emperor Maxen

MAXEN WLEDIG* was emperor of Rome, and he was the fairest man, and the wisest, and the best suited to be emperor of all his predecessors. One day he was at a council of kings; and he said to his companions, 'I want to go hunting tomorrow', he said.

Early the next day he set out with his retinue, and they came to the valley of the river that flows down to Rome. He hunted the valley until it was noon. Moreover, with him that day were thirty crowned kings, vassals of his. It was not so much for the pleasure of hunting that the emperor hunted for that length of time, but because he had been made a man of such high rank that he was lord over all those kings. The sun was high in the sky above his head, and the heat was great, and Maxen fell asleep. His chamberlains* protected him from the sun by raising shields on spear-shafts around him. They placed a gold-chased shield under his head; and so the emperor slept.

And then he had a dream. This was his dream, that he was travelling along the river valley to its source until he came to the highest mountain he had ever seen, and he was sure that the mountain was as high as the sky. As he came over the mountain he could see that he was travelling along level plains, the fairest that anyone had ever seen, on the other side of the mountain. And he could see great, wide rivers flowing from the mountain to the sea, and he was travelling to the sea-fords and the rivers. After travelling in this way for a long time, he came to the mouth of a great river, the widest that anyone had seen, and he could see a great city at the mouth of the river, and a great wall around the city with many great towers of different colours. At the mouth of the river he saw a fleet, and that was the largest fleet he had ever seen. Among the fleet he saw a ship which was much larger and fairer than any of the others: of as much of it that he could see above the water, one plank was of gold and the next was of silver. He saw a bridge of whalebone from the ship to the shore, and imagined he was walking along the bridge into the ship. A sail was hoisted on the ship, and she steered over sea and ocean. He saw himself coming to the fairest island in the world, and having crossed the island from one sea to the other he could see, at the far end of the island, steep mountains and lofty crags, and rough, rugged terrain the like of which he had never seen before. From there he saw an island in the sea, facing that rugged terrain, and between him and the island he saw a land whose plain was the length of its sea, whose forest was the length of its mountain. From that mountain he saw a river crossing the land, making for the sea, and at the mouth of the river he saw a great castle, the fairest that anyone had ever seen, and he saw the castle gate was open, and he came into the castle. He saw a hall in the castle. He thought that the roof-tiles of the hall were all of gold. The side of the hall he thought to be of valuable, sparkling stones. The floors of the hall he imagined to be of pure gold, with golden couches and silver tables. On a couch facing him he saw two young, auburn-haired lads playing *gwyddbwyll*.* He saw that the board for the *gwyddbwyll* was silver, and its pieces were of red gold. The lads' garments were of pure black brocaded silk, and frontlets of red gold on their heads holding their hair in place, with precious, sparkling stones in them, rubies and white gems alternating with imperial stones. On their feet were boots of new Cordovan leather, with bands of red gold fastening them. And at the foot of the hall-pillar he saw a grey-haired man in a chair of elephant ivory with the images of two eagles in red gold on it. There were gold bracelets on his arms, and many gold rings on his fingers; and a gold torque around his neck, and a gold frontlet holding his hair; and a noble quality about him. There was a *gwyddbwyll* board in front of him, and a bar of gold in his hand, and with steel files he was carving *gwyddbwyll* pieces from the bar.

He saw a maiden sitting before him, in a chair of red gold. Because of her beauty it was no easier to gaze upon her than it would be upon the sun when it is at its brightest and most beautiful. The maiden wore shifts of white silk with clasps of red gold at her breast, and a surcoat of gold brocaded silk with a mantle to match, and a brooch of red gold holding the mantle about her; and a frontlet of red gold on her head, with rubies and white gems in the frontlet, and pearls alternating with imperial stones; and a girdle of red gold about her; and she was the most beautiful sight to behold. The maiden got up to meet him from the golden chair, and he embraced her, and they sat down together in the golden chair. And the chair was no narrower for them both than for the maiden alone. And as he had his arms around the maiden, and his cheek against her cheek, what with the dogs straining at their leashes, and the corners of the shields touching one another, and the spear-shafts striking together, and the stamping of the horses, the emperor woke up. And when he awoke he could no longer live or breathe or exist because of the maiden he had seen in his sleep. Not a bone-joint of his, not the root of a fingernail, let alone anything larger, was not full of love for the maiden.

Then his retinue said to him, 'Lord,' they said, 'it is gone time for you to eat.'

Then the emperor mounted his palfrey, the saddest man that anyone had ever seen, and he made his way to Rome. Whatever messages he was given, no answer was received because of his sadness and moroseness. And then he arrived in the city of Rome, and he was thus the whole week long. Whenever his retinue went to drink from golden vessels and to take their pleasure, he would not accompany any one of them. Whenever they went to listen to songs and entertainment, he would not accompany them. He did nothing but sleep, for as often as he slept, he would see in his sleep the woman he loved best; when he was not sleeping, because of her he cared for nothing, for he did not know where in the world she was.

One day a chamberlain said to him (and although he was a chamberlain of his, he was also a king in Romani),* 'Lord,' he said, 'all your men are criticizing you.'

'Why are they criticizing me?' said the emperor.

The servant replied, 'Because neither your men nor anyone else has received from you either a message or an answer such as men expect to get from their lord. And that is why you are being criticized.'

'Lad,' said the emperor, 'bring the wise men of Rome to me, and I will tell them why I am sad.'

Then the wise men of Rome were brought around the emperor. He said, 'You see, men,' he said, 'I had a dream. And in the dream I saw a maiden. I can no longer live or breathe or exist because of her.'

'Lord,' they replied, 'because you have asked us for advice, we will advise you. And this is our advice to you. Send messengers for three years to the three regions of the world* to look for your dream. And since you do not know what day or night good news will reach you, your hope will sustain you.'

Then the messengers travelled until the end of the year, wandering the world and seeking news of the emperor's dream. When they returned at the end of the year, they had no more news than on the day they set out. Then the emperor was saddened to think that he would never get news of the lady he loved best. Then other messengers set off anew to search the second region of the world. When they returned at the end of the year, they had no more news about the dream than on the first day. Then the emperor was saddened to think that he would never in his life have the good fortune to find the woman he loved best. Then the king of the Romani said to the emperor, 'Lord,' he said, 'begin hunting in the forest in the direction you saw yourself go, either towards the east or towards the west.'

Then the emperor began to hunt, and he came to the bank of the river he had seen in his dream and said, 'This is where I was when I had the dream,' he said. 'And I was walking westwards, towards the source of the river.'

Then thirteen men set off as the emperor's messengers. In front of them they saw a huge mountain which seemed to touch the sky. This is how the messengers appeared as they travelled—each one had a sleeve of his cape to the front that showed he was a messenger, so that in whatever warring country they might travel, no harm would be done to them.* As they crossed over that mountain they saw great, level plains and great, wide rivers flowing through them. Then they said, 'This', they said, 'is the land that our lord saw.'

They travelled towards the sea-fords along the rivers until they came to the mouth of a river which they saw flowing into the sea, and a great city at the mouth of the river, and a great castle in the city with great towers of different colours. They saw the largest fleet in the world at the mouth of the river, and a ship that was larger than any of the others. And then they said, 'This again', they said, 'is our lord's dream.'

And in that large ship they steered over the sea and came to land in the Island of Britain. And they crossed the Island until they saw Eryri, and then they said, 'This', they said, 'is the rugged terrain that our lord saw.'

They carried on until they saw the Island of Môn facing them, and until they saw Arfon, too. Then they said, 'This', they said, 'is the land our lord saw in his sleep.'

And they saw Aber Saint,* and the castle at the mouth of the river. They saw the castle gate was open, and they came into the castle. They saw a hall in the castle. 'This', they said, 'is the hall our lord saw in his sleep.'

They came into the hall. They saw the two lads playing *gwyddbwyll* on the golden couch, and the grey-haired man at the foot of the pillar in the chair of elephant ivory carving the pieces for the *gwyddbwyll*. And they saw the maiden sitting in a chair of red gold. The messengers went down on their knees and spoke to her like this, 'Empress of Rome,' they said, 'greetings! We are messengers to you from the emperor of Rome.'

'Noblemen,' said the maiden, 'I see you bear the mark of well-born men and the badge of messengers. Why are you mocking me?'

'Lady,' they said, 'we are not mocking you at all. But the emperor of Rome saw you in his sleep. He can neither live nor breathe nor exist because of you. Lady, we will give you a choice—either come with us to be crowned empress of Rome, or the emperor will come here to take you as his wife.'

'Noblemen,' said the maiden, 'I do not doubt what you say, neither do I believe it too much either. But if it is I whom the emperor loves, let him come here to fetch me.'

By day and by night the messengers travelled back. As their horses failed, they left them behind and bought new ones. And so they reached Rome, and greeted the emperor, and asked for their reward; and they received it even as they named it. And they spoke to him like this, 'Lord,' they said, 'we will be your guides over land and sea to where that lady is whom you love best. And we know her name, and her family and her lineage.'

Immediately the emperor set off with his army, and those men as their guides. He came to the Island of Britain with his fleet, over sea and ocean. And he took the Island by force from Beli son of Manogan* and his sons, and drove them into the sea, and he made his way to Arfon. The emperor recognized the land the moment he saw it. And when he saw the castle at Aber Saint he said, 'My men,' he said, 'over there is the castle in which I saw the lady I love best.'

He came into the castle and into the hall, and there he saw Cynan son of Eudaf and Gadeon son of Eudaf playing *gwyddbwyll*, and Eudaf son of Caradog sitting in a chair of ivory, carving pieces for the *gwyddbwyll*. The maiden he had seen in his sleep, he could see sitting in a chair of red gold.

'Empress of Rome,' he said, 'greetings!' And the emperor threw his arms around her, and that night he slept with her.

Early the next day the maiden claimed her maiden fee,* since he had found her to be a virgin. He asked her to name her maiden fee. She listed thus: the Island of Britain for her father, from the North Sea to the Irish Sea, and the Three Adjacent Islands* to be held under the empress of Rome; and three major forts to be built for her in three locations of her choice in the Island of Britain. Then she asked that the prime fort be built for her in Arfon.* And soil from Rome was brought there, so that it would be healthier for the emperor to sleep and sit and walk around. After that the other two forts were built for her, namely Caerllion* and Caerfyrddin.

One day the emperor went to hunt from Caerfyrddin to the top of Y Freni Fawr,* and there he pitched his tent; and that camp has been called Cadair Faxen* ever since. Because the stronghold, on the other hand, was built by a host of men, it is called Caerfyrddin.* After that Elen decided to build great roads from one fort to the other across the Island of Britain. Because of that they are called Ffyrdd Elen Luyddog,* since she came from the Island of Britain, and the men of the Island of Britain would never have assembled those large armies for anyone but her.

For seven years* the emperor stayed in this Island. It was a custom of the Romans at that time that whenever an emperor stayed in other countries conquering for seven years, he should stay in the conquered territory and not be allowed to return to Rome. So they declared a new emperor. And he sent a threatening letter to Maxen. However, it was not so much a letter as 'If you come and if you ever come to Rome!' That letter and the news came to Maxen in Caerllion. And from there he sent a letter to the man who claimed to be emperor of Rome. There was in that letter, too, nothing but 'If I go to Rome, and if I go!'

Then Maxen travelled with his host to Rome, and conquered France and Burgundy and all the countries as far as Rome. And he laid siege to the city of Rome. For a year the emperor was outside the city; he was no closer to taking it than on the first day. But the brothers of

Elen Luyddog from the Island of Britain had followed him, with a small host. And there were better fighting-men in that small host than twice their number of the men of Rome. The emperor was told that the host had been seen dismounting near his own host and pitching its tents. And no one had ever seen a fairer host or one that was better equipped or with finer banners for its size. Elen came to look at the host, and she recognized her brothers' banners. Then Cynan son of Eudaf and Gadeon son of Eudaf went to see the emperor, and he welcomed them, and embraced them. Then they watched the men of Rome attack the city. And Cynan said to his brother, 'We shall try and attack the city in a shrewder way than this.'

Then by night they measured the height of the walls, and they sent their carpenters into the forest, and a ladder was made for every four of their men. When those were ready, every day at noon the two emperors would have their meal, and both sides would stop fighting until everyone had finished eating. But the men of the Island of Britain had their meal in the morning, and drank until they were intoxicated. While the two emperors were eating, the Britons approached the walls and placed their ladders against them, and immediately went in over the walls. The new emperor did not have time to put on his armour before they set upon him and killed him, and many others with him. They spent three nights and three days overthrowing the men who were in the city and overcoming the castle, while another group of them guarded the city in case any of Maxen's host should enter before they had brought everyone under their control.

Then Maxen said to Elen Luyddog, 'I am greatly surprised, lady,' he said, 'that it is not for me that your brothers have conquered this city.'

'Lord emperor,' she replied, 'my brothers are the wisest young men in the world. Go over there and ask for the city, and if they control it, you shall have it gladly.'

Then the emperor and Elen went to ask for the city. They told the emperor that conquering the city and giving it to him was a matter to none save the men of the Island of Britain. Then the gates to the city of Rome were opened, and the emperor sat on his throne, and all the Romans paid homage to him. Then the emperor said to Cynan and Gadeon, 'Noblemen,' he said, 'I have gained possession of all my empire. And I will give you this host to conquer whatever part of the world you wish.'

Then they set off and conquered lands and castles and cities, and they killed all their men, but left the women alive. And so they continued until the young lads who had come with them were grey-haired men, for they had been conquering for such a long time. Then Cynan said to Gadeon his brother, 'What do you want,' he said, 'to stay in this country or to return to your native land?'

He decided to return to his own country, along with many others. But Cynan and another group stayed on to settle there. And they decided to cut out the tongues of the women, lest their own language be corrupted. Because the women and their language were silenced, while the men spoke on, the Britons were called Llydaw men. And after that there have often come, and still do come to the Island of Britain, people speaking that language.*

And this tale is called The Dream of Maxen Wledig, emperor of Rome. And here it ends.

Lludd and Llefelys

ELI the Great,* son of Manogan, had three sons, Lludd and Caswallon and Nyniaw. And according to the story,* Llefelys was a fourth son. And after Beli died, the kingdom of the Island of Britain fell into the hands of Lludd, his eldest son, and Lludd ruled it successfully. He renewed the walls of London and encircled it with countless towers. And after that he ordered the citizens to build houses within it so that no kingdom would have buildings or houses like them. And what is more, he was a good warrior, and benevolent and bountiful in giving food and drink to all who sought it. And although he had many forts and cities, he loved this one more than any other, and there he lived for the most part of the year. For that reason it was called Caer Ludd, finally Caer Lundain,* and after a foreign people came there it was called Llundain, or Lwndrys.

Best of all his brothers, Lludd loved Llefelys, for he was a wise and prudent man. When Llefelys heard that the king of France had died without leaving an heir, apart from one daughter, and had left the kingdom in her hands, he came to Lludd his brother to ask him for advice and support, not only for his own benefit, but also in an attempt to increase the honour and dignity and status of his people by going to the kingdom of France to seek that maiden as his wife. His brother agreed with him immediately, and Llefelys was pleased with his advice on the matter. And straightaway they prepared ships and filled them with armed knights, and they set out towards France. As soon as they had landed they sent messengers to announce to the noblemen of France the nature of their request. After the noblemen of France and her princes had conferred, the maiden was given to Llefelys and the crown of the kingdom along with her. And after that he ruled the land wisely and prudently and prosperously, as long as he lived.

After a period of time had passed, three plagues* fell upon the Island of Britain, the like of which no one in the Islands had seen before. The first of these was the arrival of a certain people called the Coraniaid.* And so great was their knowledge that there was no conversation anywhere in the Island that they did not know about, however softly it was spoken, provided the wind carried it. Because of that no harm could be done to them. The second plague was a scream that was heard every May eve* above every hearth in the Island of Britain. It pierced people's hearts and terrified them so much that men lost their colour and their strength, and women miscarried, and young men and maidens lost their senses, and all animals and trees and the earth and the waters were left barren. The third plague was this: however much food and provision might be prepared in the king's courts, even though it might be a year's supply of food and drink, none of it was ever consumed except what was enjoyed the very first night. And the first plague was plain and clear, but the other two plagues, no one knew their meaning, and because of that there was more hope of getting rid of the first than there was of the second or the third.

Because of that King Lludd became greatly troubled and anxious, for he did not know how he could get rid of those plagues. He summoned all the nobles of his kingdom, and asked their advice as to what they should do against them. And with the unanimous advice of his nobles, Lludd son of Beli went to Llefelys his brother, king of France, to seek advice from him, for he was a wise man of remarkable counsel. Then they prepared a fleet, and did so in secrecy and silence, in case those people (the Coraniaid) or anyone else should get to know the reason for their mission, apart from the king and his advisers. And when they were ready they went in their fleet, Lludd and those he had selected with him, and they began to sail the seas towards France. When news of that reached Llefelys, since he did not know the reason for his brother's fleet, he came from the other shore to meet him with a huge fleet. When Lludd saw that, he left all his ships out at sea, apart from one, and in that he went to meet Llefelys who, in another single ship, came forward to meet his brother. And when they met they embraced and greeted each other with brotherly affection.

When Lludd told his brother the reason for his mission, Llefelys said that he already knew why he had come to those parts. Then they conferred as to how they could discuss their business in some other way, so that the wind would not catch their conversation and the

Coraniaid find out what they were saying. And then Llefelys ordered a long horn of bronze to be made, and they spoke together through that horn, but whatever one said to the other through the horn, only hateful, hostile words were heard by the other. And when Llefelys saw that, and how there was a demon obstructing them and creating trouble through the horn, he had wine poured into the horn to wash it, and through the power of the wine the demon was driven out.*

Once there was no obstacle to their conversation, Llefelys told his brother that he would give him some insects, and that he should keep some of them alive for breeding in case, by chance, that sort of plague came a second time, but he should take some others and crush them in water—that, he affirmed, was effective in destroying the Coraniaid. That is to say, when Lludd returned home to his kingdom he should summon all the people together, his own people and the Coraniaid, to one meeting, on the pretext of making peace between them; and when they were all together, he should take that powerful water and sprinkle it over one and all. And Llefelys assured him that the water would poison the Coraniaid but it would neither kill nor harm any of his own people.

'The second plague in your land,' he said, 'that is a dragon, and a dragon of another foreign people is fighting it and trying to overthrow it, and because of that,' he said, 'your dragon gives out a horrible scream. And this is how you can find out about it. When you get home, have the Island measured, its length and breadth, and where you find the exact centre, have that place dug up. And then into that hole put a vat of the best mead that can be made, and a sheet of brocaded silk over the top of the vat, and then you yourself keep watch. And then you will see the dragons fighting* in the shape of monstrous animals. But eventually they will rise into the air in the shape of dragons; and finally, when they are exhausted after the fierce and frightful fighting, they will fall onto the sheet in the shape of two little pigs, and make the sheet sink down with them, and drag it to the bottom of the vat, and they will drink all the mead, and after that they will sleep. Then immediately wrap the sheet around them, and in the strongest place you can find in your kingdom, bury them in a stone chest and hide it in the ground, and as long as they are in that secure place, no plague shall come to the Island of Britain* from anywhere else.

'The cause of the third plague,' he said, 'is a powerful magician who carries off your food and your drink and your provisions. Through his magic and enchantment he puts everyone to sleep, and for that reason you yourself must stand guard over your feasts and provisions. And so that sleep does not overcome you, have a tub of cold water at hand, and when you feel sleep getting the better of you, step into the tub.'

And then Lludd returned to his country, and without delay he summoned every single one of his own people and the Coraniaid. And he crushed the insects in the water, as Llefelys had taught him, and sprinkled it over one and all. And all the Coraniaid were thus destroyed, without harming any of the Britons.

Some time after that Lludd had the length and breadth of the Island measured, and the central point was found to be in Oxford.* He had the ground dug up there, and into that hole he put a vat full of the best mead that could be made, and a sheet of brocaded silk on top of it, and he himself kept watch that night. And as he was watching, he saw the dragons fighting. When they had grown tired and weary, they landed on top of the sheet and pulled it down with them to the bottom of the vat. And when they had drunk the mead, they fell asleep, and while they slept Lludd wrapped the sheet around them, and in the safest place he could find in Eryri he hid them in a stone chest. After that the place was called Dinas Emrys,* and before that it had been Dinas Ffaraon Dandde. Ffaraon Dandde was one of the Three Chief Officers who Broke his Heart from Sorrow.* And so ended the tempestuous scream that was in the land.

When he had done that King Lludd had an enormous feast prepared, and when it was ready he had a tub of cold water placed beside him, and he personally stood guard. And as he stood there, armed with weapons, about the third watch of the night, he heard many wonderful songs and all kinds of music, and felt drowsiness forcing him to sleep.* At that, in case his plan was foiled and he was overcome by sleep, he immersed himself in the water again and again. At last a man of enormous stature, and wearing strong, heavy armour, came in carrying a hamper,* and as had been his custom he put all the food and drink that had been prepared and provided into the hamper, and made off with it. And nothing amazed Lludd more than that so much could fit into that hamper. With that King Lludd set off after him, and spoke to him in this manner: 'Stop, stop,' he said. 'Although you have inflicted many wrongs and losses before this, you will do so no more, unless your fighting skills show that you are stronger and braver than I.' And immediately the man placed the hamper on the floor and waited for Lludd to approach. There was violent fighting between them until sparks flew from their weapons. And finally Lludd seized him, and fate saw to it that victory should fall to Lludd as he threw the oppressor to the ground beneath him. Having been conquered by strength and force, the man asked him for mercy.

'How can I grant you mercy,' said the king, 'after all the losses and wrongs you have inflicted on me?'

'All the losses that I have ever inflicted on you,' he said, 'I will restore to the extent I have taken. And I will never do this again, but will be your faithful vassal from now on.' And the king accepted that from him.

And that is how Lludd freed the Island of Britain of the three plagues. From then until the end of his life, Lludd son of Beli ruled the Island of Britain in peace and prosperity. And this story is called the tale of Lludd and Llefelys. And so it ends.

The Lady of the Well

THE emperor Arthur was at Caerllion ar Wysg.* He was sitting one day in his chamber, and with him Owain son of Urien, and Cynon son of Clydno, and Cai son of Cynyr,* and Gwenhwyfar and her handmaidens sewing at a window. And although it was said that there was a gatekeeper at Arthur's court, there was none. However, Glewlwyd Gafaelfawr* was there in the role of gatekeeper, to welcome guests and travellers, to begin honouring them, and let them know the court's conventions and customs; to inform those who might be allowed to enter the hall or the chamber, and those who might be entitled to lodgings. And in the middle of the chamber sat the emperor Arthur on a pile of fresh rushes, and a mantle of yellow-red brocaded silk beneath him, and a cushion with its cover of red brocaded silk under his elbow.

Then Arthur said, 'Men, as long as you do not make fun of me,' he said, 'I would like to sleep while I wait for my food; and you can tell each other stories, and Cai will bring you a jugful of mead and some chops.' And the emperor slept. And Cynon son of Clydno asked Cai for what Arthur had promised them.

'But I want the good story* that *I* was promised,' said Cai.

'Sir,' said Cynon, 'it is better for you to fulfil Arthur's promise first, and afterwards we shall tell you the best story we know.'

Cai went to the kitchen and the mead cellar,* and came back with a jugful of mead and a goblet of gold, and his fist full of skewers with chops on them. And they took the chops and began to drink the mead.

'Now,' said Cai, 'you owe me my story.'

'Cynon,' said Owain, 'give Cai his story.'

'God knows,' said Cynon, 'you are an older man and a better storyteller than me, and you have seen stranger things; *you* give Cai his story.'

'*You* begin,' said Owain, 'with the strangest story that you know.'

'Very well,' said Cynon. 'I was my mother and father's one and only son, and I was high-spirited, and extremely arrogant. And I didn't think there was anyone in the world who could perform brave deeds better than I. And when I had overcome every challenge in my own country, I got ready and travelled to the remote and uninhabited regions of the world. Eventually I came across the most beautiful valley in the world, with trees all the same height; and there was a river flowing swiftly along the valley, and a path alongside the river. And I travelled along the path until midday, and travelled on the other side until late afternoon. Then I came to a great plain, and at the far end of the plain I could see a great, shining castle and an ocean close to the castle. I approached the castle, and behold, two lads with curly yellow hair, and a band of gold on their foreheads, and each wearing a tunic of yellow brocaded silk, and boots of new Cordovan leather on their feet with golden buckles fastening them around the ankle. And each had a bow of elephant ivory in his hand, with strings of deer sinew, and arrows with shafts of walrus ivory, peacock-feathered, and golden tips on the shafts; and knives with blades of gold and hilts of walrus ivory as targets, and they were aiming at their knives.

'And a short distance from them I could see a man with curly yellow hair in the prime of life, his beard newly trimmed, and wearing a tunic and mantle of yellow brocaded silk, and a ribbon of gold thread in his mantle, and buskins of speckled Cordovan leather about his feet and two golden buttons fastening them. When I saw him I approached and greeted him. But he was so courteous that he greeted me before I could greet him, and he accompanied me to the castle. There was no sign of life in the castle apart from in the hall, where there were twenty-four maidens embroidering silk at a window. And I tell you this, Cai, I am sure that the ugliest one of them was fairer than the fairest maiden that you ever saw in the Island of Britain; the least beautiful was more beautiful than Gwenhwyfar, the wife of Arthur, when she is at her most beautiful ever at the Christmas Day or Easter Day Mass. And they rose to meet me; and six of them took my horse and removed my boots; and another six took my weapons and polished them in a burnisher until they were as bright as bright could be; and the third six of them laid a cloth on the table and set out food; and the fourth six removed my travel-stained clothes and dressed me in other garments, namely a shirt and breeches of fine linen, and a tunic and surcoat and cloak of yellow brocaded silk with a wide border. And they gathered underneath me and around me many cushions with covers of fine red linen. Then I sat down. The six who had taken my horse groomed him perfectly, as well as the best grooms in the Island of Britain.

'And with that there came silver bowls and water in them for washing, and towels of fine white linen, and some of green; and we went to wash, and the man I mentioned just now went to sit at the table, and I sat next to him, and all the women sat below me, apart from those who were serving. And the table was of silver, and the tablecloth of fine linen. And there was not a single vessel served at table except ones of gold or silver or buffalo horn. And our food came to us, and I can assure you, Cai, that I have never seen nor tasted food or drink that I did not see there, and the service I saw there was better than anywhere else.

'And we ate until we were halfway through the meal, and neither the man nor any of the maidens spoke a single word to me until then. But when the man thought that I would prefer to talk rather than eat, he asked me where I was going and who I was. And I said it was high time I had someone to talk with, and that the greatest fault of the court was that they were such poor conversationalists. "Sir," said the man, "we would have talked with you a long time ago except it would have interfered with your eating. But now we'll talk." And then I told the man who I was, and the journey I was making; and that I was looking for someone to get the better of me, otherwise I would have got the better of everyone.

'And then the man looked at me, and smiled gently, and said to me, "If I didn't think that you would get into too much trouble, I would tell you what you are looking for." And I felt sad and anxious because of that; and the man realized this, and said to me, "Since you would prefer me to tell you what is bad for you rather than what is good for you," he said, "I will tell you. Sleep here tonight," he said, "and get up early, and take the road over there, along the valley you came by, until you reach the forest which you passed through. A short distance into the forest, on your right, you will come across a side road. And travel along that until you come to a large clearing of level ground, with a mound in the middle of the clearing, and you will see on top of the mound an enormous black-haired man no smaller than two men of this world. And he has one foot, and he has one eye in the middle of his forehead; and he has an iron club which I assure you would take two men of this world to lift. He is not a violent man, but he is ugly. And he is keeper of that forest.* You will see a thousand wild animals grazing around him. Ask him the way out of the clearing. He will be rude to you, and yet he will tell you the way so that you will find what you want."

'And that was a long night for me. The next morning I got up and dressed, and mounted my horse and went on my way through the valley and the forest, and came to the side road the man had spoken of, and reached the clearing. And when I got there, the wild animals I saw were three times as remarkable as the man had described. And the black-haired man was there, sitting on top of the mound. The man had told me he was big, but he was far bigger than that. And the iron club which the man had said would take two men to lift, I was sure, Cai, that it would take four warriors. Yet he held it in one hand!

'And I greeted the black-haired man, but he replied discourteously. I asked him what power he had over those animals. "I will show you, little man," he said. And he took the club in his hand, and with it he struck a deer a great blow so that it gave a great bellow. And at his bellow wild animals came up until they were as numerous as the stars in the sky, so that there was scarcely room for me to stand in the clearing with them, what with all the serpents and lions and vipers and other kinds of animals. He looked at them, and ordered them to go and graze. And they bowed their heads and did homage to him as obedient men would do to their lord. And he said to me, "Do you see now, little man, the power I have over these animals?"

'And then I asked him the way. And he was rude to me, but nevertheless he asked me where I wanted to go. And I told him who I was and what I was looking for. And he showed me. "Take the road to the end of the clearing," he said, "and climb up the hill over there until you come to the top. And from there you will see a broad river valley, like a wide vale, and in the middle of the valley you will see a great tree, its branches greener than the greenest fir trees. And under that tree there is a well, and near the well there is a marble slab, and on the slab there is a silver bowl fastened to a silver chain so they cannot be separated. Take the bowl and throw a bowlful of water over the slab. And then you will hear a tumultuous noise, and think that heaven and earth are trembling with the noise. And after the noise there will be a very cold shower—a shower of hailstones—and it will be difficult for you to survive it. And after the shower there will be fine weather. And there will not be one leaf on the tree that the shower will not have carried away. And then a flock of birds will alight on the tree, and you have never heard in your own country such singing as theirs.* And when you are enjoying the song most, you will hear a great groaning and moaning coming towards you along the valley. And with that you will see a knight on a pure black horse, dressed in brocaded silk of pure black, with a banner of pure black linen on his spear. And he will attack you as quickly as he can. If you flee, he will catch up with you; if you wait for him on horseback, he will leave you on foot. And if you do not find trouble there, you will not need to look for it as long as you live."

'I followed the road until I came to the top of the hill, and from there I could see everything as the black-haired man had described to me. And I came to the tree, and I could see the well beneath the tree, and the marble slab beside it, and the silver bowl fastened to the chain. And I took the bowl and threw a bowlful of water over the slab. And at once the noise came, much louder than the black-haired man had said, and after the noise the shower. And I was sure, Cai, that neither man nor beast caught in the shower would escape alive, for not one hailstone would stop for skin or flesh, until it reached the bone. But I turned my horse's crupper to the shower, and placed the point of my shield over my horse's head and mane, and the visor over my own head, and so I weathered the shower.

'And as my life was about to leave my body, the shower stopped. And when I look at the tree, there is not a single leaf on it. And then the weather clears. And then the birds alight on the tree and begin to sing. And I am sure, Cai, that never before nor since have I heard singing like that. And when listening to the birds is at its most enjoyable, a groaning comes along the valley towards me, saying, "Knight," it says, "what do you want of me? What harm have I done to you, that you should do what you have done to me and to my kingdom today? Don't you know that the shower today has left alive in my kingdom neither man nor beast that was out of doors?"

'And with that there appeared a knight on a pure black horse, dressed in brocaded silk of pure black, and a banner of pure black linen on his spear. And I charged him, and though it was a fierce assault it was not long before I was thrown to the ground. And then the knight passed the shaft of his spear through the reins of my horse's bridle, and away he went with the two horses, leaving me there. The black man* did not take me seriously enough even to imprison me; nor did he strip me of my armour.

'I returned along the road I had travelled earlier. And when I came to the clearing, the black-haired man was there; and I confess to you, Cai, that it's surprising I did not melt into a pool of liquid for shame, what with the ridiculing I got from the black-haired man. And that night I came to the castle where I had been the night before. And I received a warmer welcome that night than the night before, and was better fed, and had the conversation that I wanted from men and from women. But no one mentioned anything to me about my journey to the well; nor did I mention it to anyone. And I stayed there that night.

'And when I got up the next morning I found a dark-brown palfrey with a bright red mane on him, as red as lichen, completely harnessed. And after putting on my armour and leaving my blessing there, I came to my own court. And I still have that horse in the stable over there, and between me and God, Cai, I would not exchange it for the best palfrey in the Island of Britain. And God knows, Cai, no one ever before confessed to a story that brought so much discredit on himself; and yet I find it so strange that I have not heard of anyone, before or since, who knows anything about this story, apart from what I have related, and strange that it should be located in the kingdom of the emperor Arthur without anyone else coming across it.'

'Men,' said Owain, 'wouldn't it be good to try and find that place?'

'By the hand of my friend,' said Cai, 'you often say with your tongue what you would not perform in deed.'

'God knows,' said Gwenhwyfar, 'you should be hanged, Cai, for speaking such insulting words to a man like Owain.'

'By the hand of my friend, lady,' said Cai, 'you have given Owain no more praise than I myself.' And with that Arthur woke up, and asked if he had slept at all.

'Yes, lord,' said Owain, 'quite a while.'

'Is it time to go and eat?'

'It is, lord,' said Owain. And then the horn called them to washing, and the emperor and all his retinue went to eat. And when they had finished eating Owain slipped away unnoticed, and came to his lodging and got his horse and his armour ready.

At dawn the next day Owain put on his armour, and mounted his horse, and set out for the remote regions of the world and desolate mountains. Finally he came across the valley that Cynon had told him about, and he was certain that it was the right one. And he travelled along the valley by the side of the river, and he travelled the other side of the river until he came to the plain. And he travelled across the plain until he saw the castle, and he approached the castle. He could see the lads aiming at their knives where Cynon had seen them, and the yellow-haired man who owned the castle standing near them. And when Owain was about to greet the yellow-haired man, the man greeted Owain, and went on to the castle. He could see a chamber in the castle, and when he came to the chamber he could see the maidens in golden chairs, sewing brocaded silk. And Owain thought that they were far more beautiful and attractive than Cynon had described. And they got up to wait on Owain as they had waited on Cynon. And Owain thought his food more impressive than Cynon had said, and halfway through the meal the yellow-haired man asked Owain where he was going. Owain told him everything about his journey—'and I want to fight the knight who guards the well.' The yellow-haired man smiled gently, and it was hard for him to tell Owain about that journey just as it had been hard for him to tell Cynon. Yet he told Owain everything about it, and they went to sleep.

And the next morning Owain found that the maidens had prepared his horse, and he travelled until he reached the clearing where the black-haired man was. Owain thought the black-haired man was far bigger than Cynon had said, and Owain asked the black-haired man for directions, and he gave them. And Owain followed the road, like Cynon, until he came to the green tree. And he could see the well and the slab near the well, and the bowl on it. And Owain took the bowl and threw a bowlful of the water over the slab. And at once, behold, the noise, and after the noise the shower. They were far greater than Cynon had described. And after the shower the sky grew brighter, and when Owain looked at the tree there was not a single leaf on it. And with that, the birds alighted on the tree and began to sing. And when the birds' song was most pleasing to Owain, he could see a knight coming along the valley. And Owain went to meet him and fought him fiercely, and they broke both their lances, and they drew their swords and began to fight. And with that Owain struck the knight a blow through his helmet and mail cap and hood of Burgundian cloth, and through the skin, flesh, and bone until it wounded the brain. And then the Black Knight knew that he had received a mortal blow, and turned his horse's head and fled.

And Owain pursued him, but did not succeed in striking him with his sword though he was not far behind him. And then Owain could see a large, shining castle; they came to the castle gate and the Black Knight was let in, but a portcullis was let down on Owain. And it struck him below the hind-bow of the saddle so that the horse was cut in half, and it went through the rowels of the spurs on Owain's heels; and the portcullis dropped to the ground, with the rowels and part of the horse outside, and Owain and the rest of the horse between the two gates. And the inner gate was closed so that Owain could not escape.

Owain was in a quandary. And while he was like this, he could see through the join in the gate a street opposite him, and a row of houses on either side of the road. And he could see a maiden with yellow curly hair coming to the gate, a band of gold on her head, and wearing a dress of yellow brocaded silk, with boots of speckled leather on her feet. And she asked for the gate to be opened.

'God knows, lady,' said Owain, 'it cannot be opened for you from in here any more than you can rescue me from out there.'

'God knows,' said the maiden, 'it's a great shame that you cannot be rescued; and it would only be right for a woman to help you. God knows I have never seen a better young man for a woman than you. If you had a woman friend, you would be the best friend a woman could have; if you had a mistress, you would be the best lover. And because of that,' she said, 'whatever I can do to rescue you, I will. Take this ring and place it on your finger, and put the stone in your hand, and close your fist around the stone, and as long as you hide it it will hide you too. And when they turn their attention to this place they will come and fetch you to put you to death, because of what happened to the man. And when they fail to see you, they will be angry. And I shall be on the mounting-block over there waiting for you; and you will see me even though I won't see you. Come and put your hand on my shoulder, and then I will know that you have come. And the road I take from there, come with me.' And with that she left Owain.

And Owain did everything the maiden had told him. And then the men from the court came to look for Owain to put him to death. And when they came to look for him they could see nothing except half the horse, and that made them angry. And Owain slipped away from their midst, and came to the maiden and put his hand on her shoulder; and she set off, and Owain with her, until they came to the door of a large, fine upstairs chamber. And the maiden opened the door, and they entered and closed the door.

Owain looked around the chamber; and there was not a single nail in the chamber not painted with a precious colour, and there was not a single panel without a different golden pattern on it. The maiden lit a charcoal fire, and took a silver bowl with water in it, and a towel of fine white linen on her shoulder, and gave Owain the water to wash. And she placed before him a silver table inlaid with gold, with a tablecloth of fine yellow linen on it, and she brought him his dinner. And Owain was certain that he had never seen any kind of food that he did not see there in abundance, except that the service he saw there was better than in any other place ever. And he had never seen anywhere so many wonderful courses of food and drink as there, and there was not one vessel from which he was served that was not of silver or gold. And Owain ate and drank until it was late afternoon.

Suddenly they heard crying in the castle, and Owain asked the maiden, 'What is that wailing?'

'They are anointing the nobleman who owns the castle',* said the maiden.

Owain went to sleep, and the excellent bed she prepared for him of scarlet cloth and ermine and brocaded silk and sendal* and fine linen was fit for Arthur himself. And at midnight they could hear dreadful crying.

'What crying is it this time?' said Owain.

'The nobleman who owns the castle has just died,' said the maiden.

And shortly after dawn they could hear tremendous crying and wailing, and Owain asked the maiden, 'What is the meaning of this wailing?'

'They are taking the body of the nobleman who owns the castle to the church.' And Owain rose and got dressed, and opened a chamber window, and he looked towards the castle. And he could see neither end nor limit to the crowds filling the streets, and they were fully armed, and many women with them on horseback and on foot, and all the clerics of the town chanting. And Owain felt that the sky was ringing because of all the wailing, and the trumpets, and the clerics chanting.

And in the middle of that crowd he could see the bier covered in a sheet of fine white linen, and many wax tapers burning around it. And not one of the men carrying the bier was of lower rank than a powerful baron. Owain was certain that he had never seen a gathering as fine as that, in brocaded silk and damask and sendal. And following that crowd he could see a lady, her yellow hair let down over her shoulders and covered with the blood of many wounds, and she was wearing a dress of yellow brocaded silk, which was torn, and boots of speckled leather on her feet. And it was surprising that the tips of her fingers were not worn away, so violently did she wring her hands together. Owain was certain that he had never seen such a beautiful woman, if she had been in her usual form. And her cries were louder than those of all the men and trumpets in the crowd. And when he saw the woman he was inflamed with love for her until it filled every part of him.

Owain asked the maiden who the lady was.

'God knows,' said the maiden, 'a woman you could say is the most beautiful of women, and the most chaste, and the most generous, and wisest and noblest. She is my mistress, known as the Lady of the Well,* the wife of the man you killed yesterday.'

'God knows,' said Owain, 'she is the woman I love best.'

'God knows,' said the maiden, 'there is no way she loves you, not in the very slightest.'

And with that the maiden got up and lit a charcoal fire, and filled a pot with water and heated it; and took a towel of fine white linen and placed it round Owain's neck, and took a bowl of ivory, and a silver basin, and filled it with the hot water, and washed Owain's head. And then she opened a wooden box and took out a razor with an ivory handle and two grooves of gold in the blade, and she shaved his beard, and dried his head and neck with the towel. And then the maiden set up a table in front of Owain and brought him his dinner. And he was certain that he had never had such a good dinner, nor better service. And when he had finished eating, the maiden made up the bed.

'Come and sleep here,' she said, 'and I shall go courting on your behalf.' And Owain went to sleep. And the maiden closed the chamber door and went to the castle.

And when she got there she found only sadness and sorrow, the countess herself in her chamber, unable to see anyone for grief. And Luned came to her and greeted her, but the countess did not reply. And the maiden lost her temper and said to her, 'What is wrong with you, why won't you talk to anyone today?'

'Luned,' said the countess, 'how can you be so bold, seeing that you didn't come and visit me in my grief? And I made you wealthy. That was wrong of you.'

'God knows,' said Luned, 'I really did think you would have more sense. It would be better for you to start worrying about replacing your husband than wish for something you can never have back.'

'Between me and God,' said the countess, 'I could never replace my lord with any other man in the world.'

'Yes, you could,' said Luned; 'marry someone as good as he, or better.'

'Between me and God,' said the countess, 'if I were not repelled by the thought of putting to death someone I had brought up, I would have you executed for proposing something as disloyal as that to me. And I will certainly have you banished.'

'I am glad', said Luned, 'that your only reason is that I told you what was good for you when you could not see it for yourself. And shame on whichever of us first sends word to the other, whether it is I to beg an invitation of you, or you to invite me.' And with that Luned left.

The countess got up and went to the chamber door after Luned, and coughed loudly. Luned looked back; the countess beckoned to her. And Luned came back to the countess.

'Between me and God,' said the countess to Luned, 'what a temper you have. But since you were telling me what was good for me, explain to me how that could be.'

'I will,' she said. 'You know that your kingdom can be defended only through military might and weapons; you must therefore quickly find someone to defend it.'

'How do I do that?' said the countess.

'I will tell you,' said Luned. 'Unless you can defend the well you cannot defend your kingdom. No one can defend the well but one of Arthur's retinue. So I shall go', said Luned, 'to Arthur's court, and shame on me,' she said, 'if I do not return with a warrior who will defend it as well as or even better than the man who defended it before.'

'That will be difficult,' said the countess, 'but nevertheless go and put your words to the test.' Luned set off as if to go to Arthur's court, but went instead to Owain in the upstairs chamber. And she stayed there with Owain until it was time for her to return from Arthur's court.

Then she got dressed and went to see the countess. And the countess welcomed her.

'Do you have news from Arthur's court?' said the countess.

'The best news I have, lady,' she said, 'is that I have succeeded in my quest. And when do you want to see the lord who has come with me?'

'Bring him to visit me at midday tomorrow,' said the countess, 'and I shall have the town cleared by then.' And she went home.

And at midday the next day Owain put on a tunic and surcoat and cloak of yellow brocaded silk and a wide border of gold thread in the cloak, and boots of speckled leather on his feet with an image of a golden lion fastening them.* And they came to the countess's chamber, and the countess welcomed them. And the countess looked carefully at Owain.

'Luned,' she said, 'this lord doesn't look as if he has been on a journey.'

'What harm is in that, lady?' said Luned.

'Between me and God,' said the countess, 'this is none other than the man who took away my lord's life.'

'All the better for you, lady; had he not been stronger than your lord, then he would not have taken his life. Nothing can be done about that,' she said, 'since it is over and done with.'

'Go home,' said the countess, 'and I shall take advice.'

And the next day the countess had her entire kingdom summoned to one place, and she told them that her earldom was unoccupied, and could be defended only by horse and armour and military prowess: 'So I'm giving you a choice: either one of *you* take me, or let me take a husband from elsewhere to defend the kingdom.' They decided to allow her to take a husband from elsewhere. And then she brought bishops and archbishops to her court to perform the marriage between her and Owain. And the men of the earldom paid homage to Owain, and Owain defended the well with spear and sword. This is how he defended it: whatever knight came there, Owain would overthrow him and ransom him at his full value. And Owain would share that income among his barons and knights, so that no one in the whole world was more loved by his subjects than he. And he stayed thus for three years.

One day as Gwalchmai was out walking with the emperor Arthur, he looked at Arthur and saw that he was sad and distressed. And Gwalchmai was extremely grieved to see Arthur in this state, and asked him, 'Lord,' he said, 'what is wrong with you?'

'Between me and God, Gwalchmai,' said Arthur, 'I miss Owain who has been gone for three years. And if I go a fourth year without seeing him, I will die. And I know for certain that it's because of the tale of Cynon son of Clydno that we have lost Owain.'

'There is no need for you to summon your kingdom on account of that,' said Gwalchmai. 'You and the men of your household can avenge Owain if he has been killed, or free him if he is in prison, and if he is alive, bring him back with you.' And they agreed on what Gwalchmai had said.

Arthur got ready to go and look for Owain, together with the men of his household. There were three thousand of them, not counting retainers, and Cynon son of Clydno their guide. And Arthur came to the castle where Cynon had been, and when they arrived the lads were shooting at their knives in the same place, and the yellow-haired man was standing beside them. And when the yellow-haired man saw Arthur, he greeted him and invited him to stay; and Arthur accepted the invitation and they went into the castle. And although they were a huge crowd, their presence was scarcely noticed in the castle. And the maidens got up to wait on them; and they found fault with every service they had ever been given except the service from these ladies. And the service provided by the grooms that night was as good as that which Arthur would receive in his own court.

The next morning Arthur set out from there with Cynon as his guide, and they came to where the black-haired man was. And Arthur thought the black-haired man was far bigger than he had been told. They came to the top of the hill, and to the plain, as far as the green tree, and until they saw the well and the bowl and the slab. And then Cai came to Arthur, and said, 'My lord,' he said, 'I know the reason for this journey, and I beg you to let me throw the water on the slab and face the first ordeal that comes along.' And Arthur gave him permission.

And Cai threw a bowlful of the water on the slab. And straight after that came the noise, and after the noise the shower. And they had never heard a noise and a shower like that, and the shower killed many of the men who were with Arthur. And when the shower stopped, the sky grew brighter, and when they looked at the tree there was not a single leaf on it. And the birds alighted on the tree, and they were certain that they had never heard a song as delightful as the one the birds sang. And with that they could see a knight on a pure black horse, dressed in brocaded silk of pure black, and travelling at a brisk pace. And Cai took him on and fought with him. And the fighting did not last long; Cai was overthrown. And then the knight set up camp and Arthur and his host set up camp for the night.

When they got up the next day, there was the signal for battle on the black knight's spear. And Cai came to Arthur and said to him, 'Lord,' he said, 'I was unfairly thrown yesterday; will you let me go and fight the knight today?'

'I will,' said Arthur. And Cai made for the knight; but at once he overthrew Cai, and looked at him, and stabbed him in the forehead with the butt of his spear so that Cai's helmet and mail cap and skin and flesh were split to the bone, as wide as the head of the shaft. And Cai returned to his companions. And from there on Arthur's retinue went in turn to fight the knight, until each one had been overthrown by him except Arthur and Gwalchmai. And Arthur put on armour to go and fight the knight.

'My lord,' said Gwalchmai, 'let me go and fight the knight first.' Arthur gave his consent, and Gwalchmai went to fight the knight, with a cloak of brocaded silk covering him and his horse, sent to him by the daughter of the earl of Anjou; because of that, no one from the crowd recognized him. And they attacked each other, and fought that day until nightfall, but neither of them came close to overthrowing the other. And the next day they went to fight with sharp spears. But neither of them overcame the other. And the third day they went to fight, each with strong, stout, sharp spears. And they were fired with rage, and on the stroke of noon they charged, and each one thrust at the other so that the saddle-girths of both horses broke, and each one of them was thrown over his horse's crupper to the ground. And they got up quickly, and drew their swords and pounded each other. And those who saw them like this were certain that they had never seen two men as strong as those, or as splendid; had it been a dark night it would have been bright with the sparks from their weapons. And with that the knight dealt Gwalchmai such a blow that the visor lifted from his face, and the knight realized he was Gwalchmai. Then Owain said, 'Lord Gwalchmai, I did not recognize you because of your cloak—you are my first cousin. Take my sword and my weapons.'

'*You*, Owain, are superior,' said Gwalchmai, 'and victory is yours; so take my sword.' And with that Arthur saw them and came up to them.

'Lord,' said Gwalchmai, 'here is Owain who has defeated me, but he will not take my weapons from me.'

'Lord,' said Owain, 'it was Gwalchmai who defeated me, and he will not take my sword.'

'Give your swords to me,' said Arthur, 'and then neither will have defeated the other.' And Owain threw his arms around the emperor Arthur, and they embraced each other. And then the host came, pressing and rushing towards them to try and see Owain and embrace him, so that men almost died in that crush. That night they all went to their pavilions.

The next day the emperor Arthur asked if he could leave.

'Lord,' said Owain, 'that would not be right. Three years ago I left you, lord, and this place is mine. And from that day to this I have been preparing a feast for you, because I knew you would come to look for me. Come with me to recover from your weariness, you and your men, and bathe yourselves.' And they all went together to the castle of the Lady of the Well, and the feast that had taken three years to prepare was consumed within just three months, and they never had a more pleasant or better feast than that.

And then Arthur asked if he could leave, and he sent messengers to the countess, asking her to allow Owain to accompany him so that the noblemen of the Island of Britain and their ladies could see him for just three months. And the countess gave her consent, but she did not find it easy. And Owain accompanied Arthur to the Island of Britain. Once he had arrived among his people and drinking companions, he stayed for three years instead of the three months.

One day as Owain was eating at table in the emperor Arthur's court in Caerllion ar Wysg, behold, a maiden approaching* on a bay horse with a curly mane that reached the ground; she was dressed in yellow brocaded silk, and the bridle and what could be seen of the saddle were all of gold. And she rode up to Owain and grabbed the ring that was on his finger.

'This', she said, 'is what we do to a deceitful cheat and traitor— shame on your beard!' And she turned her horse's head and away she went. And then Owain remembered his journey, and he grew sad. And when he had finished eating, he went to his lodging; and he was very uneasy that night.

The next morning he got up, and he did not make for Arthur's court but for the remote regions of the world and desolate mountains. And he wandered about like this until all his clothes disintegrated and his body all but gave out and long hair grew all over him; and he would keep company with the wild animals and feed with them until they were used to him. And with that he grew so weak that he could not keep up with them. And he went down from the mountains into the valley, and made for a park, the finest in the world, and a widowed countess owned the park.

One day the countess and her handmaidens went walking beside a lake that was in the park, until they were halfway round. And they could see in the park something in the shape and form of a man, and they were frightened. Even so they approached him, and touched him, and looked at him carefully. They could see his veins throbbing, and he was tossing and turning because of the sun. And the countess returned to the castle, and took a jar of precious ointment and gave it to one of her handmaidens.

'Go,' she said, 'and take this with you, and take that horse and the clothes, and place them beside the man we saw earlier. And rub him with this ointment, over his heart, and if there is life in him, he will get up as a result of this ointment; and watch what he does.' And the maiden set off, and applied all the ointment to him, and left the horse and clothes nearby, and withdrew, and retreated some distance from him, and hid and watched him.

And before long she could see him scratching his arms and getting up, and examining his flesh, and he was ashamed to see how hideous his appearance was. And he saw the horse and clothes nearby, and dragged himself until he reached the clothes and pulled them to him from the saddle, and he put them on, and with difficulty he got on to the horse. And then the maiden made herself known to him, and greeted him. And he was glad to see the maiden, and he asked her what land that was and what place.

'God knows,' said the maiden, 'a widowed countess owns the castle over there, and when her lord and husband died he left her two earldoms, but tonight all she has left is just that one house over there which has not been taken by the young earl, her neighbour, because she would not marry him.'

'That is a sad story,' said Owain. And Owain and the maiden went to the castle, and Owain dismounted at the castle, and the maiden took him to a comfortable chamber, and lit a fire for him and left him there. And the maiden went to the countess and placed the jar in her hand.

'Girl,' said the countess, 'where is all the ointment?'

'It is gone, lady,' she said.

'Girl,' said the countess, 'it is not easy for me to scold you; but it was unfortunate that I spent one hundred and forty pounds worth of precious ointment on a man without knowing who he is. Nevertheless, girl, wait on him so that he has enough of everything.' And the maiden did that, she served him with food and drink and fire and bed and bath until he was well. And the hair dropped off Owain in scaly tufts. That took three months, and his flesh was then whiter than before.

And then one day Owain heard a commotion in the castle, and great preparations, and armour being brought inside. And Owain asked the maiden, 'What is this commotion?' he said.

'The earl I mentioned to you', she said, 'is approaching the castle to try and destroy this lady, and a large host with him.'

And then Owain asked the maiden, 'Does the countess have a horse and armour?'

'Yes,' said the maiden, 'the best in the world.'

'Will you go to the countess and ask if I may borrow the horse and weapons,' said Owain, 'so that I may go and look at the host?'

'I will, gladly,' said the maiden. And the maiden went to the countess and told her everything he had said. Then the countess laughed.

'Between me and God,' she said, 'I shall give him a horse and weapons to keep, and he has never owned a better horse nor better armour. And I am glad that he is going to take them for fear that my enemies will seize them tomorrow against my will. But I don't know what he wants them for.'

And a fine black gascon horse was brought, with a saddle of beechwood on him and enough armour for a man and a horse. And Owain armed himself, and mounted the horse and set off, and two squires with him, complete with horses and armour.

And when they came to the earl's host they could see neither border nor boundary to it. And Owain asked the squires which troop the earl was in.

'In the troop with the four yellow standards over there,' they said. 'There are two in front of him, and two behind.'

'Good,' said Owain, 'go back and wait for me at the castle gate.' And they returned. And Owain rode on between the first two troops until he met the earl. And Owain pulled him from his saddle and placed him between himself and his saddle-bow, and he turned his horse's head towards the castle. And whatever trouble he had, he carried the earl along with him, until he reached the castle gate where the squires were waiting for him. And in they came, and Owain gave the earl as a gift to the countess, and spoke to her like this: 'Here is your payment for the healing ointment I received from you.'

And the host pitched their tents around the castle, and in return for his life the earl gave back to the countess the two earldoms. And in return for his freedom he gave up half his own domain, and all her gold and silver and jewels, and pledges to meet that. And Owain set off, and the countess invited him to stay and all to be his domain, but Owain wanted nothing except to travel the remote and uninhabited regions of the world.

And as he was travelling thus he heard a loud shriek in a forest, and a second, and a third. And he approached, and when he got there he could see a huge cliff in the middle of the forest and a grey rock in the side of the cliff. And there was a cleft in the rock, and a snake in the cleft, and a pure white lion near the snake. And whenever the lion tried to get away, the snake would dart towards him, and then the lion would shriek. Owain drew his sword and approached the rock. And as the snake was coming out of the rock Owain struck it with his sword so it lay in two halves on the ground, and he wiped his sword and continued on his way as before. But he could see the lion following him, playing around him like a greyhound he had reared himself. And they travelled throughout the day until evening.

When it was time for Owain to rest, he dismounted and let his horse graze in a level, wooded meadow. And Owain lit a fire, and by the time he had the fire ready the lion had enough firewood for three nights. And the lion disappeared, but then at once returned with a large, fine roebuck, and he dropped it in front of Owain, and went to lie on the other side of the fire from him. Owain took the roebuck and skinned it, and put chops on spits around the fire, and gave the whole buck apart from that to the lion to feed upon. And as Owain was doing this he heard a loud groaning, and a second, and a third, not far from him. And Owain asked whether it was a human being who was groaning.

'Yes, indeed,' said the creature.

'Who are you?' said Owain.

'God knows,' she said, 'I am Luned, handmaiden to the Lady of the Well.'

'What are you doing there?' said Owain.

'I have been imprisoned,' she said, 'because of a young man who came from the emperor's court to claim the countess as his wife, and he was with her a short time. And he went to visit Arthur's court, but he never returned. And he was the friend I think I loved best in the whole world. Two of the countess's chamberlains made fun of him in front of me and called him a cheat and traitor. And I said that the two of them together could not stand up to him alone. And because of that they imprisoned me in this stone vessel, and said that I would die unless he came to defend me by a certain day. And that day is no later than the day after tomorrow, and I have no one to look for him. He was Owain son of Urien.'

'Are you sure', said Owain, 'that if that young man knew this he would come to defend you?'

'I am certain, between me and God,' she said. And when the chops were cooked through, Owain divided them in half between himself and the maiden, and they ate. And after that they conversed until it was light the next day.

And the next day Owain asked the maiden if there was anywhere he could find food and hospitality that night.

'Yes, lord,' she said. 'Go on over to the ford,' she said, 'and take the road alongside the river, and before long you'll see a great castle with many towers. And the earl who owns that castle is the best man for providing food, and you can stay there tonight.' And no watchman ever guarded his lord as well as the lion guarded Owain the night before.

And then Owain saddled his horse and travelled on through the ford until he saw the castle. And Owain entered the castle and he was given an honourable welcome, and his horse was groomed to perfection and given plenty of food. And the lion went to lie down in the horse's manger, so that no one from the castle dared go near the horse because of the lion. And Owain was certain that he had never seen a place with such good service as that. Yet everyone there was as sad as if death were on each of them. And they went to eat, and the earl sat on one side of Owain, and his only daughter on Owain's other side. And Owain was certain that he had never seen such a beautiful girl. And the lion came to lie between Owain's feet under the table, and he fed it with every dish that he was given. The greatest failing Owain saw there was the men's sadness.

Halfway through the meal the earl welcomed Owain.

'It's high time to be more cheerful,' said Owain.

'God knows, it's not on your account that we're sad, but rather because a matter for sadness and grief has come upon us.'

'What's that?' said Owain.

'I had two sons, and yesterday they went to the mountain to hunt. And there is a monster there, and he kills men and devours them. And he has captured my sons, and tomorrow is the day set between us to hand over this maiden, or else he will kill my sons in front of me. And although he looks like a human, he is as big as a giant.'

'God knows,' said Owain, 'that is a tragedy. And which one of those things will you do?'

'God knows,' said the earl, 'I find it more honourable for him to kill my sons whom he got against my will than to give him my daughter willingly, to be raped and killed.' And they talked of other matters. Owain stayed there that night.

The next morning they heard an incredibly loud noise—it was the huge man coming with the two lads. And the earl wanted to defend the castle from him and abandon his two sons. Owain put on his armour and went out to contend with the man, followed by the lion. And when the man saw Owain in armour, he made for him and fought against him. And the lion fought much better than Owain against the huge man.

'Between me and God,' said the man to Owain, 'it would not be difficult for me to fight you if the animal were not with you.'

And then Owain threw the lion into the castle and closed the gate on him, and returned to fight as before with the huge man. But the lion howled upon hearing Owain's distress, and he climbed up on the earl's hall, and from the hall to the castle wall, and from there jumped until he was with Owain. And the lion struck a blow with its paw on the huge man's shoulder until the paw came out at the fork of his legs, so that all his entrails could be seen slithering out of him. And then the huge man fell down dead. Then Owain gave the earl his two sons; and the earl invited Owain to stay, and Owain did not want that but returned to the meadow where Luned was.

He could see there a huge blazing fire, and two handsome lads with curly auburn hair taking the maiden to throw her into the fire. And Owain asked them what they wanted of the maiden. And they told him their story as the maiden had told it the night before: 'and Owain has failed her, and so we are going to burn her.'

'God knows,' said Owain, 'he was a good knight, and I would be surprised that he did not come to defend her if he knew the maiden needed him. And if you want me to take his place, then I will.'

'We do,' said the lads, 'by Him who made us.' And they went to fight Owain. And he came to grief at the hands of the two lads, and with that the lion came to Owain's assistance, and they overcame the lads. And then they said, 'Lord, we agreed to fight with you alone, and it is harder for us to fight with that animal than with you.'

And then Owain placed the lion where the maiden had been imprisoned, and made a wall of stones at the entrance, and went to fight the men as before. But Owain's strength had not fully recovered, and the two lads were getting the better of him. And the lion was howling all the time because Owain was in trouble. And the lion tore at the wall until he found a way out, and quickly he killed one of the lads, and straightaway he killed the other. And so they saved Luned from being burned. And then Owain, accompanied by Luned, went to the kingdom of the Lady of the Well, and when he left there he took the countess with him to Arthur's court, and she was his wife as long as she lived.

And after that Owain came to the court of the Black Oppressor,* and fought against him, and the lion did not leave Owain until he had overcome the Black Oppressor. And when Owain came to the court of the Black Oppressor he made for the hall, and there he saw twenty-four ladies, the most beautiful that anyone had ever seen, but the clothes they wore were not worth twenty-four pieces of silver. And they were as sad as death itself.

And Owain asked them why they were sad. They said that they were the daughters of earls, and that they had arrived there, each accompanied by the man she loved best. 'And when we came here we were made welcome and were treated properly, and were made drunk. And when we were drunk the fiend who owns this court came and killed all our husbands, and stole our horses and our clothes and our gold and our silver. And the bodies of our husbands are in this very house, and many other bodies besides. And that, lord, is why we are sad. And we are sorry, lord, that you too have come here for fear that you shall come to harm.' And Owain was sad to hear that, and went out to walk.

And he saw a knight approaching him, greeting him with joy and love as if he were his brother. That was the Black Oppressor.

'God knows,' said Owain, 'I have not come here to seek your welcome.'

'God knows,' he replied, 'then you will not get it.'

And at once they rushed at each other, and fought each other fiercely, and Owain got the better of him, and tied him up with his hands behind his back. And the Black Oppressor asked Owain for mercy, and said to him, 'Lord Owain,' he said, 'it was prophesied that you would come here and overthrow me, and you have come and done that. And I lived here as a robber, and my house was a robber's den. But spare me my life, and I will become a hospitaller,* and run this house as a hostel for the weak and the strong as long as I live, for your soul's sake.' And Owain accepted that, and spent that night there.

And the next day he took the twenty-four ladies with their horses and clothes, and all the wealth and jewels they had brought with them, and he travelled, together with the ladies, to Arthur's court.

And Arthur had been happy to see him before when he was lost, but he was even happier now. And any of those women wishing to stay at Arthur's court were allowed to do so, and any wishing to leave were allowed to leave. And Owain remained at Arthur's court from then on as captain of the retinue, and was dear to Arthur, until he went to his own people. They were the Three Hundred Swords of Cenferchyn and the Flight of Ravens.* And wherever Owain went, and they with him, he was victorious.

And this tale is called the tale of the Lady of the Well.

Geraint son of Erbin

I T was Arthur's custom to hold court at Caerllion ar Wysg,* and he held it there continually for seven Easters and five Christmasses. Once upon a time he held court there at Whitsuntide,* for Caerllion was the most accessible place in his territory, by sea and by land. He gathered about him there nine crowned kings who were vassals of his, and with them earls and barons, because these would be his guests at every high feast unless pressure of circumstances prevented them. Whenever he was at Caerllion holding court, thirteen churches would be taken up with his Masses. This is how they would be used: a church for Arthur and his kings and his guests, and the second for Gwenhwyfar and her ladies, and the third would be for the steward* and the petitioners, and the fourth for Odiar the Frank* and the other officers. Nine other churches would be set aside for the nine captains of the bodyguard,* and for Gwalchmai above all, for he, on account of his excellent reputation for military feats and his honourable pedigree, was chief of the nine captains of the bodyguard. And not one church would hold more than we have mentioned above.

Glewlwyd Gafaelfawr was his chief gatekeeper, but he did not concern himself with the office save at one of the three high feasts; but seven men who served under him would share the duties of the year between them, namely Gryn and Penpingion and Llaesgymyn and Gogyfwlch and Gwrddnei Lygaid Cath (who could see as well by night as by day) and Drem son of Dremidydd and Clust son of Clustfeinydd,* who were warriors of Arthur's.

On Whit Tuesday, as the emperor was sitting at his feast, behold, a tall, auburn-haired lad entered, wearing a tunic and surcoat of ribbed brocaded silk, and a gold-hilted sword around his neck, and two low boots of Cordovan leather on his feet. And he came up to Arthur.

'Greetings, lord,' he said.

'May God prosper you,' he replied, 'and God's welcome to you. And do you have any fresh news?'

'I do, lord,' he replied.

'I do not recognize you,' said Arthur.

'Now I'm surprised that you do not recognize me. I am a forester of yours, lord, in the Forest of Dean. Madog is my name, son of Twrgadarn.'

'Tell us your news,' said Arthur.

'I will, lord,' he said. 'A stag have I seen in the forest, and I have never in my life seen anything like it'.

'What is there about it for you never to have seen anything like it?' said Arthur.

'It is pure white, lord, and it does not walk with any other animal out of arrogance and pride because it is so majestic. And it is to ask your advice, lord, that I have come. What is your advice on the matter?'

'I shall do the most appropriate thing,' said Arthur, 'and go and hunt it tomorrow at dawn; and let everyone in the lodgings know that, and Rhyferys (who was a chief huntsman of Arthur's) and Elifri (who was the chief squire), and everyone else.'* They agreed on that, and he sent the squire on ahead.

Then Gwenhwyfar said to Arthur, 'Lord,' she said, 'will you let me go tomorrow and watch and listen to the hunting of the stag which the squire spoke of?'

'I will, gladly,' said Arthur.

'Then I will go,' she said.

Then Gwalchmai said to Arthur, 'Lord,' he said, 'would it not be appropriate for you to allow the one who catches the stag while hunting to cut off its head and give it to anyone he wishes, either to his own lover or the lover of a friend of his, whether it is a mounted man or a man on foot?'*

'I will allow that, gladly,' said Arthur, 'and let the steward take the blame if everyone is not ready in the morning to go hunting.'

They spent the night in moderation, with songs and entertainment and stories and abundant service. And when they all thought it was time to go to sleep, they went to bed.

When dawn broke the next day they woke up, and Arthur called on the servants who were in charge of his bed, namely four squires. This is who they were: Cadyriaith son of Porthor Gandwy, and

Amhren son of Bedwyr, and Amhar son of Arthur, and Gorau son of Custennin.* These men came to Arthur and greeted him and dressed him. And Arthur was surprised that Gwenhwyfar had not woken up and had not turned over in her bed. The men wanted to wake her.

'Do not wake her,' said Arthur, 'since she would rather sleep than go and watch the hunt.'

Then Arthur went on his way, and he could hear two horns sounding, one near the lodging of the chief huntsman and the other near the lodging of the chief squire. And a full complement of all the men came to Arthur, and they travelled towards the forest. And crossing the Wysg, they made for the forest and left the highroad and travelled exposed high land until they came to the forest.

After Arthur had left the court Gwenhwyfar woke up, and she called her maidens and got dressed.

'Maidens,' she said, 'I was given permission last night to go and watch the hunt. One of you go to the stable and have brought all the horses suitable for women to ride.'

One of them went, but only two horses were found in the stable. So Gwenhwyfar and one of the maidens went off on the two horses. They crossed through the Wysg and followed the trail and tracks of the men and the horses. As they were travelling thus they could hear a mighty, ferocious noise. They looked behind them and could see a rider on a willow-grey colt, enormous in size, a young, auburn-haired, bare-legged, noble squire with a gold-hilted sword on his thigh, wearing a tunic and surcoat of brocaded silk with two low boots of Cordovan leather on his feet, and a mantle of blue purple over that with a golden apple in each corner. The horse was tall and stately, swift and lively, with a short steady step. The rider caught up with Gwenhwyfar and greeted her.

'May God be good to you, Geraint,'* she replied, 'and I recognized you when I first saw you just now. And God's welcome to you. And why did you not go hunting with your lord?'

'Because I did not realize that he had left,' he said.

'I, too, was surprised that he could have gone without my knowing,' she said.

'Yes, lady,' he said, 'I was also asleep so did not know what time he left.'

'In my opinion, of all the young men in the whole kingdom you

are the best companion to have as my escort,' she said. 'And we could
have as much pleasure from the hunting as they do, because we shall
hear the horns when they are sounded and hear the hounds when
they are unleashed and begin to bark.'

They came to the edge of the forest and there they stopped.

'We shall hear when the hounds are unleashed from here,' she
said.

Suddenly they heard a noise. They looked in the direction of the
noise, and they could see a dwarf riding a big, sturdy horse, powerful,
wide-nostrilled, ground-devouring, courageous, and in the dwarf's
hand there was a whip. Near the dwarf they could see a woman on a
horse, pale-white and handsome with pace smooth and stately, and
she was dressed in a golden garment of brocaded silk. And close to
her a knight on a great, muddy charger,* with heavy, shining armour
on him and his horse. And they were sure that they had never seen a
man and horse and armour whose size impressed them more, and all
riding close together.

'Geraint,' said Gwenhwyfar, 'do you recognize the large knight
over there?'

'No,' he replied. 'That massive, strange armour allows neither his
face nor his features to be seen.'

'Go, maiden,' said Gwenhwyfar, 'and ask the dwarf who the
knight is.'

The maiden went to meet the dwarf. The dwarf waited for the
maiden when he saw her approaching him. She asked the dwarf,
'Who is the knight?' she said.

'I will not tell you that,' he said.

'Since you are so bad-mannered that you will not tell me that,' she
said, 'I will ask him personally.'

'You will not, by my faith,' he replied.

'Why?' she said.

'Because your status is not that of a person for whom it is proper
to speak with my lord.'

Then the maiden turned her horse's head towards the knight. With
that the dwarf struck her with a whip that was in his hand, across her
face and eyes, so that the blood flowed. Because of the pain from the
blow the maiden returned to Gwenhwyfar, complaining of the pain.

'The dwarf behaved towards you in a very ugly way,' said Geraint.
'I shall go,' said Geraint, 'and find out who the knight is.'

'Go,' said Gwenhwyfar.

Geraint came to the dwarf. He said, 'Who is the knight?'

'I will not tell you,' said the dwarf.

'I will ask it of the knight personally,' he replied.

'You will not, by my faith,' said the dwarf. 'Your status is not high enough to entitle you to speak with my lord.'

'I', said Geraint, 'have spoken with a man who is as good as your lord,' and he turned his horse's head towards the knight. The dwarf overtook him and struck him where he had struck the maiden, until the blood stained the mantle that Geraint was wearing. Geraint placed his hand on the hilt of his sword and turned things over in his head, but decided that it was no revenge for him to kill the dwarf while the armed knight could take him cheaply and without armour. He returned to Gwenhwyfar.

'You behaved wisely and prudently,' she said.

'Lady,' he said, 'I shall go after him again, with your permission, and he will come eventually to a place that is inhabited, where I shall find armour, either on loan or in exchange for surety, so that I shall get the opportunity to test myself against the knight.'

'Go then,' she said, 'but do not go too close to him until you get good armour. And I shall worry a great deal about you,' she said, 'until I get news of you.'

'If I am still alive, by late afternoon tomorrow you shall have news, if I survive,' he said. Then he set off.

They travelled below the court at Caerllion and to the ford over the Wysg, crossed over, and travelled along a fair plain, very high and elevated, until they came to a walled town. At the end of the town they could see a fortress and a castle. They came to the end of the town. As the knight rode through the town the people of every house would rise to their feet to greet and welcome him. When Geraint came to the town he looked in every house to see whether he recognized anyone (but he recognized no one, nor any one him), so that he might secure a favour of armour, either on loan or in exchange for surety. But he could see that every house was full of men and armour and horses, and shields being polished and swords burnished and armour cleaned and horses shod. The knight and the lady and the dwarf made for the castle that was in the town. Everyone in the castle was happy to see them, and on the battlements and on the gates and in every direction people were craning their necks to greet and welcome them.

Geraint stood and looked to see whether the knight would stay in the castle. When he knew for sure that he was staying, Geraint looked around him. And he could see, a short distance from the town, an old, run-down court and in it a dilapidated hall. Since he knew no one in the town he went towards the old court. When he got to the court he could see hardly anything, but he saw an upper storey and a stairway of marble coming down from the upper storey. On the stairway sat a grey-haired man wearing old, worn-out clothes. Geraint stared hard at him for a long time. The grey-haired man said to him, 'Squire,' he said, 'what are you thinking?'

'I am thinking that I don't know where I shall stay tonight,' he said.

'Won't you come in here, lord?' he said, 'and you shall have the best that we can provide for you.'

'I will,' he replied, 'and may God repay you.'

He came forward, and the grey-haired man went to the hall ahead of him. Geraint dismounted in the hall and left his horse there and proceeded to the upper storey, he and the grey-haired man. And in the chamber he could see an elderly woman sitting on a cushion, dressed in old, shabby clothes of brocaded silk. When she had been in the flush of her youth he thought it likely that no one would have seen a fairer woman than she. There was a maiden beside her dressed in a smock and a linen mantle which was quite old and beginning to fall apart. And Geraint was sure that he had never seen any maiden more perfect as regards beauty and elegance and grace than she. The grey-haired man said to the maiden, 'There is no groom for this squire's horse tonight apart from you.'

'I shall give the best service that I can,' she said, 'both to him and to his horse.' The maiden took off the squire's shoes and then gave the horse his fill of straw and corn, and made her way back to the hall and returned to the upstairs chamber. Then the grey-haired man said to the maiden, 'Go to the town,' he said, 'and the best provision you can get of food and drink, have it brought here.'

'I will gladly,' she said. The maiden went to the town, and they conversed while the maiden was in the town. Soon, behold, the maiden returned and a servant with her, and a flagon on his back full of bought mead, and a quarter of a young bullock. In the maiden's hands there was a portion of white bread and a loaf of the finest wheat in her linen mantle. She came to the upstairs chamber.

'I could not find any better provision than this,' she said, 'nor could I get credit for anything better.'

'It will do very well,' said Geraint.

They had the meat boiled, and when their food was ready they went to sit down: Geraint sat between the grey-haired man and his wife, and the maiden waited on them. And they ate and drank.

When they had finished eating, Geraint began to converse with the grey-haired man and asked him if he was the first to own the court he was in.

'It is I, indeed, who built it,' he said, 'and I owned the town with the castle that you have seen.'

'Alas, sir,' said Geraint, 'why did you lose that?'

'I lost a large earldom too,' he replied. 'And this is why I lost it. I had a nephew, a brother's son, and I took possession of his kingdom and my own, and when he came to maturity he laid claim to his kingdom. But I kept his kingdom from him. So what he did was to wage war on me and take everything that was under my control.'

'Lord,' said Geraint, 'will you tell me about the arrival of the knight who came to the town earlier, and the lady and the dwarf, and why there is all the preparation that I saw for repairing weapons?'

'I will,' he said. 'It is preparation for tomorrow, for a game that the young earl plays, namely to set up two forks in a meadow over there, and on the two forks a silver rod. And a sparrowhawk* will be placed on the rod, and a tournament will take place for the sparrowhawk. And the entire crowd of men and horses and weapons that you saw in the town will come to the tournament; and the woman he loves most will accompany each man, and any man who is not accompanied by the woman he loves most will not be allowed to joust for the sparrowhawk. And the knight you saw has won the sparrowhawk for two years, and if he wins it for a third it will be sent to him every year after that, and he himself will not have to come here, and he will be called the Knight of the Sparrowhawk from then on.'

'Lord,' said Geraint, 'what is your advice to me regarding that knight and the insult that I, and a maidservant of Gwenhwyfar, Arthur's wife, received from the dwarf?'—and Geraint told the grey-haired man the story of the insult.

'I cannot easily advise you, since there is neither a woman nor a maiden that you champion in order that you might go and joust with him. Those weapons there that were mine, you could have those, and if you preferred you could also have my horse rather than your own.'

'Lord,' he replied, 'may God repay you. My own horse is good enough for me—I am used to him—together with your armour. And will you not allow me, lord, to champion that maiden over there, your daughter, at the appointed hour tomorrow? And if I survive the tournament my loyalty and love will be hers as long as I live. If I do not survive, the maiden will be as chaste as before.'

'I will agree to that gladly,' said the grey-haired man. 'And since you are decided on that course of action, early tomorrow morning your horse and armour will need to be ready, for it is then that the Knight of the Sparrowhawk will make a proclamation, namely, he will ask the woman he loves best to take the sparrowhawk: "since it becomes you best and you won it," he will say, "a year and two years ago. And if there is anyone who denies it to you today by force, I will defend it for you." And because of that,' said the grey-haired man, 'you must be there at daybreak, and the three of us will be with you.' They decided on that, and at that hour of the night they went to sleep.

Before daybreak they arose and got dressed. By the time it was day all four were standing on the bank of the meadow. Then the Knight of the Sparrowhawk was making the proclamation and asking his lady to take the sparrowhawk.

'Do not take it,' said Geraint. 'There is here a maiden who is fairer and more beautiful and more noble than you, and has a better claim to it.'

'If you consider the sparrowhawk to be hers, come forward to joust with me.'

Geraint went forward to the end of the meadow equipped with a horse, and heavy, rusty, worthless, strange armour about him and his horse. And they charged each other, and broke a set of lances, and broke the second, and broke the third set, and that alternately. And they broke them as they were brought to them. When the earl and his followers could see the Knight of the Sparrowhawk getting the better of Geraint, there would be shouting and rejoicing and jubilation from him and his followers; and the grey-haired man and his wife and his daughter would be sad.

The grey-haired man served Geraint with the lances as he broke them and the dwarf served the Knight of the Sparrowhawk. Then the grey-haired man came to Geraint.

'Lord,' he said, 'here is the lance that was in my hand the day I was ordained a knight, and from that day to this I have not broken it. And there is an excellent head to it—seeing that no lance has availed you.'

Geraint took the lance, thanking the grey-haired man for it. Then, behold, the dwarf came to his lord, he, too, with a lance.

'Here is a lance that is just as good,' said the dwarf, 'and remember that no knight has ever stood up to you as long as this one.'

'Between me and God,' said Geraint, 'unless sudden death takes me, he will be none the better for your help.'

At a distance from him Geraint spurred his horse and charged him, warning him and striking him a blow severe and keen, bloody and bold in the strongest part of his shield so that his shield splits and the armour breaks in the direction of the attack and the girths break so that he and his saddle are thrown over the horse's crupper to the ground.

Quickly Geraint dismounted and became angry and drew his sword and attacked him, furious and fierce. Then the knight got up and drew another sword against Geraint, and they pounded each other on foot with swords until each one's armour was smashed by the other and until the sweat and the blood were taking away the vision from their eyes. When Geraint had the upper hand the grey-haired man and his wife and his daughter would rejoice; and when the knight had the upper hand the earl and his followers would rejoice. When the grey-haired man saw that Geraint had received a mighty, harsh blow, he approached him quickly and said to him, 'Lord,' he said, 'keep in mind the insult you received from the dwarf. And did you not come here to try and avenge your insult, and the insult to Gwenhwyfar, Arthur's wife?'

There came to Geraint's mind the dwarf's words to him, and he summoned up his strength and raised his sword and struck the knight on the top of his head so that all the armour on his head shatters and all the flesh splits, and the skin, and it pierces the bone and the knight falls on his knees. He throws his sword away and asks Geraint for mercy.

'And my false pride and arrogance have prevented me from asking for mercy until it is too late,' he said, 'and unless I receive respite to engage with God for my sins and to talk with a priest, I am none the better for being spared.'

'I shall show you mercy on these conditions,' he said, 'that you go to Gwenhwyfar, Arthur's wife, to make amends to her for the insult done to the maiden by the dwarf—I am satisfied with what I have done to you in return for the insult I received from you and your dwarf—and that you do not dismount from the time you leave here until you are in Gwenhwyfar's presence to make amends to her as will be decided in Arthur's court.'

'I will do that gladly. And who are you?' he said.

'I am Geraint son of Erbin. And you, too, say who you are.'

'I am Edern son of Nudd.'* Then he was thrown on his horse, and he came to Arthur's court and the woman he loved most riding ahead of him, and his dwarf, amidst loud lamentation.

His story so far.*

Then the young earl and his men came to Geraint, and greeted him and invited him along to the castle.

'No,' said Geraint. 'Where I stayed last night I will go tonight.'

'Though you refuse the invitation, you will surely not refuse a plentiful supply of what I can have prepared for you in the place where you stayed last night. And I will arrange a bath for you, and throw off your weariness and exhaustion.'

'God repay you,' said Geraint, 'and I will go to my lodging.' So Geraint went, and Earl Ynywl* and his wife and daughter, and when they came to the upstairs storey the young earl's chamberlains had already arrived at the court with their service and were preparing all the rooms and supplying them with straw and fire. In a short while the bath was ready, and Geraint got into it and his head was washed. Then the young earl arrived, one of forty ordained knights what with his own men and guests from the tournament. Then Geraint got out of the bath and the earl asked him to go to the hall and eat.

'Where is Earl Ynywl,' he replied, 'and his wife and daughter?'

'They are in the upstairs chamber over there,' said the earl's chamberlain, 'putting on the clothes the earl has had brought to them.'

'Let the maiden wear nothing but her smock and linen mantle,' he said, 'until she gets to Arthur's court, so that Gwenhwyfar may dress her in whatever garment she wants'. So the maiden did not get dressed.

Then they all came to the hall and washed and went to sit and eat. This is how they sat: on one side of Geraint sat the young earl and then Earl Ynywl; on the other side of Geraint sat the maiden and her mother; and after that, each one in order of rank. They ate and were served generously, and received an abundance of various dishes. They conversed, and the young earl invited Geraint to be his guest the next day.

'No, between me and God,' said Geraint, 'to Arthur's court I will go tomorrow with this maiden. And for long enough, I believe, Earl Ynywl has been in poverty and misery, and it is mainly to try and increase maintenance for him that I am going.'

'Lord,' said the young earl, 'it is not through any fault of mine that Ynywl is without land.'

'By my faith,' said Geraint, 'he will not be without the land that is his unless sudden death takes me.'

'Lord,' he said, 'as regards any disagreement that has been between me and Ynywl, I will gladly submit to your advice, since you are impartial between us in respect of what is right.'

'I do not ask that he be given anything except what he is entitled to,' said Geraint, 'together with his various losses, from the time he lost his land until today.'

'And I agree to that gladly for your sake,' he said.

'Good,' said Geraint. 'All those here who should be vassals of Ynywl, let them pay him homage here and now.'

All the men did so, and that settlement was agreed upon. His castle and his town and his land were relinquished to Ynywl, and all that he had lost, even the smallest jewel he had lost. Then Ynywl said to Geraint: 'Lord,' he said, 'the maiden you championed on the day of the tournament is ready to do your bidding. And here she is, under your authority.'

'I want nothing,' he replied, 'except that the maiden remain as she is until she comes to Arthur's court. And I want Arthur and Gwenhwyfar to give the maiden away.'* The next day they set out for Arthur's court.

Geraint's adventure so far.

*

Now this is how Arthur hunted the stag: they assigned the hunting stations to the men and the dogs and unleashed the dogs on the stag; and the last dog that was unleashed on it was Arthur's favourite dog—Cafall* was his name. He left all the other dogs behind and caused the stag to turn. On the second turn the stag came to Arthur's hunting station, and Arthur set upon it, and before anyone could kill it Arthur had cut off its head. Then the horn was sounded announcing the kill, and then they all gathered together. Cadyriaith came to Arthur and said to him, 'Lord,' he said, 'Gwenhwyfar is over there, and she is alone except for one maiden.'

'Then ask Gildas son of Caw and all the clerics of the court to proceed with Gwenhwyfar to the court,' said Arthur. That is what they did.

Then they all set off and talked about the stag's head, to whom it should be given, one wanting to give it to the lady he loved best, another to the lady *he* loved best, and each one of the retinue and the knights quarrelling bitterly over the head. Then they arrived at the court. As soon as Arthur and Gwenhwyfar heard the quarrelling over the head, Gwenhwyfar said to Arthur, 'Lord,' she said, 'this is my advice regarding the stag's head: do not give it away until Geraint son of Erbin returns from the quest on which he has gone'—and Gwenhwyfar told Arthur the purpose of the quest.

'Let that be done, gladly,' said Arthur. They agreed on that.

The next day Gwenhwyfar arranged that watchmen were on the battlements ready for Geraint's arrival. After midday they could see a hunchback of a little man on a horse, and behind him a woman or a maiden, so they thought, on a horse, and behind her a big, hunched knight, head hanging, dejected and wearing broken armour in poor condition. Before they were near the gate one of the watchmen came to Gwenhwyfar and told her what sort of people they could see and the kind of state they were in.

'I do not know who they are,' he said.

'I do,' said Gwenhwyfar. 'That is the knight Geraint went after, and I think it likely that he is not coming of his own free will. And if Geraint caught up with him then he has avenged at least the insult to the maiden.'

Then behold, the gatekeeper came to Gwenhwyfar.

'Lady,' he said, 'there is a knight at the gate, and no one has ever seen such a terrible sight to gaze upon as he. He is wearing broken armour, in poor condition, with the colour of his blood more conspicuous on it than its own colour.'

'Do you know who he is?' she said.

'I do,' he replied. 'He is Edern son of Nudd, so he says; I do not know him myself.'

Then Gwenhwyfar went to the gate to meet him, and in he came. Gwenhwyfar would have been distressed to see the state he was in had he not permitted the dwarf to accompany him, who was so ill-mannered.

Then Edern greeted Gwenhwyfar.

'May God prosper you,' she said.

'Lady,' he said, 'greetings to you from Geraint son of Erbin, the best and bravest of men.'

'Did he confront you?' she said.

'Yes,' he said, 'and not to my advantage. But that was not his fault but mine, lady. And greetings to you from Geraint, and in greeting you he has forced me to come here to do your will for the insult done to your maiden by the dwarf. Geraint himself has forgiven the insult done to him because of what he has done to me, for he thought that my life was in danger. But he placed a firm, bold, brave, warrior-like compulsion upon me to come here and make amends with you, lady.'

'Alas, sir, where did he catch up with you?'

'In the place where we were jousting and contending for a sparrowhawk (in the town that is now called Caerdydd). And there was with him by way of retinue only three very poor and shabby-looking people, namely, a very old grey-haired man and an old woman and a beautiful young maiden, all dressed in old, shabby clothes. And because Geraint professed love for the maiden he took part in the tournament for the sparrowhawk, and said that maiden had a better claim to the sparrowhawk than this maiden, who was with me. And because of that we jousted, and he left me, lady, as you now see me.'

'Sir,' she said, 'when do you think Geraint will arrive here?'

'Tomorrow, lady, I think he will arrive, he and the maiden.'

Then Arthur came to him, and he greeted Arthur.

'May God prosper you,' said Arthur. Arthur looked at him for a long time, and was horrified to see him in this state. He thought he recognized him. He asked him, 'Are you Edern son of Nudd?'

'Yes, lord,' he replied, 'having suffered terrible misery and

unbearable wounds'—and he related the entire unhappy incident to
Arthur.

'Yes,' said Arthur, 'it is right for Gwenhwyfar to show you mercy,
from what I hear.'

'Whatever mercy you wish I will show him, lord,' she said, 'since
it is as great a disgrace to you, lord, for me to be insulted as for you
yourself.'

'Here is what is most fitting as regards the matter,' said Arthur.
'Let the man have medical treatment until it is known whether he will
live. And if he lives, let him make amends as judged by the noblemen
of the court. And take sureties on that. But if he dies, the death of a
young man so excellent as Edern will be more than enough as the
insult-price* of a maiden.'

'I am happy with that,' said Gwenhwyfar.

Then Arthur went as guarantor for him, and Caradog son of
Llŷr, and Gwallog son of Llennog, and Owain son of Nudd, and
Gwalchmai,* and many besides that. Arthur had Morgan Tud
summoned to him—he was chief of physicians.*

'Take along Edern son of Nudd and have a room prepared for
him, and prepare medication for him as well as you would prepare
for me if I were wounded. And let no one into his room to disturb
him other than yourself and your apprentices who will be treating
him.'

'I will do that gladly, lord,' said Morgan Tud.

Then the steward said, 'Who should be entrusted, lord, with the
care of the maiden?'

'Gwenhwyfar and her handmaidens,' he replied. The steward
ordered it.

Their story so far.

The next day Geraint came to the court. There were watchmen on
the battlements sent by Gwenhwyfar in case he should arrive without
warning. The watchman came to Gwenhwyfar.

'Lady,' he said, 'I think I can see Geraint and the maiden with him.
And he is on horseback but wearing walking-clothes. The maiden,
on the other hand, I see her very white, and wearing something like a
linen garment.'

'Every woman get ready, and come to meet Geraint, to greet him
and welcome him.'

Gwenhwyfar went to meet Geraint and the maiden. When Geraint came to Gwenhwyfar, he greeted her.

'May God prosper you,' she said, 'and welcome to you. And you have had a purposeful, profitable, successful, and praiseworthy expedition. And may God repay you,' she said, 'for getting justice for me in such a brave manner.'

'Lady,' he said, 'I wanted to obtain justice for you, whatever the cost. And here is the maiden on whose account you have been freed from your disgrace.'

'Yes,' said Gwenhwyfar, 'God's welcome to her. And it is right for me to welcome her.'

They came inside and dismounted, and Geraint went to Arthur and greeted him.

'May God be good to you,' said Arthur, 'and God's welcome to you. And even if Edern son of Nudd has suffered grief and injuries at your hands, you have had a successful expedition.'

'That was not my fault,' said Geraint, 'rather it was due to the arrogance of Edern son of Nudd himself for not giving his name. I would not leave him until I found out who he was, or until one of us should overcome the other.'

'Sir,' said Arthur, 'where is the maiden I hear is under your protection?'

'She has gone with Gwenhwyfar to her room.'

Then Arthur went to see the maiden. And Arthur and his companions and everyone in the entire court welcomed the maiden, and all were certain that if the provision made for the maiden were to match her beauty, they would never see anyone fairer than she.

Arthur gave the maiden to Geraint, and the bond that was made at that time between a couple was made between Geraint and the maiden. The maiden had her choice of all Gwenhwyfar's garments, and whoever saw the maiden in that chosen garment would see a graceful, fair, and beautiful sight. And that day and that night they spent with plenty of songs and an abundance of dishes and different kinds of drink and numerous games. And when they thought it was time to go to sleep, they went to bed. And in the room where Arthur and Gwenhwyfar had their bed, a bed was made for Geraint and Enid.* And that night for the first time they slept together. The next day Arthur satisfied the suppliants on Geraint's behalf with generous gifts.

The maiden became accustomed to the court, and companions of both men and women were brought to her until no maiden in the Island of Britain was better spoken of than her. Then Gwenhwyfar said, 'I did the right thing', she said, 'concerning the stag's head, that it should be given to no one until Geraint returned. And this is a fitting occasion to give it to Enid daughter of Ynywl, the most praiseworthy maiden. And I am sure that there is no one who will begrudge it to her, for there is between her and everyone nothing but love and friendship.'

Everyone applauded that, and Arthur too, and the stag's head was given to Enid. From then on her reputation increased, and because of that she had more companions than before. Meanwhile Geraint from then on loved tournaments and hard combat, and he would return victorious from each one. This lasted for a year and two and three, until his fame had spread over the face of the kingdom.

Once upon a time Arthur was holding court in Caerllion ar Wysg at Whitsuntide. Behold, there came to him messengers, wise and serious, most learned, keen of discourse, and they greeted Arthur.

'May God be good to you,' said Arthur, 'and God's welcome to you. And where do you come from?'

'We come, lord,' they said, 'from Cornwall, and we are messengers from Erbin son of Custennin, your uncle. And our message is for you—and greetings to you from him, just as an uncle should greet his nephew, and as a vassal should greet his lord—to tell you that he is growing heavy and feeble and is drawing near to old age, and that the men whose lands border on his, knowing that, are encroaching upon his boundaries and coveting his land and territory. And he begs you, lord, to let Geraint his son go to him to defend his territory and to get to know its boundaries. And to Geraint he says that he would do better to spend the flower of his youth and the prime of his life defending his own boundaries rather than in unprofitable tournaments, though he is gaining renown in them.'

'Yes,' said Arthur, 'go and change your clothes and take your food and throw off your weariness, and before you leave you shall have an answer.'

They went to eat. Then Arthur considered how it would not be easy for him to let Geraint leave him or his court. Nor was it easy or fair for him to prevent his cousin from defending his kingdom and its boundaries, since his father was unable to defend them. No less was the concern and grief of Gwenhwyfar, and all the women and maidens, for fear that Enid would leave them. They spent that day and that night with an abundance of everything, and Arthur told Geraint of the messengers' arrival from Cornwall, and of the nature of their errand.

'Well, lord,' said Geraint, 'whatever advantage or disadvantage may come to me from that, I will do what you want regarding that errand.'

'Here is my advice to you on the matter,' said Arthur. 'Although your leaving will be painful to me, go and take possession of your kingdom and defend your boundaries. And take with you the men that you want, and those you love best of my faithful followers and of your own friends and fellow knights as escorts.'

'May God repay you, and I will do that,' said Geraint.

'What murmuring do I hear between you?' said Gwenhwyfar. 'Does it concern escorts for Geraint to his country?'

'It does,' said Arthur.

'I too must think of escorts and provisions for my lady,' she said.

'You are right,' said Arthur. That night they went to sleep.

The next day the messengers were allowed to leave, and were told that Geraint would follow after them. The third day after that Geraint set out. These are the men who went with him: Gwalchmai son of Gwyar, and Rhiogonedd son of the king of Ireland, and Ondiaw son of the duke of Burgundy, Gwilym son of the king of France, Hywel son of the king of Brittany, Elifri Anaw Cyrdd, Gwyn son of Tringad, Gorau son of Custennin, Gwair Gwrhyd Fawr, Garannaw son of Golithmer, Peredur son of Efrog, Gwyn Llogell Gwŷr, court justice to Arthur, Dyfyr son of Alun Dyfed, Gwrei Gwalstawd Ieithoedd, Bedwyr son of Bedrawd, Cadwri son of Gwrion, Cai son of Cynyr, Odiar the Frank, court steward to Arthur—* 'and Edern son of Nudd, who I hear is fit to ride, I want him to come with me,' said Geraint.

'But', said Arthur, 'it is not proper for you to take that man with you, although he has recovered, until peace is made between him and Gwenhwyfar.'

'Gwenhwyfar could permit him to come with me in exchange for sureties.'

'If she gives her permission, she must do so freely, without sureties, for the man has enough troubles and tribulations on account of the dwarf insulting the maiden.'

'I agree,' said Gwenhwyfar, 'whatever you and Geraint deem to be right in this matter I shall do gladly, lord.' Then she allowed Edern to go freely; and plenty more went as Geraint's escorts.

They set off and travelled towards the Hafren, the finest retinue that anyone had ever seen. On the far side of the Hafren were the noblemen of Erbin son of Custennin, led by his foster-father, receiving Geraint gladly, and many of the women of the court sent by his mother to meet Enid daughter of Ynywl, his wife. And all the court and the entire kingdom felt great joy and happiness at meeting Geraint, so much did they love him, and so great the fame he had won since he had left them, and because he was intent on coming to take over his own kingdom and to defend its boundaries. They came to the court, where there was a splendid, abundant profusion of various dishes, and plenty of drink and generous service and all kinds of songs and games. In Geraint's honour all the noblemen of the kingdom were invited that night to meet him. They spent that day and that night relaxing in moderation. Early the next day Erbin got up and summoned Geraint to him, and the noblemen who had escorted him; and he said to Geraint, 'I am a man heavy with age,' he said, 'and while I was able to maintain the kingdom for you and for myself, I did so. But you are a young man, and in the prime of life and flower of youth. *You* must maintain your kingdom now.'

'Well,' said Geraint, 'if it were my choice, you would not be placing control of your kingdom into my hands at this moment, nor would you have taken me from Arthur's court just yet.'

'I am now placing control into your hands, and receive also the homage of your men today.'

Then Gwalchmai said, 'It is best for you to satisfy the suitors today, and receive your kingdom's homage tomorrow.'

Then the suitors were summoned to one place; and Cadyriaith came to them to consider their intention and ask each one of them what he wanted. And Arthur's retinue began to give gifts. And immediately the men of Cornwall came and they too gave. And none of them gave for long, such was the haste of each one of them to give. Of those who came there to ask for gifts, not one left there without getting what he wanted. And that day and that night they spent relaxing in moderation.

Early the next day Erbin asked Geraint to send messengers to his men to ask them whether it was convenient for him to come and receive their homage, and whether they felt angry or hurt because of anything they had against him. Then Geraint sent messengers to the men of Cornwall to ask them that, and they replied that they felt, each one of them, only sheer joy and honour at Geraint's coming to receive their homage. Then he received the homage of all those present. And there, together, they spent the third night. The next day, Arthur's retinue asked permission to depart.

'It is too soon for you to depart yet. Stay with me until I have finished receiving the homage of all my noblemen who intend coming to me.'

They stayed until he had done that, and they set out for Arthur's court. Then Geraint went to escort them, both he and Enid, as far as Dynganwyr, and then they parted. Then Ondiaw son of the duke of Burgundy said to Geraint, 'First travel the far ends of your kingdom,' he said, 'and examine your kingdom's boundaries thoroughly and keenly, and if anxiety gets the better of you, tell your companions.'

'May God repay you,' he said, 'and I will do that.' Then Geraint made for the far ends of his kingdom, and skilful guides went with him from among the noblemen of his kingdom, and he kept in mind the furthest boundary that he was shown.

As had been his custom in Arthur's court, Geraint went to tournaments, and became known to the bravest and strongest men until he was renowned in that region as in the place he was before, and until he had made his court and his companions and his noblemen wealthy with the best horses and the best armour and the best and most exceptional golden jewels. He did not desist until his fame had spread over the face of the kingdom. When he saw that, he began to enjoy relaxation and leisure—for there was no one worth fighting— and making love to his wife and being at peace in his court with songs and entertainment, and he settled down to that for a while. But then he began to enjoy staying in his chamber alone with his wife so that nothing else pleased him, until he was losing the affection of his noblemen as well as his hunting and his pleasure, and the affection of all the company at court, until there was murmuring and mocking in secret by the court household because he was so completely deserting their company for the love of a woman. Those words reached Erbin; and when Erbin heard them he told Enid, and he asked her whether it was she who was causing this in Geraint, and encouraging him to abandon his household and company.

'Not I, by my confession to God,' she said, 'and there is nothing I hate more than that.' But she did not know what to do for it was not easy for her to disclose that to Geraint. Nor was it any easier for her to listen to what she heard without warning Geraint about it. And so she became extremely anxious.

One morning in the summer they were in bed (he on the outer edge, and Enid had not slept) in a chamber of glass, and the sun shining on the bed; and the bedclothes had slipped off his chest and arms, and he was asleep. She gazed at this handsome and wonderful sight, and said, 'Woe is me,' she said, 'if it is on my account that these arms and chest are losing the fame and prowess they once possessed.'

With that, her tears streamed down until they fell on his chest. And that was one of the things that woke him up, together with the words she had just spoken. And a different thought disturbed him, that it was not out of concern for him that she had spoken those words, but because she was contemplating love for another man instead of him and longed to be alone, without him. Then Geraint's mind became disturbed, and he called on one of his squires who came to him.

'See to it', he said, 'that my horse and armour are prepared quickly, and that they are ready. And get up,' he said to Enid, 'and get dressed, and see to it that your horse is prepared, and bring with you the worst dress that you own, to go riding. And shame on me,' he said, 'if you return until you find out whether I have lost my strength as completely as you claim, and further, if it will be as easy for you as you hoped to seek a meeting alone with the one you were thinking of.' Then she got up and put on a simple dress.

'I do not know what you are thinking, lord,' she said.

'You shall not know for now,' he said. Then Geraint went to visit Erbin.

'Lord,' he said, 'I'm going on a quest, and I don't know when I shall return. Look after your kingdom, sir, until I come back.'

'I will,' said Erbin, 'but I am surprised that you are leaving so suddenly. And who is going with you, since you are not a man to travel the land of England alone?'

'No one is coming with me save one other person.'

'Now may God guide you, son,' said Erbin, 'and many a man has a score to settle with you in England.'

Geraint came to where his horse was, and his horse was fully equipped with foreign, heavy, shining armour. He ordered Enid to get up on her horse and ride ahead and keep a good lead, 'and whatever you see or hear about me,' he said, 'do not turn back. And unless I speak to you, do not utter a single word.'

They went on their way, and it was not the most pleasant and most frequented road that he chose to travel, but the wildest road and the one most likely to have thieves and robbers and venomous beasts on it. They came to the highroad and followed it, and they could see a great forest ahead of them, and they went towards the forest. And they could see four armed knights coming out of the forest. The knights looked at them and one of the knights said, 'This is a good place for us to take the two horses over there and the armour and the woman too,' he said. 'And we will get those easily as far as that solitary, downcast, melancholy, listless knight is concerned.'

Enid heard their conversation. And she did not know what she should do for fear of Geraint, whether she should mention it or keep quiet.

'God's vengeance on me,' she said, 'I would prefer to die at Geraint's hands than anyone else's, and although he may kill me, I will tell him for fear of seeing him die in a hideous way.' She waited for Geraint until he was close to her.

'Lord,' she said, 'can you hear what those men are saying about you?' He raised his face and looked at her angrily.

'You had only to obey the order you were given, which was to keep quiet. Your concern is nothing to me, neither is your warning. And though you wish to see me killed and destroyed by those men over there, I am not at all afraid.'

With that, their leader couched his lance and charged at Geraint, and he received him, but not like a weakling. He let the thrust go past, and attacked the knight in the centre of his shield so that his shield splits and the armour breaks and the shaft goes a good fore-arm's length into him and he is thrown the length of Geraint's lance over his horse's crupper to the ground. The second knight attacked him angrily for having killed his companion. With one blow Geraint overthrew him and killed him like the other. And the third attacked him and likewise did he kill him. And likewise, too, did he kill the fourth. The maiden was sad and sorrowful* to see that. Geraint dismounted and stripped the armour from the dead men and placed it on their saddles. He tied the horses together by their bridles, and mounted his horse.

'Do you see what you must do?' he said. 'Take the four horses and drive them in front of you, and travel on ahead as I ordered you earlier. And do not utter a single word to me until I speak to you. By my confession to God,' he said, 'if you will not do that, you shall not go unpunished.'

'I will do my best, lord, to obey you,' she said.

They travelled on to a forest. And they left the forest and came to a great plain. In the middle of the plain there was a bushy-topped, tangled thicket, and from that they could see three knights coming towards them, fully equipped with horses, and wearing full-length armour, as did their horses. The maiden watched them closely. When they came nearer, she could hear their conversation: 'This is a lucky windfall for us,' they said, 'four horses and four suits of armour with no effort at all. And as far as that drooping, dejected knight over there is concerned we shall get them cheaply, and the maiden, too, will be ours.'

'That is true,' Enid said; 'the man is worn out from fighting with the men just now. God's vengeance on me unless I warn him,' she said. The maiden waited for Geraint until he was close to her.

'Lord,' she said, 'can't you hear what the men over there are saying about you?'

'What is that?' he said.

'They are saying amongst themselves that they will get this booty cheaply.'

'Between me and God,' he said, 'more tiresome to me than the men's words is the fact that you will not keep quiet for me, nor do as I tell you.'

'Lord,' she said, 'I did it to prevent your being taken by surprise.'

'Be quiet from now on, your concern is nothing to me.'

With that, one of the knights couched his lance and set upon Geraint and attacked him effectively, so he thought. But Geraint received the blow nonchalantly and deflected it, and attacked him and thrust at his middle, and what with the impact of man and horse, his armour was of no use at all, so that the head of the lance and part of the shaft came out through him and he, too, was thrown the length of his arm and his shaft over his horse's crupper to the ground. The other two knights came in their turn, and their attack was no better than the other. The maiden, standing and looking at that, was on the one hand anxious, for she supposed Geraint would be wounded as he fought with the men, but on the other hand she was joyful to see him triumph. Then Geraint dismounted and stripped the suits of armour from the dead men and placed them on their saddles and tied the horses together by their bridles, so that he then had seven horses in all. And he mounted his own horse, and ordered the maiden to drive the horses, 'and it is no use my telling you to be quiet,' he said, 'because you will not obey me.'

'I will, lord, as far as I can,' she said, 'except that I cannot hide from you the horrible hateful words that I hear about you, lord, from bands of strangers that travel the wilderness, such as those.'

'Between me and God,' he said, 'your concern is nothing to me. And from now on be quiet.'

'I will, lord, as far as I can.' The maiden rode on and the horses in front of her, and she kept her distance.

From the thicket which was mentioned above just now, they crossed open land, lofty and fair, level and pleasant and prominent. Some distance from them they could see a forest, and apart from seeing the edge closest to them, they could see after that neither border nor boundary to the forest. And they approached it. Coming from the forest they could see five knights, eager and valiant, courageous and powerful, on chargers sturdy and stocky, big-boned, ground-devouring, wide-nostrilled and mettlesome, and plenty of armour on the men and the horses. When they had got closer, Enid could hear the knights' conversation: 'This is a lucky windfall for us, cheaply and with no effort,' they said; 'all these horses and suits of armour will be ours, and the woman too, as far as that solitary, spiritless, sluggish, sorrowful knight over there is concerned.'

The maiden was very worried at hearing the men's words, so that she did not know what in the world to do. But in the end she decided to warn Geraint. And she turned her horse's head in his direction.

'Lord,' she said, 'if you had heard the conversation of those knights over there, as I have, you would be more worried than you are.'

Geraint gave an angry, sarcastic, horrible, hateful laugh and said, 'I hear you going against everything I told you not to do,' he said, 'but you may yet live to regret it.'

Then, behold, her husband attacked them, and Geraint, triumph-
ant and jubilant, overcame all five men. And he placed the five suits
of armour on the five saddles and tied the twelve horses together by
their bridles. And he entrusted them to Enid.

'And I do not know what is the good of giving you orders,' he said,
'but this once, as a warning to you, I will do so.' The maiden went on
her way to the forest, and kept her distance as Geraint had ordered
her. And had it not been for his anger, he would have felt sad to see
such an excellent maiden having such trouble with the horses.

They made for the forest, and deep was the forest and vast. And
night came upon them in the forest.

'Maiden,' he said, 'there is no point in us trying to continue.'

'I agree, lord,' she said. 'We will do whatever you want.'

'It is best for us to turn off into the forest to rest and wait for
daylight before we proceed,' he said.

'Very well, let us do that,' she said. And that is what they did.
He dismounted and lifted her to the ground.

'I am so tired that I cannot help falling asleep. And you watch over
the horses, and don't go to sleep.'

'I will, lord,' she said. And he slept in his armour, and passed the
night away; and in that season the night was not long.

When she saw the dawn of day showing its light, she looked round
to see whether he was awake. And at that moment he was waking up.

'Lord,' she said, 'I should have liked to wake you some time ago.'
He said nothing to her, annoyed because he had not asked her to speak.
He got up and said to her, 'Take the horses,' he said, 'and go on your
way, and keep your distance as you did yesterday.'

Some way into the day they left the forest and came to clear, open
country, and there were meadows to one side of them, and reapers
mowing hay. And they came to a river ahead of them, and the horses
bent down and drank the water, and they climbed from the river up a
very high hill. There they met a very slender young lad with a towel
round his neck—and they could see a bundle in the towel, but did not
know what it was—and a small blue pitcher in his hand, with a cup
over the mouth of the jug. The lad greeted Geraint.

'God prosper you,' said Geraint, 'and where do you come from?'

'I come from the town there ahead of you,' he replied. 'Lord,' he
said, 'do you mind my asking where you come from?'

'No,' he replied, 'I have come through the forest over there.'

'You didn't come through the forest today?'

'No,' he replied, 'I stayed in the forest last night.'

'I am sure that you weren't comfortable there last night,' he replied, 'and that you had neither food nor drink.'

'No I did not, between me and God,' he replied.

'Will you take my advice,' said the lad, 'and accept a meal from me?'

'What sort of meal?' he replied.

'A breakfast which I was taking to the reapers over there, namely bread and meat and wine. And if you wish, sir, they shall get nothing.'

'Very well,' he replied, 'and may God repay you.'

Geraint dismounted, and the lad lifted the maiden to the ground. They washed and had their meal, and the lad sliced the bread and gave them drink and waited on them thoroughly. When they had finished, the lad got up and said to Geraint, 'Lord, with your permission, I shall go and fetch food for the reapers.'

'Go to the town first,' said Geraint, 'and get lodgings for me in the best place you know, and the most spacious for the horses. And take any horse you want,' he said, 'together with its armour, as payment for your service and your gift.'

'May God repay you,' said the lad, 'and that would be payment enough for a service greater than the one I did to you.'

The lad went to the town, and got the best and most comfortable lodgings he knew of in the town. Then he went to the court with his horse and armour. He came to the earl and told him the whole story.

'And I, lord, will go and meet the young knight to show him his lodging,' he said.

'Go gladly,' replied the earl, 'and he is very welcome to stay here, with pleasure, if that is what he wants.'

The lad went to meet Geraint and told him that he would be made very welcome by the earl at his own court. But he wanted only to go to his own lodging. He got a comfortable room with plenty of straw and bedclothes, and a spacious, comfortable place for his horses, and the lad ensured that they had plenty of provisions. When they had taken off their travelling-clothes, Geraint said to Enid, 'Go to the far end of the chamber,' he said, 'and do not come to this end of the house. And call the woman of the house to you, if you wish.'

'I will do as you say, lord,' she said. Then the man of the house came to Geraint, and greeted him and made him welcome.

'Lord,' he said, 'have you eaten your dinner?'

'I have,' he replied.

Then the lad said to him, 'Do you want drink or anything else before I go and see the earl?'

'Indeed I do,' he replied. Then the lad went into the town and brought them some drink. And they drank. Shortly after that Geraint said, 'I cannot stay awake,' he said.

'Fine,' said the lad, 'while you sleep, I shall go and see the earl.'

'Go, gladly,' he replied, 'and return here at the hour I ordered you to come.' Geraint slept, and Enid slept.

The lad went to the earl, and the earl asked him where the knight's lodging was. He told him.

'And I must go now and wait on him,' he said.

'Go,' he replied, 'and greet him from me, and tell him I will come and see him soon.'

'I will,' he replied. The lad arrived when it was time for them to wake up. They got up and walked around. When it was time for them to eat, they did so, and the lad waited on them. Geraint asked the man of the house if he had companions he wished to invite to join him.

'I do,' he replied.

'Then bring them here to have their fill, at my expense, of the best that can be bought in the town.'

The best men known to the host were brought there to have their fill at Geraint's expense.

Then, behold, the earl arrived with eleven ordained knights to visit Geraint. Geraint got up and greeted him.

'God prosper you,' said the earl. They went to sit, each one according to his rank. And the earl conversed with Geraint, and asked him what was his business.

'I am just seeing what chance brings,' he said, 'and taking part in whatever adventures I like.'

The earl looked intently and closely at Enid, and he was sure that he had never seen a more beautiful maiden, nor a more splendid one, and he set his heart and mind on her. He asked Geraint, 'May I have your permission to go to that maiden over there and talk to her? It seems to me that she is estranged from you.'

'Yes, with pleasure,' he said.

He went to the maiden and said to her, 'Maiden,' he said, 'this journey with that man cannot be pleasant for you.'

'I do not find it unpleasant, for all that, travelling the road he travels.'

'You do not have servants or maidservants to wait on you.'

'Well,' she said, 'I prefer to follow that man than to have servants and maidservants.'

'I have a better prospect,' he replied; 'I shall give you my earldom if you come and live with me.'

'No, between me and God,' she said. 'I pledged myself to that man first, and I will not break my promise to him.'

'You are making a mistake,' he replied. 'If I kill that man, I will have you for as long as I want, and when I want you no longer I will turn you away. But if you do this for me of your own free will, there will be an unbroken, everlasting agreement between us as long as we live.'

She thought about what he had said and as a result she decided to give him some encouragement in what he had asked.

'This is what is best for you, lord,' she said. 'Lest I be accused of great infidelity, come here tomorrow and carry me off as if I knew nothing about it.'

'I will do that,' he said. Then he got up, and took his leave and departed, he and his men. At the time she told Geraint nothing of the man's conversation with her, lest he should become angry or concerned, or distressed.

In due time they went to sleep. At the beginning of the night she slept a little. But at midnight she woke up and prepared all of Geraint's armour so that it was ready to wear. And, fearful and frightened, she went to the edge of Geraint's bed, and quietly and calmly said to him, 'Lord,' she said, 'wake up and get dressed; this is the conversation the earl had with me, lord, and these are his intentions regarding me,' she said, and she repeated the whole conversation to Geraint. And although he was angry with her, he accepted the warning and armed himself. When she had lit a candle as a light for him while dressing, 'Leave the candle there,' he said, 'and tell the man of the house to come here.'

She went, and the man of the house came to him. Then Geraint asked him, 'About how much do I owe you?'

'I think you owe me very little, lord,' he said.

'Whatever I owe you now, take the eleven horses and the eleven suits of armour.'

'May God repay you, lord,' he said, 'but I have not spent the value of one suit of armour on you.'

'Why bother about that?' he said. 'You will be all the richer. Sir,' he said, 'will you come and guide me out of the town?'

'I will,' he replied, 'gladly. And in what direction are you thinking of going?'

'I want to go in the opposite direction from the one I entered the town.'

The man from the lodging escorted him until he considered he had gone far enough, and then Geraint told the maiden to keep her distance in front, and she did so and went on ahead, and the towns-man returned home. He had scarcely entered the house when, behold, the loudest disturbance that anyone had heard descended upon the house. When he looked outside, behold, he could see eighty knights surrounding the house, fully armed, and the Dun Earl* was at their head.

'Where is the knight who was here?' said the earl.

'By your hand,' he said, 'he is some distance away, and he left here a while ago.'

'You scoundrel, why did you let him go without telling me?' he said.

'Lord,' he replied, 'you did not put him in my care; had you done so, I would not have let him go.'

'In which direction do you think he went?' he said.

'I don't know,' he replied, 'except that he went down the main street.'

They turned their horses' heads to the high street, and saw the horses' tracks, and they followed the tracks, and came to a wide highroad. When the maiden saw daybreak she looked behind her, and she could see behind her haze and dense mist, and it was coming nearer and nearer. And she was worried about that, and presumed that the earl and his men were coming after them. Then she saw a knight emerging from the mist.

'By my faith,' she said, 'I shall warn him though he might kill me. I would prefer to be killed by him than to see him killed without warning. Lord,' she said, 'don't you see the man coming for you, and many other men with him?'

'I do,' he replied, 'and however much you are ordered to hold your tongue, you will never be quiet. Your warning means nothing to me; and do not talk to me.'

He turned on the knight, and at the first thrust threw him to the ground under his horse's feet. And for as long as one of the eighty knights remained, at the first thrust he threw each one of them. And they came at him from best to next best, apart from the earl. And last of all the earl came at him, and broke a lance, and a second. Geraint turned on him and struck with a spear in the centre of his shield, so that his shield splits and all the armour breaks at that point, and he is thrown over his horse's crupper to the ground, and is in danger of his life.

Geraint approached him, and because of the noise of the horse the earl gained consciousness.

'Lord,' he said to Geraint, 'your mercy!' And Geraint showed him mercy. And what with the hardness of the ground where the men were thrown, and the violence of the blows they received, not one of the men left Geraint without a deadly painful, aching-hurtful, mighty-bruising fall.

Geraint proceeded along the highroad he was travelling, and the maiden kept her distance. And nearby they could see the fairest valley that anyone had ever seen, and a wide river along the valley. And they could see a bridge over the river, and the highroad coming to the bridge, and above the bridge on the other side of the river they could see the fairest walled town that anyone had ever seen. As he made for the bridge, he could see a man approaching him through a small patch of thick brushwood on a huge, tall horse, even-paced, high-spirited but manageable.

'Knight,' said Geraint, 'where do you come from?'

'I come from the valley below,' he replied.

'Sir,' said Geraint, 'will you tell me who owns this fair valley and the walled town over there?'

'I will, gladly,' he replied. 'The French and the English call him *Gwiffred Petit*, but the Welsh call him *Y Brenin Bychan*.'*

'Shall I go to that bridge over there,' said Geraint, 'or to the lower highroad below the town?'

'Do not go on to his land on the other side of the bridge,' said the knight, 'unless you wish to fight him, for it is his custom to fight every knight that comes on to his land.'

'Between me and God,' said Geraint, 'I shall go my own way despite him.'

'I think it most likely,' said the knight, 'that if you do that now you will be shamed and humiliated, fiercely, with courage and fury.'

Geraint proceeded along the road as was his intention before, and it was not the road that led to the town from the bridge that Geraint took, but the road that made for the ridge of the rough land, lofty, elevated, with a wide outlook. As he was travelling like this, he could see a knight following him on a sturdy, strong charger, bold-paced and wide-hoofed and broad-chested. And he had never seen a man smaller than the one he saw on the horse, and plenty of armour on him and his horse. When he caught up with Geraint, he said to him, 'Tell me, sir,' he said, 'was it because of ignorance or arrogance that you were seeking to take away my prerogative and break my special custom?'

'No,' said Geraint, 'I did not know that the road was restricted to anyone.'

'Since you were unaware,' he replied, 'come with me to my court to make amends.'

'No, I will not, by my faith,' he replied. 'I would not go to your lord's court unless Arthur were your lord.'

'Now by Arthur's hand,' he said, 'I insist on having recompense from you, or else you will cause me great distress.'

Immediately they charged at each other, and a squire of his came to supply him with lances as they broke. And each dealt the other hard, painful blows, until their shields lost all their colour. Geraint found fighting him to be unpleasant, because he was so small and it was so difficult to aim at him, and the blows he dealt were so severe. But they did not tire of it until the horses fell to their knees. At last Geraint threw him head-first to the ground. And then they fought on foot, and each dealt the other blows—fast and furious, bold and bitter, powerful and painful—and they pierced their helmets, and broke the mail caps, and shattered the armour until their eyes were losing their sight because of the sweat and blood. Finally Geraint became enraged and summoned up his strength and, furious and valiant, swift and ardent, bloody and resolute, he raised his sword and struck him on top of his head, a deadly painful, poisonous-piercing, violent-bitter blow, so that all the head armour is broken, and the skin and the flesh, and there is a wound to the bone, and Y Brenin Bychan's sword is thrown out of his hand to the far end of the open ground, away from him. Then in God's name he begged for Geraint's protection and mercy.

'You shall have mercy,' said Geraint, '—though your behaviour was rude and you were overbearing—on condition that you become my companion, and do not disagree with me a second time, and if you hear that I am in distress, you will intervene.'

'You shall have that, lord, gladly.' He took his oath on that.

'And you, lord,' he said, 'will you come with me to my court over there to throw off your weariness and fatigue?'

'No I will not, between me and God,' he replied.

Then Gwiffred Petit looked over at Enid, and he was distressed to see so much pain in so noble a lady. Then he said to Geraint, 'Lord,' he said, 'you are wrong not to take rest and relaxation. And if you encounter adversity in that condition, it will not be easy for you to overcome it.'

Geraint wanted nothing but to go on his way, and he mounted his horse, bleeding and uncomfortable. And the maiden kept her distance.

They travelled towards a forest which they could see some way from them. And it was very hot, and because of the sweat and the blood, the armour was sticking to his flesh. When they got to the forest, he stood beneath a tree to shelter from the heat, and he remembered the pain then more so than when he had first received it. And the maiden stood under another tree. Suddenly they could hear hunting-horns and a commotion, due to Arthur and his host dismounting in the forest. Geraint pondered which route he should take to avoid them. Then, behold, a man on foot caught sight of him. He was the steward's servant, and he came to the steward, and told him what sort of a man he had seen in the forest. The steward then had his horse saddled and took his spear and shield and came to where Geraint was.

'Knight,' he said, 'what are you doing there?'

'Standing under a shady tree and avoiding the heat and the sun.'

'Where are you going, and who are you?'

'I am just looking for adventures and going wherever I please.'

'Well,' said Cai, 'come with me to see Arthur who is close by.'

'I will not, between me and God,' replied Geraint.

'You will be forced to come,' said Cai.

Geraint recognized Cai, but Cai did not recognize Geraint. And

Cai attacked him as best he could. Geraint became angry, and with the shaft of his spear he struck him until he fell head-first to the ground. And he had no wish to do him more harm than that.

Frantic and fearful, Cai got up and mounted his horse and came to his lodging. From there he wandered to Gwalchmai's tent.

'Sir,' he said to Gwalchmai, 'I heard from one of the servants that a wounded knight has been seen in the forest over there, wearing armour that's in poor condition. And if you do what is right, you would go and see whether that is so.'

'I do not mind going,' said Gwalchmai.

'Then take your horse,' said Cai, 'and some of your armour. I have heard that that he is none too polite to those who come his way.' Gwalchmai took his spear and his shield and mounted his horse and came to where Geraint was.

'Knight,' he said, 'where are you going?'

'Going about my business and looking for adventures.'

'Will you tell me who you are, or will you come and see Arthur, who is close by?'

'I will not tell you my name and I will not go and see Arthur,' he said. And he recognized Gwalchmai, but Gwalchmai did not recognize him.

'It will never be said of me,' said Gwalchmai, 'that I let you get away without finding out who you are.' And he attacked him with a spear and struck him on his shield so that the spear was shattered and broken, and the horses forehead to forehead. Then he looked closely at him and recognized him.

'Oh! Geraint,' he said, 'is it you?'

'I am not Geraint,' he said.

'Geraint, between me and God,' he replied, 'and this is a sorry, ill-advised state of affairs.' He looked around him and caught sight of Enid, and greeted her and was glad to see her.

'Geraint,' said Gwalchmai, 'come and see Arthur: he is your lord and your cousin.'

'I will not,' he replied. 'I am in no state to go and see anyone.'

Then, behold, one of the squires came after Gwalchmai to seek news. Gwalchmai sent him to tell Arthur that Geraint was there, wounded, and would not come to see him, and that it was pitiful to see the state he was in (and that without Geraint knowing, in a whisper between him and the squire).

'And ask Arthur,' he said, 'to move his tent closer to the road, for he won't come to see him of his own free will, and it won't be easy to force him in his present state.'

The squire came to Arthur, and told him that, and he moved his tent to the side of the road. Then the maiden's heart rejoiced. Gwalchmai enticed Geraint along the road to where Arthur was encamped, and where his squires were pitching a tent at the side of the road.

'Lord,' said Geraint, 'greetings.'

'May God prosper you,' said Arthur, 'and who are you?'

'This is Geraint,' said Gwalchmai, 'and by choice he would not have come to see you today.'

'Well,' said Arthur, 'he is ill-advised.'

Then Enid came to where Arthur was and greeted him.

'May God prosper you,' said Arthur. 'Let someone help her dismount.' One of the squires did so.

'Oh! Enid,' he said, 'what sort of journey is this?'

'I do not know, lord,' she said, 'except that I must travel any road he travels.'

'Lord,' said Geraint, 'we shall be on our way, with your permission.'

'Where will you go?' said Arthur. 'You cannot go now unless you want to go to your death.'

'He would not allow me to invite him to stay,' said Gwalchmai.

'He will allow me,' said Arthur, 'and furthermore, he will not leave here until he is well.'

'I would prefer it, lord,' said Geraint, 'if you would let me leave.'

'No, I will not, between me and God,' he replied.

Then he had maidens called to attend on Enid and take her to Gwenhwyfar's tent. Gwenhwyfar and all the ladies were glad to see her, and her riding-dress was taken off and replaced by another. Arthur called on Cadyriaith and asked him to erect a tent for Geraint and his physicians, and made him responsible for ensuring that there was plenty of everything as he had been asked. Cadyriaith did everything that was requested of him, and brought Morgan Tud and his apprentices to Geraint. And Arthur and his host stayed there almost a month nursing Geraint.

When Geraint thought his flesh was whole, he came to Arthur and asked for permission to leave.

'I do not know if you are fully recovered yet.'

'I am, truly, lord,' said Geraint.

'It is not you I will believe on that subject, but the physicians who tended you.' And he summoned the physicians to him and asked them whether it was true.

'It is true,' said Morgan Tud.

The next day Arthur allowed him to leave, and Geraint set out to complete his journey. And Arthur left there that same day.

Geraint told Enid to ride ahead and keep her distance as she had done before. And she went on, and followed the highroad. As they were thus they heard, close to them, the loudest scream in the world.

'Stay here,' he said, 'and wait. And I'll go and find out the explanation for the scream.'

'I will,' she said.

He went, and came to a clearing near the road. And in the clearing he could see two horses, one with a man's saddle and the other with a woman's saddle, and a knight in his armour, dead; and standing over the knight he saw a young, newly weddded woman in her riding-clothes, shrieking.*

'Lady,' said Geraint, 'what has happened to you?'

'I was travelling here with the man I loved best, and suddenly three giants came up to us, and without regard for any justice in the world they killed him.'

'Which way did they go?' said Geraint.

'That way, along the highroad,' she said. He went to Enid.

'Go to the lady who is down there,' he said, 'and wait for me—I shall return there.' She was sad that he had ordered her to do that, but even so she went to the maiden, and it was dreadful to hear her. And Enid was sure that Geraint would never return.

He went after the giants and caught up with them. And each one of them was larger than three men, and there was a huge club on the shoulder of each one. Geraint charged at one of them and stabbed him with a spear through his entrails; and he pulled his spear out of him and stabbed another of them too. But the third turned on him, and struck him with a club so that his shield splits until his shoulder stops the blow, and all his wounds open, and all his blood is pouring out. With that, Geraint drew a sword and attacked him and struck him a severe-sharp, pitiless, fierce-furious blow on the top of his head, so that his head splits, and his neck as far as the shoulders, and so that he fell dead. And he left them dead like that and came to where Enid was. And when he saw Enid he fell from his horse to the ground as if dead. Enid gave a terrible, piercing, heart-rending scream, and came and stood over him where he had fallen.

Suddenly, behold, coming in answer to the scream, Earl Limwris* and a retinue that was with him, who were travelling the road. And because of the scream they turned off the road. Then the earl said to Enid, 'Lady,' he said, 'what has happened to you?'

'Sir,' she said, 'the man that I loved best, and will always love, has been killed.'

'What happened to you?' he said to the other.

'The man I loved best has been killed, too,' she said.

'What killed them?' he said.

'The giants killed the man I loved best,' she said. 'And the other knight went after them,' she said, 'and as you can see, he came away from them losing blood beyond measure. And I think it likely,' she said, 'that he did not leave without killing either some or all of them.' The earl saw to it that the knight who had been left dead was buried. But he thought that there was still some life in Geraint, and had him brought with him in the hollow of his shield and on a stretcher, to see whether he would live.

The two maidens came to the court. After they had come to court, Geraint was placed just as he was, on the stretcher, on top of a table in the hall. They all took off their outdoor clothes. The earl told Enid to change and put on another dress.

'I will not, between me and God,' she said.

'Lady,' he replied, 'don't be so sad.'

'It will be very difficult to persuade me on that matter,' she said.

'I am telling you', he replied, 'that there is no need for you to be sad, whatever the fate of the knight over there, whether he lives or dies. I have a good earldom; you shall have it in your possession, together with me,' he said. 'And now be happy and contented.'

'I shall never be happy, by my confession to God,' she said, 'as long as I live.'

'Come and eat,' he said.

'I will not, between me and God,' she said.

'You will, between me and God.' And he dragged her against her will to the table and ordered her several times to eat.

'I will not eat, by my confession to God,' she said, 'until the man who is on the stretcher over there eats.'

'You cannot make that happen,' said the earl. 'The man over there is all but dead.'

'I will prove that it is possible,' she said.

He offered her a goblet full of wine.

'Drink this goblet,' he replied, 'and you will change your mind.'

'Shame on me,' she said, 'if I drink anything until he drinks too.'

'Well and good,' said the earl. 'I am no better being kind towards you than being unkind.'

And he gave her a clout on the ear. She gave a loud, sharp-piercing scream and lamented far more then than before, and she thought to herself that if Geraint were alive she would not be clouted like that. Then Geraint regained consciousness at the echoing of her scream, and sat up, and found his sword in the hollow of his shield, and rushed to where the earl was and struck him an eager-sharp, venomous-hard, strong and brave blow on top of his head, so that it split and so that the table stopped the sword. Everyone then left the tables and fled outside. And it was not the living man they feared most but the sight of the dead man rising up to kill them. Then Geraint looked at Enid, and he felt sorrowful on two accounts—first on seeing how Enid had lost her colour and appearance, and secondly on realizing then that she was in the right.

'Lady,' he said, 'do you know where our horses are?'

'I know, lord, where yours went,' she said, 'but I don't know where the other went. Your horse went to the building over there.' He went into the building and led out his horse, and mounted it, and lifted Enid up from the ground and placed her between himself and the saddle-bow, and went on his way.

As they were travelling like this between two hedges, and night overcoming day, behold, they could see between them and the horizon spear-shafts following them, and they could hear the clatter of horses and the clamour of men.

'I hear someone coming after us,' he said, 'and I'll put you on the other side of the hedge.'

He did so. Then, behold, a knight rushed up to him, couching his spear. When she saw that she said, 'Lord,' she said, 'what praise will you receive for killing a dead man, whoever you are?'

'Oh, God,' he replied, 'is this Geraint?'

'It is, between me and God. And who are you?'

'I am Y Brenin Bychan,' he replied, 'coming to help you after hearing that you were in trouble. And had you taken my advice, the difficulties you have suffered would not have happened.'

'Nothing can be done against the will of God,' said Geraint.

'Much good comes from sound advice,' he replied. 'At all events,' said Y Brenin Bychan, 'I have good advice for you now: come with me to the court of my brother-in-law which is nearby, to receive the best medical treatment in the kingdom.'

'We will come, gladly,' said Geraint.

Enid was placed on the horse of one of Y Brenin Bychan's squires, and they made their way to the baron's court, and were given a welcome there, and were cared for and waited upon. The next morning physicians were sent for. And the physicians were found, and they arrived almost immediately, and Geraint was treated until he was completely well. While he was being treated, Y Brenin Bychan had Geraint's armour repaired so that it was as good as new. And they stayed there for a fortnight and a month.

Then Y Brenin Bychan said to Geraint, 'We shall go to my court now to rest and relax.'

'If you agree,' said Geraint, 'we shall travel one day more, and then return.'

'Gladly,' said Y Brenin Bychan. 'Travel on.'

They travelled early in the morning, and Enid travelled with them that day, happier and more contented than ever. And they came to a highroad and could see it branching in two. Along one of these roads they could see a man on foot coming to meet them. Gwiffred asked him where he was coming from.

'I'm returning from the country where I was doing business.'

'Tell me,' said Geraint, 'which of these two roads is it best for me to travel?'

'It is best for you to travel that one,' he said. 'If you go down this one, you'll never come back. Down there', he said, 'is a hedge of mist, and within it there are enchanted games. And no man who has gone there has ever come back. And Earl Owain's court is there, and he allows no one to take lodging in the town except those who stay with him at his court.'

'Between me and God,' said Geraint, 'we shall take the lower road.'

They followed the road until they reached the town. They took lodgings in what they considered the fairest and most desirable place in the town. And as they were thus, behold, a young man came to them and greeted them.

'May God prosper you,' they said.

'Good sirs,' he said, 'what are you planning to do here?'

'We want to take lodging and stay here tonight,' they said.

'It is not the custom for the man who owns the town to allow anyone of gentle birth to take lodging here except those who stay with him in his own court: come to the court.'

'We will, gladly,' said Geraint. They went with the squire. And they were made welcome at the court, and the earl came to the hall to meet them, and had the tables prepared. And they washed, and went to sit down. This is how they sat: Geraint on one side of the earl, and Enid on the other; next to Enid, Y Brenin Bychan; then the countess next to Geraint; everyone after that as befitted them.

Then Geraint thought about the game, and presumed that he would not be allowed to go to the game. And he stopped eating because of that. The earl looked at him and pondered, and presumed that it was because of not going to the game that Geraint was not eating; and he was sorry that he had ever created those games, if only so as not to lose a lad as good as Geraint. And if Geraint had asked him to call off that game, he would have called it off gladly for ever. Then the earl said to Geraint, 'What are you thinking of, lord, as you are not eating? If you are worried about going to the game, you will not have to go, and no one shall ever go again, out of respect for you.'

'May God repay you,' said Geraint, 'but I want nothing except to go to the game, and to be shown the way there.'

'If that is what you would like most, you shall have it gladly.'

'Indeed, more than anything,' he replied.

They ate, and received generous service and numerous dishes and great quantities of drink. When they had finished eating, they got up, and Geraint called for his horse and his armour, and armed himself and his horse. And all the people came until they were close to the hedge. And no lower was the top of the hedge they could see than the highest point they could see in the sky. And on every stake they could see in the hedge there was a man's head, except for two stakes.* And there were a great many stakes within the hedge and through it.

Then Y Brenin Bychan said, 'Is any one allowed to accompany the nobleman?'

'No,' said Earl Owain.

'In which direction does one go from here?' said Geraint.

'I don't know,' said Owain, 'but go in the direction you think easiest.'

Fearless, and without hesitation, Geraint set off into the mist. When he emerged from the mist, he came to a great orchard. He could see a clearing in the orchard, and a pavilion of brocaded silk with a red canopy in the clearing, and he saw that the entrance to the pavilion was open. And there was an apple-tree facing the entrance to the pavilion, and on a branch of the apple-tree was a large hunting-horn. Then he dismounted and entered the pavilion. There was no one inside the pavilion except a single maiden, sitting in a golden chair, and an empty chair facing her. Geraint sat in the empty chair.

'Lord,' said the maiden, 'I advise you not to sit in that chair.'

'Why?' said Geraint.

'The man who owns that chair has never allowed anyone else to sit in his chair.'

'I do not care if he doesn't like anyone to sit in his chair,' said Geraint.

Suddenly they could hear a great commotion near the pavilion. Geraint looked to see what was the cause of the commotion. He could see a knight outside on a charger, wide-nostrilled, high-spirited, impatient, big-boned, and a mantle in two halves covering him and his horse, and plenty of armour under that.

'Tell me, lord,' he said to Geraint, 'who asked you to sit there?'

'I myself,' he answered.

'It was wrong of you to shame and insult me as much as that; get up from there to make amends for you own foolishness.'

Geraint got up, and immediately they began to fight. They broke one set of lances, and broke the second set, and broke the third set, and each one dealt the other blows, hard and hurtful, fast and furious. Eventually Geraint became angry, and he spurred on his horse and rushed at him, and struck him in the strongest part of his shield so that it splits, and the head of his spear is in his armour, and all the saddle-girths break, and he himself is thrown over his horse's crupper the length of Geraint's spear and the length of his arm head-first to the ground. And quickly Geraint draws his sword, intending to cut off his head.

'Oh, lord,' he said, 'your mercy, and you shall have whatever you want.'

'I want only that this game is gone from here for ever,' he replied, 'together with the hedge of mist, and the magic and enchantment which have existed.'

'You shall have that gladly, lord.'

'Then make the mist disappear from here,' he said.

'Blow that horn,' he said, 'and the moment you sound it, the mist will disappear. And until a knight who had overthrown me sounded it, the mist would never disappear from here.'

Enid was sad and anxious where she was, worrying about Geraint. Then Geraint came and blew the horn; and the moment he sounded a single blast on it the mist disappeared, and the crowd gathered together and everyone was reconciled with each other. That night the earl invited Geraint and Y Brenin Bychan to stay. The next morning they parted, and Geraint returned to his own kingdom. He ruled it successfully from then on, he and his prowess and bravery continuing, with praise and admiration for him and for Enid ever after.

How Culhwch Won Olwen

CILYDD son of Celyddon Wledig* wanted a wife as well born as himself. The woman he wanted was Goleuddydd daughter of Anlawdd Wledig. After he had slept with her the country went to prayer to see whether they might have an heir. And they had a son through the country's prayers. And from the hour she became pregnant she went mad, and did not go near any dwelling. When her time came, her senses returned to her. This happened in a place where a swineherd was tending a herd of pigs. And out of fear of the pigs the queen gave birth. And the swineherd took the boy until he came to court. And the boy was baptized, and was named Culhwch because he was found in a pig-run.* But the boy was of noble descent, he was a cousin to Arthur. And the boy was placed with foster-parents.*

And after that the boy's mother, Goleuddydd daughter of Anlawdd Wledig, became ill. She summoned her husband to her, and said to him, 'I shall die of this sickness, and you will want another wife. And nowadays it's the wives who dispense the gifts. But you would be wrong to harm your son. This is what I ask of you: not to seek a wife until you see a two-headed briar on my grave.'

He promised her that. She summoned her chaplain and asked him to clean the grave every year so that nothing would grow on it. The queen died. The king sent a servant every morning to see if anything was growing on the grave. At the end of seven years the chaplain neglected what he had promised the queen.

One day the king was hunting; he made for the graveyard; he wanted to see the grave whereby he might seek a wife. He saw the briar. And as he saw it he took counsel as to where he could get a wife. One of the counsellors said, 'I know of a woman who would suit you well. She is the wife of King Doged.' They decided to seek her out. And they killed the king and brought his wife back home with them, together with her only daughter. And they took possession of the king's land.

One day the lady went out for a walk. She came to the house of a toothless old hag who lived in the town.

The queen said, 'Hag, for God's sake will you answer my question? Where are the children of the man who violently abducted me?'

The hag said, 'He has no children.'

The queen said, 'Woe is me that I have come to a childless man.'

The hag said, 'You need not worry about that. It is prophesied that he shall have an heir; he may have one by *you*, since he hasn't had one by anyone else. Don't be sad either—he does have one son.'

The lady went home happy, and she said to her husband, 'Why do you hide your child from me?'

The king said, 'I will not hide him any longer.'

The boy was sent for, and he came to the court. His stepmother said to him, 'It is time for you to get married, lad. And I have a daughter worthy of every nobleman in the world.'

The boy said, 'I am not old enough to get married yet.'

And then she said, 'I swear a destiny on you, that your side shall never strike against a woman until you get Olwen daughter of Ysbaddaden Bencawr.'*

The boy blushed, and love for the maiden filled every limb in his body, although he had never seen her. And then his father said to him, 'Son, why are you blushing? What's the matter?'

'My stepmother has sworn that I may never have a wife until I get Olwen daughter of Ysbaddaden Bencawr.'

'It is easy for you to get that, son,' said his father to him. 'Arthur is your cousin. Go to Arthur to have your hair trimmed,* and ask him for that as your gift.'*

The boy went off on a steed with a gleaming grey head, four winters old, well-jointed stride, shell-like hoofs, and a tubular gold bridle-bit in its mouth, with a precious gold saddle beneath him, and two sharp spears of silver in his hand. He had a battle-axe in his hand, the length of the forearm of a full-grown man from ridge to edge. It would draw blood from the wind; it would be swifter than the swiftest dewdrop from the stalk to the ground when the dew is heaviest in the month of June. He had a gold-hilted sword on his thigh and its blade of gold, with a gold-chased shield, the colour of heaven's lightning, and its rim of ivory. And there were two spotted, white-breasted greyhounds in front of him, with a collar of red gold around the neck of each from shoulder-swell to ear. The one on the left side would run to the right side, and the one on the right side would run to the left side, like two sea-swallows swooping around him. His steed's four hoofs would cut out four clods, like four swallows in the air above him, sometimes in front of him, sometimes behind him. He had a purple, four-cornered cloak about him, with a ruby-gold ball at each corner. Each ball was worth a hundred cows. The precious gold in his buskins and stirrups, from the top of his thigh to the tip of his toe, was worth three hundred cows. Not even the tip of a hair on him stirred, so light was his steed's canter beneath him on his way to the gate of Arthur's court.*

The boy said, 'Is there a gatekeeper?'

'There is. And as for you, may you lose your head for asking. *I* am gatekeeper to Arthur each first day of January, but I have deputies for the rest of the year, namely Huandaw and Gogigwr and Llaesgymyn, and Penpingion who goes about on his head to save his feet, neither looking to heaven nor to the ground, but like a rolling stone on a court floor.'

'Open the gate.'

'No, I won't.'

'Why won't you open it?'

'Knife has gone into meat and drink into horn, and a thronging in the hall of Arthur. Apart from the son of the lawful king of a country, or a craftsman who brings his craft, none will be allowed to enter. You shall have food for your dogs and corn for your horse, and hot peppered chops for yourself, and wine brimming over, and songs to entertain you. Food for fifty shall be brought to you in the hostel. There travellers from afar do eat, together with the sons of other lands who do not offer a craft in the court of Arthur. It will be no worse for you there than for Arthur in the court. A woman to sleep with you and songs to entertain you. Tomorrow, in the morning, when the gate is opened for the crowd that has come here today, for you shall the gate be opened first. And you may sit wherever you choose in Arthur's hall, from its upper end to its lower.'

The boy said, 'I will do none of that. If you open the gate, well and good. If not, I will bring dishonour on your lord and give you a bad name. And I will raise three shouts at the entrance of this gate that will be no less audible on the top of Pen Pengwaedd in Cornwall as at the bottom of Dinsol in the North, and in Esgair Oerfel in Ireland.* And all the women in this court that are pregnant shall miscarry, and those that are not, their wombs shall become heavy within them so that they shall never be with child from this day forth.'

Glewlwyd Gafaelfawr* said, 'However much you shout against the laws of Arthur's court, you shall not be allowed in until I go and speak with Arthur first.' And Glewlwyd came into the hall.

Arthur said to him, 'You have news from the gate?'

'I do—

Two thirds of my life have gone
and two thirds of your own.
I was once in Caer Se and Asse,
       in Sach and Salach,
       in Lotor and Ffotor.
I was once in India the Great
       and India the Lesser.
I was once in the battle of the two Ynyrs
       when the twelve hostages were taken from Norway.
And I was once in Europe,
       I was in Africa,
       and the islands of Corsica,
       and in Caer Brythwch and Brythach and Nerthach.
I was once there when you killed the warband of Gleis son of
  Merin,
       when you killed Mil Du son of Dugum.
I was once there when you conquered Greece in the east.
I was once in Caer Oeth and Anoeth,
       and in Caer Nefenhyr Nawdant:
       fair kingly men did we see there—

but I never in my life saw a man as handsome as the one who is at the entrance to the gate this very moment.'*

Arthur said, 'If you came in walking, then go out running. And he who looks at the light and who opens his eye and then closes it, an injunction upon him. And let some serve with golden drinking-horns and others with hot peppered chops until he has plenty of food and drink. It is a shameful thing to leave in the wind and the rain such a man as you describe.'

Cai said, 'By the hand of my friend,* if you were to take my advice, the laws of court would not be broken on his account.'

'Not so, fair Cai. We are noblemen as long as others seek us out. The greater the gifts we bestow, the greater will be our nobility and our fame and our honour.'

And Glewlwyd came to the gate, and opened the gate for him. And whereas everyone else would dismount by the gate at the mounting-block, he did not, but rode in on the steed.

Culhwch said, 'Hail, chief of the kings of this island. May it be no worse to the lower end of the house than to the upper. May this greeting apply equally to your nobles and your retinue and your battle-chiefs. May no one be without a share of it. As my greeting to you is all-encompassing, may your grace and your word and your honour in this island be all-encompassing.'

'God's truth on that, chieftain. Greetings to you, too. Sit between two of the warriors, with songs to entertain you and the privileges of a prince, heir-apparent to the kingdom,* for as long as you are here. And when I divide my bounty between guests and travellers from afar, it shall be with you that I begin in this court.'

The boy said, 'I have not come here to sponge food and drink. But if I get my gift, I shall be worthy of it and acclaim it. If I do not get it, I shall dishonour you as far as the furthest corners of the world that your fame has reached.'

Arthur said, 'Though you do not reside here, chieftain, you shall have the gift your mouth and tongue shall name, as far as the wind dries, as far as the rain soaks, as far as the sun reaches, as far as the sea stretches, as far as the earth extends, except my ship and my mantle, and Caledfwlch my sword, and Rhongomyniad my spear, and Wynebgwrthucher my shield, and Carnwennan my dagger, and Gwenhwyfar my wife.'*

'God's truth on it?'

'You shall have it gladly. Name what you want.'

'I will. I want to have my hair trimmed.'

'You shall have that.'

Arthur took a golden comb, and shears with loops of silver, and combed his hair,* and asked who he was.

Arthur said, 'My heart warms towards you. I know you are of my blood. Tell me who you are.'

'I will. Culhwch son of Cilydd son of Celyddon Wledig by Goleuddydd daughter of Anlawdd Wledig, my mother.'

Arthur said, 'That is true. You are my cousin then. Name what you will, and you shall have it, whatever your mouth and tongue may name.'

'Have I God's truth on that, and the truth of your kingdom?'

'Yes, gladly.'

'I ask you to get me Olwen daughter of Ysbaddaden Bencawr. And I invoke her in the name of your warriors.'

He invoked his gift* in the name of Cai and Bedwyr, and Greidol Gallddofydd, and Gwythyr son of Greidol, and Graid son of Eri, and Cynddylig Gyfarwydd, and Tathal Twyll Golau, and Maelwys son of Baeddan, and Cnychwr son of Nes, and Cubert son of Daere, and Ffercos son of Poch, and Lluber Beuthach, and Corfil Berfach, and Gwyn son of Esni, and Gwyn son of Nwyfre, and Gwyn son of Nudd, and Edern son of Nudd, and Cadwy son of Geraint, and Fflewddwr Fflam Wledig, and Rhuawn Bebyr son of Dorath, and Bradwen son of Moren Mynog, and Moren Mynog himself, and Dalldaf son of Cimin Cof, and the son of Alun Dyfed, and the son of Saidi, and the son of Gwryon, and Uchdryd Ardwyad Cad, and Cynwas Cwryfagl, and Gwrhyr Gwarthegfras, and Isberyr Ewingath, and Gallgoid Gofyniad, and Duach and Brathach and Nerthach, sons of Gwawrddydd Cyrfach (from the uplands of hell did those men come), and Cilydd Canhastyr, and Canhastyr Can Llaw, and Cors Cant Ewin, and Esgair Gulhwch Gofyncawn, and Drwstwrn Haearn, and Glewlwyd Gafaelfawr, and Lloch Llaw-wyniog, and Anwas Edeiniog, and Sinnoch son of Seithfed, and Wadu son of Seithfed, and Naw son of Seithfed, and Gwenwynwyn son of Naw son of Seithfed, and Bedyw son of Seithfed, and Gobrwy son of Echel Forddwyd Twll, and Echel Forddwyd Twll himself, and Mael son of Roycol, and Dadwair Dallben, and Garwyli son of Gwythog Gwyr, and Gwythog Gwyr himself, and Gormant son of Rica, and Menw son of Teirgwaedd, and Digon son of Alar, and Selyf son of Sinoid, and Gusg son of Achen, and Nerth son of Cadarn, and Drudwas son of Tryffin, and Twrch son of Perif, and Twrch son of Anwas, and Iona, king of France, and Sel son of Selgi, and Teregud son of Iaen, and Sulien son of Iaen, and Bradwen son of Iaen, and Moren son of Iaen, and Siawn son of Iaen, and Caradog son of Iaen—they were men of Caer Dathyl, Arthur's family on his father's side. Dirmyg son of Caw, and Iustig son of Caw, and Edmyg son of Caw, and Angawdd son of Caw, and Gofan son of Caw, and Celyn son of Caw, and Conyn son of Caw, and Mabsant son of Caw, and Gwyngad son of Caw, and Llwybyr son of Caw, and Coch son of Caw, and Meilyg son of Caw, and Cynwal son of Caw, and Ardwyad son of Caw, and Ergyriad son of Caw, and Neb son of Caw, and Gildas son of Caw, and Calcas son of Caw, and Huail son of Caw (he never submitted to a lord's control), and Samson Finsych, and Taliesin Ben Beirdd, and Manawydan son of Llŷr, and Llary son of Casnar Wledig, and Sberin son of Fflergant, king of Brittany, and Saranhon son of Glythfyr, and Llawr son of Erw, and Anynnog son of Menw Teirgwaedd, and Gwyn son of Nwyfre, and Fflam son of Nwyfre, and Geraint son of Erbin, and Ermid son of Erbin, and Dywel son of Erbin, and Gwyn son of Ermid, and Cyndrwyn son of Ermid, and Hyfaidd Unllen, and Eiddon Fawrfrydig, and Rheiddwn Arwy, and Gormant son of Rica (Arthur's brother on his mother's side, his father the chief elder of Cornwall). And Llawnrodded Farfog, and Nodawl Farf Trwch, and Berth son of Cado, and Rheiddwn son of Beli, and Isgofan Hael, and Ysgawyn son of Banon, and Morfran son of Tegid (no man laid his weapon in him at Camlan because he was so ugly, everyone thought he was an attendant demon; he had hair on him like a stag). And Sandde Pryd Angel (no one laid his spear in him at Camlan because he was so beautiful, everyone thought he was an attendant angel). And Cynwyl Sant, one of the Three Who Escaped from Camlan; he was the last to part from Arthur, on Hengroen his horse.

And Uchdryd son of Erim, and Eus son of Erim, and Henwas Edeiniog son of Erim, and Henbeddestyr son of Erim, and Sgilti Sgafndroed son of Erim. There were three magical qualities about these last three men. Henbeddestyr, he never found any man who could keep up with him, either on horseback or on foot; Henwas Edeiniog, no four-legged animal could ever keep up with him over one acre, let alone any farther than that; Sgilti Sgafndroed, whenever he wanted to go on an errand for his lord, he would never seek a road as long as he knew where he was going, but while there were trees, he would travel along the top of the trees, and while there was a mountain, he would travel on the tips of the reeds, and throughout his life no reed ever bent beneath his feet, let alone broke, because he was so light.

Teithi Hen son of Gwynnan, whose kingdom the sea overran, and he only just escaped and came to Arthur—and his knife had a magical attribute: ever since he came here no handle would ever stay on it, and because of that he became sick and weary during his lifetime, and of that he died. And Carnedyr son of Gofynion Hen, and Gwenwynwyn son of Naf, Arthur's foremost champion, and Llygadrudd Emys and Gwrfoddw Hen, they were Arthur's uncles, his mother's brothers. Culfanawyd son of Goryon, and Llenlleog Wyddel from the headland of Gamon, and Dyfnwal Moel, and Dunarth, king of the North, Teyrnon Twrf Liant, and Tegfan Gloff, and Tegyr Talgellog. Gwrddywal son of Efrei, and Morgant Hael, Gwystyl son of Nwython, and Rhun son of Nwython, and Llwydeu son of Nwython, and Gwydre son of Llwydeu by Gwenabwy daughter of Caw, his mother—Huail his uncle stabbed him, and because of that there was hatred between Arthur and Huail, because of the injury.

Drem son of Dremidydd, who from Celli Wig in Cornwall could see a fly rise in the morning with the sun as far away as Pen Blathaon in Pictland. And Eidoel son of Ner and Glwyddyn Saer who built Ehangwen, Arthur's hall. Cynyr Ceinfarfog—Cai was said to be his son. He said to his wife, 'If there is any part of me in your son, maiden, his heart will always be cold, and there will be no warmth in his hands. Another of his magical attributes: if he be a son of mine, he will be stubborn. Another attribute: when he carries a load, be it large or small, it will never be visible, neither in front of him nor behind him. Another attribute: no one will withstand water or fire as well as he. Another attribute: there will be no servant or officer like him.'

Henwas, and Hen Wyneb, and Hengydymaith, Gallgoig another— whatever town he would come to, though there were three hundred houses in it, if he wanted anything he would let no man sleep while he was there. Berwyn son of Cyrenyr, and Peris, king of France—and that's why it is called the citadel of Paris. Osla Gyllellfawr who would carry Bronllafn Ferllydan; when Arthur and his hosts would come to the edge of a torrent, a narrow place over the water would be sought, and the dagger would be placed in its sheath across the torrent—it would be bridge enough for the men of the Three Islands of Britain and her Three Adjacent Islands, and their booty. Gwyddog son of Menestyr, who killed Cai, and Arthur killed him and his brothers to avenge Cai. Garanwyn son of Cai, and Amren son of Bedwyr, and Eli, and Myr, and Rheu Rhwyddyrys, and Rhun Rhuddwern, and

Eli, and Trachmyr, Arthur's chief huntsmen. And Llwydeu son of
Cilcoed, and Huabwy son of Gwryon, and Gwyn Godyfron, and
Gwair Dathar Weinidog, and Gwair son of Cadellin Tal Arian, and
Gwair Gwrhyd Enwir, and Gwair Gwyn Baladr—Arthur's uncles,
his mother's brothers; the sons of Llwch Llaw-wyniog from beyond
the Tyrrhenian Sea, Llenlleog Wyddel, and Ardderchog Prydain,
Cas son of Saidi, Gwrfan Gwallt Afwyn, Gwilenhin, king of France,
Gwitardd son of Aedd, king of Ireland, Garselyd Wyddel, Panawr
Penbagad, Atlendor son of Naf, Gwyn Hyfar, overseer of Cornwall
and Devon—one of the nine who plotted the battle of Camlan. Celli,
and Cuelli, and Gilla Goeshydd—he would clear three hundred acres
in a single leap, chief leaper of Ireland.

Sol, and Gwadn Osol, and Gwadn Oddaith—Sol, who could stand
all day on one leg; Gwadn Osol, if he were to stand on top of the
largest mountain in the world, it would become a level plain beneath
his feet; Gwadn Oddaith, like hot metal when drawn from the forge
were the flashing sparks from his soles when he encountered strife—
he would clear the way for Arthur and his hosts. Hir Erwm and Hir
Atrwm, on the day they came to a feast, they would seize three
cantrefs for their needs; they would feast till noon and drink till
night. When they would go to sleep they would devour the heads
of insects through hunger, as if they had never eaten food. When
they went to a feast they left neither fat nor lean, neither hot nor
cold, neither sour nor sweet, neither fresh nor salt, neither cooked
nor raw.

Huarwar son of Halwn, who asked his fill as a gift from Arthur; it
was one of the Three Mighty Plagues of Cornwall and Devon until
he was given his fill; he never gave a hint of a smile except when he
was full. Gwarae Gwallt Eurin, the two whelps of the bitch Rhymhi,
Gwyddrud and Gwydden Astrus, Sugn son of Sugnedydd, who
would suck up the sea where there were three hundred ships until it
was just a dry beach; he had red breast-fever. Cacamwri, Arthur's
servant—show him a barn, though there would be in it the work
of fifty ploughs, he would thrash away with an iron flail until the
boards, the rafters, and the side-beams would be no better off than
the fine oats in the heap of corn-sheaves at the bottom of the barn.
Llwng, and Dygyflwng, and Annoeth Feiddog, and Hir Eiddil, and
Hir Amren—they were two of Arthur's servants—and Gwefl son
of Gwastad—on days when he was sad he would let his bottom

lip drop to his navel and the other would be a hood on his head. Uchdryd Farf Draws who would fling his bushy red beard across fifty rafters in Arthur's hall. Elidir Gyfarwydd, Ysgyrdaf and Ysgudydd— they were two of Gwenhwyfar's servants; on an errand their feet were as fleet as their thoughts. Brys son of Brysethach from the top of the black fernland in Prydain, and Gruddlwyn Gorr.

> Bwlch and Cyfwlch and Syfwlch,
>   sons of Cleddyf Cyfwlch,
>   grandsons of Cleddyf Difwlch.
> Three gleaming glitterers their three shields,
> Three stabbing strokes their three spears;
> Three keen carvers their three swords;
> Glas, Glesig, Gleisiad their three hounds;
> Call, Cuall, Cafall their three steeds;
> Hwyr Ddyddwg and Drwg Ddyddwg and Llwyr Ddyddwg
>   their three wives;
> Och and Garym and Diasbad their three grandchildren;
> Lluched and Neued and Eisiwed their three daughters;
> Drwg and Gwaeth and Gwaethaf Oll their three maidservants.*

Eheubryd son of Cyfwlch, Gorasgwrn son of Nerth, Gwaeddan son of Cynfelyn Ceudog, Pwyll Hanner Dyn, Dwn Diesig Unben, Eiladar son of Pen Llarcan, Cynedyr Wyllt son of Hetwn Tal Arian, Sawyl Pen Uchel, Gwalchmai son of Gwyar, Gwalhafed son of Gwyar, Gwrhyr Gwalstawd Ieithoedd—he knew all languages—and Cethdrwm Offeiriad. Clust son of Clustfeiniad—if he were buried seven fathoms in the earth, he could hear an ant fifty miles away stirring from its bed in the morning. Medyr son of Methredydd, who from Celli Wig could strike a starling in Esgair Oerfel in Ireland right through both legs. Gwiawn Llygad Cath, who could cut a membrane in a gnat's eye without harming the eye. Ôl son of Olwydd—seven years before he was born his father's pigs were stolen, and when he grew to be a man he traced the pigs and brought them home in seven herds. Bedwini the Bishop, who would bless Arthur's food and drink.

And also the gentle, golden-torqued ladies of this Island. Besides Gwenhwyfar, chief queen of this Island, and Gwenhwyfach her sister, and Rathtien, only daughter of Clememyl, Celemon daughter of Cai, and Tangwen daughter of Gwair Dathar Weinidog, Gwenalarch daughter of Cynwal Canhwch, Eurneid daughter of Clydno Eidin,

Eneuog daughter of Bedwyr, Enrhydreg daughter of Tuduathar, Gwenwledyr daughter of Gwaredur Cyrfach, Erdudfyl daughter of Tryffin, Eurolwyn daughter of Gwddolwyn Gorr, Teleri daughter of Peul, Indeg daughter of Garwy Hir, Morfudd daughter of Urien Rheged, Gwenllian Deg, the magnanimous maiden, Creiddylad daughter of Lludd Llaw Eraint, the most majestic maiden there ever was in the Three Islands of Britain and her Three Adjacent Islands. And for her Gwythyr son of Greidol and Gwyn son of Nudd fight each May day forever until the Day of Judgement. Ellylw daughter of Neol Cŷn Crog, and she lived for three generations. Esyllt Fynwen and Esyllt Fyngul. In the name of all of these did Culhwch son of Cilydd invoke his gift.

Arthur said, 'Well, chieftain, I have never heard of the maiden of whom you speak, nor of her parents. I will gladly send messengers to search for her. Give me some time to search for her.'

The boy said, 'Gladly, I will give you a year from tonight.'

And then Arthur sent the messengers to the far ends of every land to search for her. And at the end of the year Arthur's messengers returned with no more news or information about Olwen than on the first day.

And then Culhwch said, 'Everyone has had his gift but I am still without. I will leave and take away your honour with me.'

Cai said, 'Ah chieftain, you insult Arthur too much. Come with us. Until you admit that the maiden does not exist anywhere in the world, or until we find her, we will not be parted from you.'

Then Cai gets up.* Cai had magical qualities. For nine nights and nine days he could hold his breath under water. For nine nights and nine days he could go without sleep. A wound from Cai's sword no physician could heal. Cai was clever. He could be as tall as the tallest tree in the forest when it pleased him. There was another strange thing about him. When the rain was at its heaviest, whatever was in his hand would remain dry (and for a hand-breadth above and below), so great was his heat. And when his companions were coldest, this would be kindling for them to light a fire.

Arthur called on Bedwyr, who never feared the quest upon which Cai went. There was this about Bedwyr—no one was as handsome as he in this Island except Arthur and Drych son of Cibddar.* And this, too, that though he was one-handed, no three warriors could draw blood in the same field faster than he. Another peculiar quality of his—there was one thrust in his spear, and nine counter-thrusts.

Arthur calls on Cynddylig Gyfarwydd: 'Go on this quest for me with the chieftain.' He was no worse a guide in the land he had never seen than in his own land.

He calls Gwrhyr Gwalstawd Ieithoedd: he knew all languages.

He calls Gwalchmai son of Gwyar, for he never returned home without the quest he might go to seek. He was the best on foot and the best on a horse. He was Arthur's nephew, his sister's son, and his cousin.

Arthur calls on Menw son of Teirgwaedd, for should they come to a pagan land he could cast a spell on them so that no one could see them, but they could see everyone.

They travelled until they came to a great plain, and they could see a fort, the largest fort in the world. They walk that day until evening. When they thought they were close to the fort, they were no closer than in the morning. And the second and the third day they walked, and with difficulty they got there. And when they get close to the fort they could see a huge flock of sheep without boundary or border to it, and a shepherd on top of a mound tending the sheep, and a jacket of skins about him, and a shaggy mastiff beside him, bigger than a nine-year-old stallion. It was his custom that he had never lost a lamb, much less a grown animal. No troop had ever gone past him that he did not harm or hurt. Any dead tree or bush that was on the plain, his breath would burn them to the very ground.

Cai said, 'Gwrhyr Gwalstawd Ieithoedd, go and talk with that man over there.'

'Cai', he said, 'I only promised to go as far as you yourself would go. Let's go there together.'

Menw son of Teirgwaedd said, 'Don't worry about going there. I will cast a spell on the dog so that he will not harm anyone.' They came to where the shepherd was.

They said to him, 'You are prosperous, shepherd.'

'May you never be more prosperous than me.'

'Yes, by God, since you are supreme.'

'There is nothing that can ruin me except my wife.'

'Whose sheep are you tending, and whose is that fort?'

'You stupid men! Throughout the world people know that it is the fort of Ysbaddaden Bencawr.'

'And you, who are you?'

'I am Custennin son of Mynwyedig, and because of my wife, my brother Ysbaddaden Bencawr has ruined me. And you, who are you?'

'We are messengers of Arthur, seeking Olwen daughter of Ysbaddaden Bencawr.'

'Oh no, men. God protect you! For all the world, do not do that. No one who came to make that request has ever left alive.'

The shepherd got up. And as he got up, Culhwch gave him a gold ring. He tried to put on the ring, but it would not fit, and he placed it in the finger of his glove, and he went home and gave the glove to his wife to keep. And she took the ring from the glove.

'Where did you get this ring, husband? It is not often that you find treasure.'

'I went to the sea to look for sea-food. Behold, I saw a corpse coming in with the tide. I never saw such a handsome corpse as that, and on its finger I found this ring.'

'Alas, husband, since the sea does not tolerate a dead man's jewel, show me that corpse.'

'Wife, he whose corpse it is, you shall see him here soon.'

'Who's that?' said his wife.

'Culhwch son of Cilydd son of Celyddon Wledig, by Goleuddydd daughter of Anlawdd Wledig, his mother, who has come to ask for Olwen.'

She was in two minds. She was happy that her nephew,* her sister's son, had come to her, but she was sad because she had never seen anyone who had come to make that request leave with his life.

They made for the gate of the shepherd Custennin's court. She heard them coming. She ran joyfully to meet them. Cai snatched a log from the wood-pile, and she came to meet them to try and embrace them. Cai placed a stake between her hands. She squeezed the stake until it was a twisted branch.

'Woman,' said Cai, 'had you squeezed *me* like that, it would be useless for any one else ever to make love to me. That was an evil love.'

They came into the house and were waited upon. After a while, when everyone was milling about, the woman opened a coffer at the far end of the hearth, and out of it came a lad with curly yellow hair.

Gwrhyr said, 'It's a shame to hide such a lad as this. I know that it's not his own wrong that is being avenged on him.'

The woman said, 'This one is all that is left of twenty-three sons of mine that Ysbaddaden Bencawr has killed. I have no more hope for this one than for the others.'

Cai said, 'Let him be my companion, and neither of us will be killed unless we both are.' They eat.

The woman said, 'On what business have you come here?'

'We have come to seek Olwen for this boy.'

Then the woman said, 'For God's sake, since no one from the fort has seen you yet, turn back.'

'God knows, we won't turn back until we have seen the maiden,' said Cai. 'Will she come to a place where we can see her?'

'She comes here every Saturday to wash her hair, and in the bowl in which she washes, she leaves all her rings. Neither she nor her messenger ever comes for them.'

'Will she come here if she is sent for?'

'God knows I won't destroy my friend. I won't deceive one who trusts me. But if you give your word that you will do her no harm, I will send for her.'

'We do so.'

She was sent for. And she comes—

> with a robe of flame-red silk about her,
> and a torque of red gold about the maiden's neck,
> with precious pearls and red jewels.
> Yellower was her hair than the flowers of the broom.
> Whiter was her flesh than the foam of the wave.
> Whiter were her palms and her fingers
> than moist cotton grass amidst the fine gravel of a bubbling spring.
> Neither the eye of a mewed hawk,
> nor the eye of a thrice-mewed falcon—
> no eye was fairer than hers.
> Whiter were her breasts than the breast of a white swan.
> Redder were her cheeks than the reddest foxglove.
> Whoever saw her would be filled with love for her.
> Four white clovers would spring up behind her wherever she went.
> And for that reason she was called Olwen.*

She came into the house and sat down between Culhwch and the high seat. And as he saw her he recognized her.

Culhwch said to her, 'Maiden, it is you I have loved. And will you come with me?'

'In case you and I are accused of being sinful, I cannot do that at all. My father has asked me to give my word that I will not leave without consulting him, for he shall only live until I take a husband.* There is, however, advice I can give you, if you will take it. Go to my father to ask for my hand, and however much he asks of you, promise to get it, and you will get me too. But if he has cause to doubt at all, you will not get me, and you will be lucky to escape with your life.'

'I promise all that, and I will get it.'

She went to her chamber. They all got up to go after her to the fort, and killed the nine gatekeepers who were at the nine gates without a single man crying out, and nine mastiffs without a single one squealing. And they proceeded to the hall.

They said, 'Greetings, Ysbaddaden Bencawr, from God and from man.'

'You, where are you going?'

'We have come to seek Olwen your daughter for Culhwch son of Cilydd.'

'Where are my good-for-nothing servants and my scoundrels?' he said. 'Raise the forks under my eyelids so that I may see my prospective son-in-law.' They did that.

'Come here tomorrow. I'll give you some sort of an answer.'

They got up, and Ysbaddaden Bencawr snatched one of the three poisoned stone spears* beside him and hurled it after them. And Bedwyr caught it and hurled it back, and pierced Ysbaddaden Bencawr right through his kneecap.

He said, 'Cursed, savage son-in-law, I shall be all the worse when I walk down the slope. Like the sting of a gadfly the poison iron has hurt me. Cursed be the smith who forged it and the anvil on which it was forged, it is so painful.'

They spent that night in the house of Custennin. And the second day, splendidly, and with fine combs set in their hair, they came to the fort and into the hall.

They said, 'Ysbaddaden Bencawr, give us your daughter in exchange for her dowry and her maiden-fee to you and her two kinswomen. And unless you give her, you shall meet your death because of her.'

'She and her four great-grandmothers and her four great-grandfathers are still alive—I must consult with them.'*

'Do that,' they said. 'We'll go to eat.'

As they got up, he took the second stone spear that was beside him and hurled it after them. And Menw son of Teirgwaedd caught it and hurled it back and pierced him in the middle of his chest, so that it came out in the small of his back.

'Cursed, savage son-in-law, like the bite of a horse-leech the hard iron has hurt me. Cursed be the furnace in which it was heated, and the smith who forged it, it is so painful. When I go uphill I shall have a tight chest, and belly-ache, and throw up often.' They went to their food.

And the third day they came to the court. They said, 'Ysbaddaden Bencawr, do not aim at us again. Do not bring harm and hurt and death upon yourself.'

'Where are my servants? Raise the forks—my eyelids have fallen down over my eyeballs—so that I may take a look at my prospective son-in-law.'

They got up, and as they got up he took the third poisoned stone spear and hurled it after them. And Culhwch caught it and hurled it back as he had longed to do, and pierced him in his eyeball so that it came out through the nape of his neck.

'Cursed, savage son-in-law, as long as I live my eyesight shall be the worse. When I walk against the wind, my eyes will water; I shall have a headache and giddiness with each new moon. Cursed be the furnace in which it was heated. Like the bite of a mad dog the poisoned iron has pierced me.' They went to their food.

The following day they came to the court.

They said, 'Do not aim at us again. Do not bring harm and hurt and martyrdom upon yourself, and more than that if you wish. Give us your daughter.'

'Where is the one who is seeking my daughter?'

'I am the one who is seeking her, Culhwch son of Cilydd.'

'Come here where I can see you.' A chair was placed under him, face to face with him.

*

Ysbaddaden Bencawr said, 'Are you the one who seeks my daughter?'

'I am,' said Culhwch.

'I want your word that you will not be less than honest with me.'

'You have it.'

'When I get what I ask from you, then you shall get my daughter.'

'Name what you want.'

'I will. Do you see the large thicket over there?'

'I do.'

'I want it uprooted from the earth and burned along the ground so that the cinders and ashes fertilize it; and I want it ploughed and sown so that it's ripe in the morning by the time the dew disappears, so that it can be made into food and drink for the wedding guests of my daughter and yourself. And all that I want done in one day.'

'*It is easy for me to get that, though* you *may think it's not easy.*'*

'*Though you may get that, there is something you will not get.* There is no ploughman to till that land or to prepare it apart from Amaethon son of Dôn. He will not come with you willingly, nor can you force him.'

'*It is easy for me to get that, though* you *may think it's not easy.*'

'*Though you may get that, there is something you will not get.* Gofannon son of Dôn* to come to the edge of the land to set the plough. He will not undertake work willingly save for a rightful king, nor can you force him.'

'*It is easy for me to get that, though* you *may think it's not easy.*'

'*Though you may get that, there is something you will not get.* The two oxen of Gwlwlydd Winau, yoked together, to plough well the rough ground over there. He will not give them willingly, nor can you force him.'

'*It is easy for me to get that, though* you *may think it's not easy.*'

'*Though you may get that, there is something you will not get.* I want the Melyn Gwanwyn and the Ych Brych* yoked together.'

'*It is easy for me to get that, though* you *may think it's not easy.*'

'*Though you may get that, there is something you will not get.* Two horned oxen, one from the far side of Mynydd Bannog and the other from this side, and brought together under the one plough. They are Nyniaw and Peibiaw,* whom God transformed into oxen for their sins.'

'*It is easy for me to get that, though* you *may think it's not easy.*'

'*Though you may get that, there is something you will not get*. Do you see the tilled red soil over there?'

'I do.'

'When I first met the mother of that maiden, nine hestors* of flax seed were sown in it; neither black nor white has come out of it yet, and I still have that measure. I want to have that flax seed sown in the newly ploughed land over there, so that it may be a white veil on my daughter's head at your wedding feast.'

'*It is easy for me to get that, though* you *may think it's not easy*.'

'*Though you may get that, there is something you will not get*. Honey that will be nine times sweeter than the honey of the first swarm, without drones and without bees, to make bragget for the feast.'*

'*It is easy for me to get that, though* you *may think it's not easy*.'

'*Though you may get that, there is something you will not get*. The cup of Llwyr son of Llwyrion,* which holds the best drink; for it is the only vessel in the world able to hold that strong drink. You will not get it from him willingly, nor can you force him.'

'*It is easy for me to get that, though* you *may think it's not easy*.'

'*Though you may get that, there is something you will not get*. The hamper of Gwyddnau Garan Hir.* If the whole world were to gather around it, three nines at a time, everyone would find the food that he wanted in it, just to his liking. I want to eat from that the night my daughter sleeps with you. He will not give it willingly to any one, nor can you force him.'

'*It is easy for me to get that, though* you *may think it's not easy*.'

'*Though you may get that, there is something you will not get*. The horn of Gwlgawd Gododdin* to pour for us that night. He will not give it willingly, nor can you force him.'

'*It is easy for me to get that, though* you *may think it's not easy*.'

'*Though you may get that, there is something you will not get*. The harp of Teirtu to entertain me that night. When a man so desires, it will play itself; when he wants it to be silent, it is. He will not give it willingly, nor can you force him.'

'*It is easy for me to get that, though* you *may think it's not easy*.'

'*Though you may get that, there is something you will not get*. I want the birds of Rhiannon,* they that wake the dead and lull the living to sleep, to entertain me that night.'

'*It is easy for me to get that, though* you *may think it's not easy*.'

'*Though you may get that, there is something you will not get*. The cauldron of Diwrnach Wyddel,* the steward of Odgar son of Aedd, king of Ireland, to boil food for your wedding guests.'

'*It is easy for me to get that, though* you *may think it's not easy*.'

'*Though you may get that, there is something you will not get*. I must wash my head and shave my beard. I want the tusk of Ysgithrwyn Pen Baedd* to shave with. It will be no use to me unless it is pulled from his head while he's alive.'

'*It is easy for me to get that, though* you *may think it's not easy*.'

'*Though you may get that, there is something you will not get*. There is no one in the world who can pull it from his head except Odgar son of Aedd, king of Ireland.'

'*It is easy for me to get that, though* you *may think it's not easy*.'

'*Though you may get that, there is something you will not get*. I will not entrust the keeping of the tusk to anyone except Caw of Prydyn.* The sixty cantrefs of Prydyn are under him. He will not leave his kingdom willingly, nor can he be forced.'

'*It is easy for me to get that, though* you *may think it's not easy*.'

'*Though you may get that, there is something you will not get*. I must dress my beard to be shaved. It will never straighten out until you get the blood of the Very Black Witch, daughter of the Very White Witch, from Pennant Gofid* in the uplands of hell.'

'*It is easy for me to get that, though* you *may think it's not easy*.'

'*Though you may get that, there is something you will not get*. The blood will be useless unless it is obtained while warm. There is no vessel in the world that can keep the liquid in it warm except the bottles of Gwyddolwyn Gorr,* which keep their heat from when liquid is placed in them in the east until the west is reached. He will not give them willingly, nor can you force him.'

'*It is easy for me to get that, though* you *may think it's not easy*.'

'*Though you may get that, there is something you will not get*. Some will want milk. There's no way of getting milk for everyone until you get the bottles of Rhynnon Ryn Barfog.* No liquid ever turns sour in them. He will not give them willingly to anyone, nor can you force him.'

'*It is easy for me to get that, though* you *may think it's not easy*.'

'*Though you may get that, there is something you will not get*. There is no comb and shears in the world which can dress my beard, because of its stiffness, except the comb and shears that lie between the ears of Twrch Trwyth son of Taredd Wledig.* He will not give them willingly, nor can you force him.'

'*It is easy for me to get that, though* you *may think it's not easy.*'

'*Though you may get that, there is something you will not get.* You cannot hunt Twrch Trwyth until you get Drudwyn, the whelp of Graid son of Eri.'*

'*It is easy for me to get that, though* you *may think it's not easy.*'

'*Though you may get that, there is something you will not get.* There is no leash in the world that can hold him, except the leash of Cors Cant Ewin.'

'*It is easy for me to get that, though* you *may think it's not easy.*'

'*Though you may get that, there is something you will not get.* There is no collar in the world that can hold the leash, except the collar of Canhastyr Can Llaw.'

'*It is easy for me to get that, though* you *may think it's not easy.*'

'*Though you may get that, there is something you will not get.* The chain of Cilydd Canhastyr* to hold the collar along with the leash.'

'*It is easy for me to get that, though* you *may think it's not easy.*'

'*Though you may get that, there is something you will not get.* There is no huntsman in the world who can hunt with that dog, except Mabon son of Modron,* who was taken when three nights old from his mother. No one knows where he is, nor what state he's in, whether dead or alive.'

'*It is easy for me to get that, though* you *may think it's not easy.*'

'*Though you may get that, there is something you won't get.* Gwyn Myngddwn, the steed of Gweddw* (he's as swift as a wave), under Mabon to hunt Twrch Trwyth. He will not give it willingly, nor can you force him.'

'*It is easy for me to get that, though* you *may think it's not easy.*'

'*Though you may get that, there is something you will not get.* Mabon will never be found—no one knows where he is—until you first find Eidoel son of Aer,* his kinsman, for he'll be tireless in his search for him. He's his first cousin.'

'*It is easy for me to get that, though* you *may think it's not easy.*'

'*Though you may get that, there is something you will not get.* Garselyd Wyddel, he is the chief huntsman of Ireland.* Twrch Trwyth will never be hunted without him.'

'*It is easy for me to get that, though* you *may think it's not easy.*'

'*Though you may get that, there is something you will not get.* A leash from the beard of Dillus Farfog, for nothing will hold those two whelps* except that. And it will be of no use unless it's taken from his beard while he's alive, and plucked with wooden tweezers. He will not allow anyone to do that to him while he's alive. But it will be useless if he's dead, because it will be brittle.'

'*It is easy for me to get that, though* you *may think it's not easy.*'

'*Though you may get that, there is something you will not get.* There is no huntsman in the world who can hold those two whelps, except Cynedyr Wyllt son of Hetwn Glafyriog.* He is nine times wilder than the wildest wild beast on the mountain. You will never get him, nor will you get my daughter.'

'*It is easy for me to get that, though* you *may think it's not easy.*'

'*Though you may get that, there is something you will not get.* Twrch Trwyth will not be hunted until Gwyn son of Nudd is found—God has put the spirit of the demons of Annwfn* in him, lest the world be destroyed. He will not be spared from there.'

'*It is easy for me to get that, though* you *may think it's not easy.*'

'*Though you may get that, there is something you will not get.* No steed will be of any use to Gwyn in hunting Twrch Trwyth, except Du, the steed of Moro Oerfeddog.*'

'*It is easy for me to get that, though* you *may think it's not easy.*'

'*Though you may get that, there is something you will not get.* Until Gwilenhin, king of France,* comes, Twrch Trwyth will never be hunted without him. It is improper for him to leave his kingdom, and he will never come here.'

'*It is easy for me to get that, though* you *may think it's not easy.*'

'*Though you may get that, there is something you will not get.* Twrch Trwyth will never be hunted without getting the son of Alun Dyfed.* He is a good unleasher.'

'*It is easy for me to get that, though* you *may think it's not easy.*'

'*Though you may get that, there is something you will not get.* Twrch Trwyth will never be hunted until you get Aned and Aethlem.* They are as swift as a gust of wind; they have never been unleashed on a beast they did not kill.'

'*It is easy for me to get that, though* you *may think it's not easy.*'

'*Though you may get that, there is something you will not get.* Arthur and his huntsmen to hunt Twrch Trwyth. He is a powerful man and he will not accompany you, nor can you force him. This is the reason why—he is under my control.'*

'*It is easy for me to get that, though* you *may think it's not easy*.'

'*Though you may get that, there is something you will not get*. Twrch Trwyth will never be hunted until you get—

> Bwlch and Cyfwlch and Syfwlch,
>> sons of Cilydd Cyfwlch,
>> grandsons of Cleddyf Difwlch.
> Three gleaming glitterers their three shields;
> Three stabbing strokes their three spears;
> Three keen carvers their three swords;
> Glas, Glesig, Gleisiad their three hounds;
> Call, Cuall, Cafall their three steeds;
> Hwyr Ddyddwg and Drwg Ddyddwg and Llwyr Ddyddwg
>> their three wives;
> Och and Garym and Diasbad their three witches;
> Lluched and Neued and Eisiwed their three daughters;
> Drwg and Gwaeth and Gwaethaf Oll their three maidservants.

These three men blow their horns, and all the others come to shriek until no one could care whether the sky fell on the earth.'*

'*It is easy for me to get that, though* you *may think it's not easy*.'

'*Though you may get that, there is something you will not get*. The sword of Wrnach Gawr.* He can only be killed with that. He will never give it to anyone, either for money or as a gift; nor can you force him.'

'*It is easy for me to get that, though* you *may think it's not easy*.'

'*Though you may get that, there is something you will not get*. Sleeplessness with no rest at night will be yours seeking those things, and you will not get them, nor shall you get my daughter.'

'I will get horses, and horsemen. And Arthur, my lord and kinsman, will get me all those things. And I will get your daughter, and you shall lose your life.'

'Go on your way now. You shall not be responsible for either food or clothing for my daughter. Seek those things. And when you get those things, you shall get my daughter.'

They travelled that day until evening, until they saw a stone-and-mortar fort, the largest fort in the world. Behold, they saw coming from the fort a black-haired man, bigger than three men of this world.

They said to him, 'Where do you come from, sir?'

'From the fort you can see over there.'

'Whose fort is it?'

'You stupid men. There is no one in the world who does not know who owns this fort. It belongs to Wrnach Gawr.'

'What customs are there regarding guests and travellers who arrive at this fort?'

'Ah lord, may God protect you. No guest has ever left here alive. No one is allowed inside except he who brings his craft.'

They made for the gate. Gwrhyr Gwalstawd Ieithoedd said, 'Is there a gatekeeper?'

'Yes. And as for you, may you lose your head for asking.'

'Open the gate.'*

'I will not.'

'Why won't you open it?'

'Knife has gone into food and drink into horns, and a thronging in the hall of Wrnach. Except for a craftsman who brings his craft, it will not be opened again tonight.'

Cai said, 'Gatekeeper, I have a craft.'

'What craft do you have?'

'I am the best furbisher of swords in the world.'

'I shall go and tell that to Wrnach Gawr, and bring you an answer.'

The gatekeeper came inside. Wrnach Gawr said, 'Do you have news from the gate?'

'I do. There's a band of men at the entrance to the gate and they want to come in.'

'Did you ask if they had a craft?'

'I did. And one of them said he could furbish swords.'

'I need him. For some time I have been looking for someone who could polish my sword, but I have found no one. Let that man in, since he has a craft.'

The gatekeeper came and opened the gate, and Cai came in alone. And he greeted Wrnach Gawr. A chair was placed under him.

Wrnach said, 'Well, sir, is it true what is said about you, that you are able to furbish swords?'

'I can do that.' The sword was brought to him. Cai put a striped whetstone under his arm.

'Which would you prefer, white-bladed or dark-blue-bladed?'*

'Do whatever would please *you*, as if it were yours.' Cai cleaned one half of the blade for him and placed it in his hand.

'Does that please you?'

'It would please me more than anything in my land if it were all like this. It's a shame that a man as good as you is without a companion.'

'But sir, I *do* have a companion, although he doesn't practise this craft.'

'Who is that?'

'Let the gatekeeper go outside, and I'll describe the signs to him. The head of his spear comes away from its shaft, it draws blood from the wind and lands on the shaft again.'

The gate was opened and Bedwyr entered. Cai said, 'Bedwyr is skilful, although he doesn't practise this craft.'

And there was great arguing among those men outside because Cai and Bedwyr had entered. And a young lad came inside with them—the only son of Custennin the shepherd. He and his companions, who stuck close to him, crossed the three baileys, as though it were nothing to them, until they were inside the fort. His companions said of Custennin's son, 'He is the best of men.' From then on he was called Gorau son of Custennin.* They dispersed to their lodgings so that they could kill those who lodged them without the giant knowing. The burnishing of the sword was finished, and Cai placed it in the hand of Wrnach Gawr, as if to see whether the work pleased him.

The giant said, 'The work is good, and I am pleased.'

Cai said, 'Your sheath has damaged your sword. Give it to me to remove the wooden side-pieces, and let me make new ones for it.' And he takes the sheath from him, and the sword in the other hand. He stands above the giant as if to put the sword in its sheath. He thrusts it into the giant's head, and takes off his head with one blow. They destroy the fort and take away what treasure they want. A year from that very day they came* to the court of Arthur, and with them the sword of Wrnach Gawr.

They told Arthur what had happened to them.

Arthur said, 'Which of those wonders is it best to seek first?'

'It is best', they said, 'to seek Mabon son of Modron, but he cannot be found until we first find Eidoel son of Aer, his kinsman.'

Arthur arose, and the warriors of the Island of Britain with him, to seek Eidoel, and they came to Gliwi's outer wall where Eidoel was imprisoned. Gliwi* stood on top of the fort and said, 'Arthur, what do you want from me, since you will not leave me alone on this rock? No good comes to me here and no pleasure; I have neither wheat nor oats, without you too seeking to do me harm.'

Arthur said, 'I have not come here to harm you but to seek the prisoner you have.'

'I shall give you the prisoner, although I had not intended to give him up to anyone. And besides that, you shall have my help and support.'

The men said to Arthur, 'Lord, go home. You cannot go with your host to seek such trivial things as these.'

Arthur said, 'Gwrhyr Gwalstawd Ieithoedd, it is right for you to go on this quest. You know all languages, and can speak the same language as some of the birds and the beasts. Eidoel, it is right for you to go and seek him with my men, he is your first cousin. Cai and Bedwyr, I have hope that you accomplish the quest you are undertaking. Go on this quest on my behalf.'

They travelled until they came to the Blackbird of Cilgwri.*

Gwrhyr asked her, 'For God's sake, do you know anything of Mabon son of Modron, who was taken when three nights old from between his mother and the wall?'

The Blackbird said, 'When I first came here, there was a smith's anvil here, and I was a young bird. No work has been done on it except by my beak every evening. Today there's not so much of it as a nut that is not worn away. God's vengeance on me if I have heard anything about the man you are asking after. However, what is right and proper for me to do for Arthur's messengers, I will do. There is a species of animal that God shaped before me. I will go there as your guide.'

They came to where the Stag of Rhedynfre* was.

'Stag of Rhedynfre, we have come to you here—Arthur's messengers—for we know of no animal older than you. Tell us, do you know anything of Mabon son of Modron, who was taken when three nights old from his mother?'

The Stag said, 'When I first came here, there was only one antler on either side of my head, and there were no trees here except a single oak sapling, and that grew into an oak with a hundred branches. And the oak fell after that, and today nothing remains of it but a red stump. From that day to this I have been here. I have heard nothing about the one you are asking after. However, since you are Arthur's messengers, I shall be your guide to where there is an animal God shaped before me.'

They came to where the Owl of Cwm Cawlwyd* was.

'Owl of Cwm Cawlwyd, here are Arthur's messengers. Do you know anything of Mabon son of Modron, who was taken when three nights old from his mother?'

'If I knew anything, I would say. When I first came here the large valley that you see was a wooded glen, and a race of men came there, and it was destroyed. And the second wood grew in it, and this wood is the third. And as for me, the roots of my wings are mere stumps. From that day to this I have heard nothing about the man you are asking after. However, I shall be a guide to Arthur's messengers until you come to the oldest animal in this world, and the one who has wandered most—the Eagle of Gwernabwy.'*

Gwrhyr said, 'Eagle of Gwernabwy, we have come to you— Arthur's messengers—to ask if you know anything of Mabon son of Modron who was taken when three nights old from his mother?'

The Eagle said, 'I came here a long time ago, and when I first came here I had a rock, and from its top I would peck at the stars every evening. Now it's not a hand-breadth in height. From that day to this I have been here, and I have heard nothing about the man you're asking after. But once I went to seek my food as far as Llyn Lliw,* and when I got there I sunk my claws into a salmon, thinking that he would be food for me for a long time, and he pulled me down into the depths, so that I barely got away from him. What I did, I and all my kinsmen, was to set upon him and try to destroy him. He sent messengers to make peace with me, and he himself came to me, to have fifty tridents taken out of his back. Unless he knows something about what you are seeking, I do not know anyone who might. However, I shall be your guide to where he is.'

They came to where he was.

The Eagle said, 'Salmon of Llyn Lliw, I have come to you with Arthur's messengers to ask if you know anything of Mabon son of Modron, who was taken when three nights old from his mother?'

'As much as I know, I will tell. With every flood tide I travel up the river until I come to the bend in the wall of Caerloyw; never before in my life have I found as much wickedness as I found there. And so that you will believe me, let one of you come here on my two shoulders.'

The ones who went on the Salmon's shoulders were Cai and Gwrhyr Gwalstawd Ieithoedd. And they travelled until they came to the other side of the wall from the prisoner, and they could hear lamenting and moaning on the other side of the wall from them.

Gwrhyr said, 'Who is lamenting in this house of stone?'

'Alas sir, he who is here has reason to lament. It is Mabon son of Modron who is imprisoned here, and no one has been so painfully incarcerated in a prison as I, neither the prison of Lludd Llaw Eraint nor the prison of Graid son of Eri.'*

'Do you have any hope of being released for gold or silver or worldly wealth, or through battle and fighting?'

'What you get of me, will be got by fighting.'

They returned from there and came to where Arthur was. They reported where Mabon son of Modron was in prison. Arthur summoned the warriors of this Island and went to Caerloyw where Mabon was in prison. Cai and Bedwyr went on the shoulders of the fish. While Arthur's warriors were attacking the fort, Cai tore through the wall and took the prisoner on his back, and fought the men as before. Arthur came home and Mabon with him, a free man.

Arthur said, 'Which of those wonders is it now best to seek first?'

'It is best to seek the two whelps of the bitch Rhymhi.'

'Does anyone know', said Arthur, 'where she is?'

'She is', said one, 'at Aber Daugleddyf.'*

Arthur came to the house of Tringad* in Aber Cleddyf and asked him, 'Have you heard about her here? In what form is she?'

'In the form of a she-wolf,' he said, 'and she goes around with her two whelps. She has killed my livestock many times, and she is down below in Aber Cleddyf in a cave.'

What Arthur did was to set off by sea in Prydwen,* his ship, and others by land, to hunt the bitch, and in this way they surrounded her and her two whelps. And God changed them back into their own shape for Arthur.* Arthur's host dispersed, one by one, two by two.

And one day, as Gwythyr son of Greidol was travelling over a mountain, he could hear weeping and woeful wailing, and it was terrible to hear. He rushed forward in that direction, and as he came there he unsheathed his sword and cut off the anthill at ground level, and so saved them from the fire.

And they said to him, 'Take with you God's blessing and ours, and that which no man can recover, we will come and recover it for you.'

It was they, after that, who brought the nine hestors of flax seed that Ysbaddaden Bencawr had demanded of Culhwch, in full measure, with none missing except for a single flax seed, but the lame ant brought that before nightfall.

As Cai and Bedwyr were sitting on top of Pumlumon on Garn Gwylathr,* in the strongest wind in the world, they looked around them and they could see a lot of smoke towards the south, far away from them, unmoved by the wind.

And then Cai said, 'By the hand of my friend, look over there— the fire of a warrior.'

They hastened towards the smoke and approached the place, watching from afar, as Dillus Farfog roasted a wild boar. He, without doubt, was the greatest warrior who had ever fled from Arthur.

Then Bedwyr said to Cai, 'Do you know him?'

'I do,' said Cai. 'That's Dillus Farfog. There is no leash in the world that can hold Drudwyn, the whelp of Graid son of Eri, except a leash made from the beard of the man you see over there.* And it won't be of any use either unless it's plucked with wooden tweezers from his beard while he's still alive, for it will be brittle if he's dead.'

'What shall we do about it?' said Bedwyr.

'We will leave him', said Cai, 'to eat his fill of the meat, and after that he will fall asleep.'

While he was doing just that they made wooden tweezers. When Cai knew for sure that he was asleep he dug a pit under his feet, the biggest in the world, and he struck him an almighty blow, and pressed him down in the pit until they had plucked out his beard completely with the wooden tweezers. And after that they killed him outright. And from there both went to Celli Wig in Cornwall, and with them a leash from the beard of Dillus Farfog, and Cai handed it to Arthur. And then Arthur sang this *englyn*:

> A leash was made by Cai
> From the beard of Dillus son of Efrai.
> Were he alive, he would kill you.*

And because of that Cai sulked, so that the warriors of this island could hardly make peace between Cai and Arthur. And yet neither Arthur's misfortune nor the killing of his men could induce Cai to have anything to do with him in his hour of need from then on.

And then Arthur said, 'Which of those wonders is it best to seek now?'

'It is best to seek Drudwyn the whelp of Graid son of Eri.'

A little while before that Creiddylad daughter of Lludd Llaw Eraint* went off with Gwythyr son of Greidol, but before he could sleep with her Gwyn son of Nudd came and took her by force. Gwythyr son of Greidol gathered a host, and came to fight against Gwyn son of Nudd, and Gwyn triumphed, and captured Graid son of Eri, and Glinneu son of Taran,* and Gwrgwst Ledlwm and Dyfnarth his son. And he captured Pen son of Nethog, and Nwython,* and Cyledyr Wyllt* his son, and he killed Nwython and cut out his heart, and forced Cyledyr to eat his father's heart, and because of that Cyledyr went mad. Arthur heard of this and came to the North, and summoned Gwyn son of Nudd to him, and released his noblemen from his prison, and made peace between Gwyn son of Nudd and Gwythyr son of Greidol. This is the agreement that was made: the maiden was to be left in her father's house, untouched by either party, and there was to be battle between Gwyn and Gwythyr every May day* forever from that day forth until Judgement Day, and the one that triumphed on Judgement Day would take the maiden.

And after reconciling those noblemen in that way, Arthur obtained Myngddwn steed of Gweddw, and the leash of Cors Cant Ewin.

After that Arthur went to Brittany, and Mabon son of Mellt* with him, and Gware Gwallt Euryn, to seek the two dogs of Glythfyr Ledewig.* After he had got them Arthur went to the west of Ireland to seek Gwrgi Seferi,* and Odgar son of Aedd, king of Ireland, with him. And then Arthur went to the North,* and caught Cyledyr Wyllt, and he went after Ysgithrwyn Pen Baedd. And Mabon son of Mellt went holding the two dogs of Glythfyr Ledewig, and Drudwyn, the whelp of Graid son of Eri. And Arthur himself went on the chase, holding Cafall, Arthur's dog. And Caw of Prydyn mounted Llamrei, Arthur's mare,* and held the boar at bay. And then Caw of Prydyn armed himself with a small axe, and with fierce vigour set upon the boar, and split his head in two. And Caw took the tusk. It was not the dogs that Ysbaddaden had demanded of Culhwch that killed the boar but Cafall, Arthur's own dog.

And after killing Ysgithrwyn Pen Baedd, Arthur and his retinue went to Celli Wig in Cornwall. And from there he sent Menw son of Teirgwaedd to see whether the treasures were between the ears of Twrch Trwyth, because it would be pointless to go to fight with him unless he had the treasures. It was certain, however, that he was there. He had destroyed one-third of Ireland. Menw went to look for them. He saw them at Esgair Oerfel in Ireland. And Menw turned himself into a bird, and settled above his lair, and tried to snatch one of the treasures from him. But indeed he got nothing except one of his bristles. The boar got up in full fury, and shook himself so that some of the poison caught him. And from then on Menw was never without affliction.

After that Arthur sent a messenger to Odgar son of Aedd, king of Ireland, to ask for the cauldron of Diwrnach Wyddel, one of his stewards. Odgar asked him to hand it over.

Diwrnach said, 'God knows, even if he were the better for getting just one look at it, he would not even get that.' And Arthur's messenger came with a 'no' from Ireland.

Arthur set off with a small force and sailed in his ship Prydwen, and came to Ireland, and they made for the house of Diwrnach Wyddel. Odgar's retinue took note of their size, and when they had eaten and drunk their fill, Arthur asked for the cauldron. Diwrnach said that if he were to give it to anyone, he would have given it at the request of Odgar king of Ireland. Having been told 'no', Bedwyr got up and took hold of the cauldron and put it on the back of Hygwydd, Arthur's servant (he was a brother by the same mother to Cacamwri, Arthur's servant). His duty was always to carry Arthur's cauldron and to light a fire under it. Llenlleog Wyddel grabbed Caledfwlch and swung it round, and killed Diwrnach Wyddel and all his retinue. The hosts of Ireland came to fight them. And when all the hosts had fled, Arthur and his men boarded the ship before their very eyes, and the cauldron with them, full of Irish treasure. And they landed at the house of Llwydeu son of Cilcoed at Porth Cerddin in Dyfed. And Mesur y Pair is there.*

And then Arthur gathered together every warrior in the Three Islands of Britain and her Three Adjacent Islands, and in France, and Brittany, and Normandy, and Gwlad yr Haf,* and every choice hound and celebrated steed. And he went with all those hosts to Ireland, and there was great fear and trembling because of him in Ireland. And when Arthur had landed, the saints of Ireland came to him to ask for protection. And he gave them protection, and they gave him their blessing. The men of Ireland came to Arthur and gave him a tribute of food.* Arthur came to Esgair Oerfel in Ireland, where Twrch Trwyth was, with his seven little pigs.* Hounds were let loose on him from all directions. That day until evening the Irish fought against him. In spite of that, he laid waste a fifth of Ireland.* And the following day Arthur's retinue fought against Twrch Trwyth; he did them only harm, he did them no good. The third day Arthur himself fought against him, for nine nights and nine days. He only killed a single piglet. The men asked Arthur what was the history of that swine.

He said, 'He was a king, and for his sins God changed him into a swine.'

Arthur sent Gwrhyr Gwalstawd Ieithoedd to try and talk to Twrch Trwyth. Gwrhyr went in the shape of a bird, and settled above the lair of the boar and his seven little pigs.

And Gwrhyr Gwalstawd Ieithoedd asked him, 'For the sake of Him who shaped you in this image, if you can speak, I'm asking one of you to come and talk to Arthur.'

Grugyn Gwrych Eraint* answered; all his bristles were like wings of silver, and one could see the path he took through woods and over fields by the way his bristles glittered. This is the answer Grugyn gave, 'By Him who shaped us in this image, we will not do and we will not say anything to help Arthur. God has done us enough harm by shaping us in this image, without you too coming to fight against us.'

'I tell you that Arthur will fight for the comb and the razor and the shears that are between the ears of Twrch Trwyth.'

Grugyn said, 'Until his life is taken first, those treasures will not be taken. And tomorrow morning we will set off from here, and we will go to Arthur's land, and there we will wreak the greatest havoc possible.'

They set off over the sea towards Wales, and Arthur and his men and his steeds and his hounds went in Prydwen, and they caught a glimpse of Twrch Trwyth and his pigs briefly. Twrch Trwyth landed in Porth Clais in Dyfed. Arthur went as far as Mynyw that night.* The next day Arthur was told that Twrch Trwyth had passed by, and he caught up with him killing the cattle of Cynwas Cwryfagyl after he had killed all the men and beasts there were in Daugleddyf before Arthur arrived. From the moment Arthur arrived, Twrch Trwyth set out from there as far as Preseli. Arthur and the forces of the world came there. Arthur sent his men to the hunt, holding Eli and Trachmyr and Drudwyn, the whelp of Graid son of Eri, while Gwarthegydd son of Caw was on another flank, holding the two dogs of Glythfyr Ledewig, and Bedwyr holding Cafall, Arthur's dog. And Arthur arranged all the warriors on the two banks of the Nyfer. The three sons of Cleddyf Difwlch arrived, men who had received great praise killing Ysgithrwyn Pen Baedd. And then Twrch Trwyth set off from Glyn Nyfer, and came to Cwm Cerwyn,* and there he stood at bay. And then he killed four of Arthur's champions, Gwarthegydd son of Caw, and Tarog Allt Clwyd,* and Rheiddwn son of Beli Adfer, and Isgofan Hael. And after killing those men he stood at bay a second time in the same place, and killed Gwydre son of Arthur, and Garselyd Wyddel, and Glew son of Ysgod, and Isgawyn son of Panon. And then he himself was wounded.

And the next day, early in the morning, some of the men caught up with Twrch Trwyth and his pigs. And Twrch Trwyth killed Huandaw, and Gogigwr, and Penpingion, the three servants of Glewlwyd Gafaelfawr, so that God knows he had no servant left to him in the world except Llaesgymyn himself, a man who was no use to anyone. He also killed many men of the country, and Gwlyddyn Saer, Arthur's chief craftsman. And then Arthur caught up with him in Peuliniog,* and then Twrch Trwyth killed Madog son of Teithion, and Gwyn son of Tringad son of Neued, and Eiriawn Penlloran. And from there he went to Aber Tywi: there he stood at bay, and he killed Cynlas son of Cynan, and Gwilenhin, king of France. From there he went to Glyn Ystun,* and then the men and hounds lost him.

Arthur summoned Gwyn son of Nudd to him, and asked him if he knew anything about Twrch Trwyth. He said that he did not. Then all the huntsmen went to hunt the pigs, as far as Dyffryn Llychwr. And Grugyn Gwallt Eraint and Llwydog Gofyniad rushed at them, and they killed the huntsmen so that not one of them escaped alive apart from one man. Arthur brought his men to where Grugyn and Llwydog were, and then let loose on them all the hounds that had been named. And because of the shouting and the barking that resulted, Twrch Trwyth came and defended his pigs. He had not set eyes on them from the time they had come across the Irish Sea until now. Then Twrch Trwyth was attacked by men and dogs, and he took flight as far as Mynydd Amanw, and then a piglet from among his pigs was killed. They engaged him in mortal combat, and then Twrch Llawin was killed. And then another of his pigs was killed—Gwys was his name. And from there he went to Dyffryn Amanw, and there Banw and Benwig were killed.* Not one of his pigs lived to go with him from there except Grugyn Gwallt Eraint and Llwydog Gofyniad.

From there they went to Llwch Ewin, where Arthur caught up with Twrch Trwyth. Then he stood at bay. And then he killed Echel Forddwyd Twll, and Arwyli son of Gwyddog Gwyr, and many men and hounds besides. From there they went to Llwch Tawy. Grugyn Gwrych Eraint then separated from them, and made for Din Tywi. And from there he went to Ceredigion, followed by Eli and Trachmyr and a crowd besides. And he went as far as Garth Grugyn, and it was there Grugyn was killed in their midst, but not before he killed Rhyddfyw Rhys and many others. And then Llwydog went to Ystrad Yw,* and it was there the men of Brittany encountered him, and then he killed Hir Peisog* the king of Brittany, and Llygadrudd Emys and Gwrfoddw, Arthur's uncles, his mother's brothers. And then Llwydog himself was killed.

Twrch Trwyth then passed between Tawy and Ewias. Arthur summoned Cornwall and Devon to meet him at Aber Hafren,* and Arthur said to the men of this Island, 'Twrch Trwyth has killed many of my men. By the might of men, he will not go to Cornwall while I am alive. I shall pursue him no more but will engage him in mortal combat. You do what you will.'

This is what happened on his advice: they sent an army of horsemen, and the hounds of the Island with them, as far as Ewias,

and they returned from there to the Hafren, and ambushed him
with every experienced soldier in this Island, and drove him by
sheer force into the Hafren. And Mabon son of Modron went
with him on Gwyn Myngddwn, Gweddw's steed, into the Hafren,
and Gorau son of Custennin and Menw son of Teirgwaedd,
between Llyn Lliwan and Aber Gwy.* And Arthur fell upon Twrch
Trwyth, together with the warriors of Prydain. Osla Gyllellfawr
approached, and Manawydan son of Llŷr, and Cacamwri, Arthur's
servant, and Gwyngelli, and closed in on him. And they grabbed
him first by his feet, and soused him in the Hafren until it flooded
over him. Mabon son of Modron spurred his horse on the one
side and grabbed the razor from him, and on the other side Cyledyr
Wyllt rushed into the Hafren on another horse and snatched the
shears from him. Before they could remove the comb he found
his feet, and firm ground, and from the moment he found dry
land neither hound nor man nor steed could keep up with him
until he reached Cornwall. Whatever trouble was had getting those
treasures from him, worse was had trying to save the two men
from drowning. As Cacamwri was pulled up, two millstones pulled
him back into the depths. As he was running after the boar, Osla
Gyllellfawr's knife fell from its sheath and he lost it, and after that
his sheath was full of water; as he was pulled up, it pulled him back
into the depths.

From there Arthur went with his men until he caught up with
Twrch Trwyth in Cornwall. Whatever trouble he had caused them
before was mere play compared to what they then suffered in seeking
the comb. But after one difficulty and another, the comb was taken
from him. And then he was chased out of Cornwall and driven
straight into the sea. From then on it was not known where he and
Aned and Aethlem went. From there Arthur went to Celli Wig in
Cornwall, to bathe himself and throw off his weariness.

Arthur said, 'Are there any of the wonders we have still not
obtained?'

One of the men said, 'Yes, the blood of the Very Black Witch,
daughter of the Very White Witch from Pennant Gofid in the uplands
of hell.'

Arthur set out for the North, and came to where the hag's
cave was. And Gwyn son of Nudd and Gwythyr son of Greidol

advised that Cacamwri and Hygwydd his brother should be sent to fight the hag. As they came into the cave the hag attacked them, and grabbed Hygwydd by his hair and threw him to the ground beneath her. Cacamwri grabbed her by the hair and pulled her off Hygwydd to the ground, and she turned on Cacamwri and thrashed both of them and disarmed them, and sent them out shrieking and shouting. Arthur became angry at seeing his two servants almost killed, and tried to rush at the cave. And then Gwyn and Gwythyr said to him, 'It is not proper and we do not like to see you wrestling with a hag. Let Hir Amren and Hir Eiddil go into the cave.' And they went. But if the first two had difficulties, the fate of these two was far worse, so that God knows how any of the four could have left the place, had it not been for the way they were all put on Llamrei, Arthur's mare. And then Arthur rushed to the entrance of the cave, and from the entrance he aimed at the hag with Carnwennan, his knife, and struck her in the middle so she was like two vats. And Caw of Prydyn took the witch's blood and kept it with him.

And then Culhwch set out with Gorau son of Custennin, and those who wished harm to Ysbaddaden Bencawr, and took the wonders with them to his court. And Caw of Prydyn came to shave off Ysbaddaden's beard, flesh and skin to the bone, and both ears completely.

And Culhwch said, 'Have you been shaved, man?'

'I have,' he replied.

'And is your daughter now mine?'

'Yours,' he replied. 'And you need not thank me for that, but thank Arthur, the man who arranged it for you. If I'd had my way you never would have got her. And it is high time to take away my life.'

And then Gorau son of Custennin grabbed him by the hair and dragged him to the mound and cut off his head and stuck it on the bailey post. And he took possession of his fort and his territory.

And that night Culhwch slept with Olwen. And she was his only wife as long as he lived. And Arthur's men dispersed, each one to his country. And that is how Culhwch won Olwen daughter of Ysbaddaden Bencawr.

Rhonabwy's Dream

MADOG son of Maredudd ruled Powys from one end to the other, that is, from Porffordd to Gwafan in the uplands of Arwystli.* At that time he had a brother whose rank was not equal to his. His name was Iorwerth son of Maredudd.* And Iorwerth became greatly concerned and saddened to see the honour and power possessed by his brother, and he with nothing. So he sought out his companions and foster-brothers, and consulted with them as to what he should do about it. They decided that some of them should go and ask Madog for maintenance. Madog offered him the position of the head of the retinue,* and equal standing with himself, and horses and armour and honour. But Iorwerth refused that, and went raiding in England, and he committed murder, and burned houses and took prisoners. Madog took counsel, together with the men of Powys. They decided to place a hundred men in every three commots in Powys to look for Iorwerth. And they regarded Rhychdir Powys, from Aber Ceiriog in Halictwn as far as Rhyd Wilfre on Efyrnwy,* as equal to the three best commots in Powys. And anyone who did not succeed with a retinue in this arable land would not succeed anywhere in Powys. And those men split up as far as Didlystwn,* a small town in this arable land.

There was a man on that quest whose name was Rhonabwy. He and Cynwrig Frychgoch, a man from Mawddwy, and Cadwgan Fras, a man from Moelfre in Cynllaith, came to the house of Heilyn Goch son of Cadwgan son of Iddon* for lodging. And when they approached the house, they could see a very black old building with a straight gable end, and plenty of smoke coming from it. When they came inside they could see an uneven floor, full of holes; where there was a bump in the floor, scarcely could a man stand up, so slippery was the floor with the dung of cattle and their piss. Where there was a hole, a man would go over his ankle, what with the mixture of water and cattle-piss. And there were branches of holly in abundance on the floor, with their tips eaten by the cattle. When they came to the upper end of the hall they could see bare, dusty, dais boards, and a hag feeding a fire on one dais.* And when she became cold, she would throw a lapful of chaff on the fire so that it was not easy for anyone in the world to put up with that smoke entering his nostrils. On the other dais they could see a yellow ox-skin;* good luck would befall whichever one of them got to lie on that skin.

When they had sat down they asked the hag where the people of the house were, but she would only speak gruffly to them. Suddenly the people arrive, a red-haired, balding, wizened man, with a bundle of sticks on his back, and a little skinny, grey-haired woman, with a bundle under her arm too. And they gave the men a cold welcome. The woman lit a fire for them with the sticks and went to cook, and brought them their food—barley bread and cheese, and watered-down milk. Suddenly there was a surge of wind and rain, so that it was not easy for anyone to go out and relieve himself. And because their journey had been so troublesome, they grew weary and went to sleep. When they examined their sleeping-place there was on it only dusty, flea-infested straw-ends, mixed with bits of twig, the cattle having devoured all the straw that was above their heads and below their feet. A greyish-red blanket, rough and threadbare and full of holes, was spread on it, and over the blanket a coarse, tattered sheet with big holes, and a half-empty pillow with a filthy cover on top of the sheet. And they went to sleep. Rhonabwy's two companions fell into a deep sleep, after the fleas and discomfort had tormented them. But Rhonabwy, since he could neither sleep nor rest, thought he would suffer less if he went to sleep on the yellow ox-skin on the dais. And there he slept.

As soon as sleep entered his eyes he was granted a vision, that he and his companions were travelling across Maes Argyngroeg, and his inclination and intent, so he thought, was towards Rhyd-y-groes on the Hafren.* As he was travelling he heard a commotion, and he had never heard a commotion like it. He looked behind him, and saw a young man with curly yellow hair and his beard newly trimmed, on a yellow horse, and from the top of its forelegs and its kneecaps downwards green. And the rider was wearing a tunic of yellow brocaded silk, embroidered with green thread, a gold-hilted sword on his thigh, with a sheath of new Cordovan leather, and a thong of deerskin with a clasp of gold. And over that a mantle of yellow brocaded silk, embroidered with green silk, and the fringes of the mantle were green. What was green of the garment of the rider and horse was as green as the leaves of the pine-trees, and what was yellow was as yellow as the flowers of the broom.* Because the rider looked so fierce, Rhonabwy and his companions became frightened and began to retreat. But he pursued them. As the horse breathed out, the men moved a distance away from him; but as he breathed in, they came closer to him, right to the horse's chest. When he caught up with them, they asked him for mercy.

'You shall have it, gladly, and don't be afraid.'

'Lord, since you have shown us mercy, will you tell us who you are?' said Rhonabwy.

'I will not conceal my identity from you: Iddog son of Mynio. But usually I am not known by my name, but by my nickname.'

'Will you tell us your nickname?'

'I will. I am called Iddog Cordd Prydain.'*

'Lord,' said Rhonabwy, 'why are you called that?'

'I will tell you why. I was one of the messengers between Arthur and his nephew Medrawd at the battle of Camlan. And at that time I was a high-spirited young man, and because I was so eager for battle, I stirred up trouble between them. This is what I did: whenever the emperor Arthur would send me to remind Medrawd that he was his foster-father and uncle, and to ask for peace lest the sons of the kings of the Island of Britain and their men be killed, and when Arthur would speak to me the fairest words that he could, I would repeat those words to Medrawd in the most offensive way possible. Because of that I was called Iddog Cordd Prydain. And that is how the battle of Camlan was contrived. But three nights before the end of the battle of Camlan I left them, and came to Y Llech Las in Prydain* to do penance. And I was there for seven years doing penance, and I was shown mercy.'

Then they heard a commotion that was louder by far than the first one. When they looked towards the commotion, behold, a young lad with yellowish-red hair, without a beard or a moustache, and the look of a nobleman about him, on a large horse. From the top of its shoulders and its kneecaps downwards, the horse was yellow. The man was wearing a garment of red brocaded silk, embroidered with yellow silk, and the fringes of the mantle were yellow. What was yellow of his and his horse's garment was as yellow as the flowers of the broom, and what was red was as red as the reddest blood in the world. Then, behold, the rider catches up with them, and asks Iddog if he would give him a share of these little men.

'The share that is proper for me to give, I will do so: to be a friend to them as I have been.' The rider agreed to that and went off.

'Iddog,' said Rhonabwy, 'who was that man?'

'Rhuawn Bebyr son of Deorthach Wledig.'*

Then they travelled across the great plain of Argyngroeg to Rhyd-y-groes on the Hafren. And a mile from the ford, on each side of the road, they could see huts and tents and the mustering of a great host. They came to the edge of the ford, and saw Arthur sitting on a flat meadow below the ford, with Bedwin the Bishop on one side and Gwarthegydd son of Caw* on the other. A tall, auburn-haired young man was standing beside them, holding his sword in its sheath, and wearing a tunic and cape of pure black brocaded silk, his face as white as ivory, and his eyebrows as black as jet. What could be seen of his wrist between his gloves and sleeves was whiter than the lily, and thicker than the calf of a warrior's leg. Then Iddog, accompanied by the men, went up to Arthur, and greeted him.

'May God prosper you,' said Arthur. 'Iddog, where did you find these little men?'

'I found them, lord, up there on the road.' The emperor smiled disdainfully.

'Lord,' said Iddog, 'why are you laughing?'

'Iddog,' said Arthur, 'I am not laughing; but rather I feel so sad that scum such as these are protecting this Island after such fine men that protected it in the past.'

Then Iddog said, 'Rhonabwy, do you see the ring with the stone in it on the emperor's hand?'

'I do,' he said.

'One of the virtues of the stone is that you will remember what you have seen here tonight; and had you not seen the stone, you would remember nothing about this.'

After that Rhonabwy saw a troop coming towards the ford.

'Iddog,' said Rhonabwy, 'whose is that troop?'

'The companions of Rhuawn Bebyr son of Deorthach Wledig. And those men receive mead and bragget with honour, and get to make love to the daughters of the kings of the Island of Britain with no objection, and they have a right to that, for in each battle they lead and bring up the rear.'

Rhonabwy could see no other colour on a horse or a man in that troop that was not as red as blood. And if one of the riders broke away from that troop, he would be like a column of fire rising to the sky. And that troop encamped above the ford.

Then they saw another troop coming towards the ford. And from the horses' front pommels upwards they were as white as the lily, and from there downwards as black as jet. Behold, they saw a rider coming forward and spurring his horse in the ford so that the water splashed over Arthur and the bishop and all who were conferring with them, so that they were as wet as if they had been dragged out of the river. As the rider was turning his horse's head, the lad who was standing beside Arthur struck the horse on its nostrils with the sword in its sheath, so that it would have been a wonder had it not shattered steel, let alone flesh or bone. The rider drew his sword half out of his sheath, and asked him, 'Why did you strike my horse? Was it out of disrespect or by way of advice?'

'You needed advice. What madness made you ride so foolishly, causing the water to splash from the ford over Arthur and the consecrated bishop and their counsellors, so that they were as wet as if they had been dragged out of the river?'

'Then I shall take it as advice.' And he turned his horse's head back towards his troop.

'Iddog,' said Rhonabwy, 'who was the rider just now?'

'A young man considered to be the wisest and most accomplished in this kingdom, Addaon son of Taliesin.'

'Who was the man who struck his horse?'

'A stubborn and fierce lad, Elphin son of Gwyddno.'*

Then a proud, handsome man with eloquent, bold speech said that it was strange that a host as large as that could be accommodated in such a confined place, and that it was even stranger that those who had promised to be at the battle of Baddon by noon, to fight Osla Gyllellfawr,* should still be there: 'Decide whether you will go or not. I shall go.'

'You are right,' said Arthur. 'And let us go together.'

'Iddog,' said Rhonabwy, 'who is the man who spoke so boldly to Arthur as he who spoke just now?'

'A man who had the right to speak to him as plainly as he wished, Caradog Freichfras son of Llŷr Marini,* his chief adviser and nephew.'

Then Iddog took Rhonabwy behind him on the horse, and that large host set off towards Cefn Digoll,* each troop in its proper place. When they were halfway across the ford on the Hafren, Iddog turned his horse's head round, and Rhonabwy looked at the Hafren valley. He could see two most disciplined troops approaching the ford on the Hafren. A brilliant white troop was approaching, each man wearing a mantle of white brocaded silk with pure black fringes, and from the kneecaps and the tops of the horses' forelegs downwards they were pure black, but apart from that they were pale white all over. And their banners were pure white, and the tip of each one was pure black.

'Iddog,' said Rhonabwy, 'who is that pure white troop over there?'

'They are the men of Norway, led by March son of Meirchawn.* He is Arthur's cousin.'

Then Rhonabwy could see a troop, and each man wearing a pure black garment with pure white fringes, and from the tops of the horses' forelegs and their kneecaps downwards, they were pure white. And their banners were pure black and the tip of each one was pure white.

'Iddog,' said Rhonabwy, 'who is that pure black troop over there?'

'The men of Denmark, led by Edern son of Nudd.'*

By the time these had caught up with the host, Arthur and his host of warriors had dismounted below Caer Faddon. Rhonabwy could see that he and Iddog were going the same way as Arthur. When they had dismounted he heard a huge, dreadful commotion among the host. And the man who would be at the edge of the host one moment would be in their midst the next, and the one who would be in their midst would be at the edge. Suddenly he could see a rider approaching, both he and his horse dressed in chain-mail, its rings as white as the whitest lily, and its rivets as red as the reddest blood, and he was riding among the host.

'Iddog,' said Rhonabwy, 'is the host retreating from me?'

'The emperor Arthur has never retreated, and if you were heard uttering those words, you would be a dead man. But the rider you see over there, that's Cai;* he is the fairest man who rides in Arthur's court. And the man at the edge of the host is rushing back to see Cai ride, and the man in the middle is retreating to the edge for fear of being hurt by the horse. And that's the meaning of the commotion in the host.'

Then they heard Cadwr, earl of Cornwall,* being summoned.
Behold, he got up with Arthur's sword in his hand and the image of
two golden serpents on the sword. When the sword was drawn from
the sheath, it was like seeing two flames of fire from the serpents'
jaws. And it was not easy for anyone to look at that, because it was so
terrifying. Then, behold, the host calmed down and the commotion
ceased; and the earl returned to the tent.

'Iddog,' said Rhonabwy, 'who was the man who brought the sword
to Arthur?'

'Cadwr, earl of Cornwall, the man whose duty it is to dress the
king in his armour on the day of battle and combat.'

Then they heard Eiryn Wych Amheibyn,* Arthur's servant, being
summoned, a rough, ugly, red-haired man, with a red moustache full
of bristling hairs. Behold, he came on a big red horse with its mane
parted on both sides of its neck, carrying a large, handsome load.
The big red-haired servant dismounted in front of Arthur and
pulled out a golden chair from the load, and a mantle of damasked,
brocaded silk. He spread out the mantle in front of Arthur, with a
reddish gold apple at each of its corners. He placed the chair on the
mantle, and the chair was so large that three armed men could sit on
it. Gwen was the name of the mantle.* One of the attributes of the
mantle was that the person wrapped in it could see everyone yet no
one could see him. And no colour would ever last on it except its own
colour. Arthur sat down on the mantle; Owain son of Urien* was
standing near him.

'Owain,' said Arthur, 'do you want to play *gwyddbwyll*?'*

'I do, lord,' said Owain. And the red-haired servant brought the
gwyddbwyll to Arthur and Owain—pieces of gold and a board of
silver. And they began to play.

When their game of *gwyddbwyll* was at its most entertaining,
behold, they see coming from a white, red-topped tent—with an
image of a pure black serpent on top of the tent, and crimson-red,
poisonous eyes in the serpent's head, and its tongue flame-red—a
young squire with curly yellow hair and blue eyes, sprouting a beard,
wearing a tunic and surcoat of yellow brocaded silk, and stockings of
thin greenish-yellow cloth on his feet. And over the stockings two
buskins of speckled Cordovan leather,* and clasps of gold around his
ankles to fasten them, and a golden-hilted, heavy, triple-grooved
sword, with a sheath of black Cordovan leather, and a tip of excellent

reddish gold at the end of the sheath. And he was coming to where the emperor and Owain were playing *gwyddbwyll*. The squire greeted Owain. And Owain was surprised that the squire greeted him but did not greet the emperor Arthur. And Arthur knew what Owain was thinking, and he said to Owain, 'Do not be surprised that the squire greeted you just now. He greeted me earlier. And his message is for you.'

Then the squire said to Owain,

'Lord, is it with your permission that the emperor's young lads and squires are molesting and harassing and brawling with your ravens?* If they don't have your permission, then ask the emperor to call them off.'

'Lord,' said Owain, 'you hear what the squire says. If you please, call them off my little ravens.'

'Your move,' he said. Then the squire returned to his tent.

They finished that game and began another. When they were halfway through the game, behold, a young ruddy-faced lad with very curly auburn hair, sharp-eyed, well-built, having trimmed his beard, coming from a bright yellow tent, with the image of a bright red lion on top of the tent. And he was wearing a tunic of yellow brocaded silk down to his calf, embroidered with thread of red silk, and two stockings on his feet of thin white linen, and over the stockings, two buskins of black Cordovan leather with golden clasps. And he had a large, heavy, triple-grooved sword in his hand, and a sheath of red deerskin for it, and a golden tip on the sheath, and he was coming to where Arthur and Owain were playing *gwyddbwyll*. The lad greeted him. And Owain was put out at being greeted, but Arthur was no more troubled than before. The squire said to Owain, 'Is it against your will that the emperor's squires are wounding your ravens, and killing some and bothering others? If it is against your will, beg him to call them off.'

'Lord,' said Owain, 'call your men off if you please.'

'Your move,' said the emperor. Then the squire returned to his tent.

They finished that game and began another. As they were beginning the first move in the game, they could see a short distance from them a mottled yellow tent, bigger than anyone had ever seen, with an image on it of an eagle made of gold, and precious stones in the eagle's head. Coming from the tent they could see a squire with

bright yellow hair on his head, fair and graceful, wearing a mantle of
green brocaded silk, a golden pin in the mantle on his right shoulder,
as thick as a warrior's middle finger, and two stockings on his feet of
thin totnes cloth,* and two shoes of speckled Cordovan leather with
golden clasps. The young lad was of noble appearance—he had a
white, rosy-cheeked face, and large, hawk-like eyes. In the squire's
hand was a thick, speckled yellow spear, with a newly sharpened
head, and on the spear a conspicuous banner. The squire came
angrily, passionately, and at a fast canter to where Arthur was playing
gwyddbwyll with Owain. And they realized that he was angry. Yet he
greeted Owain, and told him that the most notable ravens had been
killed, 'and those who have not been killed have been wounded and
injured so badly that not one of them can raise its wings six feet from
the ground.'

'Lord,' said Owain, 'call off your men.'

'Play on,' he said, 'if you want to.'

Then Owain said to the squire, 'Go back, and raise the banner
where you see the battle at its most intense. And let God's will be
done.'

Then the squire rode to where the battle was at its most intense
for the ravens, and raised the banner. As he raised it the ravens flew
up into the sky angrily, passionately, and ecstatically, to let wind into
their wings and to throw off their fatigue. When they had regained
their strength and power, with anger and joy they swooped down
together on the men who had previously caused them injury and
pain and loss. They carried off the heads of some, the eyes of others,
the ears of others, and the arms of others, and took them up into the
air. There was a great commotion in the sky with the fluttering of the
jubilant ravens and their croaking, and another great commotion
with the screaming of the men being attacked and injured and others
being killed. It was as terrifying for Arthur as it was for Owain to
hear that commotion above the *gwyddbwyll*.

When they looked they could hear a rider on a dapple-grey horse
coming towards them. His horse was of a very strange colour*—
dapple-grey, and its right foreleg bright red, and from the top of its
legs to the top of its hoof, bright yellow. The rider and his horse were
dressed in strange, heavy armour. His horse's covering, from the
front pommel of his saddle upwards, was of bright red sendal, and
from the pommel downwards, of bright yellow sendal. There was a

large, golden-hilted, one-edged sword on the lad's thigh and a new bright-green sheath with its tip of Spanish latten.* The sword's belt was of rough, black, Cordovan leather with gilded cross-pieces, and a clasp of ivory with a pure black tongue. On the rider's head was a golden helmet with precious, valuable stones in it, on top of the helmet an image of a yellow-red leopard, with two crimson-red stones in its head, so that it was terrifying for a warrior, however strong-hearted he might be, to look in the face of the leopard, let alone in the face of the warrior. In his hand a spear with a long, heavy, green shaft, and from its hilt upwards it was crimson-red with the blood of the ravens and their feathers. The rider approached the place where Arthur and Owain were over the *gwyddbwyll*. They realized that he was weary, angry, and troubled as he came towards them. The squire greeted Arthur and said that Owain's ravens were killing his young lads and squires. Arthur looked at Owain and said, 'Call off your ravens.'

'Lord,' said Owain, 'your move.' They played. The rider turned back towards the battle, and the ravens were no more restrained than before.

When they had played a little they could hear a great commotion, and the screaming of men, and the croaking of ravens as they seized the men by brute force into the sky and tore them apart between each other, and let them fall in pieces to the ground. Out of the commotion they could see a rider approaching on a pale white horse, and the horse's left foreleg was pure black down to the top of the hoof. The rider and his horse were dressed in large, heavy, green armour. He wore a cloak of yellow, damasked, brocaded silk, and the fringes of the cloak were green. His horse's covering was pure black with its fringes bright yellow. On the squire's thigh was a long, heavy, triple-grooved sword, with a sheath of engraved, red leather, and the belt of new red deerskin, with many golden cross-pieces, and a clasp made of whalebone with a pure black tongue. On the rider's head a golden helmet with magic sapphires in it, and on top of the helmet an image of a yellow-red lion, its foot-long, flame-red tongue sticking out of its mouth, and crimson-red, poisonous eyes in its head. The rider carried a stout spear of ash in his hand, with a new, bloody head on it and silver rivets. And the squire greeted the emperor.

'Lord,' he said, 'your squires and young lads have been

killed, together with the sons of the noblemen of the Island of Britain, so that from now on it will never be easy to protect this Island.'

'Owain,' said Arthur, 'call off your ravens.'

'Lord,' said Owain, 'your move.'

That game ended and they began another. When they were at the end of that game, behold, they heard a great commotion, and the screaming of armed men, and the croaking of ravens and their fluttering in the sky as they let the weapons fall to the ground in one piece but the men and horses were in pieces. Then they could see a rider on a black-hoofed, high-headed horse, and the top of the horse's left leg was bright red, and its right foreleg was pure white to the top of the hoof. The rider and his horse were dressed in mottled yellow armour, speckled with Spanish latten. He and his horse wore a cloak, in two halves, white and pure black, and the fringes of his cloak were golden purple. On top of his cloak was a golden-hilted, shining, triple-grooved sword. The sword's belt was of yellow gold cloth, with a clasp made of the eyelid of a pure black whale and a tongue of yellow gold. On the rider's head was a shiny helmet of yellow latten with shining crystals in it, and on top of the helmet an image of a griffin with magic stones in its head. In his hand was a spear of ash with a rounded shaft, coloured with blue azure, with a new, bloody head on the spear, riveted with precious silver. The rider came angrily to where Arthur was, and said that the ravens had killed his retinue and the sons of the noblemen of this Island, and asked him to persuade Owain to call off his ravens. Then Arthur asked Owain to call off his ravens. Then Arthur crushed the golden pieces that were on the board until they were nothing but dust; and Owain asked Gwres son of Rheged to lower his banner. Then it was lowered and everything was peaceful.

Then Rhonabwy asked Iddog who were the first three men who had come to tell Owain that his ravens were being killed. Iddog said, 'Men who were unhappy at Owain's loss, fellow noblemen and companions, Selyf son of Cynan Garwyn from Powys, and Gwgawn Gleddyfrudd,* and Gwres son of Rheged, the man who carries Owain's banner on the day of battle and combat.'

'Who were the last three men who came to tell Arthur that the ravens were killing his men?' said Rhonabwy.

'The best and bravest men,' said Iddog, 'and they hate to see

Arthur suffer any loss: Blathaon son of Mwrheth, and Rhuawn Bebyr son of Deorthach Wledig, and Hyfaidd Unllen.'*

Then twenty-four horsemen came from Osla Gyllellfawr to ask Arthur for a truce until the end of a fortnight and a month. Arthur got up and took counsel. He went up to a large man with curly auburn hair standing a short distance from him. And there his counsellors were brought to him: Bedwin the Bishop, and Gwarthegydd son of Caw, and March son of Meirchawn, and Caradog Freichfras, and Gwalchmai son of Gwyar, and Edern son of Nudd, and Rhuawn Bebyr son of Deorthach Wledig, and Rhiogan son of the king of Ireland, and Gwenwynwyn son of Naf, Hywel son of Emyr Llydaw, Gwilym son of the king of France, and Daned son of Oth, and Gorau son of Custennin, and Mabon son of Modron, and Peredur Paladr Hir, and Hyfaidd Unllen, and Twrch son of Perif, Nerth son of Cadarn, and Gobrw son of Echel Forddwyd Twll, Gwair son of Gwystyl, and Adwy son of Geraint, Dyrstan son of Tallwch, Morien Manog, Granwen son of Llŷr, and Llacheu son of Arthur, and Llawfrodedd Farfog, and Cadwr, earl of Cornwall, Morfran son of Tegid, and Rhyawdd son of Morgant, and Dyfyr son of Alun Dyfed, Gwrhyr Gwalstawd Ieithoedd, Addaon son of Taliesin, and Llara son of Casnar Wledig, and Fflewddwr Fflam, and Greidol Gallddofydd, Gilbert son of Cadgyffro, Menw son of Teirgwaedd, Gyrthmwl Wledig, Cawrdaf son of Caradog Freichfras, Gildas son of Caw, Cadyriaith son of Saidi, and many men from Norway and Denmark, together with many men from Greece.* And plenty of people came to that counsel.

'Iddog,' said Rhonabwy, 'who is the man with auburn hair they approached just now?'

'Rhun son of Maelgwn Gwynedd, a man who has such authority that everyone goes to him for advice.'

'Why was a lad as young as Cadyriaith son of Saidi* brought to a counsel of such high-ranking men as those over there?'

'Because no one in Prydain gives more solid advice than he.'

Then, behold, poets came to perform a poem for Arthur. And no one understood the poem, apart from Cadyriaith himself, except that it was in praise of Arthur.* Then, behold, twenty-four mules arrived with their loads of gold and silver, and a tired and weary man with each of them, bringing tribute to Arthur from the Islands of Greece. Then Cadyriaith son of Saidi asked that a truce be given to Osla

Gyllellfawr for a fortnight and a month; and that the mules which had brought the tribute be given to the poets, along with what was on them, as a reward for waiting; and that during the truce they should be given payment for their singing. And that was agreed.

'Rhonabwy,' said Iddog, 'would it not be wrong to stop a young man who can give such generous advice as that from attending his lord's council?'

Then Cai got up and said, 'Whoever wishes to follow Arthur, let him be with him tonight in Cornwall.* And he who does not, let him stand against Arthur until the end of the truce.'

So loud was that commotion, Rhonabwy awoke. And when he awoke he was on the yellow ox-skin, having slept for three nights and three days.

And this story is called the Dream of Rhonabwy. This is why no one knows the dream—neither poet nor storyteller—without a book,* because of the number of colours on the horses, and the many unusual colours both on the armour and their trappings, and on the precious mantles and the magic stones.

EXPLANATORY NOTES

ABBREVIATIONS

TYP   *Trioedd Ynys Prydein: The Triads of the Island of Britain*, ed. and trans. Rachel Bromwich (3rd revised edn. Cardiff, 2006; 1st edn. 1961). References are to triad numbers or page numbers in the 3rd edition.

AOW   *The Arthur of the Welsh*, ed. Rachel Bromwich, A. O. H. Jarman, and Brynley F. Roberts (Cardiff, 1991).

LHDd   *The Law of Hywel Dda*, ed. and trans. Dafydd Jenkins (Llandysul, 1986).

THE FIRST BRANCH OF THE MABINOGI

In the White and Red Book manuscripts there are no specific titles to the Four Branches: each tale ends with a variation on the colophon 'and so ends this branch of the Mabinogi', giving rise to the current title which was popularized by Ifor Williams in his classic edition *Pedeir Keinc y Mabinogi* (Cardiff, 1930)—'The Four Branches of the Mabinogi'. However, it is not clear whether there were only four branches. In the Red Book of Hergest the words *llyma dechreu mabinogi* ('this is the beginning of a mabinogi') appear before the First Branch; similar introductions are given to the other three tales: 'this is the Second/Third/Fourth Branch of the mabinogi'. Yet, there is no closing formula informing us that the *mabinogi* has come to an end, again implying that there may well have been more than four branches originally (see also the note to p. 21 on *branch of the Mabinogion*.

     Regarding the titles of the individual tales, the First and Fourth Branches are commonly referred to by their *incipit*s—'Pwyll, prince of Dyfed' and 'Math son of Mathonwy'. The Third Branch is, in reality, a continuation of the Second, and no personal name appears in the opening lines (indeed, these may have been one branch originally); however, Manawydan is central to the plot, and it could thus be argued that 'Manawydan son of Llŷr' is a suitable title. The Second Branch begins with the words 'Bendigeidfran fab Llŷr'; until the middle of the nineteenth century this, too, was commonly known in scholarly publications as *Mabinogi Bendigeidfran* or *Brân* (another version of his name). However, the tale is commonly known today as 'Branwen daughter of Llŷr', a title bestowed on the branch by Lady Charlotte Guest. From her textual notes, it would seem that Branwen had captured Guest's imagination, and especially the 'discovery' of her grave in 1813. To the male scholars of her time it was the king who was central to the tale; to Guest, however, it was the 'unfortunate heroine', Branwen. One could surmise about whether Guest felt some empathy with Branwen who, like her, had left her homeland for foreign parts in order to get married (see Sioned Davies, 'A Charming Guest:

Translating the *Mabinogion*', *Studia Celtica*, 38 (2004), 157–78). The current
translation uses the less neutral titles, and those that emanate from the
colophons themselves.

3 *Pwyll, prince of Dyfed . . . seven cantrefs of Dyfed*: the name Pwyll means
'wisdom, caution'. Dyfed is an area in the south-west of Wales, compris-
ing today's Pembrokeshire and part of Carmarthenshire. *Cantref* was the
basic territorial administrative unit in medieval Wales: the seven cantrefs
of Dyfed were Cemais, Pebidiog, Rhos, Penfro, Daugleddyf, Emlyn,
and Cantref Gwarthaf. A cantref would be subdivided into *cymydau*
('commots'), usually corresponding to the English 'hundred'.

Arberth, one of his chief courts . . . Glyn Cuch: *Arberth* is usually equated
with the town of Arberth in Pembrokeshire (English: Narberth), while
the Cuch Valley runs along the border of Pembrokeshire and Carmarthenshire. *One of his chief courts* refers to the practice whereby the
lord, together with his retinue and officials, would circuit the land, staying at various courts of his where he would be maintained by his subjects.
Hunting was a common pastime for the noblemen of medieval Wales,
with its own terminology and legalities. The hunt is often used in medieval French and English tales and romances as well as in the *Mabinogion*
as a precursor to an encounter with the supernatural (see e.g. p. 26),
while the prince lost on a hunt is a well-known international device for
beginning an adventure. See also note to p. 8.

they were a gleaming shining white, and their ears were red: red and white
are colours traditionally associated with the supernatural in Welsh and
Irish tradition.

but I will not greet you: greeting formulae are very common in the
Mabinogion, and follow specific patterns. Usually it is the character of
lower rank who greets first, and the other responds by wishing *graessaw
Duw* ('God's welcome'). Pwyll believes that Arawn is refusing to greet
him because his status prevents it; however, when Pwyll discovers that
Arawn is a king, and therefore of higher rank, he responds immediately
with 'good day to you'. For a discussion of formulae in the Four Branches,
see Sioned Davies, *The Four Branches of the Mabinogi* (Llandysul, 1993),
32–42.

4 *I will redeem your friendship*: Pwyll has insulted Arawn by feeding his
own dogs on the stag killed by Arawn's pack. He must therefore pay
compensation to the king for injuring his honour.

Annwfn: a name for the Celtic Otherworld, derived from *an* ('in', 'inside')
+ *dwfn* ('world'). In both Welsh and Irish traditions the Otherworld was
generally believed to be located either on an island or under the earth.
Here, however, it seems to be a land within Pwyll's realm of Dyfed, while
the two Otherworld feasts that occur in the Second Branch are located
at Harlech (on the north-west coast of Wales) and on the Island of
Grassholm (see pp. 33–4). Under Christian influence, Annwfn came to be

regarded as synonymous with hell, though in modern Brittany, despite its strong Catholic heritage, *Annaon* became synonymous with paradise rather than hell (*mont da Annaon*—to go to Annaon—is a common euphemism for 'to die'). For further details, see Proinsias Mac Cana, *Celtic Mythology* (London 1983).

you must give him only one blow—he will not survive it: supernatural creatures needing the help of mortals to overcome an adversary is a theme found in Irish and Welsh literature, while the taboo that surrounds striking a monster twice is a common international motif—were the hero to strike a second time, then the monster would revive. For a list of the motifs in the Four Branches, see Andrew Welsh, 'The Traditional Narrative Motifs of *The Four Branches of the Mabinogi*', *Cambridge Medieval Celtic Studies*, 15 (1988), 51–62.

5 *I shall arrange ... I will take your place*: shape-shifting is a theme that appears several times in the Four Branches. Here, two persons exchange forms and kingdoms for a year and a day, a formula common to international folk-tale and medieval romance.

and sat like this: according to Welsh laws, everyone had to sit at a specific place at table, depending on one's status. A variable formula common to many of the tales is employed to describe the whole process, which could include the welcome and preparations (including washing before the meal), sitting at the table (including the seating arrangements), followed by eating, drinking, and conversing.

earl: the identity of this person is unclear. The title itself is not found in the medieval laws tracts, neither was it in use among the native Welsh rulers.

Time came for them to go to sleep, and they went to sleep: a common formula covering transition from one period to the next—in oral narrative, the interstices between the important and exciting occasions are almost always filled.

he turned his face to the edge of the bed: although Arawn explicitly said that Pwyll was to sleep with his wife, Pwyll declines, thus proving himself to be a true friend. In many instances of this motif, the shape-shifting takes place for the sole purpose of sleeping with the wife—compare Geoffrey of Monmouth's account of the conception of Arthur, where Uther Pendragon takes the form of Gorlois, earl of Cornwall, in order to sleep with Igerna. In the First Branch, however, the emphasis is on fidelity and loyalty, and no intercourse takes place. The episode bears a resemblance to the folk-tale of 'The Two Brothers', which involves a chaste sleeping together, sometimes with a sword of chastity, as in the Old French *Ami et Amile*.

6 *at the first attack ... suffering a fatal blow*: a formulaic description of fighting used elsewhere in the *Mabinogion*. The present tense is used invariably in this formula.

8 *Pwyll Pen Annwfn*: meaning Pwyll Head of Annwfn. This onomastic explanation is a mnemonic device, bringing the first part of the tale to a close.

Once upon a time Pwyll was at Arberth, one of his chief courts: an echo of the opening lines of the tale, signalling that a second episode is about to begin.

Gorsedd Arberth: a 'mound' or 'barrow' (*gorsedd*) which has specific properties. In this instance, Pwyll sees something wonderful; in the Third Branch, however, a walk to the mound leaves him and his four companions desolate as a mist descends on Dyfed, leaving the land bare and uninhabited (p. 36). Several locations have been suggested for the mound, including Camp Hill, less than a mile south of the town of Arberth, and the site of a circular Iron Age enclosure. Another suggestion is that Arberth and the mound should be located at Crug Mawr ('Great Barrow', near Cardigan), where there is a stream called Nant Arberth and where there once stood a hall called Glan Arberth; however, this does not fit with the geographical details given in the tale.

11 *Rhiannon, daughter of Hyfaidd Hen*: her name derives from that of the Celtic goddess Rigantona ('the Great, or Divine, Queen'). Rhiannon possesses magical qualities, and is closely associated with horses, leading scholars to associate her with the Celtic horse-goddess Epona: see Sioned Davies and Nerys Ann Jones (eds.), *The Horse in Celtic Culture: Medieval Welsh Perspectives* (Cardiff, 1997). In the Second Branch the magical birds of Rhiannon sing during the feast at Harlech (p. 33), while in 'How Culhwch Won Olwen', they are described as birds who wake the dead and send the living to sleep (p. 196). Here Rhiannon is described as being the daughter of Hyfaidd the Old.

If I could choose from all the women . . . you that I would choose: love at first sight is a common motif in the *Mabinogion*; compare, for example, Gronw Pebr (p. 59) and Owain (p. 125).

14 *Badger in the Bag*: an onomastic incident, explaining the derivation of a game which involves tying a man in a bag or sack, then beating and kicking him. This may be associated with badger-baiting: a sack would be placed over the mouth of the badger's den, and when the animal had run into the bag it would be beaten to death. The motif whereby the hero outwits his opponent by deceiving him into going inside a magic sack is widespread. Often the opponent is the devil, who is thrashed until he promises never to cause trouble again.

16 *foster-brother*: a reference to the custom whereby sons were brought up by relatives or friends, rather than their own family. This often meant that boys were closer to their foster-brothers than to their blood-brothers.

Let us kill some of the pups . . . swear that she herself destroyed her son: Rhiannon is an innocent woman who is falsely accused; in folk-tale terms, she is a Calumniated Wife. This common international motif takes many forms: sometimes the woman is accused of giving birth to a monster; sometimes she is accused of eating her child. Indeed, the fact that Rhiannon's face is smeared with blood and that the bones of the pups are placed beside her imply the latter. See Juliette Wood, 'The Calumniated Wife in Medieval Welsh Literature', *Cambridge Medieval Celtic Studies*, 10 (1985), 25–38.

17 *mounting-block*: a block of stone with steps carved on one side, from which to mount on to horseback. Rhiannon's punishment further strengthens her equine associations.

Teyrnon Twrf Liant was lord over Gwent Is Coed: Teyrnon's name derives from that of the Celtic god Tigernonos ('the Great, or Divine, Lord'). One interpretation speculates that his epithet 'Twrf Liant' (Roar of the Flood-Tide) is a reference to the rushing noise made by the Severn Bore, a tidal wave that travels up the river Severn at certain times of the year. Gwent, in the south-east of Wales, was divided into two cantrefs, Uch Coed and Is Coed. A large forest, part of which still remains today under the name Wentwood, divided Is Coed, the low-lying land along the Bristol Channel, from Uch Coed, the hillier land to the north.

May eve: the Celtic year was divided in two, as reflected in Irish sources: winter began at Samhain (1 November), and summer at Beltene (1 May); similarly, in Wales, Calan Gaeaf (the first day of winter) and Calan Mai (the first day of the summer, or May). These days took on a special significance: they were liminal periods when significant events would occur, and the boundaries between the natural and the supernatural world would be removed. The second plague to threaten Britain in 'Lludd and Llefelys' is a scream heard every May eve (p. 112), while Gwyn son of Nudd and Gwythyr son of Greidol fight for the maiden Creiddylad every May day until Judgement Day (p. 207). See A. and B. Rees, *Celtic Heritage* (London, 1961).

18 *an enormous claw*: the owner of the claw is not identified. For parallels in Irish literature, together with an analysis of this episode, see Kenneth Jackson, *The International Popular Tale and Early Welsh Tradition* (Cardiff, 1961), who argues that we have here a combination of three well-known story motifs: the Calumniated Wife, the Monster Hand, and the Congenital Animals.

and say that I have been pregnant: rather than adopt the boy, Teyrnon's wife wants to claim it as her own. The dialogue between her and her husband is in sharp contrast to the lack of communication between Pwyll and Rhiannon: here, husband and wife discuss the situation and finally agree on a plan of action.

baptized in the way it was done at that time . . . Gwri Wallt Euryn: the author acknowledges that *baptism* is an inappropriate term for the 'naming-ceremony' described here; the tales are, after all, set in the pre-Christian past. The same formula is used when naming Blodeuedd in the Fourth Branch (p. 58). *Gwri Wallt Euryn* means 'Gwri of Golden Hair'.

And before he was a year old . . . as sturdy as a six-year old: these features evidencing supernatural growth are traditionally associated with the wonder-child who develops into a great hero. In some tales, as in this instance, the hero is born at the same time as an animal, and often a special relationship develops between them.

20 *what a relief from my anxiety if that were true*: an onomastic tale whereby the boy is given a new name on account of his mother's gratitude at being relieved from her *pryder* ('anxiety').

21 *And so ends this branch of the Mabinogion*: see the Introduction (p. ix). *Cainc*, the common word for 'branch', and the title traditionally given to these four tales in translation, has been adopted here. However, it is worth noting that a different structural interpretation comes into play if one adopts the second meaning of *cainc*, namely 'strand or yarn (of a rope)', resulting in an image of interweaving episodes with a more dynamic relationship between various parts of the tale. A third meaning, namely 'song, tune', raises interesting possibilities regarding a musical context. *Mabinogion* here seems to be an error for the more common *mabinogi*, meaning 'tale'. Eric P. Hamp, on the other hand (in *Transactions of the Honourable Society of Cymmrodorion* (1975), 243–9), has argued that the term refers to a collection of material pertaining to the god Maponos or Mabon, a character who is stolen from the bed of his mother Modron in the tale of 'How Culhwch Won Olwen' (p. 198); Hamp takes his lead from earlier scholarship in identifying Mabon and Modron with the mother and son of the First Branch, namely Rhiannon and Pryderi, and suggests that the original hero of all Four Branches may perhaps have been Pryderi, the only character to appear in all four tales.

THE SECOND BRANCH OF THE MABINOGI

22 *Bendigeidfran son of Llŷr was crowned king over this island*: the name comes from *Bendigeid* + *Brân*, meaning 'Blessed Brân' (*Brân*, meaning 'crow, raven'). Later in the tale he is wounded in the foot by a poisonous spear, which has led many to regard him as the prototype for the Fisher King Bron in the Grail Cycle of medieval romance. He may also be cognate with the Irish Bran who journeys to the Otherworld. His portrayal in the Second Branch suggests that he is a euhemerized deity—he is of gigantic proportions, he owns a magical cauldron, and his severed head seems to live on after his death and when buried serves as a defence for his country.

Harlech in Ardudwy: Harlech (meaning 'high rock') is today the site of a castle built in 1283 by the English king Edward I. *Ardudwy* was a commot on the north-eastern shore of Cardigan Bay, extending from the Ffestiniog valley to the Mawddach estuary.

Manawydan son of Llŷr: the main character in the Third Branch. His name and patronymic equate him with the Irish god of the sea, Man-annán mac Lir. However, their legends are very different, and the Welsh Manawydan has no supernatural attributes. Both forms are related to

Manaw, the name given to the Isle of Man and also to the region of Manaw Gododdin, the area along the southern shore of the Firth of Forth. John Koch has attempted to identify Manawydan with the historical British chieftain Mandubracios who played a part during Caesar's invasion of Britain in 54 BC: 'A Welsh Window on the Iron Age: Manawydan, Mandubracios', *Cambridge Medieval Celtic Studies*, 14 (1987, 17–52).

Beli son of Mynogan: Beli son of Mynogan, or Beli the Great is also mentioned in 'Lludd and Llefelys' (p. 111) and 'The Dream of the Emperor Maxen' (p. 107). He and his sons Lludd, Caswallon, and Nyniaw are portrayed as legendary rulers and defenders of Britain. Major Welsh dynasties claimed descent from Beli; some scholars have argued that he is an ancestor deity cognate with the Gaulish god Belinus. Geoffrey of Monmouth refers to him as Heli in his *History*, father of Lud, Cassibellanus, and Nennius. There existed many traditions concerning Beli and his sons at one time, independent of classical accounts. His son Llefelys (see p. 111) is not mentioned in the genealogies.

23 *Branwen daughter of Llŷr*: the name also occurs once as *Bronwen*, meaning 'white breast' (see p. 24), a common female attribute: compare the heroine Olwen whose 'breasts were whiter than the breast of a white swan' (p. 192). *Bronwen* may have been the older form which was later influenced by the name of her brother *Brân*.

the Island of the Mighty: the Island of Britain.

one of the Three Chief Maidens of this Island: *rhiain* ('maiden') has also been interpreted as 'ancestor' in this context. However, Branwen is not an ancestor at this point in the story; moreover, later in the tale her only child is killed at a young age.

Aberffraw: Aberffraw was the chief court of the princes of Gwynedd, located in Anglesey.

25 *he shall have as his honour-price . . . as broad as his face*: 'honour-price' is the compensation that is paid for insult. According to the Welsh laws, the honour-price of the king of Aberffraw consisted of 'a hundred cows for every cantred he has, with a red-eared bull for every hundred cows, and a rod of gold as tall as himself and as thick as his little finger, and a plate of gold as broad as his face, and as thick as the nail of a ploughman who has been a ploughman seven years' (*LHDd* 5–6). In the Second Branch text 'his little finger', or a similar comparison, needs to be added to make grammatical sense of the sentence. This practice may reflect the original custom whereby a person's weight in gold or silver was given as compensation.

I will give you a cauldron: cauldrons played a significant part in Celtic ritual, as evidenced by both archaeological and literary evidence. Parallels have been drawn between this Cauldron of Rebirth and a scene portrayed on the Gundestrup Cauldron from Denmark, a gilded silver bowl belonging to the first or second century BC, which shows a man plunged head-first into a vat, interpreted by some as a cauldron of immortality.

26 *Talebolion*: a commot in Anglesey (see note to p. 3). Here we have an attempt—albeit incorrect—to explain the place-name: the Welsh *tâl* means 'payment' (but also 'end') and *ebolion* means foals (but also 'hollows' or 'ridges'), hence 'Payment of the Foals'. But the original meaning was probably *Talybolion*, 'the far end of the hollows/ridges'.

Llasar Llaes Gyfnewid: see note to p. 37.

a chamber completely of iron: this motif, whereby enemies are invited to a banquet and killed, appears again in the tale, when the Irish build a great house for Bendigeidfran and prepare a feast for him and his men (p. 30). There are examples of similar episodes in Irish literature. Particular attention has been drawn to the parallels between the Welsh version and the Irish tale *Mesca Ulad* (The Intoxication of the Men of Ulster). For a general discussion of the parallels between the Second Branch and elements from Irish literature, see Proinsias Mac Cana, *Branwen Daughter of Llŷr: A Study of the Irish Affinities and of the Composition of the Second Branch of the Mabinogi* (Cardiff, 1958).

27 *they are numerous, and prosper everywhere*: a possible reference to the Irish settlements in Wales.

until he avenged the insult: a legal term, *sarhad* in Welsh. It has two meanings: the act of violation, and also the fine paid for the offence.

28 *They took revenge . . . a box on the ear*: a serious offence according to medieval Welsh laws, which states that insult is done to a queen in three ways: 'One is to break her protection. A second is to strike her a blow. A third is to snatch something from her hand' (*LHDd* 6). Further instances of this insult are seen in the *Mabinogion*, in association with Gwenhwyfar, Arthur's queen (see p. 68). Branwen's story here takes on the Calumniated Wife theme; compare the fate of Rhiannon in the First Branch (p. 17).

Saith Marchog: Bryn Saith Marchog ('The Hill of the Seven Horsemen') is located between Ruthin and Corwen in north-east Wales. Seven is a conventional number, compare the seven who return from Ireland (p. 32).

Pendaran Dyfed, then a young lad: there is inconsistency here, since in the First Branch he is introduced as Pryderi's foster-father (p. 21), while in this episode Pryderi is old enough to go into battle with Bendigeidfran.

Caradog son of Brân was their chief steward: this tradition is also reflected in a triad, where Caradog is one of the three chief officers or stewards of the Island of Britain, together with Cawrdaf son of Caradog and Owain son of Maxen Wledig (*TYP*, p. 25). Caradog also appears in another triad, see notes to pp. 33 and 114.

Later the sea spread out when it flooded the kingdoms: there are several references in Welsh literature to the sea overcoming the land; see, for example, the reference to Teithi Hen in 'How Culhwch Won Olwen' (p. 185), or the modern folk-tale of Cantre'r Gwaelod which, according to legend, lies beneath today's Cardigan Bay and was drowned because Seithenyn, the keeper of the dyke, got drunk and forgot to close the sluice gates. See F. J. North, *Sunken Cities* (Cardiff, 1957).

29 *we have extraordinary news*: the motif is known as the 'Watchman Device', where watchers describe what they have seen, which is in turn interpreted by a second party. The episode introduces humour and dramatic tension into the tale, and is certainly a favourite with illustrators of the Second Branch.

There are loadstones . . . can sail across: the international motif of the 'loadstone' or 'magnetic mountain' is widely attested, one of the earliest references being that by Pliny the Elder (AD 23–79). Such rocks would pull nails out of any ships that approached, and as such were to be avoided at all costs.

30 *he who is a leader, let him be a bridge*: an attempt to explain the derivation of a common Welsh proverb. Here the words are taken quite literally.

hurdles were placed on him: perhaps a hidden explanation of the place-name Dublin—*Baile Átha Cliath* in Modern Irish, meaning 'the Town of the Ford of the Hurdles'.

31 *hung a hide bag on each peg with an armed man in each one of them*: compare the episode of the iron chamber, where enemies are tricked into attending a feast so that they can be killed. Here we also find another international motif, namely that of hiding warriors in a disguised object, the most famous example being that of the Trojan Horse. In the *Mabinogi* episode, however, the warriors are themselves killed before they can do any harm.

And then he sang an englyn . . . combat: the *englyn* is one of the oldest Welsh strict-metre forms—this is an early three-lined type. Today the four-lined *englyn* is the norm, written in full *cynghanedd* (a complex system involving the repetition of consonants and internal rhyme). In this particular *englyn* there is a play on the word *blawd*, which means not only 'flour' but also 'blossom, flower' and thence 'hero' (compare Pere-dur, who is described as 'the flower of knights' on p. 68). Efnysien is told that there is 'flour' in each bag; however, when he sings his *englyn* he is punning on the word and using it also in the sense of 'hero, champion'.

32 *Hounds of Gwern, beware of Morddwyd Tyllion*: Bendigeidfran throws out a challenge to Gwern's warriors, i.e. the Irish, referring to himself as *Morddwyd Tyllion*. The first element means 'thigh', while the second has two meanings—either 'pierced' or 'large'. If we read the latter, then we can take it as a reference to Bendigeidfran's enormous stature; the first, however, has resonances with the wounding of Bendigeidfran in the foot in the ensuing battle, and may also be associated with the wounding of the Fisher King in the groin in the Grail Cycle of medieval romance.

Pryderi: this is the only reference to Pryderi in the Second Branch.

32 *Then Bendigeidfran ordered his head to be cut off*: the cult of the head, together with head-hunting, seems to have been important in Celtic society, as reflected in archaeology and in both Graeco-Roman and vernacular literature. Here, Bendigeidfran's head serves as a talisman which will keep away invaders.

the birds of Rhiannon: In 'How Culhwch Won Olwen' they are described as birds who have marvellous powers—they wake the dead and send the living to sleep (p. 196), a motif found also in Irish literature. See note to p. 11 on Rhiannon.

Gwales in Penfro: the Island of Grassholm in Pembroke, off the coast of south-west Wales. Stories in the nineteenth and twentieth centuries associate some of these offshore islands with the supernatural. See John Rhŷs, *Celtic Folklore: Welsh and Manx* (Oxford, 1901).

And so long as you do not open the door towards Aber Henfelen: it is common for a taboo to be associated with a mortal's visit to the Otherworld: once the taboo is broken, so too is the spell. Aber Henfelen is probably the Bristol Channel.

33 *those seven men*: there are parallels here with events in the poem *Preiddiau Annwfn*, 'The Spoils of Annwfn', which tells of Arthur's disastrous expedition to the Otherworld to capture a magical cauldron, and of seven men returning. A variant is also found in 'How Culhwch Won Olwen', when Arthur sets off to Ireland in search of the cauldron of Diwrnach the Irishman (p. 208). In both *Mabinogion* versions Ireland has taken the place of the Otherworld. For a comparison of these versions, see Patrick Sims-Williams, 'The Early Welsh Arthurian Poems', in *AOW* 33–72.

And they make a four-sided grave for her: her name is preserved in *Ynys Bronwen*, 'the Island of Bronwen', the site of a cromlech known locally as Branwen's grave. It is claimed that an urn containing the calcified bones of a female were found there in 1813. Lady Charlotte Guest was particularly taken with the discovery, and includes a sketch of the urn in her translation. The publicity surrounding Branwen's grave may well have been why she gave the title 'Branwen daughter of Llŷr' to the Second Branch (see note on p. 227).

Caswallon son of Beli: brother to Lludd, Llefelys, and Nyniaw (see 'Lludd and Llefelys', p. 111). His name probably retains a memory of the historical Cassivellaunos, king of the Belgic tribe of the Catuvellauni, who led an assault against Caesar on his second expedition to Britain in 54 BC—his links with the Romans are reflected in the triads. However, in the Four Branches he conquers the Island of the Mighty during Bendigeidfran's stay in Ireland and later, in the Third Branch, receives the homage of Pryderi, reflecting Welsh traditions linking him and his family with the domination of Britain.

And he was one of the Three People who Broke their Hearts from Sorrow: *TYP* 95 notes that Branwen and Ffaraon Dandde, a character mentioned in 'Lludd and Llefelys' (p. 114), were the other two who broke their hearts.

34 *That night they stayed there ... when Bendigeidfran had been alive
with them*: these are motifs common to descriptions of the blissful
Otherworld—time lapses; humans do not age; there is no gloom, only
happiness. There is a suggestion that Bendigeidfran's head lived on, a
motif paralleled in Irish in connection with the severed heads of great
warriors.

Shame on my beard: the beard was a symbol of manhood in medieval
Wales. This is reflected in the Welsh laws, where wishing a blemish on
the beard of one's husband (i.e. casting aspersions on his virility) was a
beatable offence. See Dafydd Jenkins and Morfydd E. Owen, *The Welsh
Law of Women* (Cardiff, 1980).

*one of the Three Fortunate Concealments ... one of the Three Unfortunate
Disclosures*: these triads have been preserved in full elsewhere. The other
Fortunate Concealments are the dragons which Lludd son of Beli buried
in Dinas Emrys (see 'Lludd and Llefelys', p. 114), and the Bones of
Gwerthefyr the Blessed. A further triad tells of their disclosure, and
describes Arthur as disclosing the head of Brân the Blessed from the
White Hill, 'because it did not seem right to him that this Island should
be defended by the strength of anyone, but by his own' (*TYP* 37).

And the five provinces of Ireland still reflect that division: a reference to the
Irish word *cóiced*, meaning 'a fifth', which ultimately developed to mean
'province'. This, together with other elements in the branch, suggests
that the author was familiar with Ireland and with Irish literature. For
further details, see Proinsias Mac Cana, *Branwen Daughter of Llŷr*.

one of the Three Unfortunate Blows: this 'blow' or 'hard slap' is mentioned
in a triad (*TYP* 53), together with the blow struck by Gwenhwyfach on
Gwenhwyfar (leading to the battle of Camlan), and the blow by Golydan
the Poet on Cadwaladr the Blessed. In the triad, however, Branwen is
struck by her husband Matholwch rather than the butcher. The Second
Branch ends with a list of the constituent stories that made up the tale,
strengthening the argument that the author was drawing on a variety of
oral sources.

THE THIRD BRANCH OF THE MABINOGI

35 *After the seven men we spoke of above*: this branch does not make use of the
traditional opening formula; rather, the continuity between the Second
and Third Branches is emphasized, in written rather than in oral terms.

Caswallon: see note to p. 33.

you are one of the Three Undemanding Chieftains: in a surviving triad the
other two chieftains are named as Llywarch the Old and Gwgon Gwron
son of Peredur (*TYP* 8). The meaning of *lledyf* ('undemanding' or
'unassuming') is explained further: 'because they would not seek a
dominion, and nobody could deny it to them.' In the tale Bendigeidfran,
the king of the Island of the Mighty, is dead, as is his son Caradog, which

leaves Manawydan with a legitimate claim to the throne. However, his cousin Caswallon has seized the crown. For more details on Manawydan, see note to p. 22.

35 *The seven cantrefs of Dyfed*: see note to p. 3.

36 *Gorsedd Arberth*: for the peculiarites of the mound at Arberth, see note to p. 8. The location may be regarded as a liminal zone, where this world and the other converge.

37 *They heard a tumultuous noise ... only the four of them remained*: in the *Mabinogion* a huge noise or an uproar signals a supernatural incident; compare the disappearance of Pryderi and Rhiannon (p. 40), the appearance of the mice (p. 42), the disappearance of Teyrnon's foal (p. 18), and the events concerning the Black Knight in the tale of 'The Lady of the Well' (p. 119). Here, in the Third Branch, the noise brings in its wake a magical mist which robs the land of its people, animals, and dwelling-places; this has clear parallels with the 'waste land' theme, although Dyfed here is deserted rather than infertile.

Llasar Llaesgyngwyd: the context here suggests that the name *Llasar* means some sort of substance (perhaps blue enamel) that was used to decorate harness and weapons. In the Second Branch (p. 28), Llashar son of Llasar Llaesgyngwyd is one of the men that Bendigeidfran leaves behind to defend the Island of the Mighty, while Llasar Llaes Gyfnewid is the huge and monstrous man who brings the Cauldron of Rebirth to Bendigeidfran (p. 26). It is unclear whether these characters should be regarded as one and the same.

38 *Cordovan leather*: high-quality Spanish leather, or 'cordwain', produced in Cordoba during the Moorish period. It was used especially to make shoes.

one of the Three Golden Shoemakers: Manawydan's role as shoemaker can perhaps be explained by the connection between his name and *manawyd* ('awl'); however, this is a false derivation (see note to p. 22). In a surviving triad the other two shoemakers are named as Caswallon son of Beli, and Lleu Llaw Gyffes, 'when he and Gwydion were seeking a name and arms from his mother Aranrhod' (*TYP* 67), an incident described in the Fourth Branch (p. 56). The adjective *eur*, which literally means 'golden', can also be taken figuratively to mean 'splendid' or 'noble', the implication being that each of the high-status characters was forced at some point to adopt the humble craft of shoemaking.

39 *a gleaming white boar*: a common motif whereby the pursuing of an enchanted animal leads to an Otherworld encounter. Swine play a significant role in the Four Branches: Arawn, king of Annwfn (the Otherworld), gives swine as a gift to Pryderi (p. 48); Gwydion tricks Pryderi into parting with the swine in the Fourth Branch, an act that ultimately costs Pryderi his life (p. 51); and a sow leads Gwydion to the wounded Lleu at the end of the branch (p. 62). The boar Twrch Trwyth plays a central role in 'How Culhwch Won Olwen' (see note to p. 198).

40 *I give you God as my guarantor*: *mach* ('guarantor' or 'surety') is a legal term. Here, Manawydan is giving God as his surety, in the absence of a third party.

42 *There was a huge army of mice*: devastation of crops by supernatural creatures is a common motif. Compare also a poem on the 'Unhappy Harvest', attributed to Rhigyfarch son of Sulien, where 'a host of mice refuse to spare the fields' (see Michael Lapidge, 'The Welsh-Latin Poetry of Sulien's Family', *Studia Celtica*, 8/9 (1973–4), 68–106). Rhigyfarch was the author of the *Vita Davidis* (a Life of St David) composed about 1094. Indeed, some have argued that the Four Branches of the Mabinogi can be attributed to Rhigyfarch, or his father Sulien. A. C. Breeze, on the other hand, argues that the author was Gwenllian (1097–1136), daughter of Gruffudd ap Cynan, king of Gwynedd (see *Medieval Welsh Literature*, Dublin, 1997).

43 *a cleric*: he is followed by a priest and then a bishop, implying that 'cleric' is a man in holy orders, of the lowest rank.

I am punishing it in accordance with the law: for the laws concerning theft, see *LHDd* 156–69. If the mouse can not redeem itself through compurgation, then it can buy its way out for seven pounds. Failing that, it would be banished.

45 *Gwawl son of Clud . . . Badger in the Bag*: a reference to events in the First Branch when Pwyll tricked Rhiannon's suitor Gwawl into a bag; he was then kicked and beaten by Pwyll's men as if he were an animal (see note to p. 14). However, Gwawl promised not to seek vengeance for the humiliation.

46 *gate-hammers*: *gordd* meaning a 'hammer' or 'mallet', presumably refers here to a fixture for knocking, attached to the door. How Pryderi would have worn this around his neck is uncertain; but it is clear that the punishment was meant to humiliate him.

the Mabinogi of the Collar and the Hammer: an attempt to explain the title traditionally given to this part of the story. Indeed, at one time it may have been an independent mabinogi rather than part of a 'branch' of a mabinogi. It seems that Rhiannon and Pryderi were punished during their captivity, in retaliation for Gwawl's ill-treatment in the First Branch. It has been suggested that the noun *mynweir* ('collar') may also reflect the proper name *Gwair*, one of the Three Exalted Prisoners of the Island of Britain according to the triads, who was imprisoned in the Otherworld (*TYP* 52).

THE FOURTH BRANCH OF THE MABINOGI

47 *Math son of Mathonwy was lord over Gwynedd*: a powerful magician, as reflected also in early Welsh poetry. He has a magic wand with which he can accomplish transformations, perform a virginity test, and create a woman out of flowers. In the triads he is associated with one of the Three

Great Enchantments of the Island of Britain (*TYP* 28). It is unclear whether Mathonwy is the name of his mother or his father—the family to which Math belonged was perhaps matrilinear, as reflected in the names of his nephews Gwydion and Gilfaethwy, sons of Dôn (their mother), while at the end of the branch Lleu inherits Gwynedd through his mother, Math's sister. Or Mathonwy may perhaps be a non-person and merely a doublet of Math's own name; compare the pairs of invented names in 'How Culhwch Won Olwen': Sugn son of Sugnedydd, Drem son of Dremidydd. Gwynedd consisted of the following seven cantrefs: Cemais, Aberffraw, Rhosyr (in Môn), Llŷn, Arfon, Arllechwedd, and Dunoding.

47   *Pryderi son of Pwyll . . . Ystrad Tywi*: Pryderi is the only character to appear in all Four Branches (see Introduction). For the *seven cantrefs of Dyfed*, see note to p. 3. For details of the Welsh administrative divisions, see William Rees, *An Historical Atlas of Wales* (Cardiff, 1972; 1st edn. 1951).

could not live unless his feet were in the lap of a virgin . . . Caer Dathyl in Arfon: in the law tracts the foot-holder is listed as one of the additional officers at court: 'It is right for him to hold the King's feet in his lap from when he begins sitting at the banquet until he goes to sleep, and to scratch the King' (*LHDd* 32–3). Here, Math's very existence depends on his virgin foot-holder. *Dol Pebin* is probably in the Nantlle Valley (see note to p. 62); however, there is no certainty as to the location of *Caer Dathyl*—it is clearly a fort somewhere on the coast between Dinas Dinlle and Caernarfon (see note to p. 108). The name *Tathal* also occurs in 'How Culhwch Won Olwen', p. 184.

He was unable to circuit the land: a reference to the custom whereby a lord and his retinue would circuit the land, accepting the hospitality of his people; compare the reference in the Third Branch (p. 36).

Gilfaethwy son of Dôn and Gwydion son of Dôn: Dôn shares her name with the Celtic mother-goddess Danu, whose name is preserved today in the name of the river Donau (Danube), for example, or the river Don in Scotland. In Irish her name is commemorated in the tales of the *Tuatha Dé Danann* ('The People of the Goddess Danu'), a race of gods who populated Ireland before the Celts. In the Fourth Branch we meet her brother Math, three sons—Gwydion, Gilfaethwy, and Gofannon—and a daughter Aranrhod. Gwydion is presented as a shape-shifting magician; indeed, surviving poetry seems to suggest that there was once a large body of literature surrounding him, unlike his brother Gilfaethwy, who may well have been created solely as a catalyst for the events of the Fourth Branch. Gofannon appears again in 'How Culhwch Won Olwen', together with another son, Amaethon (p. 195).

Math son of Mathonwy's special attribute: compare the Coraniaid in the tale of 'Lludd and Llefelys' (see note to p. 112).

48   *Hobeu . . . they were sent to him from Annwfn by Arawn king of Annwfn*:

Hobeu means 'pigs' and *moch* means 'swine'. In the First Branch, Pwyll (Pryderi's father) and Arawn, king of the Otherworld, send each other 'horses and hunting-dogs and hawks' as a token of their friendship (p. 8). However, no pigs are mentioned. Pryderi is associated with the animals elsewhere: in the triads he is named as one of the Three Powerful Swineherds (*TYP* 26), when he 'guarded the swine of Pendaran Dyfed in Glyn Cuch in Emlyn'. Glyn Cuch is where his father Pwyll first encountered Arawn in the First Branch (p. 3), while Pendaran Dyfed seems to have been Pryderi's foster-father (p. 21). A variant triad adds that 'these swine were the seven animals which Pwyll Lord of Annwfn brought, and gave them to Pendaran Dyfed his foster-father'. It is clear that there existed a number of accounts regarding the introduction of pigs to Wales. The animals are often associated with the supernatural in the *Mabinogion*, and played a significant role in the mythology of the Celts (see notes to pp. 39 and 198).

They entered, disguised as poets: the reference shows that it was not unusual for poets to travel the country, and that they were most welcome at any court. According to the Welsh laws, the *pencerdd* ('chief poet') is one of the additional court officers—'it is right for him to start the song, first of God, and secondly of the Lord to whom the court belongs, or of another' (*LHDd* 38–9). See also Introduction, pp. xiii–xiv.

50 *That night they travelled ... in the town which is still called Mochdref*: an attempt to explain four place-names, three examples of *Mochdref* ('Swine-town') and one of *Mochnant* ('Swine-brook'). The author interprets the *moch-* element in all four as 'swine', reflecting the pigs' journey from South to North Wales. It is difficult to locate these places with any degree of certainty. The *Mochdref* in the *uplands of Ceredigion* may refer to a location to the north-east of Aberystwyth, in the vicinity of today's Nant-y-moch reservoir. *Elenid* is in southern Powys, and refers to the mountainous land known as Pumlumon (Plynlimon) today. *Ceri* and *Arwystli* (see note to p. 214) were a commot and cantref respectively, in the area around Newtown and Llanidloes; indeed, about 3 miles south-west of Newtown is the parish of *Mochdref*. The commot of *Mochnant* was partly in Denbighshire and partly in Montgomeryshire, while the Mochdref in the cantref of Rhos is located between Colwyn Bay and Llandudno.

Arllechwedd ... Creuwrion: an onomastic explanation associated with *creu*, the Welsh name for 'pen', possibly Cororion, situated between Bangor and Bethesda. The commote of *Arllechwedd* lay between Bangor and the Conwy river in the north, extending south to Dolwyddelan and Penmachno.

51 *Y Traeth Mawr*: meaning 'the great stretch of sand', located at the estuary of the Glaslyn and Dwyryd rivers at Porthmadog.

and he was buried in Maentwrog, above Y Felenrhyd, and his grave is there: the location is further attested in an early *englyn* in 'The Stanzas of the

Graves', a series which catalogues the resting-places of renowned Welsh heroes, both historical and legendary. *Y Felenrhyd* is a few miles to the east of *Y Traeth Mawr*, on the south side of the Dwyryd river.

52 *look for another virgin . . . in your very bed*: the author here highlights the difference between the two distinct terms—*morwyn* ('virgin') and *gwraig* ('a sexually experienced woman'). The fact that the rape took place in Math's own chamber, indeed in his own bed, only adds to the shame. The sanctity of the marital bed is emphasized time and again in the Welsh laws—expulsion from the marriage bed, for example, is regarded as one of the three shames of a wife. For further details, see Jenkins and Owen (eds.), *The Welsh Law of Women*.

good day to you: Math does not reply with the usual formula ('may God prosper you') because of his anger.

54 *Bleiddwn, Hyddwn, Hychddwn Hir*: these are the three sons conceived by the brothers Gwydion and Gilfaethwy in their animal transformations, the punishment fitting the sexual crime which they committed. The three offspring are a reminder of their life as wild beasts, their names consisting of the elements *blaidd* ('wolf'), *hydd* ('stag'), and *hwch* ('swine'); *Hir* means 'Tall'. See note to p. 31 for the metrical form.

friendship: in a legal sense, that is, a reconciliation between the two parties, Math and his nephews. Compare the First Branch, where Pwyll, having insulted Arawn, enquires as to how he may win his 'friendship' (p. 4).

Aranrhod daughter of Dôn: In the triads (*TYP* 35), she is the daughter of Beli son of Mynogan (see note to p. 22). Her name sometimes occurs as *Arianrhod*. Caer Aranrhod ('the Fort of Aranrhod') is the name given to a rock formation visible at low tide, less than a mile from Dinas Dinlleu on the Caernarfonshire coast.

That is my belief: the implication here is that Aranrhod is hiding the truth, in other words she is a *twyllforwyn*, a 'false virgin', a term attested in the legal tracts. According to the Welsh legal system, a girl was of little or no value if her prospective husband found her not to be a virgin. See Jenkins and Owen (eds.), *The Welsh Law of Women*. The context here is slightly different, since Math's life depends on her virginity.

Step over this . . . I shall know: clearly a virginity test. Other virginity- or chastity-testing objects are found in medieval Welsh literature, such as the Mantle of Tegau Eurfron ('Tegau Gold-Breast'), one of the Thirteen Treasures of the Island of Britain: 'for whoever was faithful to her husband it [the mantle] would reach the ground, and for whoever had violated her marriage it only reached her lap' (see *TYP*, App. 3).

Dylan Eil Ton . . . Three Unfortunate Blows: the triad itself has not survived. There are references to Dylan son of Wave in several medieval Welsh poems, including an elegy which implies a link between Dylan's death and a smith, although he is not named. However, Gofannon has been associated with Irish *Goibniu*, who was the smith of the Tuatha Dé

Danann. He is also one of the characters whose help Culhwch must secure if he is to marry Olwen, the daughter of Ysbaddaden (p. 195).

55 *dulse and wrack*: types of seaweed (*Rhodymenia palmata* and *Laminaria digitata*).

56 *it is with a skilful hand . . . Lleu Llaw Gyffes*: an onomastic explanation. The boy's name means 'the fair-haired one with the skilful hand'. Llew, a variant on Lleu ('the fair-haired one'), also occurs, meaning 'lion, the strong one', although this would seem to be a secondary development. Lleu is cognate with the Irish god *Lugh*, Gaulish *Lugus*, a form preserved in names of cities such as Lyons, Laon, and Leiden, and has been identified with the Roman god Mercury. Lleu is mentioned briefly in two triads: The Three Red Ravagers (*TYP* 20) and The Three Bestowed Horses (*TYP* 38). A further two triads, namely The Three Disloyal War-Bands (*TYP* 30) and The Three Golden Shoemakers (*TYP* 67), bear witness to events in the Fourth Branch, and are discussed below.

one of the Three Golden Shoemakers: in a surviving triad the other two shoemakers are named as Caswallon son of Beli, and Manawydan son of Llŷr (*TYP* 67). See note to p. 38.

57 *Dinas Dinlleu*: the author clearly associates this place-name with the character Lleu, although he does not point this out as such. Both *dinas* and *din* mean 'fortification'. Dinas Dinlle(u) is a hill-fort on the coast, a mile west of Llandwrog in Gwynedd, and about 5 miles south-west of Caernarfon.

58 *Then they took the flowers of the oak . . . Blodeuedd*: the flowers listed may well be significant. The yellow broom is often used as metaphor when describing a maiden's hair; compare Olwen, whose hair was 'yellower than the flowers of the broom' (p. 192). The flowers of the oak and the meadowsweet are both white, a colour not only associated with ideal female beauty but also with purity. For the reference to 'baptism', see note to p. 18. Here again we have an onomastic tale—the maiden is created out of 'flowers' (*blodeuedd*).

59 *Mur Castell*: known today as Castell Tomen y Mur, the site of a Roman hill-fort overlooking Trawsfynydd lake.

Gronw Pebr, the man who is lord of Penllyn: Penllyn lies to the east of Ardudwy, Lleu's realm. Gronw's epithet may be interpreted as the adjective *pybyr* ('strong') or perhaps *pefyr* ('radiant').

he asked permission to depart: this convention is seen in many of the *Mabinogion* tales, for example pp. 24 and 72.

60 *I cannot be killed indoors . . . would bring about my death*: unique vulnerability is often a characteristic of heroes (for example Achilles and Macbeth), while the secret of that vulnerability disclosed by the hero's wife has one of its most well-known examples in the biblical tale of Samson and Delilah (Judges 16). The paradoxical tasks may be associated with the international motif of the riddles which must be solved for the

heroine or hero to succeed—here, however, Blodeuedd does not need to rise to the challenge since she persuades her husband to disclose the answers.

61 *Bryn Cyfergyr*: meaning 'Hill of the Blow'—the author has omitted to draw attention to the onomastic explanation.

62 *which is now called Nantlleu*: an onomastic explanation meaning the 'Valley of Lleu'. The Nantlle(u) Valley is located along the Llyfni river, to the east of Pen-y-groes and Tal-y-sarn.

englyn: see note to p. 31. In the first stanza, 'Lleu's Flowers' is a reference to his wife Blodeuedd. The second stanza presents several difficulties, and many interpretations have been offered. The second line suggests that the oak tree in which Lleu is perched has supernatural qualities—neither the rain nor heat affects it. In the third line, the one who possesses 'nine-score attributes' is, presumably, Lleu himself; compare the magical attributes of characters such as Math (p. 47) and Cai (p. 189).

63 *until they fell into the lake and were drowned*: there is a lake in the area known as *Llyn y Morynion* ('the Lake of the Maidens/Virgins'), about 3 miles north-east of Mur Castell. However, the author has omitted to draw attention to the onomastic explanation in the text.

but shall always be called Blodeuwedd: once she is transformed into a bird, her name changes from *Blodeuedd* ('flowers') to *Blodeuwedd* ('flower-face'), to reflect the image of the owl.

insult: see note to p. 27.

64 *one of the Three Disloyal Retinues*: the story is corroborated in a triad (*TYP* 30). The other disloyal retinues or war-bands were that of Gwrgi and Peredur, and that of Alan Fyrgan who allowed him to go to the battle of Camlan alone, where he was killed (see note on p. 264).

Llech Gronw: an onomastic explanation meaning 'Gronw's Stone'. It is claimed that a stone with a hole pierced through its centre was found in the bed of the Cynfal river in 1934, while another was found in 1990, not far from a place locally known as *Bedd Gronw* ('Gronw's Grave'). There are certainly very strong associations between this branch and local topography, perhaps more so than any other tale in the corpus.

And so ends this branch of the Mabinogi: note that there is no suggestion that the Four Branches as a composite whole are at an end; indeed, there may well have been further 'branches'.

PEREDUR SON OF EFROG

65 *Earl Efrog held an earldom in the North*: *Efrog* is a place-name ('York'). Here, it is the name of Peredur's father who, in Geoffrey's *History of the Kings of Britain*, is the eponymous founder of York. The 'North' here refers to the North of Britain rather than to North Wales.

Peredur: the opening lines of the tale suggest that Peredur son of Efrog, Chrétien's Perceval, seems to have been associated with the North of Britain; indeed, he may well have been a local ruler. In the *Gododdin* poem whose subject-matter is a battle fought *c.*AD 600, his name occurs as *Peredur arfau dur* ('Peredur of steel weapons'). Indeed, it has been suggested that his name derives from *par* ('spear') and *dur* ('hard, steel')—in the earliest version of the tale (Peniarth 7), the form *Paredur* is found, as well as *Peredur*—which may well be the reason for his epithet *Paladr Hir* ('Long Spear'). He is also mentioned in 'Geraint son of Erbin' (p. 155) and 'Rhonabwy's Dream' (p. 225). See Glenys Goetinck, *Peredur: A Study of Welsh Traditions in the Grail Legends* (Cardiff, 1975), and *TYP* 477–80.

66 *Gwalchmai son of Gwyar . . . the apples in Arthur's court*: there were clearly many traditions about Gwalchmai, as attested by the early poetry and the triads, including a reference to him as one of the Three Men of the Island of Britain who were Most Courteous to Guests and Strangers (*TYP* 75), a virtue that becomes apparent in the Welsh 'romances'. Indeed, in all three tales he is the one who reconciles the hero with Arthur's men. His name, which contains the element *gwalch* ('hawk'), a common epithet for medieval lords and patrons, corresponds to the *Gauvains* of French romances, the English *Gawain*, and the Latin *Gualguanus*. According to 'How Culhwch Won Olwen', Gwalchmai is Arthur's nephew. For a detailed discussion, see *TYP*, pp. 367–71. There is ample evidence to suggest that *Owain son of Urien* was a historical character. Genealogies attest to his existence, as do poems by the sixth-century Taliesin, who refers to both Owain and his father Urien, ruler of Rheged, a kingdom which comprised the whole of modern Cumbria, extending over the Pennines to Catterick. By the twelfth century, however, Owain had developed into a legendary character and become part of the Arthurian cycle: he is the hero of 'The Lady of the Well', corresponding to Chrétien's character *Yvains fiz au roi Urien*. He also figures in 'Rhonabwy's Dream', together with his retinue known as the 'Flight of Ravens': see notes to pp. 138 and 221. For further details on *Owain son of Urien*, see *TYP* 467–72. There are no references elsewhere to the sharing of the apples in Arthur's court. For a general discussions of Arthur in medieval Welsh tradition, see *AOW*, and O. J. Padel, *Arthur in Medieval Welsh Literature* (Cardiff, 2000). 'Emperor' is his title in all three 'romances' and 'Rhonabwy's Dream'. In 'How Culhwch Won Olwen', on the other hand, he is 'chief of the kings of this island' (p. 183).

68 *a chamberlain*: one of the twenty-four officers of the king's court, according to the laws. His duties included making the king's bed, running errands between the hall and the chamber, and pouring drink for the king. See *LHDd* 19–20.

and gave Gwenhwyfar a great clout on the ear: the *Guenièvre* of the French romances. The first element of her name, *gwen*, means 'fair, beautiful'; the second element is cognate with Irish *siabair* ('phantom, spirit, fairy').

Her name therefore corresponds to *Findabair*, daughter of King Ailill and Queen Medb in the Irish epic *Táin Bó Cúailnge*. Indeed, some have argued that Gwenhwyfar was a Celtic sovereignty figure, as was Medb in Ireland, although this is doubtful since there is no reliable evidence concerning her before Geoffrey of Monmouth. In this particular scene she is insulted, a version perhaps of the abduction of Gwenhwyfar, to which there are several references in connection with Melwas (whose place is taken by Medrawd/Modred in Geoffrey's account). The many allusions to her in the triads include the Three Violent Ravagings of the Island of Britain, when Medrawd came to Arthur's court at Celli Wig and 'dragged Gwenhwyfar from her royal chair, and then he struck a blow upon her' (*TYP* 54). According to the laws, a queen was insulted legally if she were struck a blow, or if someone snatched something from her hand (*LHDd* 6). See *TYP*, pp. 376–80.

68 *on a bony, dapple-grey nag with its untidy, slovenly trappings*: this is a parody of the hero's arrival at court; compare Culhwch's arrival at Arthur's court on pp. 180–1.

Cai: in the earliest Welsh sources Cai (the Kay of later Arthurian traditions) appears as a heroic figure, one of Arthur's leading warriors. However, in the three 'romances' he is portrayed as a discourteous and contentious character, a side to him that is also apparent in 'How Culhwch Won Olwen', as he sulks and disappears from the story when Arthur sings a satirical *englyn* about him. Arthur chooses Cai to go on the quest for Olwen because he has magical attributes—he can survive for nights without sleep, and his body has great natural heat (p. 189). The epithets *gwyn* ('fair' or 'beloved') and *hir* ('tall') are constantly attached to his name. In 'The Lady of the Well' and Geoffrey's *History* he takes on the role of Arthur's steward at court. For more details, see *TYP*, pp. 308–12.

chief of warriors and flower of knights: 'flower' and 'candle' (see below) were common epithets for heroes; compare the play on words in the Second Branch (p. 31). 'Flower of Knighthood' (*Flos Militae*) is a chivalric term.

71 *And on the shore of the lake there was a grey-haired man . . . fishing in a small boat on the lake*: this grey-haired lame man has often been identified with the Fisher King of French romance. There may well be some association between him and Bendigeidfran (or Brân) of the Second Branch of the *Mabinogi*, who was wounded through the foot with a poisoned spear—the Fisher King is called *Bron* in some versions, and has been wounded through the thigh (see note to p. 22).

squire: the Welsh *macwy*, a loanword from Irish *maccoím* ('boy, young lad') is a term used for a young man, often fulfilling the role of 'page' or 'chamberlain' at court (see note to p. 68); in the Welsh Laws, the *macwyaid* are part of the king's entourage, and were probably of noble birth. Here, and elsewhere, the alternative term 'squire' is given in the

English translation, in the general sense of 'young man' rather than in any formally defined role.

73 *two lads entering the hall . . . and much blood around the head*: this is clearly a version of the Grail procession found in Chrétien's *Perceval* (or *Li Conte del Graal*), although the word 'grail' itself is not used in the Welsh text—rather, a *dysgl* ('dish' or 'platter') appears on which there is a dismembered head. In later legends the Grail is identified with the chalice of the Last Supper in which Joseph of Arimathaea collected the blood of the crucified Christ; the mysterious lance becomes the weapon used by Longinus to pierce Christ's side. In the late fourteenth century two French Grail texts were translated into Welsh as *Ystoryaeu Seint Greal* ('Stories or Histories of the Holy Grail')—versions of two French prose Grail romances of the early thirteenth century, *La Queste del Saint Graal* and the *Perlesvaus*, providing the first explicit reference to the Grail in Welsh. See Ceridwen Lloyd-Morgan, '*Breuddwyd Rhonabwy* and Later Arthurian Literature', in *AOW* 183–208.

76 *the head of the earl's retinue*: according to the Welsh laws, the head of the retinue held one of the highest offices at court; as such, he was to be the king's son or nephew. His duties included putting the harp into the hands of the bard at the three special feasts. For further details, see *LHDd* 8–11.

77 *The court steward*: another high-ranking office, whose duties included allotting lodgings and controlling the food and drink at court. See *LHDd* 12–14.

78 *the witches of Caerloyw*: these provide Peredur with training so that he can gain the remaining third of his strength; compare the Irish hero Cú Chulainn, who is taught to fight by the supernatural female Scáthach. Witches feature elsewhere in the Welsh Arthurian tradition—see, for example, 'How Culhwch Won Olwen', pp. 212–13. In that tale, *Caerloyw* (Gloucester) is where Mabon son of Modron is imprisoned, see note to p. 198.

79 *Peredur stood . . . of the woman he loved best*: this may have been inspired by the scene in the Irish tale *The Exile of the Sons of Uisnech*, where the heroine Deirdre sees a raven drinking blood from a dead calf lying in the snow, and immediately desires a man with black hair, red cheeks, and a white body. Certainly, black hair did not concur with the idealized female beauty of the period.

82 *The first night Peredur came to Caerllion to Arthur's court . . . Angharad Law Eurog met him*: the location of Arthur's court at Caerllion in all three 'romances' seems to be derived from Geoffrey of Monmouth's *History of the Kings of Britain*. In older tradition his court was located at Celli Wig in Cornwall, as evidenced by 'How Culhwch Won Olwen'. This section of the tale, concerning Angharad Law Eurog, is not found in Chrétien de Troyes's *Perceval*. The epithet *Law Eurog*, 'Golden Hand', may be a reference to her generosity.

83 *Shame on my gatekeeper's beard*: for the oath 'shame on my beard', see

note to p. 34. The *gatekeeper* (or doorkeeper) was one of the twenty-four officers of the king's court according to Welsh law (*LHDd* 25–6). See note to p. 116 on Glewlwyd Gafaelfawr.

85 *But then he spurred on his horse . . . a great distance away*: an example of the fighting formula at its most rhetorical, including a series of alliterating compound adjectives that produce an impressive, rhythmical description. Every attempt has been made to reproduce this effect in the translation.

86 *gwyddbwyll*: literally 'wood-sense', sometimes misleadingly translated 'chess'. It is listed as one of the twenty-four feats of skill performed in medieval Wales. Like chess, *gwyddbwyll* was played on a board with pawns, and refers both to the game and to the board itself. In *gwyddbwyll* the king of one player attempts to break out from the centre of the board to the edge, while the opponent's pawns attempt to stop him; compare Irish *fidceall*.

a huge, black-haired, one-eyed man coming in: this has often been translated as a 'black man'; however, this is the normal construction when describing a 'black-haired man'.

88 *and bathed it in a tub of warm water*: there are similarities between this and the Cauldron of Rebirth in the Second Branch (p. 25)—both have life-restoring powers. Here, too, a precious ointment is applied; compare the episode in 'The Lady of the Well', when Owain is rescued by a widowed countess (p. 131).

89 *India*: often used to create a sense of the exotic—compare Glewlwyd Gafaelfawr's rhetorical monologue in 'How Culhwch Won Olwen', as he describes the many places he has visited throughout the world (p. 182).

90 *Edlym Gleddyf Goch*: 'Edlym of the Red Sword'.

91 *Peredur Baladr Hir*: Peredur Long Spear. See note to p. 65 on Peredur.

94 *according to the story*: the version in Peniarth 7 ends here. Whether this was deliberate or not is uncertain; but it could reflect one of the earliest retellings of the tale in Welsh. However, the 'longer' text, found in both the White and Red Book manuscripts, has come to be regarded as the standard version of the tale.

Hywel son of Emyr Llydaw: son of Emyr of Brittany. He is also mentioned in 'Geraint son of Erbin' (p. 155), 'Rhonabwy's Dream' (p. 225), and in the Geoffrey's *History* as Arthur's nephew and close friend, Duke Hoel. See *TYP*, pp. 398–9.

a black, curly-haired maiden . . . which were stout: this maiden has been identified by many as the hideous side of sovereignty, a parody on the description of female beauty. 'Flaring nostrils' are normally associated with horses, not humans, while the reference to the flowers of the broom would surely bring to mind the beautiful Olwen, whose hair was 'yellower than the flowers of the broom' (p. 192), and perhaps Blodeuedd, who was created of flowers including the broom, suggesting her hair-colour. See Glenys Goetinck, *Peredur: A Study of Welsh Tradition in the Grail Legends* (Cardiff, 1975).

When you came to the court of the lame king ... or their cause: this is inconsistent with previous events: the first uncle was lame, according to the text, but the events described occurred at the court of the second uncle.

95 *knights ... ordained knights there*: *marchog* in Welsh can mean both 'horseman' and 'knight'; qualifying the noun with the adjective *urddol* ('ordained') removes the ambiguity.

At daybreak Gwalchmai came to a valley: the digression ends on p. 97 with 'the story says no more than that about Gwalchmai on the matter'.

On a shiny black, wide-nostrilled ... lively: the most elaborate descriptions of horses in the *Mabinogion* include a reference to the colour, size, physical features, pace, and spirit of the animal. Moreover, these features are usually expressed by means of a long string of alliterating compound adjectives, each with the same rhythm, not unlike the descriptions of fighting (see note to p. 85). Every attempt has been made to reproduce this effect in the translation. 'Palfrey' is a borrowing from the French, and refers to a light horse used for leisure, rather than the heavier war-horse which had to be capable of carrying the weight of a knight in armour. See Sioned Davies, 'Horses in the *Mabinogion*', in Davies and Jones (eds.), *The Horse in Celtic Culture*, 121–40.

100 *And the side he supported ... as if they were men*: see note on *gwyddbwyll*, p. 86. One of the Thirteen Treasures of the Island of Britain is the *gwyddbwyll* of Gwenddolau son of Ceido: 'if the pieces were set, they would play by themselves. The board was of gold, and the men of silver' (*TYP*, p. 260). In Continental versions of the Grail story it is only the pieces on one side that move automatically as they play against the hero.

102 *And that is what is told of the Fortress of Wonders*: this is clearly an ending to the final part of the tale, and not to the tale as a whole. Regarding the notion of a 'standard version' of the text, see Introduction, pp. xxiv–xxv.

THE DREAM OF THE EMPEROR MAXEN

103 *Maxen Wledig*: Maxen may be identified with Magnus Maximus, a Roman commander proclaimed emperor by his army in Britain in AD 383. *Gwledig* ('lord') in his title is often used for territorial rulers, as well as for God. Maxen invaded Gaul and defeated the emperor Gratian, but was put to death by Theodosius in 388. In the work of Gildas, and also in the *History of the Britons*, he is criticized as a leader who took all the troops from Britain, leaving the country at the mercy of foreign invaders. However, he became an important figure in Welsh historiography as someone who symbolized the relationship between Wales and Rome, and many medieval Welsh dynasties claimed descent from him. See Introduction, pp. xix–xx.

103 *chamberlains*: see note to p. 68.

104 *gwyddbwyll*: a board game, see note to p. 86.

105 *a king in Romani*: this Latin term is used both for the people (the Romans) and for the empire or kingdom of Rome.

the three regions of the world: these were Asia, Africa, and Europe.

106 *This is how the messengers looked . . . no harm would be done to them*: it was important that messengers were easily recognized to ensure a safe passage. For a general discussion, see Norbert Ohler, *The Medieval Traveller* (Woodbridge, 1989). For this particular example, see Morgan Watkin, *La Civilisation française dans les Mabinogion* (Paris, 1962), 301–3.

107 *Aber Saint*: as the messengers get closer to their destination they see the mountains of *Eryri* (Snowdonia), then *Môn* (Anglesey) and the cantref of *Arfon*, until finally they see the estuary (*aber*) of the river Saint (sometimes known as Seiont), which flows into the Menai Straits at Caernarfon. *Aber Saint* may well be a place-name here.

Beli son of Manogan: see note to p. 22.

108 *the maiden claimed her maiden fee*: agweddi is one of the many legal terms connected with marital union, defined as 'the specific sum from the common pool of matrimonial property to which the wife was entitled on a justified separation from the husband before the union had lasted seven years' (see Jenkins and Owen (eds.), *The Welsh Law of Women*). Here, however, the meaning is different in that it is a claim to be made by the bride herself as acknowledgement of her virginity prior to the union. In legal terminology, this would normally be the *cowyll*, the 'morning-gift'. The author of the tale has clearly confused the two terms.

the Island of Britain . . . and the Three Adjacent Islands: the North Sea (*Môr Udd*) is frequently contrasted with the Irish Sea (*Môr Iwerddon*) to denote the breadth of the Island of Britain. The earliest reference to 'The Island of Britain and the Three Adjacent Islands', found elsewhere in the *Mabinogion*, and in medieval poetry and the triads, can be found in the *History of the Britons*, where the islands are named as Wight, Man, and Orkney. In the triads (*TYP*, App. 1: 'The Names of the Island of Britain'), they are known as Anglesey, Man, and Wight (or perhaps Lundy, an island off the Devon coast). The concept serves to emphasize the sovereign unity of the Island of Britain, see Introduction, p. xviii.

she asked that the prime fort be built for her in Arfon: the centre of the cantref of Arfon was Caer Saint (see the Second Branch, p. 28), where the Roman fort of Segontium was located, on a hill about half-a-mile from the Menai Straits. By the end of the twelfth century this name was displaced by Aber Saint ('the Estuary of the Saint'), probably due to the location of a new site on the estuary itself, as reflected in the location of Eudaf's castle earlier in the tale (p. 104). In turn, this simple location marker was replaced by Caernarfon, the common form from the thirteenth century onwards, meaning simply 'the fort in Arfon'. As part of his military campaign against the Welsh, Edward I built a castle here in 1284, on the site of the motte built by Earl Hugh of Chester about 1090 when the Normans first advanced into Gwynedd. See Brynley F. Roberts (ed.), *Breudwyt Maxen Wledic* (Dublin, 2005), and R. A. Griffiths (ed.), *The Boroughs of Medieval Wales* (Cardiff, 1978).

Caerllion: Caerleon in Gwent, south-east Wales, and given an elevated status by Geoffrey of Monmouth. See note to p. 82.

Y Freni Fawr: one of the highest hills of the Preseli mountains in east Pembrokeshire. *Breni* ('prow of a ship') is used figuratively for a hill or mountain peak.

Cadair Faxen: meaning Maxen's Chair. An onomastic tale, although it does not seem to have survived as a place-name.

it is called Caerfyrddin: Carmarthen, in West Wales, site of the Romano-British fort Moridunum (meaning 'sea fort') which would give *Myrddin* in Welsh. According to the author of the tale, however, the place takes its name from the *myrdd* ('host') of men who built the stronghold there for Elen. Geoffrey of Monmouth locates the fatherless boy Merlinus (Welsh *Merddin* or *Myrddin*) in Caerfyrddin in his *History of the Kings of Britain*; indeed, the personal name may have been derived from the place-name. See A. O. H. Jarman, 'The Merlin Legend and the Welsh Tradition of Prophecy', in *AOW* 117–45.

Ffyrdd Elen Luyddog: the noun *lluydd* means 'host, mustering'; the adjective *lluyddog* implies 'having a host, warlike'. Elen is here attributed with building roads from one fort to another. Indeed, the major Roman road running from South to North Wales is still known today as Sarn Helen (Helen's Causeway). For traditions about Elen and road-building, see Ivan D. Margary, *Roman Roads in Britain* (London, 1957); Morris Marples, *Sarn Helen: A Roman Road in Wales* (Newtown, 1939). In later tradition Elen becomes confused with Helena, mother of the Roman emperor Constantine the Great (d. 337); according to a legend, she made a pilgrimage to Jerusalem and discovered the true Cross (see *TYP* 35).

for seven years: the Peniarth 16 version ends here; the remainder of the tale is translated from the version in Peniarth 4 (the White Book of Rhydderch), in line with Brynley F. Roberts's edition, *Breudwyt Maxen Wledic*.

110 *Because the women and their language were silenced . . . people speaking that language*: a reference to the founding of Brittany. *Llydaw* (Brittany) is explained as *lled-taw*, 'half silent'. This onomastic fabrication is also given in the ninth-century *History of the Britons*. In the triads (*TYP* 35) Cynan is mentioned as being a member of one of the 'Three Levies that Departed from this Island, and not one of them came back', while in the early prophetic poetry he is regarded as a leader who will one day return and rid the Britons of their Saxon oppressors. In Geoffrey of Monmouth's version of the legend Cynan is given the epithet *Meiriadog*, and is presented as a nephew of Eudaf and therefore a cousin of Elen.

LLUDD AND LLEFELYS

111 *Beli the Great*: see the notes to p. 22 (*Beli son of Mynogan*) and p. 33 (*Caswallon*).

And according to the story: this tale first appeared as an insertion in a thirteenth-century Welsh translation of Geoffrey of Monmouth's *History of the Kings of Britain*. This introductory phrase—'and according to the storytellers', in the Welsh translation of the *History*—refers to the fact that the author is taking the tale from native Welsh tradition and is supplementing Geoffrey's account.

Caer Ludd, finally Caer Lundain: an onomastic explanation as to how London was renamed due to Lludd rebuilding the city. *Caer* is the common Welsh word for 'fort'.

three plagues: a version of these three plagues or 'oppressions' is also found in a triad (*TYP*, p. 84), where they are listed as the Coraniaid, the Gwyddyl Ffichti (the Picts), and the Saxons. In the tale, the historical invasions have been replaced by folklore themes.

112 *Coraniaid*: the name may well have been confused with *Cesariaid* (Romans). The Coraniaid's special attribute—remarkable hearing—is a common motif, and echoes the description of Math son of Mathonwy in the Fourth Branch (p. 47).

a scream that was heard every May eve: for 'May eve', see note to p. 17. The scream is paralleled in 'How Culhwch Won Olwen', when Culhwch threatens Arthur's court with a shout so loud that pregnant women shall miscarry and those that are not shall become barren (pp. 181–2).

113 *through the power of the wine the demon was driven out*: exorcizing fairies and demons by sprinkling water (not wine) is a common motif. A well-known Welsh example is found in the sixteenth-century story of St Collen, who uses holy water to defeat Gwyn ap Nudd in his palace in Annwfn (the Otherworld).

dragons fighting: this episode is related to the account in the ninth-century *History of the Britons*, where the fatherless boy Ambrosius (*Emrys* in Welsh) explains the mystery of Vortigern's collapsing stronghold in Snowdonia: under the foundations is a pool in which there are two dragons, one red and the other white, symbolizing the native Welsh and the Saxon nations respectively. After fierce fighting the red dragon is victorious, leading to the prophecy that the Saxons will eventually be overcome and thrown out of Britain. Geoffrey of Monmouth's reworking of this account identifies the wonder-child Ambrosius with Merlin, who becomes an integral part of the Arthurian legend. The red dragon is today a symbol of Wales, and incorporated in the national flag. See note on *Caerfyrddin* (p. 108).

no plague shall come to the Island of Britain: in the triads, the burying of the dragons is linked to the talismanic burial of the bones of Gwrthefyr the Blessed and the Head of Bendigeidfran son of Llŷr, also commemorated at the end of the Second Branch (p. 34)—together they are 'the Three Fortunate Concealments of the Island of Britain', keeping the land safe from (Saxon) oppression (*TYP* 37). However, the burying of the dragons does not constitute protection as such, but rather is itself the defeating of an oppression or plague. The second part of the triad—'the Three Unfortunate Disclosures'—notes that Gwrtheyrn (Vortigern) disclosed the whereabouts of the dragons.

114 *Oxford*: it is not clear why the author should name Oxford as the central point of Britain; however, it was an important political and administrative centre in the eleventh century, which may well explain why Pryderi travels there to pay homage to Caswallon in the Third Branch (p. 36).

Dinas Emrys: *dinas* is Welsh for 'fort'; this place-name is obviously connected to the story in the *History of the Britons*. However, the naming here is anachronistic, for Emrys (Lat. Ambrosius) was only linked with the place later, after he had disclosed the whereabouts of the dragons.

Ffaraon Dandde was one of the Three Chief Officers who Broke his Heart from Sorrow: *Ffaraon* is the Welsh form of Pharaoh; *tandde* means 'fiery'. The character appears in later genealogies of Arthur as the father of Llŷr Llediaith. According to a later triad, there were Three People who Broke their Hearts from Sorrow: Ffaraon Dandde, together with Branwen daughter of Llŷr and Caradog son of Brân, both characters in the Second Branch (see p. 33).

drowsiness forcing him to sleep: sleep-inducing music is a theme in both Irish and Welsh; compare, for example, the birds of Rhiannon who, according to the giant Ysbaddaden, 'wake the dead and lull the living to sleep' (p. 196).

hamper: a hamper or vessel of plenty is a common international folk-tale motif; compare the hamper of Gwyddnau Garan Hir in 'How Culhwch Won Olwen' (p. 196). This magical object is also paralleled in the bag which Rhiannon gives to Pwyll so that he can trick Gwawl in the First Branch (pp. 12–13).

THE LADY OF THE WELL

116 *The emperor Arthur was at Caerllion ar Wysg*: see note on Arthur's court, p. 82.

Owain son of Urien . . . Cai son of Cynyr: see notes on pp. 66 and 68 for *Owain* and *Cai*. There are several references to Cynon son of Clydno in the *Gododdin*, a poem attributed to Aneirin, commemorating the heroic deeds of a war-band from the Gododdin tribe that was defeated in a battle at Catraeth (Catterick) in the North of England, about AD 600. The land of the Gododdin extended along the shores of the Firth of Forth, with its capital at Din Eidyn (perhaps Edinburgh), the epithet that appears in the name of Cynan's father, Clydno Eidyn.

Glewlwyd Gafaelfawr: means 'Brave Grey Mighty Grasp'. He appears as

Arthur's gatekeeper on special occasions in 'Geraint son of Erbin' and 'How Culhwch Won Olwen' too. In the former he fills the office only at one of the three chief festivals, while in the latter he is only there on the first of January. In the poem 'What Man is the Gatekeeper?' in the Black Book of Carmarthen, Glewlwyd is the gatekeeper of a fortress to which Arthur himself and his men are attempting to gain admittance (see Patrick Sims-Williams, 'The Early Welsh Arthurian Poems', in *AOW* 33–71). A brief reference in the triads (*TYP* 88) notes that he is the lover of Dyfyr Golden-Hair, one of the Three Famous Maidens of Arthur's Court.

116 *the good story*: the term here is *ymddiddan*, 'conversation' in Modern Welsh. The term occurs in the title of a number of dialogue poems, implying perhaps a dramatic performance between two speakers. In this context, however, *ymddiddan* is a prose monologue of some length, where Cynon narrates a personal experience to Arthur's knights but directs his comments at Cai; hence it is a dialogue of sorts, although it elicits no response from the listener.

Cai went to the kitchen and the mead cellar: this implies that Cai holds the high-ranking office of steward, one of the twenty-four officers of the king's court whose function, among other things, is 'to control the food in the kitchen and the drink in the mead-store' (*LHDd* 13).

119 *an enormous black-haired man . . . keeper of that forest*: some translators have taken this to be a dark-skinned man. However, an adjective denoting colour, when employed to describe a human, usually denotes hair colour or colour of clothing (see note to p. 86). Parallels have been drawn between this forester and the Irish Fer Caille in the tale *The Destruction of Da Derga's Hostel*. Both men are giants, and have one foot, one eye, and carry a club. Both have also been associated with the Celtic horned god Cernunnos, often portrayed as an antlered god seated cross-legged, wearing a torque and accompanied by a ram-horned snake, and sometimes a bull and a stag. See Miranda Green, *The Gods of the Celts* (Gloucester, 1986).

120 *And under that tree there's a well . . . such singing as theirs*: compare the Third Branch of the Mabinogi, where Pryderi comes across a well with marble-work around it, and a golden bowl fastened to four chains (p. 40). Indeed, many medieval poets refer to Owain as *Iarll y Cawg*, 'the Earl of the Bowl/Basin'. As in the Third Branch, too, a huge noise or an uproar precedes the supernatural incident. Birdsong is often associated with the Otherworld; compare the birds of Rhiannon who wake the dead and send the living to sleep (see pp. 33 and 196).

121 *The black man*: in this case, 'black' refers to the colour of his garments (see above).

124 *anointing the nobleman who owns the castle*: that is, administering the last rites. The death of the Black Knight is skilfully interwoven with the traditional technique of tripartite repetition.

sendal: a thin, light silk used for fine garments.

125 *the Lady of the Well*: Iarlles y Ffynnon in Welsh. *Ffynnon* is the common Welsh word for 'well'. However, in this particular context, most translators have chosen the archaic or poetic 'fountain'. 'Well', however, is a better reflection of modern usage, 'fountain' carrying with it Victorian connotations of artificial structures erected in public places. Wells, on the other hand, were associated with Celtic ritual, and many have a religious significance to this day. See Francis Jones, *The Holy Wells of Wales* (Cardiff, 1992; first published Aberystwyth, 1954).

127 *with an image of a golden lion fastening them*: this may well be in anticipation of Owain's relationship with the lion. In Chrétien's work he is known as the Knight with the Lion. See D. D. R. Owen (trans.), *Chrétien de Troyes: Arthurian Romances* (London, 1987).

131 *a maiden approaching*: there is no reason to suppose that this maiden should be identified with Luned.

137 *the Black Oppressor*: this episode seems to be an addition to the main tale. 'Black' in this context is ambiguous, but could be taken in the sense of 'wicked'; compare the 'Black Oppressor' in 'Peredur' (p. 87). They are not to be identified with each other, although the nouns in both cases mean 'Oppressor': in 'Peredur son of Efrog', the character is called the *Du Trahawg*, while here he is the *Du Traws*.

I will become a hospitaller: yspytty (hostel) occurs in 'How Culhwch Won Olwen' (p. 181), and refers to a place where guests would stay before gaining entrance to Arthur's hall. Here, however, it may well have more precise associations and refer to the Hospitallers of the Order of St John of Jerusalem (later known as the Knights of Malta), an important military order that placed great weight on hospitality and caring for the sick. However, records suggest that their hostels in Wales were centres for thieving and ill-doing, the point made here by the author of the tale. See William Rees, *A History of the Order of St. John of Jerusalem in Wales and on the Welsh Border* (Cardiff, 1947).

138 *Three Hundred Swords of Cenferchyn and the Flight of Ravens*: a reference to Owain's troops. *Cenferchyn* means 'the descendants of Cynfarch', who was Owain's grandfather. 'Raven', on the other hand, is a common metaphor for warrior in Welsh poetry, so the 'Flight of Ravens' may well refer again to his retinue. In 'Rhonabwy's Dream', however, Owain's troops are literally ravens—they swoop down and attack Arthur's men (p. 223). Owain's ravens are commemorated in the coat of arms of the family of Sir Rhys ap Thomas of Abermarlais, which claimed descent from Owain and his father Urien.

GERAINT SON OF ERBIN

139 *It was Arthur's custom to hold court at Caerllion ar Wysg*: a formula that is employed to open several episodes in the three 'romances' (see pp. 86 and 116).

139 *for seven Easters and five Christmasses . . . Whitsuntide*: these were the three major feasts of the Christian calendar, and those at which the Anglo-Norman kings held court. They are also described in the Welsh laws as 'the three special feasts' (*LHDd* 5).

the steward: one of the twenty-four officers of the king's court according to Welsh law. Cai is associated with this office in 'The Lady of the Well', see note to p. 68.

Odiar the Frank: as a common noun, *frank* means 'foreign mercenary'; here, however, it may refer mean 'Frenchman' or 'Norman'.

nine captains of the bodyguard: the captain of the household or bodyguard was a high-ranking court officer, whose duties included putting the harp 'into the hand of the bard of the household at the three special feasts'. For the full range of his duties and privileges, see *LHDd* 8–11.

Glewlwyd Gafaelfawr . . . Clust son of Clustfeinydd: 'Glewlwyd Mighty Grasp', see note to p. 116. *Gryn* does not occur elsewhere and may well be a scribal error. *Penpingion* and *Llaesgymyn* are Glewlwyd's assistants in 'How Culhwch Won Olwen' too (p. 181), while both *Drem son of Dremidydd* ('Sight son of Seer') and *Clust son of Clustfeinydd* ('Ear son of Hearer') appear in the Court List (pp. 186 and 188).

140 *go and hunt . . . and everyone else*: according to the laws, each officer was designated particular lodgings at court; for example, the chief huntsman and chief squire (or groom) were to be lodged in the kiln and the house nearest the barn respectively (see *LHDd* 21 and 29). The hunting seasons are also noted, together with the animals to be hunted in each of those seasons (ibid. 22).

would it not be appropriate . . . on foot: the laws describe how the carcass was divided into 'joints', including its loins, haunches, heart, liver, and tongue, and specify that it was an offence to carry off certain joints without the huntsmen's permission. The head itself is not mentioned (*LHDd* 184–5).

141 *the servants who were in charge of his bed . . . Gorau son of Custennin*: these seem to fulfil the role of the 'chamberlain' see note to p. 68. *Cadyriaith*, meaning 'Fine Speech', is presented in 'Rhonabwy's Dream' as someone who can understand complex praise poetry (p. 225). *Amhren* and *Gorau* appear in 'How Culhwch Won Olwen' (see note on *Gorau*, p. 202), while the latter appears in 'Rhonabwy's Dream' also (p. 225); *Amhar* is mentioned in the *History of the Britons* in the context of an onomastic tale, located in the Archenfield district of Herefordshire, where we are told that he was killed by his own father, Arthur.

Geraint: the many references to Geraint son of Erbin in early sources suggest that he may be a combination of several persons of the same name: the early fifth-century British general Gerontius; a sixth-century Geraint, named in the *Gododdin* poem; the eighth-century Geruntius, king of Domnonia (Devon); the Cornish saint Gerent; and a Gerennius, king of Cornwall (see *AOW* 46–7). In the triads (*TYP* 14), he is one of the Three Seafarers/Fleet Owners of the Island of Britain. Traditions about him were also known in Brittany; indeed, it would seem that the cognate hero of the French romance *Erec* takes his name from the Breton *Guerec*, the ruler who gave his name to *Bro Weroc*, the territory around Vannes. In the *Mabinogion* Arthur and Geraint are cousins—Erbin is Arthur's uncle—probably due to the influence of Geoffrey of Monmouth. For further details, see *TYP*, pp. 356–60.

142 *charger*: there were many terms for 'horse' in Medieval Welsh, including *cadfarch*, 'charger, warhorse'. For descriptions of horses in the *Mabinogion*, see note to p. 95. This tale is particularly rich in its elaborate descriptions, the attributes conforming to the virtues of a good horse.

145 *sparrowhawk*: hunting-birds were very important in medieval Welsh society, as attested by the laws. The hawk was worth a pound, while the sparrowhawk was worth 12 pence when young, and 24 pence with its adult plumage (*LHDd* 182–3).

148 *Edern son of Nudd*: brother to the legendary Gwyn son of Nudd, cognate with the Irish deity Nuadu. Both characters appear in 'How Culhwch Won Olwen' (pp. 184 and 207); Edern also appears in 'Rhonabwy's Dream' (p. 225).

His story so far: the author makes a deliberate attempt to show that one strand of the narrative has come to an end, and that the focus of the next section will be on a new protagonist. Cf. p. 149, 'Geraint's adventure so far', and again p. 152, 'Their story so far'.

Earl Ynywl: the name is unknown outside this tale. It may be linked to the common noun *niwl*, meaning 'mist', and the character may once have been associated with the 'hedge of mist' episode at the end of the tale (pp. 176–8).

149 *And I want Arthur . . . give the maiden away*: if a girl was given in marriage to a man by her kin, then she would be 'bestowed' by them—this was a legal agreement, associated with payments such as *amobr* (the fee payable to the woman's lord) and *cowyll* (virginity payment made to her by the husband). Here, although Ynywl the father has consented to give his daughter, Geraint wishes to postpone the marriage until he returns to Arthur's court, where Arthur and Gwenhwyfar can be the official *rhoddiaid* ('bestowers').

150 *Cafall*: he is first mentioned in the ninth-century *History of the Britons*, in the context of an onomastic tale. When hunting Twrch Trwyth (see p. 198), Arthur's dog Cabal impressed his footprint on a stone which Arthur then placed on top of a pile of stones. We are told that if the stone is taken away it mysteriously finds its way back to the place that has been called Carn Cabal (Cabal's Cairn) ever since. *Cafall* is derived from Latin *caballus*, meaning 'horse', and may well have originally been the name of Arthur's horse rather than his dog. He also plays a role in the hunt of the wild boar in 'How Culhwch Won Olwen' (see p. 210).

152   *insult-price*: see note to p. 27.

> *Caradog son of Llŷr . . . Gwalchmai*: in 'Rhonabwy's Dream', *Caradog* is presented as Arthur's nephew (p. 218). In the triad of the Three Tribal Thrones of the Island of Britain (*TYP* 1), he is linked with Arthur and his court in Celli Wig in Cornwall, and described as 'Chief of Elders', and is given the epithet *Freichfras* ('Strong-arm'), misinterpreted in the French romance as *briefbras* ('short-arm'). *Gwallog son of Llennog*, according to the triads, is one of the Three Pillars of Battle (*TYP* 5) and one of the Three Armed Warriors (*TYP* 6) of the Island of Britain. In the *History of the Britons* he is one of the four kings who fought, alongside Urien, against the Angles of Northumbria at the end of the sixth century. Surviving evidence, including early poetry, suggest he was a historical figure associated with the North of Britain. *Owain son of Nudd* seems to be a brother to Edern, Geraint's adversary, although nothing else is known of him; *Gwalchmai* is discussed in the note to p. 66.

> *Morgan Tud . . . chief of physicians*: according to the laws, the physician was one of the king's twenty-four officers at court (see *LHDd* 24–5). His role was to give medical attention free of charge, except for the three dangerous wounds for which he was paid: these were a blow to the head reaching the brain, a blow to the body reaching the bowels, and breaking one of the 'four posts' (i.e. thighs and arms). Here, Morgan Tud is a male character; however, in Chrétien's romance the name is given to Arthur's enchantress sister, Morgan le Fay, daughter of Arthur's mother by her first husband, Gorlois, duke of Cornwall. In later tradition Morgan is portrayed as Arthur's enemy, although the links with healing remain as she takes Arthur to the Isle of Avalon to be healed of his wounds.

153   *Enid*: this is the first time she is mentioned by name. *Enid* (French *Enide*) may derive from *Bro Wened*, the Breton name for Vannes (see note to p. 141 on *Geraint*). Indeed, it has been suggested that this tale is based ultimately on a sovereignty theme, whereby Erec, the founder of the Breton kingdom of *Bro Weroc*, mated with Enide, the goddess of the land. The tale was then transferred to the south-west of Britain, where the local hero Geraint replaced Erec, but Enid(e) remained unchanged. See *TYP*, pp. 349–50.

155   *Gwalchmai son of Gwyar . . . court steward to Arthur—*: many of the names occur in the lists found in 'How Culhwch Won Olwen' (pp. 184–9) and 'Rhonabwy's Dream' (p. 225). For *Gwalchmai*, see note to p. 66. The next four names form a distinct group, being the sons of rulers: *Rhiogonedd son of the king of Ireland, Ondiaw son of the duke of Burgundy, Gwilym* (i.e. 'William') *son of the king of France*, and *Hywel son of the king of Brittany. Elifri*, 'Abundance of Skills', may be identified with the chief squire mentioned earlier (p. 140); for *Gorau*, see note to p. 202; *Gwair* 'of Great Valour' is mentioned in the triads as one of the Three Enemy-Subduers (*TYP* 19), as well as one of the Three Stubborn Ones

(*TYP* 72)—he may be equated with Gwair son of Gwystyl who appears in 'Peredur son of Efrog' (p. 65) and 'Rhonabwy's Dream' (p. 225). *Peredur* is the hero of 'Peredur son of Efrog' (see note to p. 65); as for *Gwyn Llogell Gwŷr*, the epithet is obscure—for the duties of a court judge or justice, see *LHDd* 16–19. *Gwrei Gwalstawd Ieithoedd* may be identified with 'Gwrhyr Interpreter of Languages' in 'How Culhwch Won Olwen', p. 188. For *Bedwyr* and *Cai*, see notes on p. 263 and to p. 68); Odiar the Frank was mentioned earlier in the tale (see note to p. 139). For a further discussion of these names, see Robert L. Thomson (ed.), *Ystorya Gereint Uab Erbin* (Dublin, 1997), 99–100.

160 *sad and sorrowful*: a combination of two words which are to all intents synonymous and very often bound together by alliteration is a feature of most tales in the *Mabinogion* corpus. Where possible the alliteration has been preserved in the translation.

166 *the Dun Earl*: Welsh *dwn* means 'dark brown'; this probably refers to the colour of his armour; compare, for example, the Black Knight in 'The Lady of the Well' (see p. 123).

167 *The French and the English . . . Y Brenin Bychan*: an interesting reference to the bilingual context—his name in Anglo-Norman is *Gwiffret Petit* (Little Gwiffret), corresponding to Chrétien's *Guivret le petit*, while his name in Welsh is *Y Brenin Bychan* ('The Little King').

172 *a newly wedded woman in her riding clothes, shrieking*: the Welsh *morwyn-wreic* (literally someone who is both a virgin and a wife) refers to someone whose marriage has not yet been consummated.

173 *Earl Limwris*: this seems to be a foreign name, with the initial *L-* rather than the Welsh *Ll-*. *Limors* occurs in Chrétien's poem, but as the name of a castle rather than an earl.

176 *And on every stake . . . except for two stakes*: the severed heads are not explained, although it could be assumed that they are the heads of knights who have been unsuccessful at the game. For the cult of the head, compare Bendigeidfran, p. 32.

HOW CULHWCH WON OLWEN

Because of the numerous characters listed in this tale, together with the many international motifs, notes have been supplied only on the most significant features. Some additional information is provided in the Indexes of Personal and Place-Names, while further details and references can be found in Rachel Bromwich and D. Simon Evans (eds.), *Culhwch and Olwen: An Edition and Study of the Oldest Arthurian Tale* (Cardiff, 1992) (*CaO*).

179 *Cilydd son of Celyddon Wledig*: *Cilydd*, meaning 'companion', may be one of a group of names in this tale which stems from the *Gododdin* poem. *Celyddon* corresponds to Caledonia, an area covering the south-west of Scotland. The title *(G)wledig*, meaning 'lord', is given to several

characters, including Maxen in 'The Dream of the Emperor Maxen' (see p. 103).

179 *and was named Culhwch . . . pig-run*: an attempt to explain how Culhwch received his name: *hwch* means 'pig' and *cul* means 'sty, run'. However, since *cul* in this sense is not attested until the fourteenth century, the older meaning of 'slender, lean' should be read here. Culhwch may have associations with the Celtic swine-god Moccus: (see Patrick K. Ford (trans.), *The Mabinogi* (Berkeley, Los Angeles, and London, 1977).

   foster-parents: see note to p. 16.

180 *Olwen daughter of Ysbaddaden Bencawr*: her name, meaning 'white track', is 'explained' later in the story (see p. 192). *Ysbaddad* is the Welsh name for 'hawthorn' or 'thorn bush', while *Pencawr* means 'Chief Giant'. There are no references to Olwen or her father outside this story. Here, the international theme of the jealous stepmother provides the catalyst for the ensuing events, interwoven with the theme of the Giant's Daughter or Six Go Through the World (a reference to the six magic helpers that come to the hero's aid).

   to have your hair trimmed: the cutting of the hair was a symbolic act by means of which a blood-relationship was recognized and accepted. See below, p. 183, where Arthur, upon combing Culhwch's hair, recognizes him as a kinsman.

   as your gift: Culhwch is entitled to a gift (Welsh *cyfarws*) from his lord as he is accepted formally into the family.

181 *The boy went off . . . to the gate of Arthur's court*: in the *Mabinogion* characters' physical attributes are usually described by means of trad-itional formulae. However, in this tale the descriptions of both Culhwch (and his horse) and Olwen are elaborate and rhetorical, lending them-selves to a vocalized peformance. The description of Culhwch's *gorwydd* ('steed') follows the rhythmical pattern employed consistently when describing horses in the native tales (see note to p. 95), reflecting the movement of the animal itself. The four clods of earth thrown up by Culhwch's steed are paralleled by the four white clovers that grow in Olwen's track (p. 192). There may well be a play on words here, for the clods are compared to swallows, Welsh *gwennol*, where the elements of Olwen's name are transposed. Moreover, *gwennol* is also the name for the 'frog', i.e. the soft part in the middle of the horse's hoof, which may well have been the inspiration behind the author's comparison in the first place.

182 *Pen Pengwaedd in Cornwall . . . Dinsol in the North . . . Esgair Oerfel in Ireland*: *Pen Pengwaedd* can be identified with Penwith Point, near Land's End; compare the reference in the White Book version of 'The Names of the Island of Britain', which claims that the length of this island, from the promontory of Blathaon in Pictland to the promontory of Penrhyn Penwaedd in Cornwall, is 900 miles (*TYP*, p. 247). See also the note to p. 108 on *The Island of Britain*. *Dinsol* is probably Denzell, in the parish of

Padstow in Cornwall, a name that has for some reason taken the place of a location in the North of Britain, although the reference to *North* remains—if Culhwch's shout is to have any effect, it makes sense for it to be heard in places as far away from each other as possible. *Esgair Oerfel*, the 'Ridge of Coldness', seems to have been a place on the east coast of Ireland, visible from the sea. For 'The Irish Geography of Culhwch and Olwen', see P. Sims-Williams in Liam Bretnach *et al.* (eds.), *Celtic Studies in Honour of Professor James Carney* (Maynooth, 1988).

Glewlwyd Gafaelfawr: 'Glewlwyd Mighty Grasp'; see note to p. 116.

I was once in Caer Se . . . this very moment: this bombastic speech, listing exotic, faraway places, many unknown and probably invented, is characterized by repetition, alliteration, and rhyming pairs, reminiscent of metrical verse in the Black Book of Carmarthen. In the translation an attempt has been made to transmit the rhythm and essence of the oral performance visually to the printed page by dividing the prose into short lines. *Caer Oeth and Anoeth* is mentioned in the triads as a place where Arthur was imprisoned for three nights (*TYP* 52). For further references, see *CaO* 58–60.

By the hand of my friend: see note on *Cai* (p. 68). This particular oath is restricted to Cai, perhaps on account of his closest companion, Bedwyr, having lost his hand (see p. 189).

183 *the privileges of a prince, heir-apparent to the kingdom*: both manuscripts offer a gloss on the archaic term *gwrthrychiad* ('heir-apparent'): the White Book gives the legal term *edling* (from Old English *aethling*), while the Red Book gives the more general term *teyrn* ('prince').

except my ship . . . Gwenhwyfar my wife: the name of Arthur's ship is *Prydwen* (see p. 225); his mantle, according to 'Rhonabwy's Dream', is *Gwen* (p. 220), one of the Thirteen Treasures of the Island of Britain (*TYP* 258–65), which renders its wearer invisible. *Caledfwlch* ('Breach of Battle') is Geoffrey of Monmouth's *Caliburnus*, from which English *Excalibur* is derived. It is unclear whether these, together with *Rhongomyniad* ('Striking-Spear'), *Wynebgwrthucher* ('Evening-Face'), and *Carnwennan* ('Little White Haft'), take precedence over his wife *Gwenhwyfar* (see note to p. 68).

and combed his hair: see note to p. 180. As soon as he starts combing Culhwch's hair, Arthur realizes that they are blood-relatives. Compare the description in the *History of the Britons* where Guorthegirn offers to shear a young boy's head and comb his hair, only to be exposed as the boy's father *and* grandfather—Guorthegirn committed incest with his own daughter. In this tale, however, the significance of the ritual has not been understood, as Arthur agrees to Culhwch's request before realizing that they are related.

184 *He invoked his gift*: there follows an extremely long list of Arthur's companions (about 260 names in all), who are summoned by Culhwch as guarantors of the gift which he is demanding of Arthur. The list exists

within a frame, where the opening words are repeated in the closing lines (p. 189). Sections may have been taken from pre-existing lists; for example, an earlier, and much shorter, catalogue of names appears in the Black Book of Carmarthen poem 'What Man is the Gatekeeper?' (see Sims-Williams, 'The Early Welsh Arthurian Poems', in *AOW* 38–46). One can also surmise that new names were added to the list at every stage up to the writing of the surviving manuscripts, in order to bring as many characters as possible under the umbrella of the Arthurian court. In this passage, with its patronyms and epithets, alliteration and rhyme predominate, and a beat or pulse emerges when the catalogue is read out loud, so facilitating the mnemonic process. Some characters are merely named, while others carry epithets that conjure up tantalizing images; the attributes of other characters are described in concrete terms. Those belonging to this last group, such as Ear son of Hearer and Track son of Tracker, were probably invented solely for the purpose of this tale—they conform to the stereotyped magical helpers that are an integral part of this tale-type (see note to p. 180). The list should be read as a single entity, as should the second list on pp. 195–200, where Ysbaddaden describes forty tasks which Culhwch must accomplish if he is to win Olwen. However, to facilitate reading the passage has been subdivided into sections. The proper names in the translation itself appear in Welsh, but an alternative version is given below, where the epithets have been translated wherever possible, as have proper names that are clearly based on a play on words. Where a pun is not evident, the meaning of the name is noted. Further information on some of the names follows each section of the list below (for a detailed discussion of this Court List, and for more references to the individual characters, see *CaO*, pp. xxxiv–xlvi, and 67–110).

184 'Cai, and Bedwyr,[1] and Greidol Gallddofydd, and Gwythyr son of Greidol, and Graid son of Eri, and Cynddylig the Guide, and Tathal of Manifest Treachery, and Maelwys son of Baeddan, and Cnychwr son of Nes, and Cubert son of Daere, and Ffercos son of Poch, and Lluber Beuthach, and Corfil Berfach,[2] and Gwyn son of Esni, and Gwyn son of Nwyfre, and Gwyn son of Nudd, and Edern son of Nudd,[3] and Cadwy son of Geraint, and the ruler Fflewddwr Flame,[4] and Rhuawn the Radiant son of Dorath, and Bradwen son of Moren Mynog, and Moren Mynog himself, and Dalldaf son of Cimin Cof, and the son of Alun Dyfed, and the son of Saidi, and the son of Gwryon, and Uchdryd Battle-Sustainer, and Cynwas Pointed-Staff, and Gwrhyr Fat-Cattle, and Isberyr Cat-Claw, and Gallgoid the Killer, and Black and Stab and Strength, sons of Gwawrddydd the Hunchback (from the uplands of hell did those men come), and Cilydd Hundred-Holds, and Hundred-Holds Hundred-Hands, and Cors Hundred-Claws, and Esgair Gulhwch Gofyncawn, and Drwst Iron-Fist, and Glewlwyd Mighty-Grasp, and Lloch of the Striking Hand, and Anwas the Winged, and Sinnoch son of Seventh, and Wadu son of Seventh, and Nine son of Seventh, and

Gwenwynwyn son of Nine son of Seventh, and Bedyw son of Seventh, and Gobrwy son of Echel Mighty-Thigh, and Echel Mighty-Thigh himself, and Mael son of Roycol, and Dadwair Blind-Head, and Garwyli son of Gwythog Gwyr, and Gwythog Gwyr himself, and Gormant son of Rica, and Menw son of Three Cries, and Enough son of Surfeit, and Selyf son of Sinoid, and Gusg son of Achen, and Strength son of Might, and Drudwas son of Tryffin, and Twrch son of Perif, and Twrch son of Anwas,[5] and Iona, king of France, and Sel son of Selgi, and Teregud son of Iaen, and Sulien son of Iaen, and Bradwen son of Iaen, and Moren son of Iaen, and Siawn son of Iaen, and Caradog son of Iaen—they were men of Caer Dathyl, Arthur's family on his father's side. Contempt son of Caw, and Iustig son of Caw, and Fame son of Caw, and Angawdd son of Caw, and Gofan son of Caw, and Celyn son of Caw, [185] and Stalk son of Caw, and Mabsant son of Caw, and Gwyngad son of Caw, and Path son of Caw, and Red son of Caw, and Meilyg son of Caw, and Cynwal son of Caw, and Sustainer son of Caw, and Ergyriad son of Caw, and Someone son of Caw, and Gildas son of Caw, and Calcas son of Caw, and Huail son of Caw . . . and Samson Dry-Lip,[6] and Taliesin Chief of Bards, and Manawydan son of Llŷr, and Llary son of Casnar Wledig, and Sberin son of Fflergant, king of Brittany,[7] and Saranhon son of Glythfyr, and Llawr son of Erw, and Anynnog son of Menw Three-Cries, and Gwyn son of Nwyfre, and Flame son of Nwyfre, and Geraint son of Erbin,[8] and Ermid son of Erbin, and Dywel son of Erbin, and Gwyn son of Ermid, and Cyndrwyn son of Ermid, and Hyfaidd One-Mantle, and Eiddon the Magnanimous, and Rheiddwn Arwy, and Gormant son of Rica . . . And Llawnrodded the Bearded, and Nodawl Cut-Beard, and Berth son of Cado, and Rheiddwn son of Beli, and Isgofan the Generous, and Ysgawyn son of Banon, and Morfran son of Tegid . . .[9] And Sandde Angel Face . . . And Cynwyl the Saint, one of the Three Who Escaped from Camlan;[10] he was the last to part from Arthur, on Old Skin his horse.'

[1] *Cai and Bedwyr*: two of Arthur's closest companions. For Cai, see note to p. 68. There are several references to Bedwyr in the medieval Welsh sources, including the poem 'What Man is the Gatekeeper?' in the Black Book of Carmarthen (see Sims-Williams, *AOW*). In the triads he is one of the Three Diademed Battle-leaders of the Island of Britain (*TYP* 21), and is also mentioned in relation to Drystan son of Tallwch, one of the Three Powerful Swineherds of the Island of Britain. For further details, see *TYP*, pp. 286–7.

[2] *Maelwys son of Baeddan . . . Corfil Berfach*: on the Irish origin of these names, see Patrick Sims-Williams, 'The Significance of the Irish Personal Names in *Culhwch and Olwen*', *Bulletin of the Board of Celtic Studies*, 29 (1982), 607–10.

[3] *Gwyn . . . and Edern son of Nudd*: see note to p. 148.

[4] *Fflewddwr Flame*: according to *TYP* 9 he is one of the Three Chieftains of Arthur's Court. His title *gwledig* ('lord' or 'ruler') is usually

associated with Dorath, the patronymic of the next character in the list, and suggests miscopying since in the triads, and again in 'Rhonabwy's Dream', Fflewddwr has no title.

[5] *Twrch son of Perif and Twrch son of Anwas*: these are two boars (*twrch*). The former becomes one of Arthur's counsellors in 'Rhonabwy's Dream' (p. 225).

[6] *Contempt son of Caw ... Samson Dry-Lip*: Caw is listed in Ysbaddaden's list (p. 197) and plays a role in securing Olwen for Culhwch. Of the nineteen sons listed here, some are clearly farcical. Caw's son Gildas is the sixth-century Welsh and Breton saint, whose memory is preserved in two saints lives. Samson (Dry-Lip) is named as another of Caw's sons in the genealogies, again a saint and the founder of the cathedral of Dol in Brittany.

[7] *Fflergant, king of Brittany*: Alan IV, or Alan Fyrgan, duke of Brittany (d. 1119). He appears in the triads as one whose war-band was disloyal to him (*TYP* 30) and allowed him to go into the battle of Camlan alone, where he was killed.

[8] *Geraint son of Erbin*: the hero of the tale that bears his name, see note to p. 141.

[9] *Morfran son of Tegid*: 'Great Raven' son of Tegid, whose story is told in the sixteenth-century *Hanes Taliesin* ('The Tale of Taliesin'), ed. Patrick K. Ford, *Ystoria Taliesin* (Dublin, 1992). Both Ford and Lady Charlotte Guest included this tale in their respective translations of the *Mabinogion*, on the basis that it originated from the medieval period.

[10] *Three Who Escaped from Camlan*: this triad may well be an invention on the part of the redactor—no version appears in the surviving collections, although there are other references to Camlan, the supposed site of Arthur's last battle.

185   'And Uchdryd son of Erim, and Eus son of Erim, and Old Servant the Winged son of Erim, and Old Walker son of Erim, and Sgilti Light-foot son of Erim . . .

'Teithi the Old son of Gwynnan, whose kingdom the sea overran[1] . . .
[186] And Carnedyr son of Gofynion the Old, and Gwenwynwyn son of Naf . . . and Red-Eyed Stallion, and Gwrfoddw the Old . . . Culfanawyd son of Goryon, and Llenlleog the Irishman from the headland of Gamon[2] and Dyfnwal the Bald[3] and Dunarth, king of the North, Teyrnon Roar of the Flood-tide, and Tegfan the Lame, and Tegyr Talgellog. Gwrddywal son of Efrei, and Morgant the Generous, Hostage son of Nwython, and Rhun son of Nwython, and Llwydeu son of Nwython, and Gwydre son of Llwydeu by Gwenabwy daughter of Caw, his mother . . .'

[1] *Teithi the Old . . . whose kingdom the sea overran*: one of the many references in medieval Welsh to submerged kingdoms, see the note to p. 28.

[2] *from the headland of Gamon*: probably Garman in Co. Wexford, in the south-west of Ireland.

[3] *Dyfnwal the Bald*: he is mentioned in the genealogies of the 'Men of the North', and also in some versions of the Welsh laws, where he is

given the credit for measuring Britain from the headland of Blathaon on Pictland to the headland of Penwith in Cornwall (*LHDd* 120).

186 'Sight son of Seer, who from Celli Wig in Cornwall[1] could see a fly rise in the morning with the sun as far away as Pen Blathaon in Pictland[2]. And Eidoel son of Ner and Glwyddyn the Craftsman who built Ehangwen, Arthur's hall.[3] Cynyr Fair Beard—Cai was said to be his son . . .'

[1] *Celli Wig*: *Celli* ('grove') and *gwig* ('forest') is the site of Arthur's court both in this tale and in the triads. Several locations have been suggested, including Killibury hill-fort in the parish of Egloshayle, or Penwith (*Pen Pengwaedd*). For Arthur's Cornish connections, see Oliver Padel, 'Some South-Western Sites with Arthurian Associations', in *AOW* 229–48.

[2] *Pen Blathaon*: *Pen* here means 'point' or 'promontory'. See note to p. 182 on *Pen Pengwaedd*.

[3] *Ehangwen*: means 'roomy and fair'.

186 'Old Servant, and Old Face, and Old Friend, Gallgoig another . . . Berwyn son of Cyrenyr, and Peris, king of France . . . Osla Big Knife who would carry Breast-Blade Short Broad . . . Gwyddog son of Cupbearer . . . Long Shank son of Cai, and Amren son of Bedwyr, and Eli, and Myr, and Rheu Rhwyddyrys, and Rhun Rhuddwern, and Eli, and Trachmyr, Arthur's chief huntsmen [187] And Llwydeu son of Cilcoed, and Huabwy son of Gwryon, and Gwyn Godyfron, and Gwair Bird-Servant, and Gwair son of Cadellin Silver-Brow, and Gwair of False Valour, and Gwair White Spear—Arthur's uncles, his mother's brothers; the sons of Llwch of the Striking Hand from beyond the Tyrrhenian Sea,[1] Llenlleog the Irishman, and the Exalted One of Prydain,[2] Cas son of Saidi, Gwrfan Fair Hair, Gwilenhin, king of France, Gwitardd son of Aedd, king of Ireland, Garselyd the Irishman, Panawr Head of the Host, Atlendor son of Naf, Gwyn the Wrathful, overseer of Cornwall and Devon . . . Celli, and Cuelli, and Gilla Stag-Leg . . .'

[1] *Tyrrhenian Sea*: the western Mediterranean between Sicily and Sardinia.

[2] *the Exalted One of Prydain*: the proper name may have been omitted here.

187 'Heel, and Sole of Heel, and Blazing Sole . . . Erwm the Tall, and Atrwm the Tall . . .

'Huarwar son of Halwn . . . Gwarae Golden Hair,[1] the two whelps of the bitch Rhymhi, Gwyddrud, and Gwydden the Cunning, Suck son of Sucker . . . Cacamwri, Arthur's servant . . . Gulp, and Swallow, and Foolish the Bold, and Weak the Tall, and Amren the Tall . . . and Lip son of Placid . . . [188] Uchdryd Cross Beard . . . Elidir the Guide, Ysgyrdaf and Ysgudydd—they were two of Gwenhwyfar's servants . . . Brys son of Brysethach from the top of the black fernland in Prydain,[2] and Gruddlwyn the Dwarf.'

[1] *Gwarae Golden Hair*: equated with *Gwri Wallt Euryn* ('Gwri Golden Hair) in the First Branch of the Mabinogi (p. 18).

[2] *Brys son of Brysethach*: for references in the saints lives, and parallels in Irish, see *CaO* 101. As for *Prydain*, the two forms *Prydain* ('Britain') and *Prydyn* ('Pictland') are often confused in medieval Welsh texts.

188 *Bwlch and Cyfwlch ... maidservants*: Here, the acoustic dimension has taken over completely, as names are fabricated solely for the purpose of rhythm and sound, so as to make translation extremely challenging. I have divided the prose into short lines in an attempt to highlight the repetitive, alliterative, and rhyming elements of the passage. The passage, with slight changes, is repeated later in the tale, when Ysbaddaden makes his demands of Culhwch (p. 200). The first three lines play on the word *bwlch*, meaning 'gap' or 'breach'. *Cyfwlch* means 'perfect or complete', and *Difwlch* is 'without a breach'; *cleddyf* is the common word for 'sword'. *Glas* means 'grey, silver' and *Gleisiad* means 'salmon'. *Call* means 'shrewd' while *Cuall* can mean 'foolish' or 'speedy'. *Cafall*, from Latin *caballus* ('horse') is the name of Arthur's dog. The last four lines translate as follows:

> Late Bearer and Evil Bearer and Complete Bearer their three wives;
> Alas and Scream and Shriek their three grandchildren;
> Flash of Lightning and Desire and Need their three daughters;
> Bad and Worse and Worst of All their three maidservants.

188 'Eheubryd son of Cyfwlch, Big-Bone son of Strength, Gwaeddan son of Cynfelyn Ceudog, Pwyll Half-Man,[1] Dwn Vigorous Chieftain, Eiladar son of Pen Llarcan, Cynedyr the Wild[2] son of Hetwn Silver Brow, Sawyl High Head,[3] Gwalchmai son of Gwyar,[4] Gwalhafed son of Gwyar, Gwrhyr Interpreter of Languages . . .[5] and Cethdrwm the Priest. Ear son of Hearer . . . Aim son of Aimer . . . Gwiawn Cat-Eye . . . Track son of Tracker . . . Bedwini the Bishop . . .'[6]

[1] *Pwyll*: a character in the Four Branches of the Mabinogi, whose name means 'wisdom', 'caution'. His lack of sense and its repercussions in the First Branch may explain the epithet here (see p. 12).

[2] *Cynedyr the Wild*: he is later described as a son of *Hetwn Glafyriog* (the Leprous), p. 199.

[3] *Sawyl High Head*: one of the Three Arrogant Men of the Island of Britain (*TYP* 23).

[4] *Gwalchmai son of Gwyar*: see note to p. 66.

[5] *Gwrhyr Interpreter of Languages*: Welsh *gwalstawd* is derived from Old English *wealhstod*, meaning 'interpreter'. For a discussion of the *latimarii* or interpreters in twelfth-century Wales, and their possible role in transmitting narrative between the Welsh and Anglo-Norman courts, see C. Bullock-Davies, *Professional Interpreters and the Matter of Britain* (Cardiff, 1966).

[6] *Bedwini the Bishop*: the Chief of Bishops in Celli Wig in Cornwall, according to the triads (*TYP* 1). He also appears in 'Rhonabwy's Dream' (pp. 217 and 225) as one of Arthur's counsellors.

'And also the gentle, golden-torqued ladies of this Island. Besides Gwenhwyfar, chief queen of this Island, and Gwenhwyfach her sister,[1] and Rathtien, only daughter of Clememyl, Celemon daughter of Cai, and Tangwen daughter of Gwair Bird-Servant, White Swan daughter of Cynwal Hundred-Hogs, Eurneid daughter of Clydno Eidin,[2] [189] Eneuog daughter of Bedwyr, Enrhydreg daughter of Tuduathar, Gwenwledyr daughter of Gwaredur the Hunchback, Erdudfyl daughter of Tryffin, Eurolwyn[3] daughter of Gwddolwyn the Dwarf, Teleri daughter of Peul, Indeg daughter of Garwy the Tall,[4] Morfudd daughter of Urien Rheged,[5] Gwenllian the Fair, the magnanimous maiden, Creiddylad daughter of Lludd Silver-Hand, the most majestic maiden there ever was in the Three Islands of Britain and her Three Adjacent Islands. And for her Gwythyr son of Greidol and Gwyn son of Nudd fight each May day forever until the Day of Judgement.[6] Ellylw daughter of Neol Hang-Cock,[7] and she lived for three generations. Esyllt Fair Neck, and Esyllt Slender Neck. In the name of all of these did Culhwch son of Cilydd invoke his gift.' (Few of these names are attested elsewhere, and many are daughters of the men already listed.)

[1] *Gwenhwyfar . . . Gwenhwyfach*: they are associated in the triads—the Three Sinister Hard Slaps of the Island of Britain (*TYP* 53)—where it is claimed that the battle of Camlan occurred as a result of Gwenhwyfach slapping her sister. For Gwenhwyfar, see note to p. 68.

[2] *Clydno Eidin*: Clydno (meaning 'distinguished fame') was one of the leaders of the 'Old North'.

[3] *Eurolwyn*: literally means 'golden wheel'.

[4] *Indeg*: one of Arthur's Three Concubines (*TYP* 57).

[5] *Morfudd*: a twin to Owain son of Urien Rheged, while her lover was Cynon son of Clydno (*TYP* 70 and 71). Urien Rheged is the father of Owain, hero of 'The Lady of the Well' (see note to p. 66).

[6] *until the Day of Judgement*: the incident is described on p. 207.

[7] *Neol Hang-Cock*: Welsh *cŷn* ('chisel' or 'wedge') is also used in the obscene sense, as here, to mean 'penis'.

189 *Then Cai gets up*: of the long Court List, six individuals are chosen to go on the quest with Culhwch, reflecting the tale-type known as Six Go Through the World or The Giant's Daughter, where magical helpers ensure that the hero wins the giant's daughter.

Drych son of Cibddar: Drych ('aspect, mirror') is one of the Three Enchanters of the Island of Britain, according to the triads (*TYP* 27).

191 *She was happy that her nephew*: Custennin's wife is therefore an aunt to both Culhwch and Olwen, since her husband the shepherd is Ysbaddaden's brother.

192 *She was sent for . . . called Olwen*: as in Glewlwyd's bombastic speech (p. 182), the translation attempts to highlight the elaborate structure of the description by dividing the prose into lines based on repetition of syntactical patterns. The colour comparisons are conventional: see A. M.

Colby's classic study, *The Portrait in Twelfth-Century French Literature* (Geneva, 1965); but the careful structuring of the passage sets it apart from any other description of female beauty in the *Mabinogion*. For 'the flowers of the broom', see the note on Blodeuedd (p. 58) and on the hideous black-haired maiden in 'Peredur son of Efrog' (p. 94). According to the Welsh laws, a 'mewed' hawk was more valuable after it had 'moulted' and grown new plumage, whereas a 'thrice-mewed' falcon was a bird in its prime (*LHDd* 183). At the end of the passage we are given an onomastic explanation for the name Olwen—'white track'. The track she leaves behind her is paralleled by that left by Culhwch and his horse (see note to p. 181).

192 *he shall only live until I take a husband*: a common motif whereby the giant is fated to die once his daughter marries.

Ysbaddaden Bencawr snatched one of the three poisoned stone spears: when these are hurled back at him, the giant complains of the 'iron' injuring him, suggesting that the point of each spear was made of stone, or perhaps flint, while the shaft was made of iron.

194 *dowry and maiden-fee . . . must consult with them*: agweddi ('dowry') and *amobr* ('maiden-fee) are two legal terms associated with marital union: the former was given to the bridegroom by the bride's father, but could be recovered by her if the marriage lasted less than seven years; the latter was the fee payable by the girl's father to his lord on her marriage, originally perhaps payable for loss of virginity. The reference to the relatives reflects the family unit of four generations which shared legal responsibility for the maiden. See Jenkins and Owen (eds.), *The Welsh Law of Women*.

195 *It is easy for me to get that, though you may think it's not easy*: the beginning of a long list of tasks, forty in all, that Culhwch must accomplish to win the giant's daughter. The author makes use of an external frame— the list opens with the words 'When I get what I ask from you, then you shall get my daughter', and closes with 'And when you get those things, you shall get my daughter'. We are also reminded of the Court List, for Culhwch's initial reaction to Ysbaddaden is 'Name what you want' (cf. p. 183). Each task is introduced by the same formula, which is summarized in both White and Red Book versions, in various permutations, until it is eventually reduced to two words: *Hawd. Kyt* ('Easy. Although'). A second formula follows the naming of several tasks, when Ysbaddaden claims that an individual will not come of his own free will. This section is, therefore, linked together by verbal repetition which functions as a chorus of sorts, easing the process of listing, as well as listening, to the tasks; indeed, one could envisage a situation whereby the audience would join in the repetition, and so become active participants in the performance itself. Italics have been used in the translation to draw attention to this feature.

Amaethon . . . Gofannon son of Dôn: Amaethon ('Great/Divine Ploughman') and his brother *Gofannon* ('Great/Divine Smith') may reflect Celtic gods associated with agriculture and craftsmanship. See note to *Gilfaethwy son of Dôn* on p. 240.

Gwlwlydd Winau . . . Melyn Gwanwyn and the Ych Brych: the two oxen mentioned here, *Melyn Gwanwyn* ('Yellow Spring') and *Ych Brych* ('Speckled Ox') appear in the triad of the Three Principal Oxen of the Island of Britain (*TYP* 45), owned by Gwlwlydd. In the tale, the third in the triad, *Gwinau* ('Chestnut'), has become an epithet to describe the owner.

Mynydd Bannog . . . Nyniaw and Peibiaw: Mynydd Bannog ('the horned mountain') is the old Welsh name for a mountain in Scotland, surviving today only in the name Bannock Burn. The 'far side' of the Bannog refers to Pictland. *Nyniaw* and *Peibiaw* are historical characters, the sons of Erb, king of Archenfield in the sixth century.

196 *hestors*: a measure of quantity used for dry commodities, as well as the corresponding vessel.

honey of the first swarm . . . bragget for the feast: bees were regarded as a valuable commodity in medieval Wales, having come, according to the laws, 'from Paradise' (*LHDd* 183–4). 'Bragget' was a drink made of honey and ale fermented together.

Llwyr son of Llwyrion: 'Complete son of Complete.' His cup, together with the other vessels of plenty that follow, are reminiscent of the Thirteen Treasures of the Island of Britain (*TYP*, pp. 258–65); indeed, Gwyddnau's hamper and Diwrnach's cauldron are common to both texts.

The hamper of Gwyddnau Garan Hir: one of the Thirteen Treasures mentioned above, owned by Gwyddnau 'Long Shank', a legendary figure associated with the Taliesin story and the drowning of Cantre'r Gwaelod in Cardigan Bay (see note to *Later the sea spread out* on pp. 234–5). See *TYP*, pp. 391–2.

The horn of Gwlgawd Gododdin: *Gwlgawd* is mentioned twice in the *Gododdin* poem, under the form *Gwl(y)ged*, as the one 'who made the feast of Mynyddog famous', implying he was court steward to Mynyddog, leader of the Gododdin tribe.

the birds of Rhiannon: see notes to pp. 11 and 32.

197 *The cauldron of Diwrnach Wyddel*: in the Thirteen Treasures, this is listed as the cauldron of Dyrnwch the Giant rather than 'Diwrnach the Irishman', as here: 'if meat for a coward were put in it to boil, it would never boil; but if meat for a brave man were put in it, it would boil quickly (and thus the brave could be distinguished from the cowardly)' (*TYP*, pp. 259–60). A cauldron possessing a similar attribute and belonging to the Head of Annwfn is mentioned in the poem *Preiddiau Annwfn* ('The Spoils of Annwfn', see Sims-Williams, *AOW*). See also note to p. 200 on *Wrnach Gawr*.

197 *Ysgithrwyn Pen Baedd*: 'White Tusk Chief of Boars.'

Caw of Prydyn: according to the triads, the family of 'Caw of Pictland' was one of the Three Families of Saints (*TYP*, pp. 306–8); indeed, there are several references to him in the lives of the saints. Caw's nineteen sons and one daughter appear in the Court List (pp. 184–5 and 186). There is a play on words here—in both White and Red Book versions his name is rendered as *Kadw/Gado*, meaning 'to keep', since he is entrusted with the *keeping* of the tusk.

Pennant Gofid: the Valley of Grief.

the bottles of Gwyddolwyn Gorr: 'Gwyddolwyn the Dwarf.'

Rhynnon Ryn Barfog: 'Rhynnon Stiff Beard.'

198 *Twrch Trwyth son of Taredd Wledig*: the remaining tasks are associated with the hunting of this magical beast Twrch Trwyth, a king who had been transformed into a boar (Welsh *twrch*). The original form of his name was *trwyd* and not *trwyth*, cognate with the Irish *triath* meaning 'king' or 'boar'. Allusions in Welsh poetry, together with the ninth-century *History of the Britons* (see note to p. 150), suggest that traditions about Twrch Trwyth were known from an early period, and that the theme of the hunt existed independently of 'How Culhwch Won Olwen'. References to the Irish *Torc Triath*, a cognate form, suggests that both Ireland and Wales retained memories concerning a mythical giant boar. For the significance of the boar in Celtic belief, see Anne Ross, *Pagan Celtic Britain* (London, 1967). For *(G)wledig*, see note to p. 103.

Drudwyn, the whelp of Graid son of Eri: *Drudwyn* means 'Fierce White'. See p. 184 for Graid son of Eri.

Cors Cant Ewin . . . Canhastyr Can Llaw . . . Cilydd Canhastyr: all three appear as members of Arthur's Court (p. 184).

Mabon son of Modron: derived from the Celtic god *Maponos*, identified with Apollo by the Romans. In the Celtic pantheon he was the son-god, and his mother *Matrona* (*Modron* in Welsh) was the mother-goddess. W. J. Gruffydd attempted to identify Mabon with Pryderi (see note to p. 21) in his *Rhiannon: An Inquiry into the Origins of the First and Third Branches of the Mabinogi* (Cardiff, 1953). In the triads (*TYP* 52) Mabon is one of the Three Exalted Prisoners of the Island of Britain. For references to the cult of Maponos, together with variants on Mabon in continental romance, see *TYP*, pp. 424–8. On a possible link between *Mabon* and the term *Mabinogi*, see note to p. 21.

Gwyn Myngddwn, the steed of Gweddw: meaning 'White Dark Mane'. The triads note *Myngrwn* ('Arched Mane') as being Gweddw's horse, one of the Three Bestowed Horses of the Island of Britain, together with the horses of Gwalchmai and Cai (*TYP* 46).

Eidoel son of Aer: *Aer* means 'Slaughter'. Eidoel appears in the Court List as son of Ner (p. 186), possibly a miscopying. He appears later in the tale as a prisoner in the fortress of Gloucester (pp. 202–3).

Garselyd Wyddel . . . chief huntsman of Ireland: 'Garselyd the Irishman', again named in the Court List (p. 187). The *pen-cynydd* ('chief hunts-man') was one of the twenty-four officers of the king's court (see *LHDd* 21–3).

199 *Dillus Farfog . . . those two whelps*: 'Dillus the Bearded.' The whelps are probably 'the two whelps of the bitch Rhymhi' (p. 205), omitted here in Ysbaddaden's list.

Cynedyr Wyllt son of Hetwn Glafyriog: 'Cynedyr the Wild, son of Hetwn the Leprous.' In the Court List he is described as a son of *Tal Arian* ('Silver Brow') (p. 188).

Gwyn son of Nudd . . . the spirit of the demons of Annwfn: brother to Edern (p. 148). In Welsh tradition, Gwyn (meaning 'White') appears as a mythical huntsman and leader of the Otherworld (for *Annwfn*, see note to p. 4)—in Welsh folk-tales he is associated with the magical *cŵn Annwfn*, fairy dogs or 'hell-hounds', a premonition of death. Gwyn can be probably be equated with the Irish *Fionn mac Cumhaill*, who was both a seer and a poet; see Mac Cana, *Celtic Mythology*.

Du, the steed of Moro Oerfeddog: *Du* ('Black) appears in the triads as one of the Three Horses Who Carried the Three Horse-Burdens (*TYP* 44). There his full name is *Du y Moroedd* ('the Black of the Seas') and he belongs to Elidir Mwynfawr. *Moro Oerfeddog* is unknown outside this tale—some confusion may have occurred between the *Moroedd* of the triad and the *Moro* of the personal name in the tale.

Gwilenhin, king of France: 'William', generally believed to refer to William the Conqueror, included in the Court List on p. 187. In 1081 he visited St David's, to make peace, so it would seem, with Rhys ap Tewdwr, an event that could have a bearing on the tale's date of composition.

the son of Alun Dyfed: see the Court List, p. 184.

Aned and Aethlem: two hounds.

he is under my control: this is inconsistent with Arthur's behaviour—he claims that he has never heard of Ysbaddaden or his daughter—and with the sequence of events, since it is Arthur, as Ysbaddaden himself admits at the end of the tale, who has secured Olwen for Culhwch (p. 213).

200 *Bwlch and Cyfwlch . . . fell on the earth*: repetition, with very slight vari-ation, of the characters listed on p. 188 of the Court List.

Wrnach Gawr: 'Wrnach the Giant.' Compare *Diwrnach Wyddel* (pp. 208–9), and also the poem 'What Man is the Gatekeeper?' where Arthur is described as fighting with a hag in the hall of Awarnach. For a detailed analysis of the poem, see Sims-Williams, 'The Early Welsh Arthurian Poems', in *AOW* 33–61.

201 *'Open the gate'*: this dialogue echoes Culhwch's arrival at Arthur's court (p. 181).

white-bladed or dark-blue-bladed: the value of swords is discussed in the law texts: 'A sword, if it is ground on the stone, twelve pence; if it is dark-blue-bladed, sixteen pence; if it white-bladed, twenty-four pence' (*LHDd* 194). Jenkins suggests that 'the blue-bladed sword had acquired its colour in the process of tempering, whereas the white-bladed one had afterwards been polished and burnished' (ibid. 300).

202 *Gorau son of Custennin*: an onomastic explanation for the personal name *Gorau* ('Best'), which may be a corruption of *Gorneu*, meaning 'of Cornwall'—*Custennin Gorneu* is attested in several early sources. The character is also named in 'Geraint son of Erbin' (p. 155), and 'Rhonabwy's Dream' (p. 225). In the triads (*TYP* 52) he releases Arthur, his cousin, from three imprisonments. His role at the end of this tale suggests an underlying vengeance theme.

A year from that very day they came: the White Book text ends here.

203 *Gliwi*: derived from the genitive of Latin *Glevum*, the Roman name for Gloucester, and seen in Welsh as the eponym of the city—*Caer Loyw* ('Gloyw's fort'). According to Geoffrey of Monmouth, the city was built by the emperor Claudius, and the place was named after him; in the Welsh translation of Geoffrey's *History* Claudius is changed to *Gloyw*, hence *Caerloyw*. See *CaO* 141–2.

Blackbird of Cilgwri: the beginning of the tale of the Oldest Animals, which has parallels in Indian and Persian literature. Many other versions exist in Welsh, including a triad (*TYP* 92) where the Three Elders of the World are listed as the Owl of Cwm Cawlwyd, the Eagle of Gwernabwy, and the Blackbird of Celli Gadarn. Here, however, the Blackbird is associated with *Cilgwri*, probably a reference to the Wirral Peninsula.

Stag of Rhedynfre: 'Fernhill' or 'Brackenill'. Again, one cannot be certain about the location, although *Rhedynfre* may be the original name of Farndon in Cheshire, not too far from *Cilgwri*.

204 *Owl of Cwm Cawlwyd*: again, several locations possible, although the most probable is the area between Capel Curig and Llanrwst in Gwynedd.

Eagle of Gwernabwy: *gwern* is the common name for an 'alder tree', although sometimes it means 'swamp'. It may perhaps be identified with *Bodernabwy* near Aberdaron in the Lleyn peninsula, Gwynedd.

Llyn Lliw: probably the same place as *Llyn Lliwan* mentioned on p. 212, a tidal lake somewhere on the Severn estuary.

205 *neither the prison of Lludd Llaw Eraint . . . Graid son of Eri*: 'Lludd Silver Hand' is named as Creiddylad's father on p. 189. while Graid, who is mentioned on p. 184, is Gwyn ap Nudd's prisoner on p. 207. Another version of this triad is found in *TYP* 52, the Three Exalted Prisoners of

the Island of Britain, although Mabon is the only prisoner common to both. See also the note to p. 202 on *Gorau*.

Aber Daugleddyf: 'the confluence of the two Cleddau rivers', near Milford Haven in south-west Wales.

Tringad: later Twrch Trwyth kills *Gwyn son of Tringad son of Neued*. The first element may be cognate with Irish *trén* ('strong'), while the second element may be *cad* ('battle').

Prydwen: 'Fair Form', Arthur's ship; see note to p. 183.

And God changed them back into their own shape for Arthur: this implies that the bitch and her two whelps were changed back into human form.

206 *on top of Pumlumon on Garn Gwylathr*: Pumlumon (Plynlimon) is a mountain range in mid-Wales. The name *Garn Gwylathr* has not survived.

a leash made from the beard of the man you see over there: the text is inconsistent, since on p. 198 it is said that the leash of Cors Cant Ewin is needed to hold Drudwyn.

207 *Arthur sang this englyn . . . Were he alive, he would kill you*: for the use made of the *englyn*, see also the Second and Fourth Branches of the Mabinogi, pp. 31 and 62–3, and note to p. 31. As a result of Arthur's satirical verse, Cai takes offence and disappears from the story. Further *englynion* are attributed to Arthur in other sources, while in the triads (*TYP* 12) Arthur is acknowledged as one of the Three Frivolous (Amateur?) Bards of the Island of Britain.

Creiddylad daughter of Lludd Llaw Eraint: Creiddylad's name appears in the Court List (p. 189).

Glinneu son of Taran: 'Glinneu son of Thunder', see also p. 32.

Gwrgwst Ledlwm . . . Nwython: these four characters have associations with the North of Britain, suggesting that this episode originated from there. 'Gwrgwst Half-Bare', according to the genealogies, was the grandson of *Coel Hen* ('Coel the Old'), a ruler over much of north-west England and southern Scotland in the early fifth century; his son Dyfnarth may perhaps be identified with *Dunarth, king of the North*, in the Court List (p. 186), both versions of *Domangart*, grandfather of the Scottish ruler *Aedán mac Gabráin*; *Pen* ('Head') *son of Nethog* may well be a corruption and doublet of the fourth character, *Nwython*, who is associated with the area of Strathclyde.

Cyledyr Wyllt: an onomastic explanation for the epithet *(G)wyllt* ('Wild'). For an Irish parallel, see references in *CaO* 152.

every May day: for the significance of May day, see note to p. 17.

Mabon son of Mellt: 'Mabon son of Lightning', who also appears in the poem 'What Man is the Gatekeeper?' in the Black Book of Carmarthen. See Sims-Williams in *AOW*.

the two dogs of Glythfyr Ledewig: these were not specified in

Ysbaddaden's list. *Ledewig* ('Breton') suggests that Glythfyr came from Brittany.

207 *Gwrgi Seferi*: the first and only time that he is mentioned in the tale. *Gwrgi* means 'Man Hound', while *Seferi* may derive from *Severus*, a third-century emperor.

Arthur went to the North: presumably the 'Old North', namely the old Brittonic kingdoms of Gododdin, Strathclyde, and Rheged located in the North of England and southern Scotland. This, ironically, is where some of the earliest surviving Welsh poetry originates, such as the *Gododdin*, and poems associated with Owain and his father Urien of Rheged.

208 *Llamrei, Arthur's mare*: 'Grey or Swift Leaper.' Note that Arthur's horse is a 'mare'—the medieval warhorse of the West was almost always a stallion.

209 *Porth Cerddin in Dyfed. And Mesur y Pair is there*: *cerddin* is a 'rowan tree'; however, the exact location of the *porth* ('port') is unknown, although Pwll Crochan ('Pool of the Cauldron'), west of Fishguard, is a possibility, especially in view of the onomastic explanation: 'The Measure of the Cauldron is there.'

Gwlad yr Haf: the 'Summer Country', originally the whole of the south-west peninsula rather than just Somerset.

a tribute of food: the laws describe in detail the food tributes to which the king was entitled twice a year from his subjects, including flour, mead, oats, pigs, butter, and beer (*LHDd* 128–9).

seven little pigs: six of these are named as the hunt progresses: Grugyn Gwrych Eraint, Llwydog Gofyniad, Twrch Llawin, Gwys, Banw, Benwig.

a fifth of Ireland: Ireland was traditionally divided into five provinces: Ulster, Munster, Leinster, Connacht, and Meath. The closing lines of the Second Branch tell how Ireland was repopulated after the great massacre between the Irish and the men of the Island of the Mighty (p. 34).

Grugyn Gwrych Eraint: 'Grugyn Silver-bristle'. He is also referred to in this tale as Grugyn Gwallt Eraint (Grugyn Silver Hair); see p. 211. For Irish parallels, see *CaO* 158.

210 *Porth Clais in Dyfed . . . Mynyw that night*: *Mynyw* or *Menevia* is the old name for St David's, while *Porth Clais* is a harbour 5 miles south-west of the city.

Glyn Nyfer . . . Cwm Cerwyn: the Nyfer ('Nevern') valley, north-east of St David's, not far from *Cwm Cerwyn* ('the Cerwyn valley') in the Preseli mountains. For detailed geographical references to Twrch's journey, together with onomastic associations and a map, see *CaO*. See William Rees, *An Historical Atlas of Wales*, for the administrative divisions of medieval Wales.

Gwarthegydd son of Caw, and Tarog Allt Clwyd: 'Cattle-raider son of Caw' and 'Tarog from the Rock of the Clyde'; neither was included in the Court List. Indeed, several of the characters mentioned here have not been introduced previously in the tale.

Peuliniog: the land between Narberth and Carmarthen in south-west Wales.

Glyn Ystun: a wooded area to the east of the Llychwr valley (*Dyffryn Llwchwr*).

211 *Mynydd Amanw ... Dyffryn Amanw ... Banw and Benwig were killed*: 'Amanw Mountain' and 'Amanw Valley' can be linked with the name Aman, a stream which flows into the Llwchwr. There is clearly an ono-mastic association here, *Banw* meaning 'pigling', and *Benwig* being the diminutive form, 'young pigling'.

Llwch Ewin ... Llwch Tawy ... Din Tywi ... Garth Grugyn ... Ystrad Yw: many of these places are difficult to identify with any degree of certainty. *Llwch Tawy* is the old name for Llyn y Fan Fawr in the Brecon Beacons; *Garth Grugyn* Castle, built in 1242, stands in Llanilar; the commot of *Ystrad Yw* is in south-east Wales, in the cantref of Talgarth.

Hir Peisog: 'Long Tunic.'

between Tawy and Ewias ... Aber Hafren: the river Tawe flows into the sea at Swansea (*Abertawe*); *Ewias* was a cantref in the south-east, located between Talgarth and Erging. *Aber Hafren* is the estuary of the river Severn.

212 *between Llyn Lliwan and Aber Gwy*: 'Lliwan Lake' can be equated with *Llyn Lliw*, the home of the Salmon (p. 204); it was a tidal lake reached by the Severn 'bore', a fast-moving tidal wave caused by the meeting of the tidal estuary and the river. The reference to 'the estuary of the Wye' (*Aber Gwy*) implies that the lake, described in the *History of the Britons* as one of the Wonders of Britain, was situated on the Welsh side of the Severn estuary. The description below of the waters flooding over Twrch Trwyth may be a further reference to the Severn bore. Some sixty such features are found worldwide, the largest in the river Quaintang in China, personified as the Quaintang Dragon. Today, surfing the Severn bore is popular: the experience has been described, ironically, as 'Hunting Wild Bore'. See also the note to p. 17 on *Teyrnon Twrf Liant*.

RHONABWY'S DREAM

214 *Madog son of Maredudd ... uplands of Arwystli*: Madog ruled Powys from 1130 until his death in 1160. Throughout his reign he attempted to defend his lands against the power of Gwynedd, joining forces with Henry II against Owain Gwynedd in 1157. After his death Powys was shared between his heirs, namely three of his sons, his brother Iorwerth, and his nephew Owain Cyfeiliog, leading to internal strife. Powys in the twelfth century consisted of today's Montgomeryshire and parts of the counties of Merioneth, Denbigh, and Flint. Porffordd can be identified with Pulford in Flintshire, 5 miles south of Chester. The exact location of Gwafan is uncertain, except that it was somewhere in the cantref of Arwystli in south Montgomeryshire. The author emphasizes, therefore,

that *all* of Powys is under Madog's rule. For a detailed map of the places mentioned in the tale, see Melville Richards's Welsh-language edition of the tale, *Breudwyt Ronabwy* (Cardiff, 1948). See also William Rees, *An Historical Atlas of Wales*.

214 *Iorwerth son of Maredudd*: or *Iorwerth Goch* ('Iorwerth the Red'), according to historical sources. Iorwerth was a *latimari* ('translator') for the king, and was given the lordship of Chirk Castle for his services. He joined his brother in 1157 against Owain Gwynedd. But in 1165 he fought *with* Owain Gwynedd for a short period, against Henry II; but then restored his allegiance to the English Crown once more. The tension between Iorwerth and his brother is representative of the fragile situation in medieval Wales, where male relatives would fight for supremacy.

head of the retinue: the *teulu* ('retinue') was integral to the role of any ruler; it would not only defend him, but also promote his cause in the bloody political sphere. The *penteulu* ('head') was usually a close relative, as attested by the Welsh laws (*LHDd* 8–11).

Rhychdir Powys . . . Efyrnwy: the *Rhychdir* (meaning 'arable land') is the area around Oswestry. The river Ceiriog flows into the Dee at Aber Ceiriog, not far from Chirk; nearby is Halton (*Halictwn*). *Rhyd Wilfre* refers to a ford (*rhyd*) on the river Efyrnwy (English: Vyrnwy), between Llanymynech and Melverley.

Didlystwn: Dudleston, to the south-east of Aber Ceiriog.

Rhonabwy . . . Heilyn Goch son of Cadwgan son of Iddon: Rhonabwy's two companions are from Powys: Cynwrig *Frychgoch* ('Freckled and Red') comes from Mawddwy, a commot in north-west Powys; Cadwgan *Fras* ('stout') comes from Moelfre in the commot of Cynllaith, 6 miles to the west of Oswestry. No details are given about Rhonabwy himself. Heilyn, like Cynwrig, is 'Red', presumably a reference to the colour of his hair.

215 *A very black old building . . . on one dais*: a vivid description of a medieval house, quite unlike the sumptuous halls of the 'romances'. The building is unlikely to be a hall-house (which might have a raised dais at one end of the hall for the main table), and probably represents a building lower down the social scale, such as a medieval long-house with combined cattle/living quarters, where the dais may refer to low built-in benching along the walls, either side of the central hearth, for sleeping and sitting on. My thanks to Mark Redknap, Amgueddfa Cymru/National Museum Wales. See also John B. Hilling, *The Historic Architecture of Wales* (Cardiff, 1976), 90–104.

yellow ox-skin: in Irish sources sleeping on an ox-hide was a precursor to a dream, very often a prophetic vision.

Maes Argyngroeg . . . Rhyd-y-groes on the Hafren: *Maes Argyngroeg* is the level land near Welshpool, retained in the name Gungrog today. *Rhyd-y-groes* ('Ford of the Cross') is probably at Buttington near Welshpool.

216 *and saw a young man . . . as yellow as the flowers of the broom*: the first of many formulaic descriptions which, although highly elaborate, follow the traditional pattern found in most of the other tales. The horse is often an integral part of the description in 'Rhonabwy's Dream'. Powys was famous for its horses in the Middle Ages, as witnessed, for example, by Gerald of Wales, who emphasizes their 'majestic proportions' and 'incomparable speed': Lewis Thorpe (trans.), *The Journey Through Wales and The Description of Wales* (Harmondsworth, 1978) 201. See Sioned Davies, 'Horses in the *Mabinogion*', in Davies and Jones (eds.), *The Horse in Celtic Culture*.

Iddog Cordd Prydain: an onomastic tale, explaining how Iddog received his nickname 'Agitator of Britain'. He is almost unknown outside this tale, although he is included in a fifteenth-century version of the triad the Three Men of Shame (*TYP* 51) as one who caused strife between Arthur and Medrawd at the battle of Camlan. For further triads reflecting a strong Welsh tradition concerning Arthur's last battle, see *TYP*, pp. 167–70, as well as the many references in 'How Culhwch Won Olwen'. See note to p. 68 for further details of Medrawd. This reference to Iddog would suggest that the battle of Camlan has already taken place; however, Arthur is then introduced later in the story. Rather than read this reference to Iddog as an anachronism, it could be viewed as a deliberate attempt at parody on the part of the author, where the expected chronological sequence of events is reversed. On the notion of the story 'running backwards', see Edgar Slotkin, 'The Fabula, Story, and Text of *Breuddwyd Rhonabwy*', *Cambridge Medieval Celtic Studies*, 18 (1989), 89–111.

Y Llech Las in Prydain: the Grey Rock in Pictland.

217 *Rhuawn Bebyr son of Deorthach Wledig*: Rhuawn the Radiant, one of the Three Fortunate Princes of the Island of Britain (*TYP* 3), appears in Arthur's Court List as Rhuawn Bebyr son of Dorath (p. 184).

Bedwin the Bishop . . . Gwarthegydd son of Caw: Bishop Bedwin is mentioned in Arthur's Court List (p. 188), while Gwarthegydd ('Cattle-raider') is killed while hunting Twrch Trwyth (p. 210).

218 *Addaon son of Taliesin . . . Elphin son of Gwyddno*: Addaon (sometimes Afaon) appears in the triads as one of the Three Bull-Chieftains (*TYP* 7), and one of the Three Battle-Rulers (*TYP* 25); his death was one of the Three Unfortunate Slaughters of the Island of Britain (*TYP* 33). Elphin is associated with the saga of Taliesin; see note to *Morfran* (p. 264).

battle of Baddon . . . Osla Gyllellfawr: this was traditionally one of Arthur's famous battles (see *AOW* for references in Welsh sources). Osla 'Big Knife' plays a prominent role in the hunting of Twrch Trwyth, where he is portrayed as one of Arthur's own men rather than his enemy (p. 212).

Caradog Freichfras son of Llŷr Marini: Caradog Strong Arm appears in the triads, and also in 'Geraint son of Erbin' (see note to p. 152).

219 *Cefn Digoll*: Long Mountain, south of Welshpool.

March son of Meirchawn: the King Mark of the Tristan romances. Welsh
sources suggest that there existed many traditions about him. In *TYP* 14,
for example, he is one of the Three Seafarers/Fleet Owners, which perhaps explains his association with the men of Scandinavia in the dream—
they were renowned for their seafaring exploits. He is also associated with
the Three Powerful Swineherds of the Island of Britain (*TYP* 26)
through his nephew Trystan. For a discussion of 'The *Tristan* of the
Welsh', see Rachel Bromwich in *AOW* 209–28.

Edern son of Nudd: a character who appears in 'Geraint son of Erbin'
(p. 148) and also 'How Culhwch Won Olwen' (p. 184).

Cai: one of Arthur's foremost warriors, who appears in five of the
Mabinogion tales. See note to p. 68.

220 *Cadwr, earl of Cornwall*: a borrowing from Geoffrey's *History of the Kings
of Britain*.

Eiryn Wych Amheibyn: Eiryn the Splendid, son of Peibyn.

Gwen was the name of the mantle: a reference is made to Arthur's mantle
in 'How Culhwch Won Olwen' (p. 183); it is also listed as one of the
Thirteen Treasures of the Island of Britain—'whoever was under it
could not be seen, and he could see everyone' (*TYP*, p. 240)—compare
Caswallon's mantle in the Second Branch (p. 33).

Owain son of Urien: one of Arthur's men, and the hero of the tale 'The
Lady of the Well'. See note to p. 66.

gwyddbwyll: a board game not unlike chess; see discussion in the note to
p. 86. The chess motif is often used to parallel real battles; however, here
Arthur and Owain are on the same side, although ironically, when they
begin to play their men begin to fight.

Cordovan leather: see note to p. 38.

221 *your ravens*: Owain is traditionally associated with ravens; compare the
ending of 'The Lady of the Well', where reference is made to the 'Flight
of Ravens' (see note to p. 138). 'Raven' is a common metaphor for warrior in Welsh poetry. Here, in the dream, Owain's troops behave literally
like ravens who swoop down and attack Arthur's men. Owain's ravens are
commemorated in the coat of arms of the family of Sir Rhys ap Thomas
of Abermarlais, which claimed descent from Owain and his father Urien.

222 *thin totnes cloth*: twtnais, from Middle English *totenais*, a type of cloth
from the town of Totnes.

His horse was of a very strange colour: it is difficult to know whether the
descriptions of this horse, and the two that follow, should be taken at face
value. Ambiguity arises as to whether the colours, here and elsewhere in
the tale, refer to the horses themselves or to their apparel. Some have
attempted to link the colours with thirteenth-century heraldry, while
others argue that the colours themselves are not important—this is all
part of the author's attempt to parody the formulaic descriptions of

medieval narrative. See Sioned Davies, 'Horses in the *Mabinogion*', in Davies and Jones (eds.), *The Horse in Celtic Culture*, 121–40.

223 *Spanish latten*: a yellow metal, either identical with, or very like, brass.

224 *Selyf son of Cynan Garwyn . . . Gwgawn Gleddyfrudd*: Selyf was king of Powys at the beginning of the seventh century; he lost his life fighting the Northumbrians at the battle of Chester (*c*.615). His reputation as a fierce warrior is reflected in the triads, where he is named as one of the Three Battle-Rulers of the Island of Britain (*TYP* 25). Gwgawn Red Sword, too, is comemmorated as someone who holds his ground in battle (*TYP* 24). According to the genealogies, he was a local ruler in Ceredigion, in West Wales (see *TYP*, p. 384).

225 *Blathaon son of Mwrheth . . . Hyfaidd Unllen*: for Blathaon, compare the place-name (see note to p. 182 on *Pen Pengwaedd*); Hyfaidd One-Mantle appears in Arthur's Court List (p. 185).

Bedwin the Bishop . . . many men from Greece: compare the lists in 'Geraint son of Erbin' (p. 155) and 'How Culhwch Won Olwen' (pp. 184–9). It would seem that the author has borrowed extensively from the latter, and also from the triads. The following names do not appear in the above lists, neither are they mentioned elsewhere in the dream: Gwenwynwyn son of Naf (one of the Three Fleet Owners, *TYP* 14); Daned son of Oth, Gwair son of Gwystyl (meaning 'hostage', one of the Three Diademed Battle-Leaders, *TYP* 21); Dyrstan son of Tallwch (for Trystan, see note to p. 219 on *March*); Granwen son of Llŷr; Llacheu son of Arthur (mentioned in the triads, see *TYP*, pp. 408–10); Rhyawdd son of Morgant (a 'frivolous/amateur bard', according to *TYP* 12); Gilbert son of Cadgyffro (son of Battle Tumult, see *TYP*, pp. 360–1); Gyrthmwl Wledig (see *TYP*, p. 383); Cawrdaf son of Caradog Strong Arm (see *TYP*, p. 308).

Rhun son of Maelgwn Gwynedd . . . Cadyriaith son of Saidi: Maelgwn, king of Gwynedd (d. 547), is one of the five rulers of sixth-century Britain condemned by Gildas for his crimes. His son Rhun is mentioned in more than one source regarding a dispute with Maelgwn's son-in-law Elidir Mwynfawr (see *TYP*, pp. 491–2). For Cadyriaith ('Fine Speech') see note to p. 141.

it was in praise of Arthur: the author is probably satirizing the court poets here—their poetry is so complex that no one understands! Madog himself was a renowned patron of poets: eulogies were composed to him by men such as Gwalchmai ap Meilyr and Cynddelw Brydydd Mawr.

226 *in Cornwall*: a memory of the older, pre-Geoffrey of Monmouth tradition that associated Arthur with Celli Wig in Cornwall.

neither poet nor storyteller . . . without a book: a much-quoted phrase in any discussion regarding the relationship between the poet and the story-teller. This could well be a doublet, and does not necessarily prove that poets and storytellers were two autonomous groups. The reasons given for dependence on a book are hardly plausible, considering the mnemonic feats of the medieval storytellers; moreover, the elaborate descriptions found in the dream, although detailed, all follow a similar pattern, so facilitating the task of committing them to memory. *Without a book* probably refers to the fact that this tale had always been a literary tale, and had no dynamic oral life prior to its being committed to manuscript, although the author certainly draws on traditional sources. It is perhaps appropriate that this is the last tale in our *Mabinogion* 'collection', for with it medieval Welsh narrative moves in a new direction.

INDEX OF PERSONAL NAMES

This list is not meant to be exhaustive. For the names included in the Court List and Ysbaddaden's list of tasks in 'How Culhwch Won Olwen', see pp. 184–9 and 195–200.

Cadwri son of Gwrion a member of Geraint's escort to Cornwall 155

Cadyriaith son of Porthor Gandwy 'Fine-speech' son of the porter Gandwy, one of Arthur's chamberlains; his patronymic varies—he is sometimes the son of Saidi 140, 150, 156, 171, 225

Cai son of Cynyr sometimes portrayed as the steward at Arthur's court; he is often given the epithet *Gwyn* ('fair') or *Hir* ('Tall') 68–71, 74, 79–82, 85, 116–21, 129, 155, 169–70, 182–3, 184, 186, 188, 189–92, 201–2, 203, 205, 206–7, 219, 226, 246 n., 254 n.

Caradog son of Brân one of the men left behind to guard Britain when Bendigeidfran (Brân) and his troops go to Ireland to wage war 28, 33, 234 n.

Caradog son of Llŷr Arthur's cousin, sometimes known as Caradog Freichfras (Strong Arm); he acts as guarantor for Edern son of Nudd 152, 218, 225

Caswallon son of Beli he usurps the crown of Britain while Bendigeidfran is waging war in Ireland 33, 111, 233 n., 236 n.

Caw of Prydyn Caw of Pictland, who is entrusted with the keeping of the tusk of Ysgithrwyn Pen Baedd ('White Tusk Chief of Boars') 184, 185, 186, 197, 208, 210, 213, 217, 225, 270 n.

Cigfa daughter of Gwyn Gohoyw or Gloyw, wife of Pryderi 21, 35–6, 40–2

Cilydd son of Celyddon Wledig father of Culhwch; *Cilydd* means 'companion', *(G)wledig* means 'lord' 179, 183, 189, 191, 193, 194, 259–60 n.

Clust son of Clustfeinydd Ear son of Hearer, a gatekeeper at Arthur's court 139, 188

Creiddylad daughter of Lludd Llaw Eraint 189, 207

Culhwch son of Cilydd and Goleuddydd; his stepmother swears a destiny on him that he shall marry no one except Olwen daughter of Ysbaddaden Bencawr (Ysbaddaden Chief Giant) 179–84, 189, 191, 193–5, 206, 208, 213, 260 n.

Custennin son of Mynwyedig a shepherd, uncle to Olwen and to Culhwch 191, 202, 212, 213

Cyledyr Wyllt Cyledyr the Wild, who is forced to eat his father's heart 207, 212

Cymidei Cymeinfoll wife of Llasar Llaes Gyfnewid, the original owner of the Cauldron of Rebirth; they escape death in Ireland and flee to Britain 26

Cynan son of Eudaf brother to Elen wife of Maxen; founder of Brittany, according to 'The Dream of the Emperor Maxen' 107, 109–10, 251 n.

Cynddylig Gyfarwydd Cynddylig the Guide, one of Arthur's men 184, 190

Gwallog son of Llennog one of Arthur's men who acts as guarantor for Edern son of Nudd 152, 258 n.

Gwarthegydd son of Caw cattle-raider son of Caw, one of Arthur's men 210, 217, 225

Gwawl son of Clud betrothed to Rhiannon 12–15, 45

Gwenhwyfar wife of Arthur 68, 70, 85, 116, 117, 121, 139–43, 145, 147–56, 171, 183, 188, 245–6 n.

Gwern son of Matholwch, king of Ireland, and Branwen, sister of Bendigeidfran; he is thrown into the fire by Efnysien, his mother's half-brother 27, 30, 32

Gwiffred Petit he is called *Y Brenin Bychan* ('The Little King') by the Welsh 167, 169, 176

Gwilym William, son of the king of France; he accompanies Geraint to Cornwall 155, 225

Gwrddnei Lygaid Cath Gwrddnei Cat-Eye, a gatekeeper at Arthur's court 139

Gwrgi Gwastra one of Pryderi's men, given as hostage to Math son of Mathonwy 51

Gwrhyr Gwalstawd Ieithoedd Gwrhyr Interpreter of Languages, one of Arthur's men 188, 190, 192, 201, 203–5, 209, 225, 266 n.

Gwri Wallt Eurin the name given to Pryderi when he is found and adopted by Teyrnon Twrf Liant and his wife 18, 20, 231 n.

Gwydion son of Dôn nephew to Math, king of Gwynedd, and uncle to Lleu Llaw Gyffes 47–58, 61–3, 240 n.

Gwyn Llogell Gŵyr perhaps Gwyn 'Protector of Men'; a member of Geraint's escort to Cornwall and court judge to Arthur 155

Gwyn son of Nudd one of Arthur's men who fights Gwythyr every May eve for the hand of Creiddylad 184, 189, 199, 207, 211, 212–13, 271 n.

Gwyn son of Tringad a member of Geraint's escort to Cornwall 155, 210

Gwythyr son of Greidol one of Arthur's men; he saves an anthill from fire 184, 189, 205, 207, 212–13

Hafgan one of the kings of the Otherworld 4, 6

Heilyn son of Gwyn (Hen) son of Gwyn (the Old); he opens the forbidden door on the Island of Grassholm 32, 34

Huandaw one of Arthur's gatekeepers 181, 210

Hychddwn Hir the son of the brothers Gwydion and Gilfaethwy, conceived and born while they were in the shape of a wild boar and a wild sow; his name means 'Dark-red Pig, the Tall' 53–4

Hyddwn the son of the brothers Gwydion and Gilfaethwy, conceived

INDEX OF PLACE-NAMES

This is not meant to be an exhaustive list. For place-names associated with the Court List in 'How Culhwch Won Olwen', and also the Hunt of Twrch Trwyth, see pp. 184–9 and 209–12.

Common place-name elements include *caer* ('fort'), *din* ('fort'), *rhyd* ('ford'), *aber* ('estuary' or 'confluence').

Medieval Wales was divided into large territorial divisions known as *gwledydd* or *gwladoedd* (sing. *gwlad*): these were Gwynedd, Powys, and Deheubarth. The *gwlad* was divided into several *cantrefi*, and each *cantref* consisted of two or more *cymydau* ('commots'). The situation was, of course, fluid, and boundaries would often change. For detailed maps, see William Rees, *An Historical Atlas of Wales* (Cardiff, 1972; 1st edn. 1951).

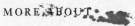

The Oxford World's Classics Website

www.worldsclassics.co.uk

- Browse the full range of Oxford World's Classics online

- Sign up for our monthly e-alert to receive information on new titles

- Read extracts from the Introductions

- Listen to our editors and translators talk about the world's greatest literature with our Oxford World's Classics audio guides

- Join the conversation, follow us on Twitter at OWC_Oxford

- Teachers and lecturers can order inspection copies quickly and simply via our website

www.worldsclassics.co.uk